The Blood of the Land

"Noel-Anne Brennan masters inner struggle and explores many traditional conflicts of today's women through the lives of female rulers . . . an excellent choice for readers who enjoy exploring human emotion, difficult choices, or richly designed twists in any genre."   —*Gothic Revue*

"With its strong female protagonist, this tale will be appreciated by readers of Victoria Strauss and Caroline Stevermer."   —*Kliatt*

"Brennan shines at characterization."   —*Romantic Times*

The Sword of the Land

"Brennan's characters are neither all good nor all evil, which makes them more interesting, and their story that much more entertaining."   —*Chronicle*

"An engaging story with a wonderfully strong protagonist."   —*Booklist*

"A very entertaining fantasy."   —*Midwest Book Review*

"Noel-Anne Brennan is a sensitive writer whose intense tale of honor and sacrifice is definitely a keeper. Strong characterizations coupled with exceptional plotting result in a heartwarming epic."   —*Romantic Times*

Ace books by Noel-Anne Brennan

THE SWORD OF THE LAND
THE BLOOD OF THE LAND
DAUGHTER OF THE DESERT

Daughter of
the Desert

NOEL-ANNE BRENNAN

ACE BOOKS, NEW YORK

THE BERKLEY PUBLISHING GROUP
Published by the Penguin Group
Penguin Group (USA) Inc.
375 Hudson Street, New York, New York 10014, USA
Penguin Group (Canada), 90 Eglinton Avenue East, Suite 700, Toronto, Ontario M4P 2Y3, Canada
(a division of Pearson Penguin Canada Inc.)
Penguin Books Ltd., 80 Strand, London WC2R 0RL, England
Penguin Group Ireland, 25 St. Stephen's Green, Dublin 2, Ireland (a division of Penguin Books Ltd.)
Penguin Group (Australia), 250 Camberwell Road, Camberwell, Victoria 3124, Australia
(a division of Pearson Australia Group Pty. Ltd.)
Penguin Books India Pvt. Ltd., 11 Community Centre, Panchsheel Park, New Delhi—110 017, India
Penguin Group (NZ), Cnr. Airborne and Rosedale Roads, Albany, Auckland 1310, New Zealand
(a division of Pearson New Zealand Ltd.)
Penguin Books (South Africa) (Pty.) Ltd., 24 Sturdee Avenue, Rosebank, Johannesburg 2196,
South Africa

Penguin Books Ltd., Registered Offices: 80 Strand, London WC2R 0RL, England

This is a work of fiction. Names, characters, places, and incidents either are the product of the author's imagination or are used fictitiously, and any resemblance to actual persons, living or dead, business establishments, events, or locales is entirely coincidental. The publisher does not have any control over and does not assume any responsibility for author or third-party websites or their content.

DAUGHTER OF THE DESERT

An Ace Book / published by arrangement with the author

PRINTING HISTORY
Ace edition / April 2006

Copyright © 2006 by Noel-Anne Brennan.
Cover art by Bleu Turrell.
Cover design by Annette Fiore.
Interior text design by Stacy Irwin.

ISBN: 0-441-01394-5

ACE
Ace Books are published by The Berkley Publishing Group,
a division of Penguin Group (USA) Inc.,
375 Hudson Street, New York, New York 10014.
ACE and the "A" design are trademarks belonging to Penguin Group (USA) Inc.

PRINTED IN THE UNITED STATES OF AMERICA

10 9 8 7 6 5 4 3 2 1

For Jim

ACKNOWLEDGMENTS

My thanks to Sirikanya B. Schaeffer, the real Sirikanya, and to Ann Martin, for help with some of the names.

ONE

*I*T WAS ONLY THE LIGHT OF DAWN, SAFFRON and rose, showing through her window, not fire in the night. Forentel sat up, pushing back sweat-streaked coppery bronze hair. She was not only tired, she was tired of being tired, of having the dreams. When she was younger she had cried and screamed, but she had quickly learned better. Crying had brought her the attention of her parents, who were far from comforting. She had long ago learned not to even mention the dreams. Now when they came she simply endured and tried to hide her exhaustion.

She stretched, pushing herself out of bed. The Tirdar girl was late bringing her breakfast, or more likely had forgotten altogether. Forentel knew she wouldn't complain and wouldn't bring it to the attention of her parents. She had attempted to explain her attitude to her father once, but

Nedriff thought she was feeling sorry for the Tirdar. She had not felt sorry for them; what she felt was empathy. Fortunately, she had realized in time that this was not something she should point out.

"You shouldn't feel sorry for them," her father had said. "Without us, without the Virsat," he had amended, "the Tirdar would be nothing but savages. Superstition-ridden savages."

Forentel had stared at him uneasily, hearing something, she was not sure what, beneath the words. Of course "us" meant the Virsat. Who else would it mean? And the Tirdar *were* superstition-ridden savages. She had let the matter drop. There were times when her own family seemed incomprehensible to her, and there were too many things she could not ask about, for reasons she could not fathom, only sense. The passing years had not clarified much.

She felt uneasy around her father, but she told herself it was simply because of the nature of his work. Nedriff was a commanding general of the Virsat, a confidant of the king and of the king's heir. Although she came from a ruling family, most things to do with the government made Forentel edgy.

Now she padded to the window, barefoot, and looked out. The sun was not yet up over the city of Tireera, but the east was flushed with light. The house was built on the edge of one of the rust-red rock formations, and from her window Forentel could look down on a portion of the desert city's streets. People were already going about their business in the cool of the early morning, and as she watched, a covered litter approached the big formal door of her house, the Tirdar out-walkers waving their huge feathered fans. It was the litter of the High Judge of Tireera, come to take her mother to the Temple of Justice. Forentel was later than she thought.

She pulled on her striped silk pants, fuming that she

needed to waste time tying them at the ankles as good taste and decency required, pulled on a short-sleeved striped silk shirt which by sheer good luck matched the pants, crammed her feet into her sandals, and ran her fingers through her unruly long copper bronze hair, tying it back with a ribbon without combing it. She would be late, and she would be blamed for it, even though it was the fault of the Tirdar servant who had failed to wake her.

By the time she reached the courtyard, the center of the family's house, the morning offering was in its final stages. She slipped in as quietly as she could, hoping her tardiness would not be noticed. She stood beside the fragrant wisa bush, half hidden behind the masses of pink and lavender flowers. She watched as her father poured the dish of red wine, symbolic of the blood of captives, down the side of the altar and into the stone drain. Forentel saw Sheesa, one of the younger and more imaginative of the Tirdar servants standing at the edge of the courtyard, flinch back and tremble slightly. Forentel knew she was imagining a human sacrifice on the altar, even though human sacrifices were rarely offered anymore, and certainly not at a house altar.

Even as she thought this, Forentel felt the cold, tingly, distanced sensation, the feeling that came with the dreams. She saw her father, much younger than he was now, standing before a stone slab, with a Tirdar captive kneeling before him. Behind him, flames shot upward toward the sky. There was no sound, but Forentel knew that if she wished, she could hear the screams. She blinked, banishing the vision. It was a vision from her dreams, a recurring dream, more completely out of place now in the morning sunlight than it was at night.

"I expect my children to be present at the morning sacrifice, not just at the end, but at the beginning." Nedriff stood in front of her, hands clasped behind his back, frowning. Distracted by her vision, Forentel had not seen him finish the rite and approach. "You must make an effort to be here in time, as Dreena does."

Forentel glanced at her younger sister, who stood slightly behind her father, smirking. Dreena was only two years younger than she, with long golden hair and a heart-shaped face. She was beautiful, and their father's favorite, and she knew it. She was insufferable.

"There are new suitors for Dreena's hand in marriage," her father continued, "so I will have a decision for you, probably tonight. I cannot permit Dreena to marry until you are married first. Forentel, look at me! I am speaking to you. I said I will have a decision tonight as to whom you will marry. There is someone very rich and powerful who has an interest in you."

Forentel stared at him. She knew this had been under discussion, but she had not believed it was serious. She still could not believe it. Surely her father knew she did not wish to marry, not yet. All the eligible Virsat boys she knew were just that, boys. Furthermore, none were interested in her.

"She is not marrying, Nedriff, not yet. We have talked about this." Forentel's mother Mareg put her hand briefly on Forentel's shoulder. "She will be my junior, and my heir."

"You have decided then, daughter." Nedriff was surprised. "I did not know." He looked darkly at her mother, not pleased at being the last to know.

I'm surprised, too, thought Forentel. She had not come to any such decision and had not even been giving it serious thought. She had meant to think about it, but she just hadn't.

"Yes," she said, "I have decided." She saw her mother smile and immediately resented it. Her mother had never been slow to take any advantage that presented itself to her. In that she was like her husband. It was a Virsat trait.

"Come to the temple with me now," said Mareg, "and we can begin with your preparations. The sooner we begin, the sooner initiation will be."

"I will come soon, Lady Mother." Forentel hoped to hide her unhappiness and resentment beneath a cloak of formality, but she could see that her mother was not deceived.

"Don't take too long. Forentel," she added, her voice pitched to reach only her daughter and not her husband, who had walked away to discuss something with the Tirdar house foreman. "You are suited for this. You have a mind for the law. It will not be so bad. You will enjoy it, and it will save you from marrying some foolish boy your father picks out."

Before Forentel could answer, Mareg turned away, headed for the outer door and the litter that would take her to the temple. Forentel, trailing behind, saw her mother helped into the litter in a swirl of saffron and fuschia silks. She hung back, watching as the litter bearers, six strong Tirdar men, swung the litter poles onto their shoulders and trotted off down the steep, winding street into the lower town, the out-walkers waving their fans and crying, "Make way for the High Judge."

"Don't tell me you ate, because I know you didn't." Forentel turned to find Dreena behind her. "You are covering up for the slaves again. And don't tell me you really want to be temple apprentice, either. I know better. You are going to make a mess of this, just the way you do everything. I wish you would marry. At least then you would be out of the house."

"And out of your way," muttered Forentel. She didn't think her sister had heard her, but she was wrong.

"Yes!" said Dreena. She tossed her head, sending her blonde hair flying and jingling the little silver rings tied into her tiny braids. "If you work for Mother in the temple you will still live here. And you are an embarrassment! No one wants to court me with you hanging around. Why don't you just get married! Go live with some poor man who won't know what he's getting until it's too late, someone Father chooses for you."

"You have a black spot on your front teeth, Dreena." Forentel watched as her sister hurried away to find her mirror. Once she might have been amused at how easy it was to distract her, but not today.

The truth was that Dreena was right. Forentel frequently felt like an outsider in her own family, and an embarrassment not only to her sister but to her father. Today, her sister's words seemed to mesh with the strange feeling left over from her dreams, making her unsettled.

She decided to walk to the Temple of Justice, which would take her some time, and to buy herself breakfast on the way. It would be late morning before she reached the temple, enough time, perhaps, for her to sort out some of her thoughts. She would go alone, without a bodyguard, without out-walkers. Even so, her clothing would proclaim her a Virsat, and if she kept to the better streets no one would dare to harm her. Suiting action to the thought, she ran back inside to her room, snatched up her money pouch and her comb. It would not do to arrive at the temple with her hair in disarray. She managed to avoid all but one Tirdar servant as she hastily left the house through the kitchens.

At the last moment she changed her plan. She wanted to be anonymous on the streets, and what better way than to go as a Tirdar. No Virsat would deign to stoop so low, but to Forentel, flush with resentment and rebellion, it seemed the perfect idea. She snatched the house foreman's cloak, plain gray slashed with her house colors of saffron and fuschia, and pulled it around her.

The streets were busy even though the sun had not yet risen above the line of cliffs to the east of Tireera. No one

paid any attention to the young woman who walked unattended. She found the pastry vendor at his usual corner beside the water vendor, and bought an an olive and cheese
roll, which she ate as she walked. She stood aside for a Virsat noble and his out-walkers, contriving to look busy in
case she were recognized. She needn't have worried. The
out-walkers almost pushed her aside when she stood too
close to the path of the noble, but they did not glance twice
at the presumed slave in her house colors.

The sun was up now, shedding golden light along the
streets, which were rapidly heating up. By midday it
would be brutally hot. Forentel had wandered without
thinking toward the gardens of the king, a watered park
where the plants were tenderly cared for by a corps of
Tirdar gardeners. Tirdar other than the king's servants
were generally not permitted within the park's grounds.
Immersed in her own thoughts, Forentel was in the deep
shade of the small grove of golden fringe trees when she
was noticed.

"You there!"

She blinked stupidly. It took a moment to realize that
she was being addressed. It took a moment more to realize
that she was being addressed by king's guards, who were
striding toward her with their hands on their swords. She
remembered she was dressed as a Tirdar. She did not stop
to think. She ran.

"You! Tirdar! Halt in the name of the king!"

They had fanned out and were coming at her from three
sides. Forentel dodged, leaped a low ornamental wall, and
headed toward the small grove that bordered one side of
the park. She was a good runner, accustomed to racing
with the dogs and the younger children on the grounds of
her father's estate. Now she put that speed to use.

It occurred to her to stop, to remove her Tirdar cloak, to
explain herself. What could she have said? Something

buzzed by her ear: an arrow. Any notion of stopping and explaining vanished. She increased her speed, running almost doubled over, dodging. The grove was closer now, but she saw with a sense of shock that she wouldn't make it. Another pair of the king's guards was coming out of the trees, preparing to cut her off. They had drawn swords. As she hesitated, another arrow barely missed her.

"This way! Psst, Frelenya, this way!"

Forentel stumbled, turned toward the voice, and saw a young woman in dirty gray clothing motioning to her from behind an artfully positioned tumble of rocks, over which ran an elegant waterfall. Forentel dodged behind the structure. The woman grasped her by the hand and yanked her forward.

"What is the matter with you! Hurry up, Frelenya— don't dawdle—they'll catch us!"

Forentel wasn't dawdling; she had no idea where to go. The woman pulled her hand impatiently, and Forentel followed her through a little twisty passage into the rocks, right under the waterfall. Then they had to get down on their knees and crawl through a little tunnel where the dirt was shored up by rocks and wood, and then they were out again in the sunlight.

Forentel stood up and blinked. They were on a street, the one that ran behind the garden. They had come out in a tiny alley between two buildings, and Forentel stared around her and then across the street at the garden. King's guards roiled along the edge of the garden, and she could hear them shouting.

"You're not Frelenya. You look like her, but you're not." Her rescuer was examining her more thoroughly. "Who are you? What were you doing there?"

What was she doing there? What was this strange young woman, obviously a Tirdar, doing there? And the secret passage beneath the ornamental waterfall—why did it ex-

ist? Forentel moved toward her rescuer and then stopped.
The other woman was staring at her. Forentel looked down
at herself. Her cloak had fallen open, showing clothing that
was obviously better than any Tirdar could afford. And on
her wrist flashed the golden bracelet, the sign of the Virsat
nobility.

"What are you doing, Lelat; who is this? What—"

Forentel turned to see who the newcomer was. She
turned and then froze. There was a third woman in the tiny
alley. Forentel stared: at the burnished bronze colored hair,
shorter than hers and more unkempt, but the exact same
shade, at the long legs and rather boyish figure that so disappointed her father, at the oval face and green eyes that
were exactly her own.

"She's a Virsat! She's a Virsat spy! Frelenya, run!"

Frelenya did not run. She stared at Forentel with the
same wonder and astonishment that Forentel knew were on
her own face.

"You," said Forentel softly. "I've seen you in my
dreams." The dreams of fire, the dreams of blood, those
dreams, and in those dreams the sound of screaming and
the sense of loss, greater than the terror, the sense of being
torn away. Forentel took a step forward. She opened her
mouth to say, *I know you.*

She wasn't sure what she would have meant by that, but
she never got the chance to say the words. She extended a
hand toward the other woman and saw her mirror the gesture. Just as Frelenya reached out slowly toward her there
were more shouts, closer now. The guards from the garden
had seen them somehow and were crossing the street.

"Run! Frelenya, run! We'll be caught!" The third
woman, Lelat, grasped her friend by the shoulder and
shook her. Forentel and Frelenya both started, as if awakened from a trance.

"They have us! We can't get away!" Lelat was desperate.

"I will stop them." Forentel reached up and unclasped her cloak, swinging it away from her. Frelenya took it and bundled it into her arms. "Go!" said Forentel. She drew herself up and stepped forward toward the street, toward the guards. At the last moment she looked back. "How will I find you again?" There was no answer. Both young women were gone, hurrying away.

Forentel stepped out into the street. The guards saw her and stopped short, surprised. She drew herself up, calling on the illustrious nature of her family, her Virsat heritage.

"May I be of help to you?" she asked imperiously. At the same time she managed to block the guardsmen from edging around her into the alleyway. The sun was lighting up the buildings around them now, driving off any remaining chill of dawn. Forentel brushed back her hair, letting the light flash off her Virsat bracelet.

"Tirdar rebels," said one of the guards shortly. "They were in the garden and ran out."

"Rebels?" Astonishment and polite disbelief edged Forentel's voice. "No one has mentioned rebels to me. Are there rebels in the city itself?" The Tirdar sections of Tireera were thick with resistance in the form of rumors, superstition, and tales, but not with outright rebellion.

"Your pardon, lady, but we must search." The guards' leader was impatiently trying to get her to move.

"I saw two street urchins, that is all. I am sure my mother, Lady Judge Mareg Friltera of Pentrat, would be interested in news of any rebels, as would my father, Lord General Nedriff Pentrat."

She saw their eyes widen. The guard captain drew himself up straighter. Forentel could see the questions in his eyes, although the other guards were simply shocked. He did not venture to ask any questions, however. A good thing—she wasn't sure how she would have explained being alone with no out-walkers.

"The general will have a report, will he not?"

"Of course, lady." The guard captain all but saluted.

"Very well." Forentel nodded at him and turned. "I am on my way to the Temple of Justice," she said. Fortunately, she could see it, its platformed terraces catching the light of the newly risen sun. "I will not require an escort." She knew he was anxious to give her one. "I am seeing the city and its streets for myself, to give the High Judge my observations." She was pleased with herself for thinking of this. "Be assured I will mention you and your vigilance. Captain—?"

"Restu. Captain Restu." He looked both pleased and concerned.

Forentel strode quickly away before he could recover, before he could insist on giving her an escort. She did not look back. She was on the busier streets now, streets full of Virsat of all classes, many of them going to the Temple of Justice for their own reasons.

Just outside the gates of the temple complex Forentel stopped. Her thoughts were jumbled, and when she rubbed at her eyes to try to clear her mind, she discovered that her hand was shaking. She needed to be calm before she saw her mother. She drew a deep breath, filling her lungs, and then expelled it slowly, remembering as she did so the advice of her Tirdar nurse. The woman had vanished one day when Forentel was eleven, and no one had told her why. But she had taught Forentel a few things, tricks, Forentel labeled them, that were extremely helpful. This breathing exercise was one. She could hear her nurse's voice. "Breathe in, and think of calm, think of the cool, golden light of the just-risen sun flooding through you, relaxing you. And then breathe out, and let all the bad things go. Do this three times, Forentel. Three times."

Forentel did it three times. Then she opened her eyes. It had helped, as it almost always did.

She looked up at the Temple of Justice. The building rose in a long series of steps, broken by flat terraces dotted with statues and dry-land trees in pots. Up and up, terrace after terrace, each terrace guarded by armed temple servants, nine terraces in all. And at the very top, the huge entrance, the dark gateway to the temple itself, like a cave in the dark gray stone. Her mother was within the temple, preparing to listen to the cases brought before her, the most important and desperate of cases, as befitted the highest of Virsat judges. According to tradition, according to law, and according to the hope of all who appeared before her, the High Judge would have the answers. Forentel certainly hoped so, since she had what she thought were some very difficult questions. Without further delay she began to climb the steps to the temple.

Two

I AM SURE THERE IS A CONNECTION; THERE must be. You showed me this yourself; look, Filfa, look at the map." Erba, younger son of King Rellaff of Tireera, drew his finger along the parchment. "Look at the place names. Up here, the Tirdar call this place," he jabbed at the map, "Visla, *the big falls*. Where the river comes through the canyon. Not surprisingly. And then down here, very far to the south, is Fizla. We don't know what it means, but I can guess, can't you? I know the reports are sketchy. Few travel that far and return, but there must be a connection. A Tirdar connection. Think, Filfa, what this could do for your theories on the origins of the Tirdar, and perhaps on the nature of their abilities."

Filfa, tutor to the younger prince, regarded his charge with a mixture of amusement and satisfaction. The prince was twenty-one years of age, four years younger than his brother Mirta, the heir. Both brothers were known for their intelligence, but Filfa was convinced that Erba was more intelligent than his elder sibling. He simply tended not to show it as much, since he also possessed charm and blond good looks and a certain naive enthusiasm that did not suit his station in life. It was an enthusiasm that Filfa had never hesitated to use for his own purposes, however.

"You may very well be right. You probably are, since you are an apt linguistic pupil, but there is no way we can find out for ourselves. Your father will not allow the funds for an expedition, and he will certainly not permit you to go."

"My father has nothing to say on these matters." Erba walked to the window and looked out on the garden below. Tirdar gardeners were carrying precious water to the tender plants in the ornamental beds. "It is all in my brother's hands now."

"Even less, then, are we likely to obtain what you wish." Filfa did not bother to deny it. King Rellaff suffered from a wasting disease, and much of the government was in the hands of his heir. "Prince Mirta is not kindly disposed to studies of the Tirdar." The Tirdar believed the disease was the judgment of the gods.

"My brother believes most study that has no obvious and immediate benefit is a waste of time. Because the Tirdar are lesser beings, he can see no value in learning more about them. He is shortsighted."

"Do not bring up the subject of an expedition with your brother again, Prince; that is my advice to you." Filfa had long since regretted kindling his charge's interest in this area.

"You worry too much, Filfa." Erba smiled at his tutor. "No, I mean it, I give you my word. I will not push it. I know how far I can go with my brother, and I will go that far and no farther."

In the gardens below, the Tirdar had finished with watering the flower beds. Erba watched them, pulling at the multiple braids in his blond hair. There were those who claimed the conquered race was not even truly human, but he did not believe this. They were, perhaps, a different order of human, but he did not believe they were a different sort of creature altogether. After all, he knew of cases where Virsat and Tirdar had managed to produce children. Such children were never formally acknowledged by the Virsat, but they didn't seem much different to Erba than children of pure Virsat ancestry.

"They must be somewhat like us," he murmured to himself. "After all, there are children—"

"You had best not mention your theories on Tirdar and Virsat mixing, at least." Filfa seemed to know what he was thinking. "Your brother has a horror of anyone of mixed blood."

"Please don't worry, Filfa," said Erba again. "Now I had better go; it won't do for me to be late for the midday meal. My brother has commanded my presence."

Filfa preceded the prince from the room, and once out in the palace corridor, turned in the other direction. He paused, watching the prince stride away from him. As soon as his charge was out of sight, he turned back, hastening through the servants' hallways, anxious to reach Mirta, the elder prince, before Erba did.

MIRTA, HEIR TO the throne of Virsat Tireera, carefully tucked the napkin into the collar of his father's shirt. He allowed no one else, and certainly no servant, to do this small task. An appearance of filial love was important, not just to his image but to his plans. He wanted there to be no reason for anyone to question his dedication to his father. He solicitously cut the meat on his father's plate into small cubes and placed the spoon—not a knife, but a spoon like a child's—in the king's hand.

Mirta held no animosity toward his father, but he had no patience with him, either. He himself was a strong and active man, a self-proclaimed warrior who kept himself fit, and his father's weakness annoyed him. Weakness to Mirta was a sign of moral deficiency, although he did not consider his own fondness for wine to be a weakness. Even though he knew his father had never been weak in any sense until his illness, and had never shirked the more difficult decisions that came with power, Mirta battled disgust every time he looked at the king.

"My lord, the scholar Filfa wishes to see you." The servant was a Virsat, as were all palace servants but the very lowest, and the gardeners, of course, who dealt with the soil. "I told him you were about to begin your meal, but he insisted I give the message that he is here. Should I send him away?"

"No." Mirta was slightly annoyed at the timing. "Send him in."

"Your Majesty." Filfa bowed to Rellaff, whose head bobbled, either in response to the greeting or as a result of his disease. Filfa was in almost before the servant had left the room; he must have been listening at the door, Mirta thought.

"My lord prince." Filfa bowed to Mirta, his eyes shifting back to the door.

It was obvious what was on his mind, at least in one respect. Mirta was tempted to drag this out, just to see the man squirm. Mirta held a certain resentment of learned men. Most, in his opinion, looked down on men of action, which was what he considered himself. Mirta was not foolish enough to indulge his whim, however. He waved the servants out and turned back to his brother's tutor.

"I gather that my brother is on his way; you had best make this brief," he said.

"He intends to ask about an expedition to the south again," said Filfa.

"To the mythical lands that supposedly spawned the Tirdar, yes," said Mirta. He was tempted to yawn. "This is nothing new."

"What is new," replied Filfa, "is that I believe he intends to mount this expedition, or at least attempt to do so, without your backing. He has, I believe, enough support from some of the younger nobles to do this."

"He will not succeed, certainly not without support from the elder nobles. And he will never have my blessing or my permission." Mirta slammed his fist against the table, making the place settings jump. The thought of his younger brother attempting to evade his control was intolerable. "There is nothing to be found to the south, nothing that is of any benefit to us."

"Perhaps he should go."

The words were so soft that for a moment Filfa wasn't sure he had actually heard them. It was only when he saw Mirta frown with annoyance that he realized the king had spoken.

"He is not a fool, my younger son." Rellaff's voice was a hoarse whisper. "He needs something to occupy him. Chasing this fantasy will purge it from his mind. You know very well that he cannot succeed." The king began to cough, and for a few moments was unable to say more. Mirta went to his aid, holding him up in his chair so that the force of the spasm would not knock him to the floor. "He will find nothing of value out in the wilderness," gasped the king. Mirta eased him back into his seat as the spasm ended.

"My lords." The servant was at the door again. "Prince Erba has arrived."

Mirta smiled briefly at Filfa's discomfort. He motioned for the scholar to leave through the hidden door behind the wall hanging. Erba knew the door was there, and he might even guess that someone had just used it, but he could scarcely check or even question this in the presence of his father and brother. Mirta expected Filfa to leave immediately, but he was surprised when the tutor lingered a moment.

"The wilderness is dangerous, sirs," he said, "even for one as young and strong as Prince Erba. I have no wish to see any ill befall him."

"Go, old man." Mirta's annoyance was surfacing again. Old relics like his father and Filfa were a strain on his patience.

He turned and nodded to the servant before Filfa was completely behind the tapestry, and Erba entered, followed by servants with crystal carafes of wine and water and servants bearing huge feather fans, for the day was becoming hot. It was a private meal, which meant that only family and servants were in attendance.

"Sit down, brother," said Mirta, smiling, after Erba had said his greetings. "Sit down and tell our father of your newest theories."

The ruling family of Tireera was a small, odd group. Outwardly, the brothers were similar. Both were tall, robust, and handsome, although Erba was blond and Mirta had dark hair. The resemblance was obvious in the broad, square shape of their faces and in the dimple at the right corner of their mouths. These traits were echoes of the king's face. Even Rellaff's wasted form showed traces of the physical power and strength that had once been his. But where Erba's manner was open and forthright, both Mirta and the king had an air of reserve and of secrecy.

"I have no new theories," said Erba easily, ignoring the edge of sarcasm in his brother's voice. "You have heard them all already. I have decided to put study aside for the time being and go hunting this afternoon. There are reports of a herd of gazelles near the Tirdar ruins beyond the old well. Have you heard? Will you join me?"

"I had not heard." For a moment, interest flickered in his Mirta's face. He loved to hunt. In particular, he loved dangerous prey, which was hard to find in the environs of Tireera, but gazelles, although not dangerous, were certainly a challenge requiring skill, and for a moment he was tempted.

"No," he said at last, "I will not join you, not this time."

Erba nodded. He had not expected Mirta to accept the offer and was pleased he had not. He intended to use the ruse of the hunting trip to begin to set up his planned expedition. "What a shame," he said.

"It is," agreed Mirta. *A shame I will not be able to witness the surprise I have in store for you, Brother,* he thought. He had intended to wait, but it was apparent now, in light of Filfa's information, that waiting was a strategy that might end in failure. It was better to seize this opportunity.

The rest of the meal was taken up by discussion of the resistance movement among the Tirdar. It was not a rebellion. The conquered race, despite its claims of special and uncanny abilities, did not have the resources or the organization for outright revolt. The Tirdar hopes seemed to be pinned, not surprisingly, Mirta thought, on magic. It was a quasi-religious movement, based on some sort of prophecy. The city was awash in magic and prophecy.

"They are waiting, my sources tell me, for the Delass. *Delass* is not a word that my Tirdar slaves claim to know, but then they wouldn't, of course. Some stupid Tirdar superstition," Mirta said. "Waiting for a savior, a warrior, I suppose, who will set them free."

"It's an old word," said Erba, "archaic. But it doesn't mean *warrior.* As best I can tell, it means *bridge.*"

Mirta laughed. "What could a bridge have to do with helping the Tirdar?"

"Not much, I would think," said Erba. "Perhaps I am wrong."

Through all of this the king watched his sons with half-closed eyes. Occasionally Mirta lifted meat on a spoon to his lips, and Rellaff chewed the pieces slowly. Drool ran down from the corner of his mouth, and Mirta wiped it away.

After his brother left, Mirta sat with his father, carefully giving him sips of cooled wine. He couldn't wait much longer. If Nedriff didn't come soon, the plan would have to be postponed. It could be done just as well any other day, but Mirta had worked up his courage to do it today, this afternoon.

"My lords, the Lord General Nedriff asks your permission to enter." The servant stood in the doorway.

"Send him in," said Mirta, hiding his relief.

"Your Majesty," said Nedriff, with a slight bow to the king, "and Lord Prince." He motioned behind him, and a servant entered, a Tirdar carrying a basket packed with straw. "New wine," said Nedriff, "from my estates. For your pleasure, my lords." He waved, and the servant placed the basket down and unpacked several tall, slender bottles.

"Nedriff, my friend, you are thoughtful, as always. Shall we have some now?" Mirta rose and went to the long sideboard where the bottles had been placed. He glanced down at them. Sure enough, the third bottle had a little star scratched into it.

"Would you care for some, Father?" When the old man attempted to nod, his head bobbling, Mirta took the bottle and poured a little into his own cup first. "Excellent!" he said, smiling.

He poured a cup for Nedriff, who drank. Then he poured for his father. Inside the bottle, just under the lip, was a tiny packet of waxed paper. As he poured, Mirta broke this with his fingernail, mixing the tiny amount of clear powder with his father's wine. He nodded at the two servants, dismissing them, knowing they had seen him drink first, and had seen Nedriff drink from the same bottle.

After a little conversation and wine, Nedriff and Mirta left, and the king was escorted to his chamber for his afternoon rest. It was much later that Prince Mirta was informed that his father could not be roused, that he was lying in bed with foam on his lips and his eyes open and unblinking.

ERBA PAUSED BEFORE the statue of the Falcon God outside the stable and bowed. Around him, the horses snorted, waiting, and his companions shifted. It was the expected ritual before setting out on a hunt, and he did it without much thought. His mind was instead on the preparations for his expedition. He wanted to meet his friends Feffar and Nenndat, two young men of his own age who had inherited a vast fortune and were taken with the idea of riches and slaves to be found in the unknown lands of the south. There would be some gazelle hunting also, of course, but the main purpose of this excursion was to discuss their venture. It would be a great adventure, possibly with wealth at the end, as his friends hoped, but certainly with fame, which Erba craved.

So Erba bowed, sprinkled the incense, and stood back lost in thought as his two Virsat servants also bowed. All three were dressed in leather trousers for riding and light cotton shirts for comfort, and all had canteens of water slung across their saddles, along with bows with quivers full of arrows. Erba carried his sword and his long knife as well, because a Virsat nobleman should never be without them.

Erba could not hunt unattended, but with servants he

could ride ahead and speak privately with his friends, something he could not do with Virsat of equal rank. He swung up into the saddle, and the servants followed suit. They set off at a gentle pace through Tireera's streets. Unlike his brother, Erba did not believe in scattering the citizens, and only when they were through the gates, having accepted the salutes of the gate guards, did he break into a canter.

The sun was hot, and the sky was the pale, washed-out blue that it became at the height of the day. It was not the best time to hunt, but Erba was happy to be out. The palace often felt stifling, no matter what the weather. It was the intellectual climate, he told himself, or lack of it.

The road led out and upward into the scrubby hills around the city. There were few dwellings on the northward side of the city where they rode now. It was too dry here; the farmsteads tended to cluster near the river, a bright green strip of fertile land. Out here were only the hot wind, the thorn bushes, and farther out still, the Tirdar ruins.

The ruins were said to be haunted, but they fascinated Erba. They were all that remained now of a small complex where the Tirdar holy women had lived, in the days before the conquest, back in his grandfather's time. The women had served the shrine, which was farther out in the scrub desert. In fact, one "holy woman" still lived in the shrine itself, although Erba could not imagine the sort of life that must be. She was by report at least half crazy. Free Tirdar from the city brought her food and supplies from time to time in return for her blessings, and there was a small, deep well at the shrine, so she had water.

The Virsat left her strictly alone. In part this was because she did no harm and gave the Tirdar a harmless focus for their superstition, but the Virsat also had no desire to tangle with the desert cats that prowled the area. The Cat

Goddess of the Dawn had been the focus of the shrine's worship, but the cats were not the small variety that caught rats in the streets of the city. These animals were large tawny animals, dangerous predators, hunting either singly or in small prides. The Tirdar legends claimed that the prophet of the shrine had some bond or communion with them, but Erba considered this myth; he doubted that any of the cats had ever been tamed.

Mirta had attempted to hunt these cats but had never been successful, much to his disgust. The cats had done better against Mirta. Two of the stragglers from his hunting party had been killed by the cats on one afternoon, although no one else in the party had seen it happen. After this unfortunate accident the cats and the desert they prowled had been left alone. Erba briefly considered hunting the cats today, but he realized that it would have been not only unwise, it would have distracted him from his objective.

His friends were waiting for him, mounted and armed, with their own small party of servants. They both wore cloaks, which the rising wind whipped out behind them. Feffar and Nenndat were brothers. Feffar was the elder, but only two years separated him from Nenndat. The two had the same birthday, unlikely though this was, and they looked so similar that strangers sometimes mistook them for twins.

"Ha!" shouted Nenndat, as he saw Erba approaching. "We were beginning to think you would not come! That you had forgotten us!"

Erba grinned. "The family meal was deadly as always, just longer," he said when he was close enough to be heard by only the brothers. And then, more loudly, "Besides, I could never forget you."

The three of them spurred their horses and rode slightly away from their escort. Erba cast a practiced glance to the horizon. The sky was darkening there slightly, even though it was only early afternoon. A storm might be brewing, but since it was not the brief rainy season, it would be one of the strange, dry desert storms that consisted mostly of wind and lightning and stinging sand. He frowned and saw that the others had followed his glance.

"We'd best keep an eye on that," said Feffar. "Were you able to talk any sense into your esteemed brother, my prince?"

Erba snorted indelicately. "No. I could not bring the matter up with him; I could see he would not hear me. Filfa warned me against speaking to him, so I can only imagine that Mirta had some words with him about it, but of course Filfa would never say. I am afraid that we shall have to proceed on our own."

"The prize will be all ours, then," said Feffar. "There is great wealth far down the river in those distant lands."

They were riding under a line of broken hills covered with tough, short grasses. Not far beyond this point the land opened up to an expanse of hard-packed, baked earth, where nothing grew. On the other side of the desert, more hills began again, bleaker and more barren than the hills under which they rode.

"We can be ready within three months, by the beginning of the rainy season," said Nenndat.

"My brother will certainly know by then, and I will have to be the one to tell him. Three months gives him plenty of time to attempt to stop us. Can we not start sooner?" Erba fretted. He wasn't sure he could ever bring Mirta to back him, so proceeding sooner was better.

"Not without turning our mother against us. I know, I know," Feffar made a dismissive motion, "the estate is all in our hands, but it would not do to have Mother object. Right now she is willing to go along with us. In three months' time the revenues from the farms downriver will be in, and she will not feel the cost of this venture."

Erba began to nod and opened his mouth to reply. When he thought back on this later, he still could not understand how it happened. One moment everything was fine. He was a favored prince of the land, riding with his two noble friends. He had every advantage. And then, in the blink of an eye, he was a fugitive, hunted himself, with nothing but his life.

They were still riding beneath the low scrub hills. Jagged slabs and tumbles of rock broke from the earth here and there, sometimes creating shade for the occasional thorn bush. The attack came from behind one of these rock tumbles. The first Erba knew of it was the choked cry that came from behind him, from one of the escort. That and the whining song of arrows.

"Attack! We're under attack!" cried Nenndat. He rose in the saddle to point at the hills, and it was the last thing he ever did. An arrow buried itself in his throat, and he toppled from his horse.

Feffar screamed, a hoarse cry of agony and disbelief. He leaped from his horse, disregarding the flying hooves, to catch his brother up in his arms. Erba leaned down across the neck of his own horse, reaching after his fallen friend, and it was this that saved his life. The arrow meant for him caught his horse in the neck, and it went down. Erba threw himself free just in time, as the big animal hit the ground, thrashing and screaming. Erba rolled away from the hooves. He grabbed Nenndat by the back of his shirt and tried to drag him into the cover of a tumble of rocks and a thorn bush. Feffar saw what he was doing and tried to help. There was the *thunk* of another arrow. Feffar stiffened and then collapsed, an arrow protruding from his eye.

Erba looked down. Nenndat's eyes were open, but blood soaked his clothing, soaked Erba's hands, soaked Erba's shirt and trousers. Lying flat on the ground, Erba felt for his friend's pulse. There was none. He looked back

down the road. None of his escort remained alive, or if
they were alive, they were still. Bodies were sprawled in
the road, both men and horses. The wind had picked up,
and dust was swirling around them, half obscuring the
horror.

In disbelief Erba raised his eyes to the rocky scree that
had hidden the archers. Someone was standing there now,
looking down at the slaughter in the road through the dust
and the rising wind. The distance was not great. Erba could
see that whoever it was wore a uniform, the uniform of the
king's personal guard. The guard's eyes swept over the figures lying in the road and came to rest on Erba. Erba met
the guard's gaze. Slowly, without breaking the gaze, the
guard reached behind his back and drew another arrow
from his quiver. Still not taking his eyes from Erba, he
nocked the arrow into the bow.

Erba couldn't breathe, couldn't move. He didn't understand. His friends were dead. His escort was dead. And this
man, this man who wore the uniform that meant he should
protect the royal family, this man was going to kill him. As
he watched, frozen, a second and then a third archer came
out of the rocks, all of them wearing the king's uniform.

Erba knew that if he didn't move he was dead. He
looked for his quiver and his bow, but they were trapped
beneath his dead horse. He had his sword, but that was of
no use against archers. He let go of Nenndat's body and
crawled, belly to the ground, to the body of his horse. As
he moved, he heard the arrows fly past him. He reached the
horse and crouched behind it, wondering, *What next?* He
could not break cover, and if he stayed where he was, his
attackers had merely to surround him to finish him off.

At this moment the storm broke. The winds shrieked
and dust swirled everywhere. Erba could not see his hand
in front of his face. The dust and the pressure of the wind
made it hard to breathe. Erba yanked off his shirt and

wrapped it around his face, shielding his mouth and nose from the dust. Bits of sand and stone and plant matter stung against his bare skin. He half closed his eyes. He yanked the water canteens from the back of the saddle, pulling so hard that the leather straps snapped. Then he crawled in what he hoped was the direction of a rock pile farther back down the road toward the city.

THREE

$\mathscr{F}$ORENTEL SAT IN HER MOTHER'S CHAMBER IN the temple. The High Judge, she had been informed, was out, discussing a matter with the priests. She would return shortly. For a time, she waited in the outer chamber, under the bored gaze of the temple guard and of the secretary, a young Virsat junior priest assigned to the High Judge. He knew Forentel, and apparently had heard that she was going to apprentice to her mother, because after a while he showed her to the more comfortable inner chamber.

Forentel sat on the couch where Mareg sometimes slept when her duties kept her at the temple. She stared out the window, noting that the sky was beginning to get the odd yellow cast that came before one of the dust storms that blew in from the desert. The storms were not too bad in the center of Tireera, which was protected by buildings and the city walls, but visibility became bad, and the winds were nasty. Out in the desert it was a different matter.

She looked around her mother's chamber. Against one wall, away from the window, were shelves piled with scrolls and papers. Most of them concerned the criminals and heretics her mother had sentenced or pardoned, but Forentel had once heard Mareg say that papers concerning their family were also stored in these shelves. Forentel walked over to the shelves and stood looking at them, and after a moment, their organization became apparent. The scrolls of law and religion were on the right, the scrolls and papers of the cases of the High Judge were in the middle, and down on the left, many of them covered with dust, were other papers. Slowly she bent down and reached out a hand to touch them.

"What are you doing, Forentel?"

Forentel turned to face her mother. She made no effort to move away from the shelves or to hide what she had almost done. She saw something in her mother's face and then, with the insight that sometimes came to her and always at the worst of times, she saw beneath her mother's expression, saw what was in her mind. She made a tiny sound and stared at her mother.

Her mother glanced from her to the shelves, saw they had not been disturbed, and then looked back at her daughter's face. The color drained from her face, and she drew a deep breath.

"You know." It was scarcely louder than a whisper. When Forentel said nothing, Mareg went and gently took her hand, intending to lead her back to the couch. Forentel pulled away.

"I have a sister," she said. "And I do not mean Dreena. I have a twin."

"Yes."

Forentel stared at her mother, but it seemed no explanation was to come. Her mother looked terrible, gray, and suddenly drained, almost ill. In some dim corner of her mind Forentel felt a flash of alarm, but she pushed it back. She was numb. Without realizing it, she had come to certain conclusions.

"I am not my father's child." She knew how her father looked at her, and suddenly it made sense. She was always second in his heart to Dreena, and there could be only one reason for it. Her mother had borne her to some other Virsat noble, and her father resented her for this. Somehow her mother had been able to keep her, to convince her father, no not her father, Nedriff, to accept her, but not her twin. Why not? What had happened to her twin? Why was her twin dressed as a Tirdar? Could her father be that vindictive—?

"Why do you say that? Of course you are Nedriff's child." Mareg pushed at her hair, a habit she had when she was unsettled. "You are his child in the way that Dreena is mine, but you are my child in the way that Dreena is his." She sighed, seeing that Forentel did not understand her. Now was not the time for legal riddles. "I did not give birth to you, but you are Nedriff's own."

Forentel stared. "What—" she whispered. "What," she tried again, "what do you mean? And what about Dreena?"

"I gave birth to Dreena; she is my child and your father's. I meant only that although I did not bear you, you are my favorite child. As Dreena is your father's. I have always loved you from the second I saw you."

"Not my mother?" Forentel's voice was tiny. "You are not my mother? Then who is?"

"I am your mother, and I have been your mother since the day—since you were very small." Mareg felt that her heart was breaking. Forentel looked so lost. She went to put her arms around the girl.

At first Forentel did not respond. She stood within the

circle of Mareg's arms like a block of stone. "Were you ever going to tell me?" she whispered. She did not seem to realize that tears were running down her face.

"I don't know," said Mareg. She took the sleeve of her gown and gently wiped Forentel's face. "But I see now there is no way I could have avoided hurting you, which is the last thing I ever wanted. You should know everything, and you will, but I cannot be the one to tell you. Please don't ask me yet. Your father must join me in this. He will not want to speak, but he will, I promise you." Mareg did not seem to realize that she, too, was crying, until Forentel at last put her arms around her.

The junior priest was startled but said nothing when Mareg informed him that she and her daughter were leaving. They looked ill, and the secretary assumed this was the reason. Mareg herself sent a messenger to find her husband and call him from the palace back to the house.

Mareg called for her litter, and Forentel made no objection, climbing in and settling herself among the cushions. Neither of them spoke as they traveled through the city streets. Forentel stared out through the curtains, seeing the king's gardens with their guards, seeing the streets she had so recently left under such different circumstances. She glanced sideways at her mother, wondering what she would say if she knew the strange adventure her daughter had just had. *No,* thought Forentel, *she is not my mother.* The thought made her feel hollow.

Their litter pulled to the side for a party of horsemen. It was the younger prince with some companions; Forentel could see them through the curtains. The prince bowed slightly toward their litter, knowing it to be the litter of the High Judge. Prince Erba was far better liked than his elder brother the heir. Many of the younger Virsat would prefer to see him inherit, but of course that was not possible. Forentel did not know the prince personally, although she had met him twice at formal functions. Now, wrapped in her thoughts, she barely noticed why the litter had stopped.

When they arrived home, they were informed that Nedriff was waiting for them, but Forentel went immediately to her room. Mareg told her to stay there and rest, that she would send for her soon. She sat on her bed, staring out the window, seeing nothing. Her Tirdar maid came in and was sent away.

"They said you were in here. I don't know what it is you did, but it must be pretty bad since Father came back from the palace."

"Dreena, go away." Forentel did not turn from staring out the window.

"It looks as though Mother has been ill. What did you do?"

"Dreena, go away."

"Honestly, Forentel, I don't understand you. No one understands you! It's almost as if you are a changeling, one of those ugly things left by the desert spirits in place of a real child. You don't belong here, you know that?"

"Yes," said Forentel. She turned and looked into the smug and taunting eyes of her younger sister. "Yes, I do know that. You are right. I don't belong here, and I never have. Now go away."

Dreena had opened her mouth to make another remark. When she saw that Forentel meant what she said, her eyes widened, her mouth stayed open, and she forgot what had been going to say. When Forentel turned away from her again, she put out a hand.

"Forentel. What is it?"

Forentel would not answer. She could not answer, and eventually Dreena left. Forentel stared out at the street until she realized that the sky had darkened further and the first winds of the storm had risen. Then she closed the window and looked around the room. She was tired of waiting. She got to her feet and went out quietly into the hallway. There were no servants around, and she walked down the hall but saw no one. The servants had gone to close up the house against the storm winds and any dust that might blow in off the desert, and her sister, for once, was elsewhere. Outside of Nedriff's study she stopped. She raised her hand to knock, but she could hear raised voices within.

"She does have a right to know the rest, Nedriff. We should have told her before."

"*You* had no right to tell her anything! Not without my permission! It was my decision to keep her! What she knows is my decision, what becomes of her is my decision!"

"You saved her for me, Nedriff, when she was tiny. You gave her to me. So don't tell me now that I have no rights. She is my child by law now, as much as yours."

There was silence for a moment, and Forentel did not have to see to know what her father was doing. He was standing, fists clenched, in front of Mareg, but he was looking away from her. He would never admit to being wrong, but he was backing down. Forentel had seen him do this more times than she could count.

"What exactly does she know? And how?"

"She must have seen the other one, her twin. I don't know where or how she saw her, but she is obviously in the city. No, Nedriff, I did not ask her. Don't look at me like that, and don't you dare raise your voice to me again. I did not ask her. We will call her down here, and we will tell her everything. Then and only then we can ask her."

"Forentel is a strange one. If we tell her everything, Mareg, how do you think she will take it?"

"Badly. At least at first. How else could she take it? How would anyone take it? But we must do it. We will do it, Nedriff, both of us."

"I should have had the other killed. No one should have been left alive who knew. How do you think she will react when she learns her mother, her true mother, was a Tirdar?"

There was a crash. Her father's temper had risen again; he had smashed something to the floor.

"You are the one who cares most about that." Although Mareg sounded calm, there was an icy undertone to her voice that meant that she was truly angry.

"I brought you the child because you could not conceive. I gave in to your foolishness and let the twin live, even though twins are bad luck. I sent the mirror child away, where I hoped she would die, or at least do no harm. I was a fool. I let you keep Forentel even after you did conceive. And I have raised her as my own."

"She *is* your own, Nedriff. You should remember that. And there is no way—by law or any other way—that you could have taken Forentel from me!"

Standing in the dim hallway, with the winds of the storm outside buffeting the house, Forentel felt a rush of warmth. Mareg was her mother, whatever woman of whatever kind had given birth to her. Some of the ice around her began to melt. But she was a Tirdar woman.

Certain things made sense to her now. The dreams. Some Tirdar had dreams in which the future or the past became clear, or so they claimed. She had never wanted to believe this, but she had always had a sneaking fear that her dreams were of this sort. If what she saw in her dreams was real—

"Very well, then! I will tell Forentel, after I have taken care of matters. I will tell her what I think she should know, and then I will tell her what it is she will do. You realize she will have no future if this gets out. I know where the double, the twin is. Her name is Frelenya. Ah, I see you know that already! Did you know that she is connected with the Tirdar rebels?"

"They are not rebels, Nedriff. There are no rebels. They are superstitious savages, hoping for magic to save them, heretics, perhaps—"

"Without a doubt. And heresy is rebellion. You prosecute and condemn heretics, Mareg, you do it all the time. Frelenya is one. Destroying her destroys an enemy and solves a problem we should have taken care of years ago. No, I will not blame you. *I* am the one who should have taken care of this. When I found that this Frelenya was still alive, I should have done it. And now I hear that she was part of this new and dangerous religious movement."

"It's not dangerous, Nedriff. It's only savages and their superstitions. These superstitions do no harm, they—"

"Of course it's dangerous. How do you think Forentel will react when she learns the truth of who she is, of who her twin is? Frelenya is dangerous." Nedriff's voice was grim. "I intend to see that nothing worse comes of this. I will do tonight what I should have done when the children were born."

Mareg made an inarticulate sound, and there was the noise of a scuffle. Then there was a crash. Her mother said nothing more, but Forentel could hear her father breathing hard.

"I am not going to hurt you, Wife, nor will I hurt Forentel, but I will not allow you to interfere. You will stay here, in this room, and I will send my men to guard you until this is finished. Forentel will be placed under guard, and she will not leave her room. I will send more men to the Tirdar quarter, to find Frelenya and kill her, to do what should have been done long ago. I will have the double's blood, and then I will tell Forentel what I wish her to know. Afterwards she will do as I say, and I will give her in marriage to Brezat. She cannot refuse once she knows her true heritage."

"Brezat is almost your age!" Mareg's voice sounded muffled.

Forentel drew a deep breath, flattened herself against the wall beside the door, and tried to peek through the crack. When she couldn't see well, she pushed the against the door gently, and the crack widened. She could see her father, red-faced, standing over her mother, who was in a chair. With a flash of horror she realized that her father had bound her mother in the chair with her own scarves and with the rope from the curtains. Her voice was muffled because Nedriff had his hand partly over her mouth. As Forentel watched, Mareg leaned forward and bit Nedriff on the hand. Nedriff shouted and drew back.

"His first two wives died, Nedriff! I can't prove it, but he killed them, I know it! I will not let you do this to my child—" Her words were cut off as Nedriff raised his hand and slapped her. Then he took his handkerchief from his pocket and stuffed it into her mouth. Forentel smothered a gasp. She had never seen her father strike her mother before.

"Brezat has said he wants Forentel, and have her he shall. I need his support with Prince Mirta, for more funds for my troops. Forentel will do as she is told, once she learns she has Tirdar blood. As a Tirdar in our household she can be sold, if I so order it. She will be pleased to marry instead, and marry a Virsat noble. She will keep her silence, and she will obey me. What Brezat does with her is his business, but I doubt he will kill her if she pleases him. And you will say nothing. How will it look to Prince Mirta if he discovers the High Judge has knowingly kept a Tirdar in her husband's house, has raised that thing as her husband's child, as a Virsat? They will think you bore the child to a Tirdar father. That is what I will say, Mareg, and you cannot prove otherwise. Even if you could, it would not matter. Lord Brezat and the prince will believe me, or they will say they do and back me, either way. And Brezat will still have Forentel, only then he will not use her gently."

Nedriff finished binding another scarf around Mareg's mouth, keeping the handkerchief gag in place. Then he leaned over and kissed her forehead. "I am sorry I struck you. You will thank me when this is done, Mareg," he said gently. "You have no family left since your father and brother died in that accident. You have only me. And your place in the temple, which I will see that you keep. I have always taken care of you, given you everything you desired. But this must be different. It is for the good of us all."

Forentel could not move. She wanted to, but she simply couldn't. Now many things were clear. Her father had given her as a toy to Mareg, when Mareg could not conceive, and then had wanted to take her away when Mareg did conceive, when she conceived Dreena, a true, pure Virsat child. Her father planned to give her to Brezat, a man only three years younger than he, a man who looked at her with hot and predatory eyes, a man who was known for cruelty to his Tirdar slaves. Her father thought of her, his own child, as less than human, as property. He was willing to threaten his wife, another Virsat noble, to further his plans. And what had happened to her Tirdar mother, the woman on whom Nedriff had fathered her? Forentel knew without a doubt that Nedriff had killed her. She saw again her recurring vision of fire and terror.

Her mind reeled. She wanted to rush in to help her mother, but she knew she couldn't. Her father would simply seize her and tie her up as he had Mareg. To tie up another Virsat like that was to court revenge from the injured party's family. Except, as Nedriff had pointed out, Mareg had no family left. What was even worse was that many Virsat would agree that Nedriff was doing the wise thing.

Forentel glanced up through the crack in the door and right into her mother's eyes. Mareg saw her. She did not jerk or struggle or do anything to give away the fact that Forentel was at the door. But Forentel, looking into her eyes, heard a message as clearly as if Mareg had spoken. *Run,* said Mareg's eyes. *Run now.*

Forentel wanted to ask where to run, where she could get help, what she could do. She stared back at her mother, feeling desperate.

Go, daughter, go. Hurry! If only I could speak to you! Oh Forentel, run!

Forentel backed up, away from the door. As she did, her father turned and saw that the door was open a crack. He did not see her, but he knew, Forentel could feel it. It was not as clear as her mother's thoughts, but it was there, the knowledge of her, and also anger and shock.

She ran back up the hallway toward her room but veered away before she reached it. If she went there, he would find her, and she could not get out, short of leaping from the window. She ran toward the kitchen. She had only the most general of ideas, not a plan at all: go to the Temple of Justice and get someone to help, the high priest, perhaps, or an under-judge, or anyone she could find who was willing. But then she remembered: her father was going to kill her twin, the sister she hadn't known she had, Frelenya. She had to stop that from happening first.

As she dashed into the kitchen she ran headlong into Lofa, the head cook, a plump, middle-aged Tirdar woman she had known from childhood. She paused, gasping, looking around wildly. From behind her came shouts, not just from her father. Forentel glanced behind her. She knew what had happened: her father had called out the guards he had brought with him from the palace. She looked around desperately, saw the long bread knife on the cutting board, and grabbed it up. It was not very sharp.

"Not that way." The cook took Forentel by the shoulder. "You can't fight them off, lady. Forentel, sweetheart, look at me. You have to leave. You must get help. And you must save yourself."

Forentel let go of the knife. She looked up at Lofa. "What can I do, where can I go? They have my mother; they are going to kill—" She couldn't explain.

Lofa was wrapping her in a cloak, a Tirdar cloak, not patterned with house colors, but a plain gray cloak, and she was handing her a small package of food and a canteen full of water.

"Hurry," she said.

"Where shall I go? What can I do?"

"Go where you are called, and bring help—for all of us. Go!" Lofa pushed her out the kitchen door.

For a moment Forentel stood in the small kitchen garden that Lofa and her assistants tended so carefully. The winds of the storm whipped around her, hot and dry and dusty. The plants had been covered with white cloth as soon as the servants knew the storm was coming, so it seemed now as if Forentel stood in a garden of snow. She heard shouts in the kitchen now, so she turned and ran.

There were few people out in the streets. Most had gone to shelter out of the winds of the storm. Even here, in this protected part part of Tireera, the winds were harsh, flinging bits of sand and other matter like a stinging hail. Forentel pulled the cloak over her head and wrapped it around her, pulling it across her mouth. She squinted her eyes, but she ran ahead, into the yellow, dusty light. She needed to find Frelenya before her father's soldiers found her. Frelenya would be in the Tirdar quarter, and she could at least go there, but she had no idea what to do after that. She didn't know what Lofa meant when she had told her to go where she was called, and she could not ask now.

The winds were worse in the Tirdar quarter, toward the edge of the city. Virsat often referred to the Tirdar as slaves, but not all of them were. Some were free Tirdar who lived in this quarter, the poorest section of Tireera, where they survived by selling services to others of their kind or by contracting with Virsat. The quarter was a maze of alleys and poorly kept streets. Buildings of mudbrick and straw, and only occasionally of stone, leaned haphazardly against one another.

Forentel looked around for someone who might help her. Although most people were in shelter somewhere, there were some still out, bundled into cloaks as she was, hurrying somewhere, or having no place to go despite the storm. Forentel tried to stop one of them, a young man, but he pulled away from her with a muffled curse and disappeared into the yellow haze. It did not help matters that the day was turning toward evening, and the light, what there was of it, was beginning to fail.

Crouching in a ruined doorway she found an old woman. She almost overlooked her as part of the blowing trash and the heaps of stone, but the woman's bright eyes caught hers. Forentel crouched beside her and shouted above the wind.

"I'm looking for someone—Frelenya. Do you know her?" The old woman stared back at her as if turned to stone. "Frelenya!" shouted Forentel. "I need to find her!" Her errand seemed hopeless; how could she ever have thought she could do anything here? It would have been better to go straight to the temple.

"Looking for Frelenya." It seemed the old woman had a voice after all, but it was barely audible. Forentel leaned closer. This close, even with the wind, she could smell as well as hear her.

"You are the one with the dreams. We knew you would come." Suddenly the old woman reached up and grabbed Forentel by the front of her cloak. "I will tell you, but beware they do not catch you, too. Then go to the prophet in the desert. In the shrine." The woman grinned, and Forentel saw that her bottom front teeth were missing.

"The shrine! Will you do it? You must! Swear it, woman, swear it, for the sake of us all!"

Forentel nodded, then croaked, "Yes." She would have said anything to make the crazy woman let go. The old woman did let go, looking satisfied.

"That way," she pointed with a bent finger toward a twist of alleyways. "Keep always to the left in the turnings. After five turns is the street where she—your mirror," she laughed when Forentel started, "lives."

"Thank you," said Forentel, backing away.

The old woman began to laugh, a high shriek that mixed with the sound of the storm. Forentel turned and ran, with the woman's laughter riding the wind behind her.

The alleys were dark and getting darker in the failing light. No one emerged from the buildings, and no one, inside or out, dared to light a lamp in this wind. Forentel felt her way along the outer walls of buildings, counting the turns, keeping always to the left. She knew before she got there that she was at the right place. She knew because now there was light and noise. There was screaming.

She came to the end of the last alley and peered around the corner. Despite the wind, someone had lit torches, and the flames streamed out and away, licking perilously near to the thatched straw of some of the rooftops. Forentel stared. In some ways this was very like her vision.

Soldiers were there, Virsat troopers in uniform. They had dragged Tirdar from their houses out into the windy evening, and even as Forentel watched, more were dragged out. The soldiers surrounded them with drawn swords, and some with spears. Forentel swallowed, looking for Frelenya. She did not see her, and she felt a momentary relief.

"Where is she!" the captain was demanding. "We know she is here. Bring her out now, or you will all die, one by one."

People were screaming and sobbing, and as she watched, a trooper pulled a child away from a woman and ran the little boy through. The child fell into the street, and the wind whipped dust over his body and the rapidly forming pool of blood. The mother screamed and threw herself across her dead child, but the trooper yanked her up.

"Stop!" Someone was pushing people aside, working her way forward through the crowd. It was Frelenya.

Of course it was, Forentel thought. She couldn't seem to catch her breath.

"What do you want with me?" Frelenya stood in the flickering, streaming torchlight. She had thrown back her cloak, and the light played across her face, making strange patterns. "I am here. I am Frelenya; why do you seek me?"

The captain said nothing, merely nodded at his men. One seized Frelenya and twisted her arms behind her back. Another grabbed her hair, pulled her head back, and cut her throat.

Forentel screamed. The sound cut through the cries of the Tirdar and rose above the sound of the wind. Before she had time to think, one of the troopers was at the mouth of the alleyway. He grabbed her by the arm and drew her out. Forentel stumbled as she came into the light, and the captain reached out and grabbed her chin, turning her into the torchlight. Forentel heard his indrawn breath.

"Magic!" the captain said. "Tirdar evil magic!"

The Virsat soldiers drew back, one of them making the sign against evil, and even the captain seemed stunned. The Tirdar had quieted, except for a few sobs. Forentel took advantage of the captain's confusion. She gave him a swift, hard kick in the shins with edge of her foot and followed this up with a knee to the groin. The captain shouted and let go of her, doubling over. Forentel ran. She dodged into another alley, with no idea where she was going.

Behind her she heard shouting, and then a roar; a soldier, deliberately or not, had touched his torch to one of the straw roofs. The fire caught immediately and, fanned by the wind, began to spread. If it were not stopped, the whole quarter would burn. There were cries for water, and now people were coming out of the buildings, racing toward the fire, desperate to put it out. Glancing behind her, Forentel saw that not everyone was involved with trying to put the fire out. Some of the soldiers had come into the alley and were pushing through the crowds of people, looking for her.

"This way!" Someone had grabbed her by the cloak. Forentel fought to pull her cloak back.

"I need to get to the temple!" she said. "The Temple of Justice!"

It was a young man who had her by the cloak, and he was paying no attention. "We have to get out of the city!" he cried. "They will kill us!" Still holding her by the cloak, he began to run, and with no choice in the matter, Forentel stumbled after him. The crowd drew Forentel inexorably toward the gates.

The city gates had been closed against the storm and the night, but the guards were distracted, looking inward toward the fire. Several of the Tirdar rushed the pedestrian gate and pushed it open, even as the guards began to shout. Forentel was shoved out. The young man who had grabbed her cloak was long gone. She found herself outside the gates, just as the guards slammed them shut from behind.

She was alone outside the gates. The storm was over, and the stars were beginning to come out. The air was cooling rapidly, and soon it would be cold. She found she was shaking not from the cold but from emotional reaction.

She moved quickly away from the gates and off the road. Now that she had a moment to think, she realized she could not go back in. Not yet. She could pound at the gates, and the guard would come, but they would almost certainly kill her, thinking she was Frelenya, and if they realized who she really was, they would take her back to her father.

She needed someplace to hide, someplace she would be safe, where no one would look for her. Then, when it was a little safer, she would go back. She had to believe that her father would not keep her mother prisoner once the word came back that Frelenya had been killed as he ordered. He would probably have troops looking for her, but with any luck it would take a little time for him to organize that search in the confusion following the fire.

She couldn't think where to go. She had a few friends, but none could hide her from her father, especially not once it was known that he was looking for her. She couldn't stay out here in the desert. She shivered and drew the Tirdar cloak more tightly around her. This reminded her of the old woman. "Go to the shrine," she had said. Forentel knew which shrine that was: the Shrine of Dawn, the Shrine of the Cat Goddess. The haunted, dangerous Tirdar ruin out in the desert. The ruin inhabited by ghosts, predators, and a madwoman.

FOUR

HE COULDN'T GO BACK TO TIREERA, NOT UN-
til he had a better idea of what was happening. Erba shivered, hidden in a tumble of rocks far from the road. He
twitched nervously, wishing for some light. Scorpions
were known to shelter in the rock tumbles, but he could
not afford to strike a light and reveal where he was. Even
if he dared, he had nothing with which to make a light: no
matches, no tinder, no fire-striker. He had, in fact, nothing except for his cloak, his sword, and a canteen of
water.

He had spent the storm huddled as best he could in a
rock tumble that was home to a small thicket of tough
desert bushes. He had pulled his cloak over his head and
wrapped it tightly around him to keep out the sand, not dar-
ing to open the cloak even when it became hard to breathe.

After the storm passed he had found that he was not far off the road.

He crept back toward the place of ambush, keeping low. He saw the troopers return to carry away the bodies of his friends and his servants. He heard them laughing and talking, but he had not dared to get close enough to hear what they said. It was lucky he had gone no closer, for between him and the road, he had seen several troopers, fanned out in a search pattern. His breath had caught, and he had slithered away like a rodent, pushing his way into a tight cluster of thorn shrubs. The search had gone past him, but now he was cut and torn, and if he were unlucky, some of the thorn poison could fester.

Erba strained to listen for anyone or anything out in the desert. There was nothing but the wind, the ordinary cold night wind, at least, and not the storm. He needed shelter, and he he needed help for the thorn poison. He couldn't go back to Tireera, back to the palace. He trusted no one now. His friends would either be suspect or be under watch by his enemies. He shied away from the thought of just who these enemies might be, but at last he forced himself to think the unthinkable. It was Mirta. The knowledge had worked its way to the surface, and now he couldn't hide from it.

His brother had always been jealous. It did not matter in the least that there was nothing of which to be jealous. Erba was younger; he was not the heir. He was, he knew, the more popular and perhaps even the more intelligent of the brothers, but he had never challenged Mirta's will. The younger Virsat nobles liked him, even though he was interested in study, in history, and in tales of far-off places. He was interested in culture. None of this should have been threatening to Mirta. All the same, it was. Erba knew it was. And he knew his brother's nature, knew how he couldn't stand to be overshadowed in anything. Nonetheless, Erba had never dreamed Mirta would take things this far. Would try to kill him.

He found that his teeth were chattering. The temperature was dropping precipitously, as it did at night in the desert. He was in shock. He had seen the victims of hunting accidents and of mishaps in military practice, and he knew the signs. He saw them now in himself. He felt distanced, slow, and clumsy.

He forced himself to stand and to move out of the rock tumble. He uncapped the canteen and carefully drank a little of the water. Now that the storm was gone and the stars were out, his eyes were adjusting to the darkness. In another hour or so, if he were not mistaken, the moon would rise. That would make it easier for him to see, but it would also make it easier for anyone tracking him, and he knew his brother. Mirta would have told his guards not to give up but to persist until they found him and killed him.

That was not going to happen. Erba knew a place where he would not be found, where no one would think to look for him, at least for a while, and by then he would be gone. He had only to reach there safely, not an easy task. He drew a deep breath and set off in what he hoped was the direction of the ruined Tirdar shrine.

FORENTEL FOLLOWED THE road for a while, but the road would not take her to the shrine. She knew that. She also knew that if anyone were to search for her outside of the city, they would start by following the road. She had only a vague idea of where the shrine was, since she had never been there. It was to the east; it was, after all, the Shrine of the Dawn. It was on a cliff on the high, rocky terrain beyond the city, close to some of the villages on the

river. Forentel looked behind her at the road, shining in the
moonlight, and then at the scrubby desert. She took a deep
breath and stepped off the road, feeling that she was leaving her entire life behind her.

It was hard going on the open desert, and she had to
watch her footing. There were cracks and rocks and sharp
little thorn plants that she did not want to step on. After a
few hours of this sort of travel she was exhausted. There
was no sign that she was any closer to the shrine. She had
no idea how to find it, except to head in an easterly direction and hope, and she realized now how foolish that was.
She wrapped her cloak around her, sat down wearily on a
large rock, and pulled the cork from the canteen Lofa had
given her what seemed like years ago. The water made her
feel better, so she opened the package of food. Lofa had
given her a whole small round of cheese and a small loaf of
bread. She broke off some of both and ate them, feeling
suddenly ravenous.

It was while she was eating that she got the strange
prickly feeling of someone watching her. She looked up,
startled. There was nothing: flickering moonlit shadows on
the desert. She took another bite of bread and chewed it.
The feeling was stronger, so strong that she felt the hair
rise on the back of her neck. Hastily she tied up the food
package again and stood. Two yellow eyes glowed at her
from the top of a rock tumble only a few yards away.

She jumped to her feet and only at the last second kept
herself from running. Whatever it was watching her had
not yet attacked. If it was a predator, fleeing might bring
about the attack she feared. She was unarmed and wished
desperately now that she had brought the kitchen knife after all, however dull it was. She looked around for a
weapon, but there was nothing, only a few broken pieces of
rock near her feet. Keeping her eyes on the thing that
watched, she bent to pick up the pieces of rock.

The thing moved. It was so fast that she felt rather than saw it. She rose hastily, clutching the rocks. The animal was only a few feet away now, and she could see it clearly in the moonlight. It was a tawny desert cat, one of the kind that had killed two of Prince Mirta's hunters only a year or so back. She froze.

The cat glided toward her. It was at least three feet long with a much longer tail, and as it turned its large head, she could see that its eyes were green gold, reflecting the moonlight. When it rose from its crouch, it came up to waist height on her. Forentel swallowed and gripped the rocks, shifting one to her right hand. She would have to be extremely accurate with her throw if it was to be of any use, and even then she wasn't sure if she might not antagonize the animal rather than scare it off.

The animal stared at her, straight in into her eyes. Then its gaze shifted to the rock in her hand. It drew back slightly, then looked up at her again.

Forentel stared. She had never heard of one of the desert cats behaving in such a way, but then not much was known about them other than that they were secretive, fearless predators. This one seemed intelligent, but then they had to be, to be successful out here in the desert. The cat flowed toward her, and she tensed. Then it stopped, looked into her eyes, and gave a hoarse cry, a sort of meow. It turned and trotted away from her. A few feet away it stopped, turned its head back to look at her, and meowed again. As if in a dream Forentel dropped the rocks and followed it. The cat continued, glancing back occasionally to be sure that she was still following.

Sometimes she wanted to stop, but she could not. The cat would not let her. If she paused, it would come back and stare at her with its eyes glowing in the reflected moonlight. She got a sense of urgency from it, or perhaps from her tired and overwrought mind, for surely an animal could not communicate such a feeling to her. Nonetheless, there it was, turning back for her every time she stopped. She began to stumble over rocks in her exhaustion, and once a thorn poked up through the side of her sandal, causing her to cry out. Finally, the cat stopped, and Forentel stopped, too. She stood blinking in the moonlight, unsure at first that what she saw was real.

It was a mass of broken walls and impossible crumbled spires standing in the desert. Terraces eroded into tumbled debris. Dark spaces that might have been windows or doors gaped blackly. When she looked more closely, Forentel could see that the structure was actually built into the edge of a cliff. Had she kept walking, following the cat in a trance, she would have walked off the edge of this cliff.

It was the Shrine of the Dawn, the shrine of the Cat Goddess, but it was far larger than anything Forentel had imagined. This was not a simple and crude remnant of a savage people; this had been an architectural marvel. For the first time Forentel felt a glimmer of wonder about the Tirdar, and then the beginning of a sort of pride. This was her heritage, too.

She tore her eyes away from the shrine to look for the animal that had guided her here, but the cat was gone, vanished into the shifting desert shadows. Now that it was gone, she perversely wished it back, feeling even more alone. Then she squared her shoulders, settled her cloak, and set off toward the shrine.

When she reached the shrine, it was even more imposing. The shattered columns showed evidence of having been smashed, and not just by the erosion of the dry desert heat and wind. A statue that was part woman, part desert cat had had its face hacked and chiseled away. Defacing it had been better than simply destroying it completely in the eyes of the Virsat conquerors, but it was still beautiful. In daylight it would have been a warm honey gold in color, like many of the desert cats themselves.

"Is anyone here?" Forentel's question echoed back from the hollow rooms and terraces of the shrine. She stopped dead. She could understand why none of the Virsat came out here. It was not that the place was destroyed and had no value to them, or not entirely. The shrine was eerie. There was no sign that anyone or anything had been here recently. If in fact a Tirdar madwoman had once lived here, she had probably died long since.

Just as well, thought Forentel. What was she doing here anyway? Why had she come all the way out here, following the advice of an old woman in the Tirdar quarter, someone undoubtedly just as mad as the rumored prophet in the shrine? Now that she thought about it rationally, she had no desire whatsoever to meet some toothless old hag. She was a Virsat, after all. She would wait here until the sun rose and then make her way back to the city and the Temple of Justice, where she could surely find someone to help. The Virsat gods would help her.

"So you have finally come."

The voice came from behind her, and Forentel jumped, turning to look for the speaker. Whoever it was stood in the shadow of a broken column, impossible to see clearly.

"This is a place for Tirdar. All others stand in peril." The voice was forbidding, cold.

"I am Tirdar," whispered Forentel.

"Are you?" The tone implied knowledge of Forentel's prior thoughts, but there was an edge of laughter to it. The speaker came forward into the moonlight, smiling. To Forentel's surprise, it was a young woman, a woman not all that much older than she, perhaps in her midtwenties.

"Not much is as you expected, is it? That is what life does to us."

"What do you know of life? You are not much older

than I." Forentel tried to speak with Virsat haughtiness, but
she succeeded only in sounding rude, and she winced.

"Oh, I am much older than you, my friend. But come inside. It is not polite of me to keep you out here when the
night is chilly and you are tired and hungry."

Forentel felt her face heat up and was glad the darkness
hid it. It was embarrassing to have her rudeness answered
not just with courtesy but with hospitality.

"Who are you?" she said.

"I'm the prophet," said the young woman matter-of-
factly. "I'm the madwoman who keeps the shrine." She
turned to grin at Forentel.

They had entered a low doorway, pushing through some
thick hangings that kept out the cold and the dust storms.
Forentel found herself in a small room where an oil lamp
burned. Not a torch and not a fire of dung, such as most
Tirdar used, but an actual oil lamp. Oil was expensive and
not easy to procure, but she pushed the questions down.

The room was very sparsely furnished with a low bed
made up primarily of cushions with a few blankets, a stool,
and a rickety table. Through a door at the back Forentel
caught a glimpse of another room. In the brief flash of light
from the oil lamp her hostess held up, she saw a wavering
reflection on a wall, and then it was gone again.

"My name is Illiana." The woman spoke as if there had
been no break in the conversation.

"I thought you were Raffa," said Forentel. It was what
she had always heard.

"Illiana is my name. Raffa is my title, my life, what I do
and what I am." She smiled again.

She had long, dark hair, braided in back, and she wore a
calf-length saffron-colored tunic. She looked perfectly normal, Forentel thought, like anyone she might meet in Tieera.

"As Forentel is your name and Delass is your life, what
you are and what you will be."

"I don't understand." Forentel took the offered cushion and sat down. "I came here—" She stopped. Why had she come here? Because an old woman in the city had told her to? Because she was lost, because she needed help—but she didn't want to say that.

"You do understand. You are fighting against your understanding. Eat first, and then I will show you. You have a long journey ahead of you."

The food she was offered was clear water, fresh bread, and a warm vegetable stew with hunks of antelope meat in it. It was delicious, and Forentel tried not to wolf it down. She was famished. She wondered where the meat came from; Illiana did not look much like a hunter.

"The cats bring me gifts from their hunting," the other woman said. She smiled faintly when Forentel started, as if reading minds was usual for her. "There are no cats here now," she said reassuringly, "not even White Ears, who brought you."

Forentel finished eating in silence, trying to guard her thoughts. Illiana let her eat and seemed quite comfortable with the silence. When Forentel had finished the meal, Illiana rose.

"I wish I could let you rest, but events will not permit it. There are times I wish I could change what is to be, not merely foresee it, but we do what we can. Come, Forentel."

The room to the rear where Illiana led her was dim, but when the Tirdar woman raised the oil lamp, reflections bounced back from water. There was a small pool within the room, filling a natural basin, a sight so surprising that Forentel gasped.

"There is a spring beneath us that comes to the surface just here. The Virsat tired to block it when they destroyed this place, but it rose again past the blockage. Sit here."

Illiana took her to a curved indentation in the stone side of the basin. She placed the oil lamp so that the light shimmered back from the water, and Forentel sat as she was told. Then, unable to help herself, she leaned forward and looked into the water.

At first she saw only brilliant ripples, but they mesmerized her, and she could not take her eyes away. Then the shimmers began to form pictures: Nedriff as a younger man, laughing with friends, riding out into the desert. Her mother, standing before her mirror, alone in her room, running her hands over her nude body, with a look of such sorrow in her eyes that Forentel wanted to cry out. But she could say nothing and do nothing except watch.

She saw her father with a young woman with dark hair. They were together in a small adobe house that she knew, somehow, was outside the city, in a tiny village. *That's not my mother,* she thought. *What is my father doing with a woman not my mother?* And then she realized, *She is my mother.* She saw her father visiting this woman, her mother; she saw them laughing. The woman's stomach grew and swelled, and then the woman was in bed with two babies in her arms. Virsat soldiers swept down during the night. There was fire, and her father, riding to the house, ripping one of the children from the woman's arms, handing the child to a soldier. The other infant was lying on the bed, and a soldier lifted his sword, but Nedriff stopped him. And then gave the second child to a sobbing Tirdar woman. *My father saved her.* Forentel thought. *He saved Frelenya, he saved us both. It was chance that he took me home and not Frelenya.*

There was more fire. It was just as in her dreams, but it was not a dream now; it was clearer, even more real and somehow immediate. She swallowed dryly, and then she could hear, too. She heard the screaming, and the shouts of the soldiers, and her father's commands to burn the houses, to kill all within, except for this child, and to let one woman go with the other baby. Her father stood by while a soldier tied the door closed on the house, trapping her mother within, before he lit the house afire.

Someone was screaming now, loudly. It hurt her ears, and it hurt her throat. Forentel felt herself pulled away from the pool. Illiana shook her and then enfolded her in her arms.

"Shh," she murmured. "There is nothing you can do to change the past. Shh."

After a moment Forentel stopped shaking, and now she sat quietly, absolutely still. "I don't understand," she said. "Why?" She reached up and wiped her eyes; she hadn't realized that she had been crying. This angered her. "And what did you do to me?"

"I did nothing to you. You have seen this before, if not as clearly. You have this ability, Forentel. As to why," she shrugged, "killing is what the Virsat do." She looked at Forentel for a moment, and then amended, "It is not all they do, of course, but they do it too much. They claimed they thought there was a rebellion in the village, but that was not the truth. They had heard the prophecy that one born in the village would change things, would bring the peoples together. The Virsat have always been afraid of us, odd though that sounds. We even knew they would come for us, but we could not change it. One cannot change what the gods decree. I remember Fira—your mother—saying she wanted to save her babies. That was you and your sister—"

"How could you know my mother?" Forentel broke in. "You are barely older than I."

"I told you, I am older than I look. Fira wanted to send her daughters away, but she was not quick enough. You were only a few days old when they came, and Fira died that night. That is what you remember, Forentel."

"Frelenya is dead now, too. I saw her die. My fa—

General Nedriff sent soldiers to kill her. All those years and I never knew, and now she is dead." Forentel looked up, her face expressionless. "Why do I have these dreams, Illiana? Do all Tirdar?"

"Not all, no. Some. A few can see the past, a few can see the future, or several possible futures. It would seem that you are one of those who can see the past. And there is another thing. One more thing that some of us can do. Listen, Forentel."

Forentel looked at her. Illiana said nothing. Forentel stared, then opened her mouth to question, but Illiana held up her hand, and still she said nothing.

I wish we had more time. You need more time to learn. I am sorry that time is so short.

Forentel jumped. She knew quite well that Illiana had not spoken, yet she had heard her. It was clear, clearer even than when she had overheard Mareg.

"How did you do that?"

"I don't know. A few of us can do it, those of us blessed by the Goddess, She of the Silence. It does not always work."

"Only Tirdar?"

"Yes. Until now. It runs in our blood, in the blood of some of us. Very few of us."

"What do you mean, 'until now'?"

"You. You are Tirdar and also Virsat."

"I am no longer Virsat. I renounce them, and all my Virsat heritage. It is no longer mine!"

"Even Mareg, your mother? Yes," Illiana said, "your heart mother if not your birth mother. Would you deny her also?"

Forentel opened her mouth and shut it again. *I wanted to get help for her,* she thought.

"You cannot help her by going back to Tieera. There is another journey on which you must leave, and soon."   .

"Stop it!" Forentel rose to her feet. It was suddenly too much. The shocks of the past day were overwhelming. She had lost everything, and she was exhausted. "You cannot tell me what I can and cannot do! I am going on no journey." She stopped. What would she do?

"I am sorry. You have learned things this past day that would be difficult for anyone. There is one place you can go that will bring help to your mother and to the Tirdar as well. To all of us, even Virsat. You must go to the source of our people, the hidden homeland from which we came. We Tirdar are an offshoot of a greater people. You must find the hidden city to the south, Dreffir, the place from which we came generations ago, long before the Virsat came to this land. Most think it is only legend, but it is real, and they understand there the source of our abilities. And they will help you, the Delass, to understand your own abilities and to learn what you must do. You cannot help Mareg by remaining here, and you cannot help yourself. It will be a hard journey. You will see things no one from this land has seen in generations. You will be tempted sometimes to cease in your quest, for I see not only hardship and strangeness before you, but betrayal. There is also love, as perilous in its way as other dangers."

"I will give you what I can of food and some water, and a blanket. There is no map, but you must follow the stars and the river. Come and greet the dawn with me, and then you must leave, before the Virsat soldiers arrive."

Forentel said nothing more. She followed Illiana, feeling dazed. Soldiers were coming. She trusted Illiana on that, and she did not have to be a prophet to understand this much. Somehow, her father had tracked her. Would he now kill her the way he had her sister? All the same, she thought it would take them a little time to figure out where she had gone. Surely she would have another day at least to rest and to find out just what Illiana meant. Hidden cities and lost ancestral lands, surely the woman did not expect her to believe that?

It was indeed almost dawn. Forentel could clearly see the first faint flush on the eastern horizon as she followed Illiana out into the courtyard. The view from the shrine looked out across the desert from the cliff's edge, and now that the sky was paling, it was a stunning sight. Illiana did not pause to look; for her, this was ordinary. There was a crumbling staircase cut into the cliff at the rear of the courtyard, and Illiana began to climb. After a moment's hesitation Forentel followed.

The staircase led to a tiny winding path along the very edge of the cliff. Illiana did not pause or even look back, and Forentel edged carefully along after her. Down below them the desert fell away in a dry, rolling pattern of rust and red and gold, without shimmer now in the predawn light. At last the tiny path widened slightly, and they came to a small, flat space set back against the cliff wall. A natural stone bench jutted out from the wall. Illiana strode to this, climbed up on it, and stood facing the east. From somewhere in her saffron robe she pulled out a twist of grass and two stones. Forentel watched in amazement as she struck the stones together, producing a spark, and lit the grass. When the grass was smoldering, a sweet, light scent drifted on the rising breeze, and Illiana began to chant something in a musical voice.

Forentel couldn't understand the chant. The words were not in Virsat, and they did not seem to be in the dialect the Tirdar spoke among themselves; she had learned a little of this from the servants. If she listened closely, she could hear a relationship with some of the Tirdar words that she did know, but if she let her mind simply flow with the sound something stranger happened: she saw pictures in her mind. She saw the shrine, not as it was now but as it had been, with columns and statues gleaming in the dawn light, with worshippers standing in the courtyards. She saw the desert cats of the dawn goddess prowling the edges of the courtyards, leaving the worshippers alone but staring out across the desert like sentries.

Forentel opened her eyes, shaking off the spell of sound. Whatever magic Illiana employed, she wanted no part of it. She opened her eyes and saw several of the desert cats gazing back at her. They were not visions of the chant; they were real, sitting in the tiny open space. One of them was on the little crumbling path, where it sat unconcerned with its nearness to the edge, scratching its ear with its hind foot. As they didn't seem about to attack her, Forentel warily ignored them as best she could and looked beyond them, out over the desert. There was a column of dust rising from the direction of Tireera, and closer than that, almost at the ruined shrine itself, two men struggled across the broken ground. In a few minutes they would be here.

Illiana had finished her chant. She extinguished the grass incense and stepped down from the stone bench.

"Let us greet our visitors," she said. "We haven't much time before the troops get here. So many soldiers for one poor old woman." She smiled slightly, pushing the dark hair away from her young face. As she walked down the little trail to the lower levels of the shrine, the desert cats padded beside her. Forentel hesitated only a moment before following.

FIVE

$\mathscr{H}$E MUST HAVE TAKEN A FAIR DOSE OF THORN poison. He was shivering and sweating alternately. Normally, he would have gone to the palace physician, who would have an antidote. That was not possible now. He had heard that if the dose of poison was not too great, the effects would diminish after a few days, but he could not afford to wait and hope. And not only that, but the cuts from the thorns hurt. He was exhausted. It wasn't fair; he was a prince of Tireera, after all. He found himself staggering through the moonlit desert, and when he heard a voice and realized it was his own, he knew he was in trouble. He tripped and sprawled full length on the hard desert floor without any more strength.

"Get up, Erba, Prince, you must get up! Here, drink this, you must."

Someone was holding a water canteen to his lips, someone was attempting to wrap him in a clean cloak. It was not another hallucination. Someone was trying to make him sit up.

"Thank all the gods I found you!"

"Filfa?" Sheer surprise caused Erba to push himself away from the hard ground. As he did, Filfa caught him and half dragged him up to a sitting position. "What are you doing here?" He gulped the water Filfa gave him.

"What happened to you?" Filfa pulled the canteen away. "You must not drink too much at once; you know this."

"Sandstorm. And poison. The thorns . . . my foot."

Filfa was holding his foot and turning it to see it better in the moonlight. Erba stared at him owlishly. Then the older man was rubbing something on his wounds, something cool and tingly. Erba recognized the feel of a healing ointment. Then there was a bandage. Erba blinked.

"Not too tight, not too much. Must walk. Must get away."

"Drink this." A different canteen.

It was not water, it was broth. Not very warm, but it helped. After a moment, Erba took the canteen himself, drank a little more, and then stoppered it. When he looked up, his eyes were clearer.

"How did you find me? And why are you here?"

"Let me tell you as we walk. We need to get you some help. But you must not be found."

"The shrine," said Erba. "That old Tirdar shrine, the ruin, no one will go there."

Erba attempted to make sense of things as they walked. Filfa had overheard Mirta ordering out the squad to kill his brother.

"I was in the anteroom waiting to see Prince Mirta, but I was unannounced. He did not know I was there, thank the gods, or I would not be alive now. I took what I could from my rooms for supplies, but I took too long. When I went to find you, I found that I followed the squad, not preceded it; I was too late. And then the storm came up. I saw you when the troopers killed Feffar and Nenndat." Filfa's voice cracked slightly. "I saw it all, but I could not stop it, and I could not get to you. And then after the storm—thank all the gods I found you again."

Erba said nothing, but he leaned on his tutor's arm for a time. He still felt weak, and sometimes the desert seemed to shimmer in front of him, but at least he was up and moving again. At least he was no longer alone.

"He will not stop," he said. "My brother will send more men. He will not give up."

"I know," said Filfa. "I know. We will be away. Hidden, for you to recover from the poison, and then away."

"Why?" whispered Erba. "Why must he kill me?" There was something that was eluding him, something he should know. He shook his head, frustrated, annoyed with himself. The poison had slowed his mind. "And where can I go?" he whispered. Filfa had no answer.

They walked all night. Erba did not become better; he became worse, having taken more poison than he realized. Nonetheless, as dawn approached, they saw the ruin of the Tirdar shrine, growing slowly closer. Erba stopped, swaying slightly as he regarded it.

"Look," he said. "It's beautiful."

Filfa said nothing for a moment, looking at the young man who had been in his care for so long. The prince might not survive, and the news might make him worse, but that did not matter. It had to be said.

"I have worse news," he said, "and you must know. Erba, listen to me. Your brother—your father—"

"I know," said Erba. His voice was thin and bitter and full of sorrow. "My brother would never have dared to

come for me had my father been alive." He looked at Filfa
with eyes filled with pain from more than his wounds.
"Never."

Filfa could think of nothing to say. He merely pulled the
young man's arm across his shoulders and half dragged,
half carried him toward the shrine.

FORENTAL RECOGNIZED ERBA as soon as Illiana
helped him through the ruined gate. The two men had
come to what had been the shrine's formal gate in times
past. Now it was a mass of rubble, difficult for a wounded
man to negotiate. Illiana helped the older man bring Erba
inside. It was indeed the prince. She had seen him only a
few times before; she had never been a friend or even really an acquaintance. And he was not the polished, well-
dressed noble she had seen. He leaned against the older
man, who looked vaguely familiar.

The prince was wounded. Forentel could see it: a hot,
sick, red purple color pulsing through his foot, and worse,
pulsing upward through his leg, reaching toward his heart.
If it kept going it would kill him.

"You need to take care of that poison," she said.

The two men stared at her with astonishment.

"What poison?" asked Illiana.

"Thorns," said Forentel shortly. "Bring him over here
and let me see."

When she thought about it afterward she could neither
understand nor believe her behavior, but that was later. All
she knew then was that she had to act. Erba was stretched
out on the flat stones of the courtyard, and Forentel bent
over him. She unwrapped the bandage around his foot and
gasped when she saw that it was puffy and blue, with
streaks rising up through the ankle.

"Get me water. And stretch that leg out; stop pulling it

back." She knew she was giving orders to a prince of the city, but that was unimportant. She sat down on the stones and took Erba's foot in her lap. Although his skin was waxy and sweat stood out on his forehead, he began to protest. He cut it short with a gasp as she touched the swollen skin.

"What are you doing, woman, don't harm him!" Filfa was alarmed.

"It will be all right." Illiana put her hand on the older man's arm and gently drew him aside. "Give her your water; we can refill your canteens. She will heal him."

Forental placed her palm against the swollen tissue. It seemed to her that she could feel the poison doing its work, corrupting flesh and nerve, working toward the very bones, and reaching outward for more. She drew in a breath. As she did, she felt the poison pull back toward her. She concentrated on this, feeling the alien substance pool under her hand. She heard Erba say something in a surprised voice, but the words did not register.

"Is she a witch? The poison responds to her!" Erba said softly to Filfa.

"Witches are superstition," responded the tutor, his gaze locked on the odd procedure.

"Knife," said Forentel shortly, holding out her hand. She did not take her eyes from Erba's wound. A knife appeared from somewhere, and she took it and without hesitation sliced into the swollen, puffy flesh. She heard Filfa make a shocked sound, but the prince himself said nothing, merely gasped and shuddered. Greenish yellow liquid drained from the wound, and Forentel gently massaged the foot, encouraging more liquid to spill out.

"Water," she said, again holding out her hand. A canteen was placed into it, and she began to wash away the infection. Finally she looked up.

"Done," she said, "for now. It will need to be washed

every day and kept clean, and sand and dirt must be kept from it, but it will heal. It would be best if you stay off the foot for a few days." She blinked, coming back to herself. What was the prince doing out here, at this forgotten place? She felt drained, utterly exhausted. She needed rest as much as the prince did.

"I'm afraid that won't be possible," said Illiana, as if reading her thoughts. "You need to leave, and soon. All of you. This healing took too much time."

Too much time? Forentel blinked. The sun was much higher in the sky. How long had that healing taken? And how had she known what to do? There were too many questions, and she opened her mouth.

"I know," said Illiana, gently, "but I cannot answer you now. You are a healer, among other things, and I wish there were time; you need to know so much. But the soldiers are almost here."

Forentel remembered the column of dust she had seen leaving the city. The prince would be fine; the soldiers would take him home. But she must leave. To her surprise, she saw alarm on the men's faces. Understanding flashed through her. The prince was on the run.

"Where can we go?" Erba was grim.

"To the river," said Illiana, "and down the river to the lost city that haunts your dreams. You may find answers there. And you, my young friend," she looked at Forentel, "you will find your answers there, too. You must go to Dreffir, the homeland to the south. It's there," she grasped Forentel by the shoulders to stop her from turning away. "It's always been there. It's no legend, but it's hidden and hard to find." She looked at Forentel intently. "There are those who would use us. You understand me." She spoke softly. "But they will help you in Dreffir, and help you learn your powers. You must go there. All of us depend on it. Yes, your mother, too, child, and even these Virsat here."

She put her arms around Forentel and gave her a quick hug. "I am sorry I cannot go with you," she said more loudly, "but hurry."

She set off at almost a run. With an exchange of startled glances, the others followed her. Illiana bypassed her own quarters and led them to a small, cool chamber in the rock. She went to a chest and began to pull things from it.

"Here," she said, "quickly."

She handed them rolled blankets, a package of bandages, and then, hurrying to the other side of the chamber, began to pull packets from a stack and give them to the others. Bread, Forentel saw, and some packages that looked like cheese and dried meat. She tossed them two bags such as hunters used, and as they hastily stuffed the items into them, she grabbed several canteens. They ran from the chamber, following her. At the back of the temple where it melded with the cliff was a dark opening. In this natural cave was a well of clear water. Forentel wondered if the same stream fed this well as fed the pool of images in Illiana's quarters. They filled the canteens. As the older man leaned over, filling his, Forentel watched him. He looked familiar, and she knew she must have seen him in her brief visits at court, but she could not place him.

"Come out! You cannot hide from us!" The shout boomed and echoed from the stone around them.

Forentel gasped and put a hand to her mouth. Erba, still shaky, drew his sword, but Illiana stepped forward and put her hand on his sword arm.

"No," she whispered. "There are too many of them; you cannot fight them, sick as you are. This way!" She turned once to make sure they followed.

It was a twisting passageway into the cliff, a strange tunnel, half-natural, half-carved. Forentel held back for a moment, feeling a dry wind blowing from the darkness. She heard Erba draw in a breath behind her.

"Here." There was a scratch and then a flare of light. Illiana had lit a torch. "The passage goes through the cliff. It will take you out into the desert far from here, or far enough. The Virsat do not know of this." She smiled faintly at the two men. "I will deal with the soldiers; they will not follow you if I can prevent it. Find the river and go south. Find Dreffir."

The shouts from outside were closer, and they could hear the stamp of feet. Filfa had taken the torch and now he held it up, the flame streaming back, illuminating the rough stone of the passageway. Forentel shivered and drew her cloak around her. When she looked back, she caught a brief glimpse Illiana. Forentel blinked. The prophet looked suddenly ancient. Before Forentel could say anything, she was gone.

"I am here; why do you disturb an old woman!" Illiana's voice carried back to them from just outside the cave's mouth. It had a quavery sound to it, the sound of extreme age.

The soldiers were close. No matter what Illiana said to distract them, if they did not go, they could be caught. Since both men just stood there, Erba with his hand still on his sword, Forentel strode forward. She took the torch from Filfa's hand and pushed ahead.

"Come if you are going to," she said, "or stay here. It's all one to me. I am going." She hoisted one of the bags of provisions in her left hand and slung it over her shoulder. Holding up the torch in her right hand, she edged along the passage. After a moment she heard the men behind her.

The tunnel twisted downward and then leveled off. It was cool here, as if the heat of the desert never made it to the heart of the cliff. The sides of the tunnel had chisel marks on them. Forentel wondered how long ago the passage had been made and why the Tirdar, or perhaps those who came before them, had carved it. She was so involved with studying the walls that she tripped over uneven rock on the floor and almost dropped the torch.

"Here, give me that." Erba kept his voice low lest the sound carry back upward to the light and the soldiers. "Let me take it."

Forentel resisted, keeping her hand around the base of the torch. She was very aware now of the stone around them, and the darkness, and the fact that these two men had no reason to help her.

"What do you think," said Erba impatiently, "do you believe I will leave you here in the darkness because you are Tirdar?"

It was exactly the sort of thing a Virsat noble would do. It was the sort of thing her family would do. It was an odd and uncomfortable realization.

He looked down at her, his hand touching hers on the shaft of the torch. "I do not repay my debts in such fashion." Before Forentel could respond, he pulled the torch from her. Then he held out his hand to guide her.

Forentel looked at him. "No thank you," she said quietly.

He withdrew his hand without further comment but made a point of seeing that she was always within the circle of torchlight. They continued in silence, but for the sound of the wind in the underground tunnel. The darkness, the stone, and the quiet made Forentel feel as if they walked in one of her dreams, and her skin crawled.

After some winding turns of the passage, the ground began to rise again. Forentel had the impression they had been walking for hours, but she couldn't be sure. She only knew that she was desperately in need of rest, but when she saw light gleaming ahead, some of her exhaustion lifted. She moved ahead more quickly now, pushing past the men in her eagerness to reach the light. Erba put out a hand to stop her.

"Wait," he said, his voice low. "We don't know who or what is out there." He extinguished the torch and placed it in his pack. He drew his sword, and they crept cautiously toward the jagged opening in the hillside.

With his back to the side of the cave, Erba peered out into the daylight and then motioned them forward. Coming up cautiously behind him, Forentel stepped out of the dimness and into the full desert sun.

There was no one and nothing before them but desert, the hard-baked red land with a few scrubby thorn bushes. Standing watching them was a lizard, one of the large green ones with the purple frill at its neck. The frill opened and closed, and then the lizard turned and scuttled away. Forentel saw that it was on a sort of path, a path very faintly outlined, as if it had been made long ago.

"Where are we?" She looked around, seeing nothing but desert, and behind them, the bulk of the cliff. From where they stood now, they could not see the shrine.

"Not far from the ruins of the old village," said Filfa, "the old Tirdar village on the river. The river cuts through the dry lands and splits. One branch goes through Tireera, that's the Drell, the other, the Red, goes out into the swamps and then rejoins the Drell later, downstream. The—"

"Look!" Erba was pointing. "We have to go!"

It was a cloud of dust, of haze, from around the bulk of the cliff, coming from the direction of the shrine. Forentel stared at it, afraid it was another storm. But it couldn't be another storm. With a shock she realized it was the dust raised by the passage of a large group of people on horseback. The soldiers had seen them, or had somehow guessed where they were and would see them soon.

"Where's the river? Filfa, do you know?" Erba had never been out this way.

Forentel glanced at the older man. So he was Filfa, the

prince's tutor. She had never met him, but she knew who he
was. Her father had once said something about him, she
couldn't remember what.

"Don't stand there, woman; come on!" Erba grabbed
her arm.

They ran. Filfa led the way, since he seemed to know
where they were going. Glancing back, Forentel could see
figures in the cloud of dust now, horses and men. They
were running over the flat, red land, dodging through thorn
bushes, and the prince was limping. There was no sign of
any ruined Tirdar village or of the river.

"We can't make it!" gasped Forentel. Her arm hurt;
Erba had not released his grip on her. "They will catch us if
we can't find a place to hide!"

"Can you hide us?" Erba's lips were pale, and he had
begun to slow. He shouldn't be doing this, Forentel
thought, not with the infection in his foot.

"Do you know Tirdar magic to hide us?" Erba persisted.
The prince obviously believed in Tirdar arcane powers, at
least when in suited him, and from Filfa's silence she suspected he did, too.

"I can't," she said shortly.

Erba stopped. He was panting slightly, and sweat stood
out on his face. His wounded for dragged slightly.

"Go," he said. "You and Filfa. Run, hide in the thorn
scrub if you have to. I'm the one they want." He drew his
sword and turned to face the oncoming cloud.

"Don't stop!" cried Filfa. "Look!"

Ahead of them low shapes rose out of the desert.
Forentel realized what they were looking at: the remains of
mudbrick dwellings. The remains of the destroyed Tirdar
village. The river could not be far.

They ran through the ruins, but now Filfa was half supporting Erba. Forentel glanced at the ruined dwellings,
many of them not so much ruined as abandoned. Odd

thoughts came to her: visions of children playing, of someone carrying a string of fish to one of the houses, of a
woman pounding dry wheat for flour. The past. Illiana had
said she had a gift for seeing the past. She shook her head,
banishing the visions.

"I can't, really, I cannot, Filfa. You take the woman and
run, find the river, go find the lost city. I will hold them off
as long as I can. You can get away." Erba was no longer just
pale, he was waxy in color, and his lips looked like paper.
He was pulling at his sword again, trying to get it free. It
said much about his state that he could not seem to draw it.

"Stop it," said Forentel sharply. "I will carry you." She
wasn't quite sure why she cared, except that she had in-
vested something of herself in him when she had treated
his wound. It wasn't until she saw how he looked at her that
she realized what she had said and how it would sound to
them. She stepped up to him and pushed the weapon back
in its sheath while he gaped at her. He truly was ill, she
thought. She could feel how abnormally cool his skin was.

She had seen her father's troops in training, the same
troops that now chased them. There had been exercises
where they had to practice carrying wounded comrades
from the field of battle, where healthy men lay limp on the
ground and joked with their "rescuers." Erba was taller
than she, and heavier, but it did not matter. The technique
had less to do with strength than leverage. She turned her
back to him and grabbed one of his arms, pulled it across
her chest, and hauled him unceremoniously across her
back. Then she reached around and grabbed him under a
leg, attempting to hoist him higher. She gritted her teeth.

"Let's go." She staggered forward.

She managed to carry him a short way, despite his
protests. They could hear the thunder of hooves behind
them now, and then the shouts of the troop leader.

"Halt! In the name of the king!"

She would have had no choice, but for one thing: she saw the river. And not just the river, but a boat on the stony bank of the river, a boat that had no business being there. An arrow whistled by, and she gasped.

"Put me down!" Erba's voice was weak but furious.

She did put him down. She dumped him into the boat. Filfa tossed in their packs, and together they pushed the boat out into the river and clambered in. At least the boat was sound and seemed to have no leaks.

There were more shouts behind them. She looked back and saw the troop of horsemen on the shore, not regular troops, but the King's Guard. They were no longer shooting at them, and Forentel wondered why they weren't, until she looked at the river. The current was carrying them along strongly. Upstream was the broad river and the stony beach that had once been the landing for the town's fishermen. Downstream the river narrowed and the current quickened, racing around sharp, needlelike rocks that crested above the river. There was no way to avoid the rocks; the only possibility was to thread their way through, and that only if they were excellent boatmen.

"Oars!" she cried. "Get the oars!"

Erba was lying in the bottom of the boat, but Filfa had been looking under the seats.

"There are no oars!" he said.

Forentel looked back at the receding shore. The guard captain was standing on the stony beach with an oar held upright in his hand. She wasn't sure, but she thought he was smiling.

SIX

$\mathcal{T}$HE CURRENT SWUNG THEM SIDEWAYS, AND there was a crash as the boat smashed into the first rock. Forentel was almost flung from the boat, but Filfa grabbed her and hauled her back. They huddled on the bottom, clutching the sides to keep from being thrown into the river. They hit another rock, and water poured in over the side, and then the boat rammed again. Forentel lifted her head and risked a glance. The rapids stretched out ahead of them, and little waves crested and boiled around the rocks. There was a grinding sound as they momentarily caught on another rock and then were pulled free by the current. Part of the thwart was smashed, and Forentel found splinters in her hand where she had been gripping the wood.

They were awash in water but still afloat. Their bone-jarring progress continued until the flat bottom of the boat scraped along a partially submerged rock, spun sideways into another rock, and wallowed and tipped, throwing them all into the river.

Forentel felt the water close over her head and she clawed desperately for the surface. The river dragged and pulled her along, scraping her over rocks and then pulling her into an eddy between two rocks. No matter how she fought, she could not get free. She couldn't breathe, and the dark water sucked her down, dragging her deeper and deeper. She flailed, kicking out, hoping to find the bottom, and then her head hit the side of a rock. Lights flashed before her, she lost control of her limbs, and the world grayed.

Something grabbed her by the hair and pulled her up. She broke the surface, and something pulled her away, out of the eddy. She felt the water still tugging at her, and she tried to thrash. Someone had her pinned, with an arm across her chest.

Occasionally, water lapped across her face. Panic rose and she fought automatically.

"Hold still," said Erba. "We're almost to shore."

"I can't swim," she tried to say.

She was being dragged now, but there was land under her. Erba hauled her out of the water, crawled forward, and collapsed. She couldn't breathe. Someone loomed over her, and a hand turned her face to the side. Someone pushed on her stomach. Forentel coughed and then threw up, heaving up what seemed to her like half the river. When she had finished she was shivering and her throat was raw, but she felt much better. She looked up into Filfa's concerned face. Only one thing seemed of immediate importance.

"Where did you learn to do that?" she croaked.

"When I was a boy," said Filfa, "my family had a large pond on our estate. I saw one of the Tirdar save a child this way—my sister. We thought she had drowned. That was a very long time ago."

Forentel sat up. Filfa looked exhausted, and Erbra was lying on the shore shivering. They were on a small sandy beach beyond the rapids, which foamed in the near distance. Behind them the beach gave way to crumbling red cliffs, but near them was wood cast up by the river, a rarity.

"We need a fire." Forentel was looking at Erba. "He needs to get warm. And I need to look at his foot again. The river may have done it more damage." She didn't say it, but she wanted the fire, too. She felt chilled to the bone.

"We can't." Erba pulled himself up. "We have to move, now." He waved off Forentel's protests before she could voice them. "The guards will hope the river has finished us, but they won't assume it, and they will come downstream to check. It will take them some time. The river flows into the gorge below the city, and they will have to get around the cliffs and the broken ground, but they will come. We had best be away from here before then and hope they find the remains of the boat and draw their conclusions from that."

They took some of the driftwood with them for a fire later if Erba deemed they were safe enough. Filfa made a bundle of it and tied it across Forentel's back. No one asked her—they assumed she would carry the firewood, and she didn't have the strength to object.

The trek away from the river was difficult. At first they shivered despite the heat, but then, after the sun had warmed them, exhaustion and thirst became a problem. One of their water canteens had been lost in the river. Luckily, most of their meager supplies had survived, and Forentel carried these as well.

The sun beat down, and not far from the river the land was completely dry. They needed to find the Red River, to get out of the desert and follow it, avoiding lands and set-

tlements close to Tireera. They stumbled along until the
heat of the day was too great and Filfa insisted they rest.
They made their way to a rock pile in the near distance, but
before they took shelter under the overhang, Filfa inspected the sand in the cool shadows for any scorpions that
had had similar desires.

Forentel fell asleep almost as soon as she tucked herself
into the shade. Her Tirdar cloak had dried, and she folded
this under her head for a pillow. Just as she was dozing off
she felt someone shaking her, and looked up to see Filfa.

"Drink," he said, holding out the waterskin. She sat up
long enough to gulp some of the warm water before falling
back into sleep.

When she woke, it was dusk. She sat up, feeling even
more thirsty now. Disorientation hit her, and for a moment
she couldn't understand where she was or why, but then recent events came back to her in a flashing tumble. She
looked around, but she was alone under the shelter of the
rocks. Disappointment hit her throat in a burning rush, and
she swallowed, but why should two Virsat nobles stay with
a fugitive Tirdar? Then she heard low voices. Peering out
from under the rocks she saw the two men seated on the
hard-packed earth close by, speaking softly. She must have
made some sound, for they both turned, and Filfa motioned
for her to come.

"When it is full dark we can go," said Filfa, as she came
up to them. "But first there are some questions you must
answer."

Forentel lifted her head, ignoring her thirst. "My question first," she said. "I need to look at his foot. I need to see
if the poison has drained."

She nodded at Erba, just barely refraining from saying
his name. They had not told her their names, and they obviously did not expect her to know who they were. What

surprised her more than anything else was that she really did want to know, first and foremost, about the infection in Erba's foot. She expected that the day's travel would have aggravated the wound, but that did not seem to be the case. The time in the river had cleaned it, and walking on it did not seem to have harmed it. Forentel wrapped the foot again in some material she ripped from her cloak.

"It would be better to let it rest," she told him, "but obviously you do not intend to follow that advice. At least the poison has drained, and the swelling is going down. You are very lucky."

Erba leaned back, regarding her as he tucked his foot back into his sandal. He said nothing, but Filfa moved closer, peering into her face in the dusk.

"Who are you, wearing the cast-off clothes of your mistress?" he asked. "And what are you running from, Tirdar?"

"I could ask you the same," she shot back. And then, as an afterthought, "Virsat."

Filfa stood up. Even in the gathering darkness she could see his face flush. He drew a ragged breath, and for a brief moment she wondered if he would hit her as she had seen her father hit Tirdar servants. He was obviously not accustomed to retorts from those he considered lesser beings.

"Sit down," said Erba. "Uncle." His tone was mild, but there was an edge of both command and amusement to it, and Forentel noticed that the older man promptly obeyed.

"She has as much right to ask of us as we do of her," said Erba. "We already know she is one of their healers, and I owe her my life."

"As I owe you mine." Forentel said. "You pulled me from the river."

"Well, then, we are even." Erba smiled slightly. "A fair trade."

"It is not a barter. I did not save your life so that you

would owe me. I did what I did because it was right."
Forentel snapped her mouth shut. *Where did that come
from?* she wondered. Her newfound ability to heal made
her uneasy, but it was less unsettling and more useful than
visions.

"I know that. That is the way Tirdar healers are, or are
said to be. I never thought I would actually meet one. Some
now believe your kind are only stories."

Forentel flinched. She felt a little like she thought the
desert fox must have, the one her cousins had caught and
kept in a cage for a time.

"That would explain why you are a fugitive," Erba went
on. "And why you didn't want to tell us, since trained Tirdar healers have a price on their heads. Not that anyone
thought they—you—truly existed anymore. Don't be concerned, I will hardly turn you in to the King's Guard." His
mouth twisted bitterly.

"I'm not trained to heal." She knew what Illiana had
told her, but more than that, she knew what she felt. She
was, or would be, a healer. Someday, perhaps, but not yet.
"I'm going to the lost—I'm going to Dreffir to learn." She
supposed she was, among other things.

"What's your name, healer?"

"For—Frelenya." She watched them both as best she
could in the dim light, but there was no reaction.

"Frelenya," said Erba in acknowledgment. "I'm Erret
and this is my uncle Filfa." Filfa started slightly. Obviously
he had not expected to give out his real name, but just as
obviously Erba remembered that the name had already
been given. "We have some family trouble in Tireera. As
I'm sure you realize, we Virsat have our feuds. Right now it
is not safe for us in the city."

The weight of anger and sorrow in his voice made
Forentel draw back.

"I have to tell you, for your own sake, that you may be in

more danger with us than alone." Erba shifted uncomfortably on the hard ground. "I am a wanted man. I hope my—
enemies—believe I am dead, and my uncle with me, but if
they do not, they will hunt me without ceasing. If you wish
to strike out on your own, we certainly understand that. Although I for one would like you with us"—he paused, and
then shrugged, having decided on a certain amount of
honesty—"for your skills."

Forentel knew she should tell them she had no real
skills, not yet, that what she had done was guesswork and
luck, but the fear that ran up her neck was foremost. He
was a prince of the city.

"Who hates you so much that they would hunt you so?"
she whispered.

"I told you we Virsat have our family feuds." Erba
looked into the distance. The sun had set in a blaze of saffron, and stars were pricking through the deepening blue
of the night sky. The temperature was beginning to fall
again.

"My brother." Erba bit the words off. "It is my brother
who hates me so. Hates me and would kill me, as he
killed our father." His voice was low and bitter, full of
grief and fury.

Forentel gasped. The king was dead, he had to be, old
Rellaff killed not by the wasting disease but by Prince
Mirta, his son and heir. What would happen to Tireera
now? And what of her family? Her father was close friends
with Prince Mirta. But her mother—what would happen
now to her mother, High Judge with so few allies? If her father would not protect her mother, and all because of her—
She looked up to find the men regarding her strangely.

"It's terrible," she said, "for a brother to do this, and for
a son to kill his father!" The shock in her voice was real,
and the situation appalling enough that she hoped they did
not suspect what she knew. Of course Mirta would hunt

his brother, considering what he had already done. She shuddered.

"So you see now why it may not be safe with us." Erba's voice was still bitter.

"She will stay with us," said Filfa. "We should keep her. We may find her useful. You belong to us now, woman."

Forentel rose to her feet. "I am not your property. I am no one's property." The words had a quiet force that surprised the men, that even surprised her.

"She is a free Tirdar," said Erba.

"Even free Tirdar belong to Virsat who need them. We can claim her," Filfa began, but Erba cut him off.

"Frelenya decides how she travels. Although," Erba looked at her, "I would like you to travel with us."

"Why are you going to Dreffir?" Forentel asked. Nowhere in Tireera was safe for them, she knew that, but certainly there must be somewhere they could find refuge.

"I have nowhere else to go," said Erba shortly. "No one believes the lost city is more than a tale, so even if my brother suspects I live, he will not look for me there. And," he paused, "I have always wanted to see if there was any truth to this legend. I have searched through all of Virsat writings and maps. Or rather, Filfa and I have. And I believe there are clues to the existence of Dreffir. Now we will find out."

"You say you looked all through Virsat writings. Did you ever ask any Tirdar?"

Both men regarded her with astonishment, which was answer enough. Then Erba had the grace to look thoughtful.

Forentel sighed and shook her head, and then glanced at their meager supplies. There wasn't much: the two bags Illiana had given them, two waterskins, her Tirdar cloak, Erba's sword. She didn't have much hope that any of them would reach the hidden city, alone or together. She wrapped her ragged cloak around her. It was cold now that the sun had set. She didn't much like the idea of moving at night, but she agreed that it would be best to put as much distance between themselves and Tireera as they could, as fast as they could. Beyond all of these considerations she remembered how Illiana had told her she was a healer, and how she—*they*—would find their answers in the city.

"I will travel with you," she said, "as an equal companion, nothing less."

Filfa looked annoyed and Erba looked amused, but they both nodded, accepting her. They had been looking out over the darkened desert, and Forentel had a sudden flash of unease.

"You *do* know which way the Red River is?" she said.

"It should be that way." Filfa pointed across the flat land. "Since the sun set there."

None of us know, she thought. She looked across the dark land with them. The stars were bright overhead, and thorn bushes and the occasional rock tumbles made darker shadows against the night. As she had the previous night— was it only last night?—she felt something watching them. It felt wild and strange and not very friendly, and Forentel shivered.

"Let's go, then," she said. She didn't know where the river was, and she wasn't sure she truly wanted to go to the lost city. All she knew was that she didn't want to stay there, exposed in the desert, any longer.

"HE'S DEAD. THEY'RE both dead. I trust Vrellir. He's one of my better captains." Mirta leaned back in his carved chair before the large window. He hadn't been sleeping well. Wine had not helped to banish the evil dreams of his father, so now he was not only tired but edgy.

There was a faint emphasis on the word *my*. Nedriff, King's General, did not miss it. The King's Guard was not under the authority of the army. Nedriff succeeded in masking a frown, but he regarded his new king with a certain skepticism.

"I hope you are right, my lord, but I still wish you would let me pursue this." Nedriff stood facing the big window, right where the sun hit his eyes. Mirta had arranged it this way, making his point about who was in charge, just in case Nedriff had any doubts.

"There is nothing to pursue, as I keep telling you. Vrellir had some pieces of the boat brought for my inspection. It was smashed almost beyond recognition. My brother and the tutor and the Tirdar slave will be in similar condition. Too bad about Filfa," Mirta shrugged, "but he was not too great a price to pay, considering the gain."

"How did there happen to be a boat there?" Nedriff was not about to drop the subject.

"I don't know, nor do I care. A remnant from some fisherman." It was obvious that Mirta wished the subject closed. "Some lone fisherman living in the deserted village."

"A Tirdar fisherman, perhaps, someone who could have helped your brother escape."

"There is no one who could have helped my brother escape! Vrellir questioned the old hag in the ruins. She is as insane as they say, and she knew nothing, and there was no one else. But I believe you have good reason to understand the Tirdar better than most, General, and to be wary of their trickery. You know of that from your own family's experience." Mirta did not smile when he saw the flicker on the general's face. Mirta had in fact taken steps to have his brother tracked. If he had escaped, Mirta wanted him hunted down. But he had reasons for keeping this from his ally. "But let us move on to other topics. Have you news yet of your own runaway, your daughter?"

"No word," said Nedriff curtly. He had not told the new king that his child was half Tirdar, despite his threat to

Mareg. It would not reflect well on him, and he was saving the fact as a ploy of last resort, but now it appeared that Mirta knew, or guessed, at least, that something was not right, so any future advantage was lost. The question was, how did Mirta know?

"This must be an ordeal for your esteemed and charming wife, the judge. I heard she has been absent from the temple for the past several days, and I hope she will feel well enough to return soon to her duties. The Goddess of Justice needs her. As does Tireera."

Nedriff stared at the younger man, this time unable to hide his astonishment. Of course the king knew that Mareg had been absent from the temple, but he could not know why, any more than he could know of Forentel's true heritage. Not unless someone had told him, and that someone had to be Mareg herself. Somehow his wife had gotten word to Mirta and given him information. Why had she done it? *How* had she done it? He had confined her to her room and permitted no visitors, only Tirdar servants to care for her. She had no way to get a message out, as no Virsat had seen her. The idea that she had given information to a Tirdar servant was simply unthinkable. Mareg, daughter of a noble family, would not have stooped so low, not even if she had suspicions about the accident that had killed her father and brother.

"She has been ill," croaked Nedriff, seizing on the excuse implied by the king.

"Perhaps I will make a call, myself, on your noble wife." Mirta was enjoying himself. "It might aid in her recovery. Yes, that is exactly what I will do, my friend, if she is not well in another day or so. No need to thank me. A king must give of himself to his people, after all."

"I am sure she will be well, my lord," Nedriff muttered, "and returned to her duties by tomorrow." He squinted uncomfortably into the sun, trying to see Mirta's expression.

Perhaps it had not been so wise after all, to back Mirta, but Rellaff had been dying slowly, by inches. It was either Mirta or Erba, and Erba would never have acted against his father. The younger prince fancied himself a scholar. Nedriff, as a warrior, had an unflattering opinion of scholars. Beyond that, Mirta was far too fond of wine, which would be useful in time. In any event, the choice had been made; the deed was done. Nedriff could not afford to go against Mirta now, not so soon.

"I am sure she will be well," agreed Mirta. He looked at Nedriff thoughtfully. The general was upset and more than unhappy; perhaps he had gone too far. After all, Nedriff had been instrumental in securing the throne for him. He was a valuable ally, albeit one one who needed to be kept in check.

"Come, my friend." Mirta rose from the chair and moved away from the window, allowing Nedriff to move away as well. "Perhaps you will join me for lunch. We need to discuss your plan for solidifying our control and expanding our influence."

"Of course, my lord, thank you." Nedriff smiled, but he was not fooled. Mirta trusted him no more than he trusted his new king.

SEVEN

$\mathcal{W}$HEN THE DOOR TO HER ROOM SLAMMED open, Mareg, High Judge of Tireera, was not in the least surprised to see her husband there. She put aside the scroll book she had been reading, patted her dark hair to be sure it was still in its coils, and looked up calmly.

"The king has expressed a concern for your health and a desire to see you back at your duties in the temple," said Nedriff shortly.

"How kind of him." Mareg rose and smoothed her her long tunic of striped silk. She placed the book on the table beside a bowl of ripe pears, rose, and walked to the window. It was open, although the bars to keep out thieves had been locked in place, and the key was in Nedriff's possession.

"Enough games." Nedriff stood before her. Although Mareg was a tall woman, Nedriff loomed over her. "You got word out to Mirta. I want to know how you did it, and I want to know it now!"

"Certainly." Mareg did not appear in the least shaken, either by having been held prisoner by her own husband or by his attempt to intimidate her now.

"And I want to know why you told the king that Forentel is half Tirdar!" Nedriff wasn't sure which shocked him most, his wife's revealing this information to the king, or her political gamesmanship. Mareg had never before evinced any interest in political manipulation. She had certainly been aware of the currents around her, but she had always held herself aloof in the interests of the goddess she served.

"I did not tell the king that Forentel is half Tirdar, and he does not believe any such thing."

"But you—but he told me—" Nedriff paused. Mirta had very carefully not mentioned Forentel's heritage. "He implied that he knew Forentel has Tirdar blood."

"What I told him," Mareg walked around her husband and closed the door behind him so they would not be overheard, "is that *you* threatened to tell this lie in order to control me." Mareg carefully did not smile at Nedriff's astonishment. "I told him that you wished Forentel to marry now rather than the enter the temple as my apprentice, and I told him who it was that you chose for her. I reminded our new young king that after only two years as my apprentice Forentel will be again eligible for marriage, but then she will have even more worth in the eyes of the gods than she does now. And that she will have the backing of the Temple of Justice, as well as the support of our family and its wealth. You do realize, husband, that Mirta is himself still unmarried, but at some point he must take a noble wife."

Nedriff moved to a chair and sat down heavily, sinking

into the cushions. He passed a hand in front of his face and then stared at his wife.

"Are you hungry? Would you care for a pear?" Mareg offered him the bowl, and when he did not respond, she took one herself and bit into it. "They're good. Never let it be said that you do not provide for your wife when she is *ill,* Nedriff."

"How did you convey all this to Mirta?" asked Nedriff hoarsely.

"I wrote it. I gave it to one of the Tirdar servants. Never mind which one; I will not have you destroy one of my servants, Nedriff. And you know quite well they cannot read. Nonetheless, I took care to code the message. Yes, my dear, it is a code that Mirta knows, as did Rellaff. How unfortunate Rellaff died, from, ah, from a seizure, I understand."

Mareg resumed her former chair and looked thoughtfully at her husband. He looked slightly ill, and his eyes were glassy. She felt briefly sorry for him.

"I have long given information to Rellaff in this code," she said, "and when he became ill, I gave it to Mirta, who handled these matters for him. What I sent in the past had to do with temple matters, nothing more."

"I see." Nedriff sat up in the chair. He had been stunned, but it had not taken him long to recover. He had not risen to command over the army by failing to adapt to sudden shifts of fortune. "How long have we been married, Mareg?"

"Twenty-three years come the rainy season, Nedriff."

"How is it I did not realize your many talents in all that time?"

"I will assume that is a rhetorical question. I never took action before because I never needed to, but don't be concerned." Mareg allowed herself to smile openly now. "We have the same ends in mind. You know my father was a good friend of Rellaff's father, as well of Rellaff himself. Rellaff always regretted the hunting accident that killed his friend. While Rellaff regretted my father's fatal accident, I did not. I never did hold my father in much devotion, not the way a daughter should. I have told you how he treated me. And my brother was no better. I consider their fate an act of the gods." She looked straight at him. "Or the agents of the gods. Forentel is another matter. My daughter. Our daughter, Nedriff. Our Virsat daughter."

"Yes," agreed Nedriff. He knew when to retreat, when to change his strategy, and how to plan for the future. Mareg did not appear to realize that Mirta's hold on the throne was tenuous.

"Is there any sign of her? You are close to finding her? Aren't you?" Mareg could not hide her worry. The last two days of uncertainty and concern for her child had taken their toll, and now that she thought she had her husband's support, she let it show.

"None." Nedriff did not attempt to hide the truth. "I don't see how she could have vanished the way she did. I have squads out searching, and they will find her, never fear."

Nedriff wasn't as certain as he wanted to sound, however. His daughter, a young woman with no experience in desert ways, who, half Tirdar or not, had never been out of the lap of luxury, had disappeared. He had tracked her to the Tirdar quarter—that had not been difficult—and there had been reports that she had been seen near the city gates, but that was as far as it went. He tried not to show his own concern. Now his plans were upset, and it appeared that his wife had plans of her own.

"If she is out alone in the desert, how she will she survive?" Now that Mareg had started down this road she could not seem to stop.

"She has always been resourceful," Nedriff said gruffly. His anger at his wife dissipated like the brief morning

mists on the river. He remembered their early days together and was overcome by a wash of tenderness. He considered putting his arms around her, but glancing around
the room in which he had so recently imprisoned her, he
thought better of it.

"I will find her," he assured his wife. "When she is
safely home again she will be your apprentice, and I will
tell her she need not worry about marriage, not yet." He
considered what Mareg had said about Mirta. It was true,
the king would need a wife. But that wife would not be
Forentel, nor would the king be Mirta.

"I am happy to hear it." Mareg rose and walked to her
husband. She stood over him and put a hand on his shoulder.

"You had best prepare and go to the temple." Nedriff
could not look her in the eye.

It was all she would get in the way of an apology, and
Mareg knew it. Nedriff had never been able to admit when
he was wrong.

"It's too late for the temple today. The priests will not
expect me."

Mareg reached up and unpinned the heavy coils of hair
from above her ears. Her hair was one of her best features,
long and thick, with only a little gray mixed with the dark
brown. As it tumbled down around her face she smiled at
Nedriff, seeing the fire kindle in his eyes. She walked to
the door and locked it, this time from the inside. Now that
she had her freedom again, she would be able to attend to
her own search for her daughter, with her own private resources. Her husband had a lot to answer for. She had been
a very patient woman, but patience had its limits. She
smiled at Nedriff and led him to the bed.

SHE WAS ALMOST accustomed to moving at night now,
scanning the shadows of the moonlit desert, looking for

hazards. What it would be like when the moon waned, Forentel did not want to contemplate, but perhaps by then they would be safe in the hidden city, wherever it was. Or in any event, safe somewhere.

They had been doing this now for night after night for weeks. Forentel had lost track of the time. They slept during the day in whatever shade they could find, covering themselves from the sun. Filfa knew where water could be found, near the base of some of the thorn bush thickets. It was hard to dig down to it, and the water was brackish and foul-tasting, but it was wet, and it had to suffice.

They were low on food, and they rationed out their now stale bread and the hard cheese. Erba caught a desert rabbit in a snare and skinned it. There was pitifully little meat on the animal, and Erba tried to insist that they eat it raw, as he was afraid a fire might draw pursuers to them. Filfa was able to persuade him that a fire now, for the amount of time it would take to cook the rabbit, was a risk they could afford, and Forentel was grateful. Filfa did not feel they were being pursued, but Forentel could not shake the feeling that they were being watched. Sometimes she wished that whatever watched them would make itself known, especially if it had food and clear water.

"We have gone around the city," Erba told her. "We will make our way back to the river, the Red River, south of the city, far south."

"How much longer, Erret?" Forentel did not forget to use the prince's alias. She smiled slightly at him. They had become almost friends. They would have been friends if they both hadn't been conscious of what that might mean. Erba seemed to remember every so often that Forentel was Tirdar and not an equal, and Forentel was afraid he would realize she wasn't Tirdar. It made for an awkwardness.

"Another day?" Erba glanced at Filfa and shrugged; it was obvious that he wasn't certain.

"But once we find the river, Frelenya," said Filfa, "we will have water, and food should be easier to find. And we will be more certain that we are not pursued." He sounded as if he were lecturing. When he spoke to her he always sounded that way.

"At least your foot is healed," she said tartly to Erba. She had detected the condescension in Filfa's voice, and it nettled her. She had no reason to take it out on Erba but she did.

"Yes," said Erba, "it is." He smiled at her. "Thank you," he said pointedly, with a glance at the older man.

Filfa turned away. He made no secret of his dislike of Forentel, or of his disapproval of her growing rapport with Erba.

It didn't matter to Erba. He would often walk beside her in the starlit dark and point out the constellations.

"That one is the Ladder," he said. Under the guise of pointing it out to her, he took her hand.

"I used to think," said Forentel, "that when it almost touched the horizon, in the rainy season, I could find where it comes to earth. If I could just run to the edge of the sky I could find it and climb it and get away from everything. Of course I never could. My father wouldn't allow it." She stopped, embarrassed.

Erba didn't notice. "I thought the same thing," he said. "My father would not allow me to search, either." He fell silent then, thinking of his father.

In the darkness Forentel gently squeezed his hand. It did not matter to her then that he was a prince, only that he was in pain.

Toward dawn the the thorn bushes thickets began to appear more often, and they were denser. Then a scrub-willow appeared, and some of the tough, long grass that grew on the hard land in the presence of even small amounts of water. They were nearing the river, or at least some river.

SHE WOKE IN the dusk. Her companions were both asleep. Filfa was supposed to have the watch, but the older man had drifted off, and now there was no one on guard. Forentel was not sure what had awoken her. She saw nothing but the scrub willow thicket in which they rested, the long grass around a tumble of rocks, and the sunset, fading in the west. She strained for a sound, but there was only the wind, chittering softly in the grass.

Then it came to her again. It wasn't a sound so much as a feeling, a call in her mind. It was not in words or even in pictures. It was an impression of wildness, and of need.

Forentel sat up, and then stood. The feeling was still there. It was stronger as she turned toward the rock tumble. With a glance behind her to be sure the two men were still sleeping, she walked toward the tumble. This was what she had felt for the past days, out in the desert, and now whatever it was, was there in the rocks.

Bright eyes were watching her, golden, with a faint hint of green. Forentel stopped and stared. There was a flash of reddish fur. It was an animal, with red brown fur, and those beautiful eyes, and it seemed to want to her to come closer.

"Frelenya!"

Erba was shouting, and then from close behind her a stone skimmed into the rock tumble, and then another. Now Filfa was shouting, too. The animal vanished.

"Stop it! What are you doing!" Forentel darted in front of Erba as he raised his hand to throw another stone. "Why did you chase it off! It meant no harm!" She felt an intense sense of loss. The fox had wanted something, and now she wouldn't know what it was. She felt like crying.

"Do you know what that was?" Erba was furious. His anger surprised him, the more so because he realized it came from fear for Frelenya. Concern made him want to shake her, a contradiction of feelings so unaccustomed and confusing that he trembled.

"A fox." She spat the words at him. "A fox, an animal that would do no one harm."

"It was a wolf. A desert wolf, although I have never seen a red one before. They are usually gray. I had one once in my menagerie."

Forentel stared at him. She had heard tales of the desert wolves. They were sly, intelligent, and deadly, living mostly in packs but capable of living alone. They had been known to make off with hunters separated from their companions. In their own way they were as dangerous as the desert cats.

"It was trying to entice you closer; you were its prey," said Filfa, who had come up beside the prince. He seemed almost disappointed it had not succeeded.

"They are evil," Erba added, glancing at his tutor.

"If they are so evil, why did you have one in your menagerie?"

"To study it, of course," said Erba in surprise. He had taken Forentel by the arm and was attempting to lead her back to their makeshift camp in the thicket. "It died." He shrugged. "It had plenty of food and water, but after a time it refused to eat. Who knows why. I will have to catch another someday." Actually, he had been very sorry, but this was something he would not admit now, especially in front of Filfa.

Forentel hoped he would not catch another. She had never seen a desert wolf before, but the from the glimpse

she had had, it was beautiful. She had the impression that
the wolf had not been their only follower, that in fact it had
been protecting them from something else. She pulled
aside from Erba, trying to be unobtrusive about it. As she
did, her eyes, night-adjusted now, saw something in the
tough grass.

"A trail." When the others continued ahead toward the
thicket, she said it again. "There is a trail here, and it is
more than an animal trail."

"She's right." Filfa came up beside her and stood looking down. Even in the glimmering starlight the path was
obvious now that they looked for it. It wound past the scrub
willow thicket in which they had sheltered before without
seeing it, and off past more rock tumbles and another
thicket.

"There should be a village near." Erba's hand had gone
to his sword as he looked at the path. "Hunters and fishers,
who live on the borders of the marshes."

"What sort of people are they?"

"They are dregs. A mixture of people, of Virsat and Tirdar. Neither one nor the other."

It was just an offhand remark, but Forentel felt herself
flush and was glad it was dark.

There was an odd sound, a cry like a night bird's, and
then the long grass on either side of the silvery starlight
trail erupted, and armed men poured forth. Erba drew his
sword with a shout. Filfa cried out and drew a long knife
from his belt.

Forentel screamed. Her first thought was that her father's troops had found her; her second was that Mirta's
soldiers had found Erba and Filfa, and that she would die
with them. But their attackers were not soldiers. They were
dressed in hides and short, woven cloaks. They did not
fight like soldiers, but they were effective enough. She
turned to run, but someone grabbed her from behind. She

kicked and tried to bite the arm that was around her throat, but whoever had her began to squeeze, and she had to fight to breathe. Panicked, she flailed wildly as the world began to gray. Then it went dark.

WHEN FORENTEL WOKE, her head was throbbing. The room was dark, and her bed was not comfortable. Then she realized it was not her bed, it was a pallet of dried grasses and rushes, and she remembered traveling through the desert with Erba and Filfa. She remembered the attack, and abruptly tried to sit up. She managed it, although it made her head hurt worse.

The room she was in was actually a one-room hut, woven from scrub willow branches and daubed with mud-brick. There was a fire pit in the center of the hut, beneath a smoke hole, but no fire was currently lit. In various corners were woven rush pallets. *Rushes,* Forentel thought. *We really must be near the river.* Near the fire pit was a large pot, and in one corner was a huge water storage jar. At least Forentel hoped it was a water jar; she was desperately thirsty. She managed to stand and stagger over to the jar. It was tall, chest high on her, and it did indeed hold water. She began to scoop water up in her hands and drink it. Finally she leaned over and slurped up water directly from the jar. When she had finished she ran her wet hands over her face and head. The cool liquid felt wonderful, both on her parched and dried skin, and sloshing within her.

Only then did she realize that she was alone. The owners of the hut were not present, nor were her companions. The almost-empty provision bags Illiana had given them were not in sight, either. Forentel went to the hut's door, which was covered by a cured goatskin. Cautiously, she pulled skin slightly to one side and peered out.

It was late afternoon, and the sun was setting behind a

circle of huts similar to the one she was in. In the center of
the large circle was an open space, where a fire was lit, despite the heat of the day. People dressed in skins and
coarsely woven cloth, with a few in tattered remnants of
what looked to be cloth of city weaving were busy around
this fire, carrying pots, bundles of twigs and wood, and jars
that held either water or possibly beer. It looked as though
they were preparing for a celebration. There was no sign of
Erba or Filfa. Easing the skin back from the doorway a little more, she stuck her head out to get a better view. Staring back at her was a boy of about fourteen summers.
When he saw her, he put his hand on the long knife
strapped prominently to his belt.

"You stay, Virsat woman."

She could understand him, but his accent was strange,
the vowels rounder somehow. For the first time it occurred
to Forentel that if she reached Dreffir she might not be able
to speak to the people there.

"Who are you, and where are my, my traveling companions." She had almost said "friends," but at the last moment
she realized that might not be wise. She wasn't convinced
they were her friends, even Erba, for all that they were
traveling together.

"Wait." The boy pointed at her authoritatively. "Do not
leave the house. You understand?"

When she nodded her agreement, he strode off across
the open space, disappearing into another, slightly larger
hut. He emerged again after a few moments with an older
woman behind him, both of them striding toward Forentel.
They stopped in front of her, and the woman pushed
Forentel's chest with one hard extended finger.

"You," she said. "What is your name?"

"For—Frelenya."

The woman's eyes narrowed. She was a tall woman with
graying black hair in a long braid that fell down her back.

Her face was lined from weather and age, but she seemed strong.

"Married?"

"No." Forentel was startled.

"Good. Virgin?"

Forentel stared at her, feeling heat coming to her face. She opened her mouth to say something indignant, but the woman laughed.

"I see yes. Good, again. Very good. Although," she grinned, "not virgin for long." When Forentel took a step back, she laughed. "Don't worry, you will be married soon, Virsat woman. Married here, in our village. If you bear children you will live, and in time you will be one of us. I see that does not please you. It is better than your friends get. Your friends die tonight, in the fire." She nodded toward the center of the open space where the preparations for the celebration were continuing. "Your friends die, but you live. A hard fate, you think, for a Virsat woman?" She grinned again. Forentel saw that one of her front teeth was missing.

"I am not a Virsat," she said.

The woman looked her up and down. "You are," she said with finality. "City woman." She grinned again. "Don't worry. A few of us have Virsat mothers, and we do not hate them for it. We would kill all Virsat who come here," she said conversationally, "but we need women. Need more children, since the swamp takes too many. Virsat women can be tamed. Like you." She patted Forentel on the arm. "Come." When Forentel did not follow, she grabbed her arm, and Forentel found herself being dragged out into the village.

She was dragged to the edge of the huge fire pit, and many of the villagers stopped their work to stare at her. Most of the villagers were boys in their teens or slightly older men. There were very few women of any age and no old men. A few children playing in front of one of the of the huts stopped their game to gape at her.

"Sit." The woman pointed to a large flat stone near the side of the fire. Forentel sat.

"Hungry?"

Forentel was, and she accepted the slab of hard, flat bread.

"What is your name?" she asked between mouthfuls. She had no intention of cooperating with this woman's plans, but a show of friendliness or at least interest would be helpful, as would more information.

"Kandika. I am the chief here."

Forentel was surprised but did not show it. It was unusual for a woman to be chief, but she had no doubt this woman could do the job.

"I am the mother, the oldest, with the most living children," Kandika continued. "It is my sons you will marry." She tilted her chin in the direction of the men.

Forentel looked. Several of the men looked back at her speculatively. All of them were rough, bearded, and thin, but tough. Most of them were working on constructing a sort of cage from thin, dried branches.

"For your friends," said Kandika. "We will roast them in the fire, for your wedding feast."

It was a joke. It had to be, but Forentel couldn't smile. Kandika smiled instead and patted her on the knee.

"We get very few Virsat here. The gods will be pleased with their spirits, and if the word gets out, the Virsat will never come here. They will be afraid."

More likely they will come and kill you all, Forentel thought. She said, "Why are there so few women and children, and even older men?"

"The will of the gods." Kandika rose abruptly. "They are angry with us and send the shivering sickness. The children die first, and pregnant women. And often women cannot bear more than one child. The old men die. My only daughter is ill with this sickness. So tonight we will give the gods a sacrifice, and perhaps they will relent."

The shivering sickness had been a problem in Tireera for generations. It carried away many people every year until one of the priests, working with the sick, had discovered that boiling all river water before drinking it solved the problem. Water from the few underground wells and springs near the city had always been pure, but the river itself was infested with evil spirits. Boiling drove them away and stopped the sickness. Forentel glanced around. There was no sign in the little village of a well. It was a reasonable guess that these people's water came from the river itself, or from the marshes, of which she had heard nothing good.

"I know the shivering sickness, and I can help you." Forentel tried to look impressive, like a priestess or a Tirdar magician, not that she had ever seen one, except for Illiana. She had no way to know if her attempt to look portentous and mysterious succeeded, for at that moment the hangings in the doorway of a nearby hut were pushed aside. Two young men armed with spears came out, pulling and prodding two bound captives: Erba and Filfa.

EIGHT

WHEN THEY CAME TO GET HIM ERBA WAS almost glad. At least he would be able to move now, and after hours of being bound in one position his muscles were cramped. He knew better than to think they might give him a drink, but he still hoped. They took Filfa, too, and the older man looked to be in much worse condition than he was. The old woman had told them what was going to happen: they were to be sacrificed to these savages' strange gods. Erba had other ideas about that, but it was hard to know what it might be possible to do when you were tied up and helpless in a stinking hut. He wondered where Frelenya was. He needed to know. If they were to escape, he would not leave her behind. He couldn't imagine not having her with him. He would miss her intelligence and humor.

As they emerged, staggering into the sunlight, the first thing he saw was Frelenya, sitting on a large, flat stone at the edge of the huge fire pit. She seemed to be in conversation with the old hag who was in charge here; they were talking together as if they were old friends. Erba pushed down the flush of anger and a surprised sorrow and confusion. It would not serve him now. If Frelenya had betrayed them, she would have something to answer for later, once they were out of here. He refused to entertain the possibility that they might not escape.

Filfa's legs buckled, and with some unkind laughter two of the men shoved the older man onto the ground. Others lowered the large woven cage that swung on a pole near the fire, and then opened it.

"In you go," said one of the men, holding open the door to the cage. They cut Filfa's bonds, and as he was rubbing his arms, attempting to restore the circulation, two of them picked him up and swung him into the cage. Filfa sprawled across the tightly woven branches that formed the floor of the cage, eliciting more laughter from the men.

"You next."

He was going to have to fight, even though he was not in much better shape than Filfa. Erba gathered himself to rush the man who held the spear, waiting to prod him into the cage. If he could get the spear for himself, the situation would improve tremendously. He might not be able to fight his way out, but at least he would give a good account of himself before he died, and he could spare Filfa the humiliation of a death at the hands of savages. He drew a breath, preparing to lunge.

"Let them go! Get him out of that cage!"

The words were spoken with the utmost authority, and Erba was astonished to see that it was Frelenya who had spoken. For a moment it almost looked as if the savages would obey her.

"Let them go," Forentel repeated, "and I will help you so the sickness will not harm you again. I have been sent by the gods."

Erba stared at her. They all did. She stood with the light of the setting sun behind her, flaming in her bronze-colored hair, which framed her face in tight spirals. She stood straight as a spear beside the fire, and her eyes flashed. Sent by the gods? It seemed almost possible. Erba drew in an astonished breath, and he heard the others around him do the same. She had the power of command, but she did not look like a Tirdar mystic. *No Tirdar could command that presence,* he thought. In a flash of illumination, Erba realized that he had seen her before. He knew who she was. He had seen her with her mother in the temple.

"You have nothing to lose," Forentel continued. "I tell you now that your gods can wait for their sacrifice. If I am wrong, if I lie to you, you will have them. And me. But I can save you from the shivering sickness. I have that power."

The people were shifting uneasily, but the men holding Erba did not relax their grip. If there had been an opportunity for grabbing the spear from his captor, Erba realized, it was when Frelenya, no, *Forentel,* had made her announcement, and that opportunity had passed.

"How will you end the shivering sickness?" Kandika scowled at Forentel.

Forentel swallowed. Boiling the water would not immediately eradicate the illness; it would take time for the benefits to be felt. She could teach these people some Virsat prayers and chants, and she could make up others to form ritual trappings to go with the simple act of boiling, but none of these things would be immediately helpful, no matter how impressive.

"I have a ritual," she said weakly. "It will take time."

"You will heal my daughter," said Kandika, "and you

will heal her now. If you are truly sent by the gods, you can do this. Then we will let your friends go. And you. If not—" She did not finish.

Forentel knew with a sudden certainty that they would not let her go. Whatever the fate of Erba and Filfa, these people meant to either kill her or keep her.

"Come," said Kandika.

She had no choice. As she stepped away from the fireside, the sun set with equatorial abruptness. Surrounded by armed men, Forentel followed the headwoman to a hut. She glanced behind her once, but Erba and Filfa were still being held.

The interior of the hut was dim and incredibly hot. There was a fire lit in the fire pit, giving off far too much heat but very little light. On a pallet of grass and rushes in a corner lay a woman who at first glance appeared ancient. As Forentel knelt beside the pallet, however, she realized that the woman was in reality not much older than she. It was the ravages of the shivering sickness that made her seem old. Her eyes were sunken, her black hair matted and brittle, and her skin seemed pulled tightly across her bones. One of the signs of the sickness was that it seemed to devour its victims, melting their flesh away. Families would try to get patients to eat, but no matter how much they ate, the sickness consumed more, and the victims starved.

"Riessa. Riessa, wake." Kandika's voice was full of tenderness as she knelt beside her daughter. She gently stroked the hair back from the young woman's brow with a gesture that was more eloquent than anything she might have said. For the first time Forentel felt sympathy for these people. Eventually, the sick woman's eyes opened.

"This woman says she can heal you," Kandika told her daughter. "I think she lies, but if you wish it, we will let her try."

"Let her try." Her voice was stronger than Forentel expected. "I am dying now. Let her try what she wishes. It does not matter, the gods will have me soon."

Kandika leaned over and whispered something to her daughter. Even Forentel, close as she was, could not hear what she said, but Forentel could see the tears in Kandika's eyes.

"Cure her, Virsat woman." The headwoman had no trace of tears when she rose to her feet. She crossed her arms and stared at Forentel.

Forentel looked around the hut. As many of the people as could manage had crammed themselves inside and were adding to the heat and stuffiness of the small space. There was no way Forentel could escape, but strangely she did not even wish to. She frowned at the crowd.

"Clear some of the people out. Open the door and let some fresh air in. And bring a torch for some light." People shuffled and grinned, staring back at her. "Do it!"

Someone pulled back the hide that closed the door, and cooler night air began to blow in. Someone else brought a torch and grounded it beside the bed, where it cast a flickering light over the sick woman and the spectators. Forentel pushed the sweaty hair out of her eyes and sat down on the ground. Riessa stared at her with pain-filled eyes, and Forentel looked back. Without the faintest idea of what to do, she reached out and took Riessa's hand.

It was as if the spectators vanished, and the room, and all her surroundings with them. What was important was the woman she sat beside. Forentel could feel the fever in her, the heat that burned, eating up all the resources in the now-frail body. This inner fire burned for a reason. Riessa's body was trying to burn out invaders.

The invaders were in Riessa's blood, and Forentel could feel them. She was not sure how, but she could feel them crawling through the other woman's veins. She closed her eyes and reached deeper. Wherever the warm red blood flowed, it carried these tiny but powerful invaders. As Forentel watched, they multiplied, despite the fever heat that tried to destroy them. Forentel opened her eyes.

"Get me some cool, water-soaked cloths," she said. She noted in a detached way that the villagers were staring at her with awe, and even Kandika watched her, wide-eyed, with dawning hope.

Forentel did not speak again. When the damp cloths were brought, she placed them on Riessa's forehead, took the ill woman's hand again, and closed her eyes. She hoped the coolness of the water would help, but she had no way to be sure. She only knew what she felt: that she had to somehow increase the heat to drive out the invaders, out of Riessa's blood, and into—into where? Into her own blood, her own body. The realization almost made her stop. But she could not stop, not now. It had nothing to do with Erba and Filfa and their freedom, nothing to do even with her own freedom or her own life. She had to do what she could to drive this sickness out. There was nothing else now that mattered.

The heat she needed came from within her. She drew it up from somewhere deep within her mind and body. She envisioned it as tiny tongues of flame, small, hot lances, and she sent them into Riessa, into the bloodstream of the other woman. She directed them toward the small invaders in the blood. At first she tried to lance each invader with her tiny flames, but there were too many of them, and eventually she found that she could simply release the lances and let them go. They would seek out the small evil spirits within the blood on their own, as long as her will was behind them.

Somewhere outside her she was aware of Riessa moaning and crying. She heard people muttering, heard Kandika order them back.

"She is a healer; I have seen one once, and this was how she worked. She battles the demons! Do not touch her!"

Forentel was grateful, in some far corner of her mind. The invader spirits were dying, but not fast enough. Riessa's fever was too great, and Forentel could feel the fever heat beginning to burn in the other woman's brain. A higher fever would kill the invaders in the blood, but it might also kill Riessa. Desperate, and not knowing what else to do, Forentel opened herself to the things in Riessa's blood.

She felt as if a bottomless drop had opened up beneath her, and then a wave of attack so strong that Forentel was pushed over. She felt herself collapse on the ground of the hut, but she could not move. The evil spirits were crawling in her blood now. They had left Riessa, all that were still alive, and they were within her. She could feel them, eating away within her. Someone screamed. As if from a distance, Forentel recognized her own voice. She built up the fire within herself and drew what heat she could from Riessa. The tiny invaders died. She focused her inner gaze on them and killed them. When at last she was sure they were dead, she dampened the heat and opened her eyes.

She was lying on the floor beside Riessa's pallet, and she was drenched in sweat. Riessa was sitting up, clasped in her mother's arms. They were watching her, as were all the villagers, but no one made a move toward her. Shakily, Forentel pushed the sweat-drenched hair from her eyes. She felt weak and wobbly, and when she tried to sit up, she could not.

"Water," she whispered. Then she remembered how the shivering sickness was spread. "Wait," she whispered. She cleared her throat, trying to strengthen her voice. "From this day forward," she said, "you must boil all water from the river before you drink it. That will kill the evil spirits that bring the shivering sickness. Now bring me boiled water."

Eventually they did, and Forentel tried to prop herself up to drink it. It was still warm, but she drank it anyway, thirsty as she was. As she did, she monitored herself with that inner sight she had discovered. The sickness spirits were dead. She could see some of the dead ones drifting still within her blood, and she realized her blood had been changed. She could now drink the unboiled river water if she wished, for she would never again need to worry about the shivering sickness.

When she felt a little stronger, she sat up and looked around her. The villagers were still staring at her with awed faces and big eyes. Forentel looked at Riessa, then put her hand weakly against the other woman's brow. She could feel it: the sickness was gone.

"The sickness is gone from this woman," she said, "and it will not return."

The villagers sighed together, as if they were one being. Kandika smiled down triumphantly at Forentel.

"Frelenya was sent by the gods; she spoke true. Hila village has a true healer now! The gods have indeed blessed us. And you have heard the healer's command. All water from the river must be boiled before we drink it, from this day forth. Help Frelenya up. We must take her out and give her food from the feast."

At Kandika's command several villagers hurried forward and assisted Forentel to her feet. She was amazed at how weak and shaky she was. She needed to lean on the villagers as they left the hut. Riessa followed her, and the villagers outside who had not witnessed the healing began to cheer and then to sing. Forentel was seated in a large chair woven of rushes. They brought her wine, which she did not touch, and water, carefully boiled, which she

drank. Then they brought her food. She could see that Erba
and Filfa had been released. They were feasting also, sitting at a large wooden table some distance from her, under
the sputtering light of torches. They tried several times to
come speak with her, but villagers always prevented them,
and after a few attempts the men ceased to try. Kandika
saw her watching them.

"We will let your friends go. We do not go back on our
word."

Of course you don't, Forentel thought sourly, *and the
next thing you will say is that you will not let me go, contrary to your promise.*

"You will stay here in Hila, where the gods have sent
you," Kandika confirmed, not hearing the irony in her own
words. "You need not marry until you are ready; far be it
from any of us to force a healer from the gods. But my sons
are very worthy mates," she continued hopefully.

"I am sure they are, but you promised me my freedom
along with that of my companions."

"That was before we knew you had truly been sent by
the gods, as you claimed. Before we knew you for a true
healer. You cannot leave this place of your destiny. You will
be well treated here, and you will make Hila famous. No
other village has a true healer. People will come from
everywhere when they learn of this. We will grow rich."
She paused, hearing how she sounded, and glanced at
Forentel. "You will grow rich, also."

"I don't care to become rich." Forentel heard the irritation in her voice and made no attempt to hide it. Perhaps it
was not wise to annoy her captor, but she could not help it.

"Of course not," said Kandika, misunderstanding. "You
care only for the healing, and for the gods."

The attentions of the villagers kept her away from Erba
and Filfa for the remainder of the night. Several times she
said she wished to speak to them, but she was always kept

from them. She told herself it was all right; Erba, at least, would not leave without her. She was exhausted from the healing, and the food and drink that the villagers kept offering her only increased her exhaustion. Finally, unable to stay awake any longer, she let the villagers lead her to a hut that had been prepared for her. Soft, clean hides had been spread over a bed of rushes, there were new clothes laid out and a new water jar in the corner.

"Filled with boiled water," Kandika told her proudly. "This whole hut is yours. If you desire anything, you have only to ask for it."

Forentel was tempted to ask to see Erba and Filfa, just to test Kandika's word, even though she knew she would not be permitted to. It didn't matter. She was tired, and there would be time later to see them, after she awoke. They were resourceful. When the time was right, they would find a way to come to her, and they would escape. Surely nothing would happen, in any event, for another day or so, until they all had a chance to recover from the feasting, and she from the healing.

Forentel discovered that there was an actual cotton sheet on the bed. She drew this over her to keep out the little biting insects that came from the swamp. She was asleep almost before she finished pulling it up.

When she awoke it was broad daylight. Someone had drawn back the hide from the doorway of the hut, and light spilled in. Forentel sat up and yawned. A young girl was placing something near the bed: a pottery bowl holding a large slab of bread with honey, and some sort of blue fruit Forentel had never seen. The girl smiled shyly when she saw Forentel was awake, bowed, and hastened from the hut.

Forentel emerged from the hut a little while later. She felt much better after some sleep, and after washing and putting on some of the clothes left out for her. The cotton leggings and the strange, soft shoes of hide were more comfortable than she had imagined. Breakfast had helped, too. The blue fruit seemed to be some sort of sweet melon. She hoped to be able to take some with her when they left this place.

She looked around the small village. People nodded to her but continued with their tasks. A few women were pounding grain, two boys carried firewood, and a man, one of Kandika's sons, she remembered, had a string of fish. Since she did not see them, she set out to find Erba and Filfa. It did not take long to make a complete journey around the little village, but she could not look into the huts with closed door skins. She frowned, standing in the shadow of a hut. It did not escape her that in her explorations she had never been alone. When she caught someone's eye there was a pleasant nod and sometimes a smile, but she was always under scrutiny. And now someone had alerted Kandika, for the headwoman was striding toward her.

"If you are looking for your friends," said Kandika, "we kept our promise to you. They were escorted to the marsh at dawn. We even gave them food and a boat and showed them the main channel. You know they are looking for riches and slaves to take home to their people." She laughed. "They won't find them."

"What?" Forentel was distracted. She supposed Kandika was correct. Erba, or at least Filfa, would be looking for much more than just the satisfaction of finding the source of a legend, for being the first to find the lost city. She should have realized that. She couldn't believe they had just left her here. They were on their way with a boat, and she was left behind. She remembered Filfa telling Erba they might have a use for her. They had. They had traded her for their safety and their freedom.

"You could not go with them." Kandika was studying her. "You understand that."

"I just wanted to wish them farewell." Forentel

shrugged. "But now they are gone. It does not matter. I traveled with them as the gods arranged, to help me find your village. Your village is my home now."

Kandika looked at her sharply, but Forentel kept her expression bland. She had learned long ago to hide both tears and fear from her father, and the skill served her now. It helped that she was furious with the prince and his tutor. She had traveled with them for weeks, she had saved Erba's life, *twice,* she thought, and he and Filfa had saved hers, and yet they had abandoned her without a second thought when it was convenient for them. They were not friends, she knew better than that, and yet she had thought there was some loyalty there. *Virsat do not have loyalty, except to their own kind,* she thought. And she had taken pains to let them think she was not of their kind. Thinking of Erba brought tears to her eyes. She fought them back.

"Healer," said a tentative voice, "can you help me? My child is ill."

"Go with her," Kandika told her.

The child had a sniffle. Forentel had no need to draw on the strange inner vision she had used the previous night, a good thing, as its use had left her exhausted. What would happen if she had to use this inner sight again? Could she? Had she used it all up this one time? If she tried to use it again, would she become ill herself? She certainly now felt as if she would. She wished there were someone she could ask, and now that it was impossible, she would have given much to be able to speak to Illiana again, even for a few moments. But this child only had a sniffle, and Forentel recommended that she rest, and drink boiled water, and neither play nor help her mother with the fish drying for several days. The mother was incredibly grateful for this piece of obvious advice and thanked Forentel profusely and sent her out with two of the blue melons in thanks.

She was almost tempted to stay in Hila. It was good riddance to Erba and Filfa, she decided, despite an odd pain
that came when she thought of Erba. She could manage on
her own, and her life was probably safer and simpler without them. As for finding Dreffir, it was a legend, and a far
and difficult legend at that. She placed the blue melons in
her hut and asked to see the fishing. Two of the older children offered to take her.

The marsh was not far, and the first sight of it made
Forentel gasp. She had heard of marshes, but she had never
imagined the reality of so much water all in one place.
They followed a winding path down a steep embankment,
and then there it was: on the one side, the dry embankment,
and then below that a vast sea of glimmering water and
green rushes. And over all of it a slight haze, the haze of
water. Birds called harshly somewhere on a tiny island.
Just what was water and what was land was difficult to tell.

"It goes on forever," said one of the children, a boy of
about thirteen. "All the way to the end of the earth."

"Full of fish and animals," said his sister. "It is the
mother of us all; the marsh feeds us."

"And takes us back when we die," said the boy. He
looked at his sister and she back at him.

"It keeps our ghosts," she whispered, "the ghosts of
those lost or drowned or cast out." Despite the warmth of
the day the child shivered. "You can see the ghosts at dawn
and dusk, and sometimes in the night."

Savage superstition, thought Forentel, but she felt a
shiver, too. "Have you seen them?" she asked. "What do
they look like?"

"They look like mist." The girl's eyes were big. "I've
seen them just before dawn, over the marsh."

Forentel said nothing. A mist over the marsh in the
morning did not seem supernatural to her, and she wondered why it would to people who lived near the marsh.

But then the girl said, "And I have felt them watching me."

A prickle ran up Forentel's neck. She could feel something watching them, watching her, right now. She tried to look around surreptitiously, but she saw nothing unusual. There were not even other villagers paying them any particular attention. Nonetheless, the feeling intensified throughout the rest of the day.

It remained with her the day after and the day after that, as she tried to settle into the life of the village. She found herself bandaging cuts and prescribing heated rocks wrapped in hides for sore muscles. Just where this knowledge came from, she was not sure, except that it seemed like common sense to her, and she could not fathom why everyone was so grateful. But this was all she had to do, this and wander the village, meeting the villagers, learning their way of life. Always there was the sense of being watched and a sense of urgency, the sense that she needed to be elsewhere. She thought of her mother, and she thought of Tireera. And she thought of Erba and Filfa. What would they do if they did indeed find Dreffir? Would they go back to Tireera and lead warriors against the lost city to bring back riches and slaves?

Despite the warnings about ghosts, she went one evening to sit on the embankment overlooking the marsh. The people had stopped following her everywhere, now that it seemed she had accepted life in the village. The fishermen were gone, their shallow little skiffs pulled well up onto the shore, overturned, covered with hides and weighted down for the night. It seemed like a lot of unnecessary work to Forentel, but they told her it was tradition.

Darkness drifted over the marsh, and the little biting insects that lived there were out in swarms. Forentel had brought a torch, and moths were attracted to its flickering light, while out in the marsh something large splashed, and there was an animal cry.

She was a Virsat. She needed to get help for her mother, her Virsat mother, and she had a duty to her people. And she was Tirdar, with a duty to her long-dead Tirdar mother and her enslaved people. Hiding in a tiny village at the edge of the swamp would not help her. As she thought this, she looked up and into two yellow eyes.

It was the wolf. It was the same wolf; she knew it. It sat just outside the circle of light cast by her torch. She couldn't cry out, and she could barely breathe. The wolf made no threatening moves but simply looked at her. She felt the same odd sense of attraction that she had felt before. Was this really a way these animals lured prey to them? She stared into its yellow eyes.

The the wolf cocked its head to one side and panted. Then it whined. It stood up, turned, and then looked back over its shoulder at her.

The sense of urgency, which had never left her, was intensified. The animal wanted her to follow it. Abruptly Forentel stood up. If the wolf had wanted to kill her, it had had ample opportunity.

"Wait," she said to it. "I will come back. I want to get a few things from my hut first." She was speaking to an animal, expecting it to understand her. For a moment her Virsat sensibilities flared, but she pushed them aside.

She turned her back on the animal and began to walk back to the village. It was a foolhardy thing to do. She was giving the wolf the perfect opportunity to attack her from behind, and she knew it. When nothing happened, she risked a look back. The wolf sat where it was, gazing after her. Forentel turned back to the path.

NINE

"YOU'RE LEAVING, AREN'T YOU."

Forentel started so violently that she dropped the clothing she was rolling up to put in her pack. She hadn't seen Riessa in the hut when she came in, but the other woman had been waiting for her, hidden in the shadows. Riessa was still gaunt, but the drained and fevered look, the look of imminent death, was gone. She was regaining her strength.

"I knew you would leave." She walked into the light of Forentel's torch. "Don't worry, I won't call anyone. You saved my life, and I won't repay you that way. You have some urgent reason to be gone. I know it."

"I'm sorry, Riessa. I would like to stay, but I can't. Maybe I can come back someday, after I'm done—" *With what?* she thought. It was nonsense. The other woman knew it.

"Take me with you."

"What!"

"Take me with you. We can go quickly. I can help you. I can—"

"You don't know where I'm going, you don't know what I will be facing, and you would be leaving everything behind here. Your mother, everything."

"I can't stand Hila another day." Riessa kept her voice low. "You don't know what it's like—well, maybe you are beginning to. There is nothing here but fish, and the swamp, and dying children. Of course they will not die now, not after you said to boil the water," she added hastily. "But I can't stay here. Relt, my husband, died, and my mother wants to marry me off again. She thinks I can have children. Many children. She wants me to marry old man Berro."

Forentel shook her head, unsurprised. Kandika had marrying on her mind, for certain. "Surely you can take some control over your own life here." Even as she said it, she knew it was hollow. She had been unable to control her life back in Tireera, except by running.

"I cannot marry Berro! He's old and filthy. I have always wanted to see other places, to have a life out in the big world. I will not become headwoman after my mother in some tiny little village, and I will not marry some man I do not choose for myself. I simply will not."

"Riessa, I can't take you." Forentel struggled to think of some way to make the rejection more gentle, but nothing came to mind. "I barely know what I am doing or where I am going myself."

"It's all right." Riessa turned toward the door without further argument and pulled aside the skin hanging. "I had to try." She smiled faintly. "I am sorry I startled you. I meant what I said before. I will not tell anyone you are leaving. I wish you well." She turned and was gone.

Forentel stared after her for a second and then returned to packing her belongings. She wanted to believe Riessa, but she would take no chances. It was better to be as far from Hila as possible before the headwoman's daughter had a chance to change her mind and tell someone.

A few minutes later she hoisted her pack across her shoulder and opened the door again. She had extinguished her torch and placed it in her pack, deciding to navigate the village and the path to the embankment by starlight. There were shadows and things hidden in the shadows, but they all proved to be only items left by the residents: storage jars and fishing nets. The village's few dogs were already accustomed to her and did not bark.

The pack was heavy, and she stumbled a few times before she reached the embankment. Once there, she risked lighting her torch again; she wouldn't dare the steep slope to the swamp in the darkness.

The wolf was still there. She felt the animal before she saw it, so the yellow eyes blinking out of the darkness did not surprise her. It glanced at her and then preceded her down the embankment.

Forentel stood looking at the swamp, wondering which of the fishermen's boats to take. Now that it was time to follow through with her escape, she realized that she would be depriving one of the villagers of his livelihood, and she hesitated. Finally she shrugged. She needed a boat. She moved toward the closest one and began to pull the stones from the hide weighting it down. The wolf growled.

It was low and short, but she stopped what she was doing and looked at the animal. It sat back on its haunches, regarding her with a quizzical look. When she turned back to the boat, it growled again. She hurried, tossing the stones into a pile. In a flash the wolf was beside her. There was a snap as the wolf's teeth closed on the cloth of her sleeve, missing her arm. The animal pulled, dragging her away from the boat.

Forentel gasped. The wolf looked up at her, teeth still locked on her sleeve. She knew what the animal wanted.

"All right," said Forentel. "You've made your point. How am I supposed to manage the swamp without a boat?"

The animal released her sleeve, looked at her, and then trotted toward the swamp, glancing back at her occasionally. Forentel followed.

There were paths in the marsh, at least near to the village. The wolf kept to them at first, pausing every now and then to look back at her, but soon enough they were away from the paths. She was glad; it would make it harder for the villagers to find her.

Forentel had no desire to be walking in the marsh at night, but there was no choice; the wolf would not permit her to stop. She couldn't believe she was following a wolf, but now that she was committed, she was afraid it would leave her. The flickering torch seemed to attract biting insects, but the thought of extinguishing it was unbearable.

She tripped over roots, and more times than she could count she stepped into water. Her soft leather shoes squelched softly on the ground. Some of the stands of long grasses had razor-sharp edges, and and before long her arms and hands were cut and bleeding. She could not shake the feeling that she and the wolf were being followed. By the time the first flush of dawn showed in the east she was exhausted, filthy, and lost.

It came to her how incredibly foolish it was to be wandering in this swamp. Surely Erba and Filfa had been right. The wolf had attracted her the way the insect-eating flowers attracted their prey. She had been weak and helpless enough to fall for it. Perhaps the wolf was leading her to its pack, where she would prove to be dinner. Or breakfast, she thought, watching the sun poke its fiery rim over the horizon. She sank down, exhausted and hopeless, on a tuft of marsh grass in the midst of what proved to be a small island. She was trying not to sob, but she put her face in her hands.

She did not look up when she felt the breath of the wolf on her hair. *Might as well eat me now and get it over with,* she thought. The wolf did no such thing. It snuffled and and licked at her face. Forentel found this oddly comforting, and after a moment she sighed and sat up.

"What's your name?" It was ridiculous to ask the animal; she knew it, and yet it didn't feel ridiculous. "What's your name, girl?" Why did she think it was female?

It was female, but definitely not a girl. Too old for that. And she would not harm Forentel. As for a name—there was an impression of the sun rising in red glory over the desert.

Forentel blinked. None of this had been in words, but it had been the wolf and not her imagination, for a moment she was sure of it. She shook her head, trying to dispel the strangeness. Perhaps her mind was affected by hunger. She had been slogging all night through the swamp without food, after all. She reached for her pack and took out the waterskin and some cheese and a little of the blue melon, which she had been unable to resist bringing. The wolf looked at her quizzically, then vanished into the swamp grass. She relaxed and concentrated on eating and trying to think of where to go next. Unfortunately, she could not go back to Hila now, even if she wanted to. She was lost, and she desperately regretted not having stolen a boat.

A sound made her look up. The wolf was back, and it held something in its mouth. Her mouth. Whatever it was squeaked once, but then the wolf bit down and began to eat. Forentel put her cheese and melon away, no longer hungry.

As she was doing so, she became aware again of the

feeling that someone was nearby. She looked up to find
that the wolf had vanished again, but the feeling was
stronger. She hastily looked through her pack, cursing the
stupidity that had made her put her knife away. The long
grass behind her rustled, and too late she realized that she
should have at least tried to hide.

Someone came through the grass and into the little
clearing where Forentel crouched, someone wearing soft
colors of tan and gray and pale green, colors that blended
with the swamp. Someone with a long knife drawn and at
the ready. Forentel prepared to run.

There was a flash from the grass behind her. The wolf
reappeared, as if from thin air. With uncanny speed, she
had the newcomer pinned against the ground. Saliva
dripped from her mouth.

"Stop!" screamed Forentel. "Stop! Stop, don't kill her!
She's a friend!"

The wolf looked up and snarled. The sound raised the
hair on the back of Forentel's neck.

"Please," she said. "Sunrise." She tried out the name.
The wolf looked up at her and then backed off her victim,
but stayed close. Forentel edged over and helped Riessa to
sit up.

"I didn't know you were protected." Riessa edged
slightly away. "I should have guessed."

"It was you I felt behind us."

"You were not that easy to find." Riessa pushed her hair
out of her eyes and glanced warily at the wolf. The wolf
looked back without moving. "But I know the marsh, and I
know tracking. Even so, I had to work to stay on your trail.
I thought you would need me to help you through, but I see
I was wrong." She looked nervously at the wolf again.
"You need to know, Frelenya, if I can find you, so can others. Even with the protection of one of the Marsh Lady's
Guardians. My people will want you back, and they will

come after you." She hesitated. "And after me. It won't take them long. You can't stay here. They aren't that far behind me."

"You had better go, then."

"Frelenya, I can get us a boat. And I can help you get to Dreffir. I know the legends. I know that's where you're going." She smiled at Forentel's surprise. "I heard the Virsat men talking."

"A boat? Where?" A boat would make all the difference now.

There was an island near the one on which they rested. It was home to a small and temporary fishing camp, used on and off by the men and women of Hila. They had to slog their way to the island through knee-deep water, and then they had to swim. Since Forentel couldn't swim, she had to trust Riessa to tow her. Reluctant though she was to do this, there was no choice. As Riessa pulled her along, she thought she felt something move in the depths beneath her. She said nothing but clambered gratefully ashore through the long reeds. The wolf had swum with them and climbed up onto the drier ground beside her. The animal then trotted ahead along the shoreline, stopping beside a small, flat swamp skiff. Forentel wondered if the wolf had been leading her here all along. Sure enough, the animal jumped right in and settled herself comfortably. Riessa looked askance at this, but Forentel said nothing. So far the wolf had proved herself a better friend than the woman.

IT WAS COOL on the upper story of the Temple of Justice. Mareg stood at the window of the small meditation room looking out over the terraced gardens. She knew by now that her daughter had left the city, but there was no sign of her. King Mirta had secured her freedom for her, but Mirta did not truly care about her daughter, and to be truthful, Mareg had good reasons for not wishing to enlist his aid in finding her missing child. Mirta was dangerous. He was also an untrustworthy ally, something his father had never been. The young king was edgy, and he drank more than usual. Mareg knew these were signs of guilt, and she knew why the king felt guilty. It had suited Mirta to help her occasionally in return for a check on Rellaff's influence, but this was a dangerous road to travel.

Mareg sighed. The temple was a peaceful place right now, or at least this quiet meditation room was. She was sick of all the intrigue that went along with her position, that went along with Virsat nobility. Even the service of the Lady of Justice did not exempt her from this: Mareg was powerful in her own right, but none of this power would help her find her daughter. Forentel was not wise in the ways of the desert and had no experience living on her own. Since she had not reentered Tireera, there was only one place Mareg could imagine she might have gone for help. She might, in fact, still be there.

Mareg turned her back on the window. She walked briskly down the stairs to her chamber, informed the junior priest that she would be gone for the day, and collected her cloak. When she reached home, there was no one there but the Tirdar servants. She went to her room and took a small purse of gold coins. Then she went to the kitchens and took a waterskin. She ordered the cook to make her up a small package of cheese, bread, and dried fish. Although the woman did not dare to ask why, she could see her curiosity. She informed the cook that she was going to the king's gardens to think, and that no, she did not want an escort. This was unusual, but she could not afford for anyone to know what she planned. At least no one would be much concerned if they thought her in the gardens, and she planned to be back well before dark. Nedriff had finally reached the conclusion that she was up to nothing unusual, and for the past few days she had been able to go to the temple without being followed.

She strode through the city streets until she reached the gardens. Just in case she was wrong and someone was following her, she made a show of going in and settling herself on a bench. When she was certain no one was watching her, she rose and slipped quickly and quietly through the bushes and flowering plants. Reaching the tiny hut far back on one of these paths, she let herself in. She wasn't sure the person she hoped to find would be there, but luck was with her.

"I heard you left the temple earlier, and I thought you might come here. What do you need?"

"A horse, my friend. And soon."

"A horse that you can get to quickly and secretly, and that will not be missed, and that you return later in the same way."

The speaker came out of the shadows, smiling. He was a small old man, stooped from the years of his work as a gardener, wizened by the sun, but tough. He was, in fact, the king's head gardener and descended from a long line of Tirdar nobles, but that was not well known. He had become a friend of the Virsat High Judge many years previously, when she was a only a girl with an interest in the growing things of the garden. It was an odd friendship, but one that had endured.

"Bilop, my friend." Mareg embraced him. "It is good to see you again."

"And you." The old gardener's eyes lit with genuine affection. "I wish you would come more often. But I know there is no time to waste. Come along, and let's get you your horse."

Behind the hut was a pile of old pots, a rake, and other

equipment. There was also a shed, set right up against the fence, with a gate nearby. Bilop took deliveries here for his supplies. There was a small desert horse saddled and waiting. Mareg glanced at the old man, wondering again if he had some of the powers for which the Tirdar were fabled. He grinned at her.

"Do you have any idea how many of your visits to me have resulted in a way to leave the city and do something in secret? Beginning with that time you and your friend Eliss wanted to find the fox burrow out near the old road in the desert and bring home the kits. Of course I did not know what you intended at the time."

"But you did help with the kits." Mareg smiled. "And cleaned my bite and kept it from becoming infected."

"You had a soft heart," said the old man, "I know you could not bear the thought of the kits being hunted." He helped her mount the horse. "Wrap yourself in this." He handed her a light gray cloak. "At least until you leave the main gate. And Mareg, I hope you find your child. But be careful with the old woman; she is not what she seems."

Mareg drew back slightly, reining in the horse, surprised and suspicious.

"It's not magic, child. It's deduction, of the kind you practice in your temple. Many of us know your daughter is missing. We know you have had the city searched, or rather your husband has. You have inquired by other methods. We know you have inquired of the fishing village. There is one place you have not checked, one place alone but for the wide desert. The blessings of the gods on your search."

The main gate was open for traffic, as it was still the height of the day. With her nondescript cloak pulled up across her head, riding her ordinary horse, Mareg attracted no attention. She rode sedately through the gate with a crowd of both Virsat and Tirdar, headed for the estates on the city's edge. Once out on the desert road, Mareg picked up her pace, but she waited until she had passed most of the other travelers before she broke away from the road and headed across the desert at a faster pace. She had never before been where she was going, but she knew quite well how to find it.

It was late afternoon when she saw the shrine rise up out of the desert. She stopped, pushing back the cloak from her head, staring at the cliff, thinking it was truly beautiful even now, destroyed and in ruins. The shrine faced east, toward the dawn, and now the sun was edging over the cliff into which the shrine had been built, beginning to cast the desert below into shadow. From somewhere within the shadows, something moved.

The horse shied, and Mareg looked down into the wild amber eyes of the largest cat she had ever seen. It was a pale buff in color, and it reached almost to saddle height. Its tail twitched slightly.

Mareg drew back tightly on the reins, certain the horse would bolt. With her other hand she reached slowly for the knife at her waist. She kept her movements calm and slow, not wanting to provoke the attack she was sure would come anyway.

The animal watched her hand and drew its lips back in a snarl. Its eyes met hers, and it backed away. When she closed her hand on the knife hilt, it snarled again, then turned and ran. Mareg blinked. The cat had seemed to flow, melting into the desert. She was more alert now as she approached the shrine, remembering that not only was it the shrine of the dawn, but sacred to the Tirdar cat goddess.

The shrine was in shadows by the time she entered the gate. Mareg cursed herself for her foolishness in setting out immediately, today, instead of waiting for morning. She had not realized how long it would take to get here, and the desert was even more dangerous, not just at night, but in the dusk, when she would be returning to the city.

"Sometimes a mother's heart will not allow her to wait."

The words came from deep in the shadows. Mareg could not see the speaker, but she resisted the urge to mount her horse again and ride away as fast as she could. The speaker had to be the person she had come to see, the prophet of the shrine. She didn't know whether or not to feel like a fool.

"So you know why I'm here," she said. "I think perhaps all of Tireera must know."

"Not all of the city. But word does travel. Faster than you."

Mareg heard the smile in the words, and the voice was youthful. Whoever this person was and whatever she knew, Mareg wanted to waste no more time with her.

"I am in a hurry," she said. It was true. The sun was all but gone, and darkness would descend abruptly. "I want to see the prophet. Where is she? Bring her to me." As soon as the words left her mouth she knew she had made a mistake.

"I had expected better of the mother of the Delass."

The woman who stepped out of the shadows was so old that Mareg wondered how she kept to her feet. She was wrinkled and stick thin and bent, but her eyes were bright. And the voice—that voice was the same, the young girl's voice that had greeted her moments before.

"Are you the prophet?" And then, because she knew the answer, "I am sorry for my words. They were discourteous."

"They were, and not only to a prophet but to anyone. What is it you wish, High Judge?"

Mareg bit back the first answer that came to her. This woman obviously knew why she was here, but the words needed to be said.

"I came to find my daughter. I came to ask your help in finding her. I have searched the city for her, and she is not there. She can only be here. Please, prophet." Now that she had spoken her hope aloud, she realized how desperate she was. "Please, tell me, is she here? Is Forentel here?"

"No, she is not."

Mareg wanted to call the old woman a liar, but part of her calling as High Judge was to ascertain truth, and she heard it now. All the strength ran out of her. She could think only that Forentel was lost in the desert, had died in the desert.

"Come and sit."

The old woman took her arm, and her grip was surprisingly firm. It was not that Mareg allowed herself to be led away, it was more that she could not resist. The old woman took her to a small room back within the cliff, part of the original shrine. There was a torch already lit, and a small fire. Mareg sank onto a bench.

"Drink this; I am sure you have not eaten since morning."

Mareg took the cup and drank. It was some sort of cold tea, and it must have a stimulant property, for she felt much better and more alert.

"She was here." The old woman spoke softly.

It took a moment for the words to sink in, and then Mareg dropped the cup. The old woman held up her hand.

"She is not dead, but she is gone, following her fate. Surely you knew you could not keep her here. You have known since she came to you that she would be called out into the wider world."

"Where has she gone?"

"To Dreffir. The lost city. To find her heritage."

"She knows her heritage! It is here, in Tireera!"

The old prophet held up her hand again. "Her other heritage. Do you know her lineage?"

"Of course I know her lineage; I am her mother."

The prophet smiled gently. "Yes, you are," she said, "a truer parent in many ways than her father, whose blood runs in her veins. It is your love that has brought her this far, but it is not your blood within her. She has another heritage and another lineage beyond the Virsat, one as noble, more noble than that of the city's conquerors."

Mareg wanted to comment that a Tirdar heritage could not possibly be more noble than Virsat, but something about the woman stopped her. In the flickering light of the torch she seemed suddenly young. Mareg shivered slightly.

"What is your name?" She had a sudden need to know more about this person. "And what do you know of my daughter's—other—heritage?"

"My name is Illiana. I am the Raffa, the Prophet of the Dawn."

Mareg blinked. Now the other woman seemed not much older than Forentel. She rubbed her hand across her eyes. The ride across the desert had tired her. And perhaps there had been something in the tea; it was foolish of her to have accepted it. When she looked up, Illiana was as ancient as she been moments before.

"I am old, yes," said Illiana with a faint smile, "and I have seen much. And I am, of course, Tirdar myself. I know Forentel's mother's line. I knew your child's blood mother and her mother before her and her mother before her. She comes from the royal line of Dreffir. It is fitting that she go to seek her fate there." She smiled faintly at Mareg's expression.

"Dreffir is a myth! My child went out into the desert alone to seek a mirage! How could you let her!"

"How could I stop her?" Illiana gently put her hand on the other woman's shoulder. "Dreffir is neither myth nor illusion. She will find the city, and she will return to Tireera. When she does, what will she find here?"

"What do you mean? She will find what has always been here." What she wanted to ask was how the old woman knew her daughter would be safe, knew her daughter would return.

"That would be a pity. Tell me, High Judge, you have given your life to the Lady of Justice. Do you believe there is true justice in Tireera?"

Mareg opened her mouth to reply that of course there was, and then paused. In the flickering light from the fire and the torch Illiana seemed to command the truth. Her eyes looked into Mareg's. Was there justice in Tireera? Sometimes there was, but frequently there was not. There was sometimes justice for the Virsat, for those who could afford the sacrifices to the temple. For those who could afford gifts to the priests there was more justice. Mareg had long fought against this in a silent attempt at impartiality, but it was not always possible. King Rellaff had occasionally made her wishes known on a matter, and when he had, the goddess had smiled upon his wishes. Mareg knew in her heart that King Mirta would make his wishes known more frequently. When Tirdar came to the temple, which was rarely, the goddess did not smile upon them as often. Mareg looked up to meet Illiana's gaze.

"No," she said. "There is justice for some, but without justice for all, there is no true justice, only an affront to the Lady."

The words seemed to hang in the air. The fire snapped in response. Then Illiana nodded.

"You are the High Judge," she said. "You are not bound by the vows of the priests."

"I have my own vows." Mareg thought for a moment. "Vows to place the service of the Lady above service to all else." Including the king. Including even her family. But by truly serving the Lady of Justice she would be serving all, including her daughter. Her half-Virsat, half-Tirdar daughter. Changing Tireera in this way would be far from easy. It would also be dangerous, and she would have to be careful how she went about it. She could lose her freedom and possibly her life if she were not careful. She wondered what the city would be like if she succeeded. She had a brief vision of a very different place. She spoke none of this aloud.

"Exactly," said Illiana, just as if she had.

TEN

$\mathscr{I}$T WAS MUCH EASIER IN THE BOAT THAN IT
was slogging on foot through the swamp, and Forentel was
grateful. Riessa knew how to use the long pole to steer and
propel the boat forward, although sometimes they had to
use the oars if the water was deep. Sunrise dozed in the
bottom of the shallow craft. Both women tried to keep their
distance from her as best they could in the small space, but
Forentel, although cautious, was not afraid of the animal.
That bothered her. It reminded her constantly of her un-
Virsat abilities. These abilities were just what seemed to
reassure Riessa, however.

"How much of this swamp do you know?" Forentel
yawned. She was hot and tired, and she hoped the swamp
would end soon. She couldn't believe how much of it they
had already traveled through.

It was late afternoon now, with no sign of pursuit. They had pulled the boat in close to one of the reedy little islands, and Riessa had dropped a line over the side, baited with some of the little iridescent green flies that swarmed over the surface of the water. Several fish had already been caught by this method, and Forentel heard her stomach rumble. The wolf sat up and yawned hugely, eying the fish on the bottom of the boat.

"I have traveled four days away from the village though the swamp, and I know it fairly well for that distance." Riessa pushed a strand of black hair away from her eyes. "That's farther than most of the fishermen ever go. There are things beyond there that are dangerous." She paused.

Forentel frowned, not liking the sound of this. "How far is Dreffir?"

Riessa stared at her in surprise. "I don't know. Much farther. No one's ever been there. But the legends say it's a month beyond that. Or a thirteen-month. Or more."

"Nice and precise," Forentel muttered. "But even if it's a year away, why hasn't anyone gone there?"

"Let's pull over here and cook these fish; I'm starved." Riessa poled the boat in to the shore. The wolf leaped out first and stood on the shore watching them. "Come on, get out and help me beach the boat. We can build a small fire and then move on again before dark. If anyone is following, they won't find us."

"You didn't say why no one has gone to Dreffir." Forentel got out to help with the boat. Weedy water squelched under her feet.

"If anyone found Dreffir, they have not returned. It is said that there are too many obstacles in the way. And"— Riessa glanced around her—"that farther downriver the swamp is haunted."

"Haunted how?" Forentel wanted to sound skeptical. The truth was that she was not. Although the sun was still bright and the afternoon was hot, there was something about the marsh that lent itself to the idea of hauntings. There was a haze over the water, and a wading bird cried nearby, a harsh, lonely sound. Despite the heat and despite herself, Forentel shivered.

"There are many things in the marsh," said Riessa in a low voice. "Spirits of the lost. Spirits of the drowned. And some things—demons—that were never human," she ended in a whisper. "Your magic should protect us," she went on a little more strongly. "And perhaps the wolf's." She looked sideways at Sunrise, who was scratching behind her ear with a hind foot, her tongue lolling out. At that moment, anything less magical was difficult to imagine.

"Perhaps we should get out of the marsh and avoid all those things." Forentel picked up the string of fish. "What's beyond the marsh?"

"I don't know. No one knows."

Someone has to, thought Forentel.

"I think you should know." Forentel lay the fish down across the side of the boat. "My name is not Frelenya. It's Forentel. Frelenya was my sister." It felt odd to say that, even now.

"Was?" Riessa had managed to start a fire. Forentel couldn't see where she had managed to come up with enough dry wood for burning.

"She died." Forentel realized she didn't want to say more than this. "She was my twin. I use her name sometimes, because, well, to remember her." That wasn't quite right, of course, since she had never known her. "To keep her alive."

Riessa stared at her, eyes huge, while the fish, which she had been gutting, slipped from her hands. Forentel leaned forward and rescued it. Riessa made an odd sign with her fingers.

"Double souled," she whispered.

Forentel sighed. She had heard the term before from
Tirdar servants. Twins, identical twins, were thought to
share a soul. If one died, the survivor was crippled unless
he or she could somehow recapture and keep alive the portion of the soul held by the twin. Twins were magical. It
was typical Tirdar superstition.

"I always wanted a sister," said Riessa. "I had one, once.
She was eighteen moons younger than I." She glanced at
Forentel. "About your age. But she died when I was only six
summers, of the sickness. We were not double souled, but
sometimes, sometimes," she sighed, "it felt as though we
were. But we were not magical. I swore then that I would do
something with my life, that I would live for her, for Siella,
that I would see the world for her, as well as for myself. I
would do anything to get out of Hila, anything to make a
place in the world. And all I did was marry and stay in Hila.
Until you came." She smiled quickly at Forentel. "You
could be my sister, perhaps, except that you are magic."

Later, as they sat near the fire, Forentel decided to try to
clear the air. The fire had been banked but not extinguished.
Neither of them could quite bear to lose it, not for its warmth
but for what it represented in the middle of the trackless
swamp. A dinner of fresh fish had made a difference in how
Forentel felt, and finding Dreffir now seemed more possible.

"I'm not magical, Riessa. I'm no different than you."

"You are a healer."

"I suppose so"—she still wasn't accustomed to thinking
of herself that way—"but that isn't magical, it's—"

Whatever she thought it was remained unsaid. The wolf
had wandered off, ignored by the two women, but now she
was back. She whined, and then barked, a sudden sharp
sound.

"What's wrong with her?" Riessa edged away.

Forentel shrugged; she had no idea. The wolf barked
again, and then she knew.

"Someone is coming!"

They stared at each other for a moment. Then they turned simultaneously to gather up their things, packing away what remained of the fish.

"The boat!" said Forentel. "We have to get back to the boat."

"Put out the fire first!" Riessa was kicking soil over the fire.

"Never mind." Forentel caught her arm. "He's nearby. He will find the fire anyway and know we are close. Let's go. Now, before he finds us."

They stared at each other briefly and then turned to run. Forentel glanced around for Sunrise, but the wolf was gone again.

"Don't run." The voice came out of the darkness just beyond the wan circle of light cast by the dying fire. "If you run, I will kill you."

Both women stood frozen, and Riessa whimpered slightly.

"Who are you?" Forentel did her best to sound brave. "Come out where we can see you. We mean you no harm." Forentel realized she held the knife with which she had been spearing her cooked fish, and she made a show of sheathing it at her belt.

There was a crash, as someone large stumbled toward the fire and then fell. Forentel and Riessa both flinched, and then Forentel went forward cautiously.

It was a big man, lying on the ground, breathing heavily, with the swamp insects buzzing around him. He couldn't have killed anyone, Forentel thought, unless perhaps he fell on them. She nudged him with her toe and he groaned. Clutched in his right hand was a bow, and there was an almost full quiver strapped on his back.

"Get a torch," said Forentel. "I need more light." She knelt beside the man and managed by dint of grunting and heaving to get the quiver off and to roll him over. He did nothing to help her and seemed barely conscious.

Riessa brought a lit torch. By its light Forentel saw that he also had a sword, a knife in his boot, a full pack, and several water canteens. She stripped his weapons from him and put them in a little pile.

"He's Virsat," said Riessa.

"Yes," said Forentel shortly. "From the city." She did not mention what else she could tell from his clothing: that he was military, and not just any soldier. Around his neck was the bronze medallion of the King's Guard.

"I can't see what's wrong with him." She was struggling to look through his clothing. "There are no obvious wounds." She put her hand against his brow. "He's burning with fever. Help me get him nearer the fire. And stoke it up again, please; we may need it."

They struggled and heaved with the inert body before finally getting him near the fire. Forentel hadn't realized how difficult it was to move someone without help from the person being moved. As she rested, panting, wondering what to do next, the man's eyes suddenly snapped open. Riessa let out a little scream.

"Bitten," he said. "Knife lizard. If you harm me I will kill you." His hand spasmed as if trying to grasp a weapon, making Forentel very glad she had taken them, even though he was in no condition to use them.

"What's a knife lizard?" she asked Riessa.

"Nasty little creature. They live in the reeds. If you step on them, they bite you, and it's poisonous. It doesn't usually kill you, but it makes you very sick." She paused. "I say we take his weapons and his food and whatever else we can use, maybe his clothes, and leave him."

"He'll die!"

"Maybe, but maybe not. I just said, they don't always."

Forentel wasn't shocked. She wasn't even surprised.

She looked at the man in front of her, seeing the sheen of sweat on his face. In the torchlight his lips looked blue. She couldn't tell how sick he really was, not without reaching deep within herself to that strange place, and that took so much energy.

"I want to know what he's doing here."

"What does it matter?" Riessa was impatient. "He's Virsat. Whatever he's doing, it's not good. I'm not saying we kill him, just leave him."

"Please." The object of their discussion whispered. "Don't—"

"That's a far cry from 'I'll kill you.'" Forentel placed her hand against the man's cheek. She agreed with Riessa. They should take this man's weapons and goods and leave. It would be safer still to kill him. But she could not overcome the feeling that she must help him. "If I don't at least try to help him I will have failed," Forentel said.

Riessa frowned but said nothing. It was clear she had expected this, and Forentel wondered again just why Riessa wanted her company. Surely she could have left her village on her own at any time and survived. And just as surely she was no replacement for Riessa's lost sister.

"Look around his ankles. You'll find the bite there, most likely." Riessa grounded the torch and watched as Forentel pulled back the man's short boots.

"That doesn't look too bad." Riessa was leaning over, peering at the bite mark just above the man's right ankle. It was puffy and red and oozing slightly. "It's oozing, which means some of the poison is leaking out. He will live, even if you do nothing."

"I'm helping him." Resentment and a perverse sense of pride overcame good sense.

"If you have taken the healer's vow, then I suppose you must," said Riessa sourly.

Forentel didn't answer. She was already reaching down

into herself for whatever it was that helped her to heal. She
remembered what she had done with Riessa. This time it
was easier. She felt the weakness in her patient, a simple
poison. He was a strong man. It didn't take much of her
own powers to encourage his own healing abilities, which,
as Riessa had implied, were already at work.

It was almost a pleasure to feel the poison recede. She
could feel the sick tissue regenerate, feel the strength flowing back into the man. It was power. It was wonderful.

Something grabbed her wrist. Forentel opened her eyes
to look into the eyes of her erstwhile patient. He was kneeling beside her now, and he had his knife, the same knife
she had stripped from him only moments ago. He held the
knife almost casually, but it would take very little for him
to pull her around and have the knife at her throat. Riessa
stood back slightly away from them, her eyes wide in the
torchlight, her hands pressed to her breast. Not much help
from her, Forentel thought.

"I told your friend," Forentel's patient glanced at
Riessa, "that I can catch her and kill her before you draw
your last breath." A flash of torchlight reflected from the
knife blade into Forentel's eyes, and she squinted. "She believed me, so she won't do anything stupid. And you won't,
either. Will you?"

He told Riessa? Forentel thought. When? She hadn't
heard him. She had been so locked in the healing trance
that she hadn't even heard her patient speak. How was that
possible?

"Will you?" The knife was now at her throat.

"No," she said.

"Who are you?" The knife eased fractionally away from
her throat, and she could breathe again. "And what are
you? I thought you were Tirdar, but there is something
about you that is not right. And you are not one of these

swamp villagers," the contempt in his voice made Forentel flinch slightly, "so don't tell me you are."

Forentel shifted slightly to try to get a better look at him. He felt her move and pressed the knife harder against her throat. Suddenly rage washed through her. It rolled over her like one of the brief but vicious rainstorms of home.

"I saved your life!" she snapped. The fury lent her courage, and also a speed and skill she did not realize she had. Probably it was only luck, but she pulled away from the knife, twisting aside and slapping his hand down and away in one continuous movement. "I think you owe me your name first! I owe you nothing!" She was on her feet, somehow, looking down at her patient.

He stared up at her with astonishment and a rather grudging respect, while in the corner of Forentel's vision Riessa moved slightly, trying to come around her to the other side of their adversary. A damp wind had picked up, and Forentel saw Riessa shiver.

"Answer me. I saved your life," she repeated.

"Perhaps, but I think I would have lived in any case." He made some sort of rapid movement, too fast for Forentel to follow, and the knife vanished. "No need to try to rush me," he smiled slightly at Riessa. "Jumping me would be unfortunate for you, and as you can see, I am harmless now."

Forentel barely refrained from snorting in disbelief. "Give me the knife," she said.

"I can't do that. But I will do this; I will promise not to attack you or harm you, either of you, without reason. If you refrain from attacking me, that should keep you safe." He smiled again, this time with obvious humor. "I apologize for my behavior, honored lady. Forgive me." He made the courteous half bow of one Virsat noble to another, and without thinking, Forentel returned it. As soon as she did, she could have kicked herself; she could see he missed nothing.

When he smiled he was charming, and he obviously knew it. His dark brown eyes sparkled with humor, and the quirk at the corner of his mouth made him look boyish. His dark hair had been pulled loose from its restraining leather thong and curled around his face. If he didn't look exactly harmless, he looked at least like someone who wouldn't wish to cause harm. Forentel was not reassured.

"My name, honored lady, is Kelern Drilini."

She knew the name, his family name. They were minor Virsat nobility whose sons usually went into the military.

"I'm Frelenya."

"I am honored." But he straightened, his eyes sharp, and Forentel knew without a doubt that he had realized who she was. "I'm Forentel," she said, "Forentel Pentrat."

"The general's daughter," he said, "and the daughter of the High Judge. I heard that you were missing."

Riessa gasped, and they both turned to look at her.

"This is Riessa," said Forentel.

"Daughter of the headwoman of Hila village," said Riessa. She drew herself up, and Forentel blinked. She looked regal, despite the mud and sweat and dirt, despite her disheveled clothes. "Your equal, and more." She stared hard at Kelern.

Kelern turned from her back to Forentel. "I know you are running from something, Lady Forentel." When Forentel frowned, he smiled a little grimly. "It is my business to know things."

Forentel waited. If he knew about her ancestry, if he knew what her father had said to her mother, why her father sought her—she pushed the thought down.

"I heard rumors of a marriage," Kelern continued, oblivious to her turmoil, "one that I can understand a young woman would not wish."

Forentel drew a breath. She was conscious of Riessa behind her now, and of the other woman's surprised scrutiny.

"I am not concerned with that. That's not—" He paused.

"I'm not the one you are hunting," said Forentel. "I saw your medallion. King's Guard. King's man. King's hunter." She turned and glanced at Riessa. "He hunts men," she said.

He nodded. "Yes," he said quietly, "I do. But you are correct. I have not been sent for you. I am hunting others. Perhaps you have seen them. The prince and his tutor. Prince Erba and Lord Filfa."

"Yes," said Forentel. "I was with them. But they left me in the village weeks ago." She felt odd telling him, but she owed the prince nothing, she thought, and more than that, she wanted this man gone, despite all his charm. She could not regret healing him, but danger flowed off him in waves. Erba and Filfa could take care of themselves, and it was unlikely he would find them. Nonetheless, she felt guilty.

"They went into the swamp. I don't know where they are."

"But you know where they are going." It was not a question.

"No," she began.

"They are looking for Dreffir," said Riessa, "as are we."

Forentel wanted to slap her. "Looking for a legend," she said acidly, glaring at the Hilan. "Following dreams."

"Dreffir is dangerous enough even as a legend." Kelern had retrieved his pack and was rummaging in it. "Perhaps you will allow me to share some of my provisions in return for your—help."

Forentel knew he was wondering how it was that a Virsat noblewoman had skills suited to a Tirdar healer. But he had dried meat in his pack, and some dried vegetables. With those and what was left of their fish, they made some stew.

Kelern told Riessa tales of Tireera, of its beauty and riches, and she hung on every word. Forentel was bored and ate her stew looking off into the marshes. Kelern had wine in one of his skins, too, which Riessa accepted. Forentel did not.

"I am not going to drug you, lady. I am instead offering you my protection on your journey." He stretched out his legs to the fire and slapped at one of the bloodsucking insects. It was hard to believe that he had not that long ago been delirious and ill.

"Why?" Forentel wished she had followed Riessa's advice, that they had run when they had the chance. Too late now. Riessa was sleeping, overcome by the wine.

"Because you and I are going to the same place, and I would not leave a noble lady alone in such a land."

"And perhaps because once you have found the prince you would not object to bringing me back also, for whatever my father might give you?"

Kelern chuckled. "Believe me, lady, I was not hunting you, and I will have no need of any reward that your father might offer for you. Once I have the prince and the tutor, my charge is accomplished and my duty fulfilled. And I will have all the riches I might desire." He smiled at her.

Forentel felt cold. She could guess why he hunted Erba, and what the king's charge was. Erba and Filfa would never return to Tireera alive. And since she knew this, she would not live, either. She tried to keep the knowledge from showing in her eyes.

The sun was rising now, and the mist over the swamp was beginning to dissipate. The dawn reminded Forentel of the wolf. Sunrise had vanished when Kelern appeared and had not returned. It shouldn't matter, but it did, and for reasons she couldn't entirely understand, Forentel felt abandoned. She was also exhausted. The night without sleep, the stress of the healing, and the anxiety were taking their toll. Kelern obviously planned to stay with them, and she couldn't think of a plan now to lose him.

"My boat sank," he told them cheerfully. "It rammed a stump and filled with scummy water. I was lucky to make it to this island and find you."

He stowed his gear in their boat, and they climbed in. Forentel determined to let him pole and paddle in her place; the least he could do, she decided, in return for her healing.

Just before they pushed the boat out into the marshy channel, Sunrise appeared. Kelern dropped the boat pole and reached for his knife, but the wolf ignored him. She jumped into the boat and curled up in the stern beneath the seat. When neither woman commented on the presence of a large predator in their boat, Kelern let out a low whistle and resheathed the knife.

It was afternoon when Forentel awoke. There was a low murmur of voices. Turning her head, she looked into the yellow eyes of the wolf, who lay near her. The wolf yawned. Beyond the wolf, Riessa and Kelern sat together in the bow of the boat, talking softly. The boat drifted gently in a current, and Forentel realized they must have found the main channel.

"So you will truly be wealthy," Riessa was murmuring. Forentel knew she was not meant to overhear this, but the water carried the sound.

"Wealthy enough to leave the army, if the king permits," said Kelern. "Although I don't see myself managing an estate outside Tireera, I suppose I could get used to it."

Forentel blinked and eased herself up on her elbows. She peered over the side of the boat and saw that they were indeed caught in the current, which carried them along gently. The river had widened, too. It now seemed to have actual banks, although there were many low islands and mud flats, and there were branches and channels that meandered away in all directions. The light of the westering sun sparkled back off the water and tinged it slightly red. Still more water, she thought irritably. She had slept most of the day, and she had hoped, perversely, to be away from the river soon.

No one but the wolf had noticed that she was awake. Forentel leaned back again in the boat and tried to think. Her abilities were not only potentially dangerous, they were apparently out of her control. She had no real knowledge of how to use them, or even exactly what they were. The healing, yes, she understood a little part of that, but not all of it. But the ability to relate to the wolf—she glanced sideways at the animal.

The wolf, Sunrise, she told herself, or was it Dawn, looked back at her and panted, tongue out. Which is it, she thought, Sunrise or Dawn? There was no answer. Perhaps whatever it was that she felt with the wolf was not her doing at all, but the animal's. That comforted her for only a moment, until she realized that it took both of them to communicate, on whatever level they were doing it. This was not something a Virsat did. Even the healing was frightening. The strange joy and power she had felt in the trance when she healed Kelern had been, after the fact, terrifying. The healing power had controlled her. If only she could have had time with Illiana, if only she had known to go to the shrine for help when she was younger, if only she had never had the visions and the dreams. If she could rid herself of them, she could be true to her Virsat heritage.

Forentel was overcome by a wave of grief that mixed with her fear. She would never see Tireera again, she was sure. She missed her mother, and she missed her father, and she even missed her sister. She had given them up because she must, and she could not go back until she learned not only who she was but what she was.

Something cold and wet touched her hand. The wolf was pushing at her hand, and then gently began to lick it. Forentel swallowed the lump in her throat and put her arms around the animal. The wolf lay down beside her, and she rested her head against the animal. She didn't think she was still tired, but she must have been, because when she opened her eyes again, it was dark.

The first thing that struck her was not the darkness but the silence. The wolf was still beside her, breathing softly, but there were no other sounds but for the rush of water and the occasional cry of a night bird. She was ravenously hungry, and she wondered at herself for having slept so long. Undoubtedly it was a result of the loss of energy from the healing trance.

"Riessa, where is that fish? We have some left, don't we?"

Silence answered her. In the light of the stars she strained to see, certain she was wrong. They couldn't be gone, both Riessa and Kelern. Where could they go? But it was true. She was alone in the boat with only a wolf for company, carried along down a strange river.

ELEVEN

$\mathcal{E}$RBA DRIFTED BACK INTO CONSCIOUSNESS. IT was damp and clammy, and his arms hurt. He felt nauseated, and his head ached. After a moment it began to come back to him: following the directions of the villagers as best they could through the swamp to where the river at last developed an actual current, and then letting the current carry them. The island had loomed out of the dawn, attractive, compelling, like a song in his head, silent but irresistible. He had wondered about his sanity, and if Filfa heard it, too. He had seized the oars and pulled hard for the shore, despite Filfa's shouts.

"I am the prince," he remembered saying, "and I command that we go." He had kept Filfa from the oars, ignoring the older man's protests.

Erba raised his head to look for his tutor. It was difficult to see in the dim light, and it hurt to move his head. He groaned. He was afraid that both his arms were broken. The movement sent sharp spikes of agony through his arms up into his shoulders, and he almost vomited. He gritted his teeth to keep from crying out, while spots swam in front of his eyes. After a few moments, his vision stabilized.

"Filfa," he whispered hoarsely, "are you there? Can you hear me?" There was no response, but a lump of clothing nearby shifted slightly, as if it were breathing.

They were in what might have been a cellar or a cave. It was damp stone and even moister earth. Something scuttled out from the damp and rotting vegetation on which he lay. He had never imagined such wet misery was possible. It was a far cry from what he had seen when he heard the silent song. He should have known the visions of comfort, of luxurious feasts, and beautiful women were false, but how could he have been expected to evaluate something so unexpected, let alone resist it? The villagers had said nothing of this trap when they had given him the boat. Perhaps they hadn't known.

At least Forentel wasn't here. If he had insisted on sneaking back to Hila for her she would be here, too, in this horrible place. But the Hilans had said that she wished to stay with them. The headwoman had been quite clear about that. Forentel was a healer, and this was what she had been meant to do. It wasn't a good argument as far as he was concerned, but the headwoman had insisted. And Filfa had agreed. If only he could have spoken to her, to be sure she had chosen for herself, he could have set his mind at ease. He had tortured himself silently ever since they left. Was he a coward for not having risked his new freedom to try to speak to her? And the deeper truth was that he missed her. But now he was glad she was safe in Hila.

He managed to sit up despite the pain. Although his arms hurt, he could move them, so perhaps they weren't broken. His legs were chained. This surprised him, but he looked down the chains to their termination at a ring in a large boulder. The effort made him groan again, but it also helped him remember.

The silent song had become stronger as they approached the island. The urgency to reach the island was almost unbearable. They beached the boat and jumped out into mud, which squelched around their feet. Not far back from the shore was a bank of flowers that seemed to vibrate with color. Everything was brighter, clearer, more wonderful. It had seemed just the way it was meant to be, as if the world were made for him. Breathing was a delight. Even when they saw the strange men in animal skins carrying knives and clubs he hadn't been alarmed. The men were little, surprisingly so. They looked funny, and he had laughed. He knew that he should draw his sword, but it wasn't with him. He had left it in the boat. At least he should have drawn his knife, but he couldn't seem to care enough to do that. It didn't matter. Filfa had tried to drag him back toward the boat, but he had resisted, laughing. He had smiled, right up until one of the men had hit him on the back of the head with a club.

He remembered waking again later, with his captors around him, and with Filfa bound nearby. One of the odd little men, a wizened fellow with dark, braided hair, had nodded at him, smiling, and said something unintelligible. Erba had promptly thrown up and then lost consciousness again.

When he had woken for the second time he had been on a relatively comfortable bed made of skins and rushes. Someone had helped him sit up and had given him something to drink, and he had begun to feel better. When he looked around he found he was in a hut, surrounded by the small people, men and women both, and Filfa was on a bed similar to his, nearby. Erba could feel the strange song in his head again, but a little dark woman smiled at him and gave him something to drink, and the song faded, and he knew he was in trouble. Eventually they found someone who could speak Virsat.

"You have been called," the little man told him. He was strong-looking despite his small size, and even if Erba had felt completely well he would have hesitated to attack him. "She called you. You are attuned to her. If she accepts you, you will serve her. You will speak to her for us."

He had still been under the spell of the silent song. Even though it no longer sang in his mind, he knew it was there, and he could feel it somewhere within him. He knew the little man spoke of the singer, and if these people wanted him to speak to the singer for them, he would be glad to do so. Still groggy from the blow that had rendered him unconscious, he had been taken to see the singer. They had left Filfa in the small room, still unconscious.

He had found it hard to walk, and he knew that this was not good, that he was still recovering from the blow that had rendered him unconscious, but also that he was under the influence of whatever drug they had given him. Always in the background was the strange song. It was a Tirdar-like ability to hear something like this, an evil magic, something no Virsat should be subject to, but he could not become alarmed. He imagined a woman, unlike any woman he had ever met, a goddess, waiting just for him.

When they took him into a small cave on a hill over-looking the marsh, he thought he was prepared. His guides stopped, holding his arms. There was a passageway leading down, and the song was louder. He pulled free of his escort, and he saw the way they looked at one another, but he didn't care. He half staggered downward, through the stone tunnel, knowing they were behind him.

The stone passage opened out into a lower, damper cave. There was a smell, a stench: something rotting. The faint

cry of alarm that sounded at the back of his brain almost
woke him from his trance, and it jarred him enough so that
he came to a dead stop before the source of the song.

It was not a woman, and it was not even human. It reminded him of an orchid, but enormous, nothing like the
ones carefully nurtured in his father's greenhouse. It tow-
ered over him. He stopped dead and stared at it. The shimmering haze that had begun to form around him was
shattered, and he saw the odd oily streaks down the side of
the plant. He realized the smell was coming from it, as well
as the song.

"You hear her, yes?" His small interpreter had come up
beside him. "She needs you. Go to her."

"For what?" Despite himself Erba was fascinated, but
the sense of danger prickled along his neck.

"You speak to her for us, and to us for her. She protect
us." The little man took his hand and patted it. "She protect
us," he said again, "and we feed her. We do not have the ability you have. We cannot talk to her. Only those born with extra magic here," he touched his head, "can talk to her."

Erba stared. Surely the blast of silent song he had heard
could be heard by anyone with a mind. Although not by
Filfa, he remembered uneasily. The little man seemed to
understand what he did not say.

"She send out very strong song to call her new consort.
Very strong. And she find you, but it make her weak. So
talk to her, and she will tell you what she needs."

He was going to refuse. It did not matter what they did
to him, he would still refuse. Talking to some plant was not
a thing a Virsat did, and certainly not a prince. This horror
in front of him was just that: damp, rotting, and in no way
capable of thought of any sort. He turned to tell them he
would not do it, and that they were all superstitious fools.

The song came back. It engulfed him and filled his
brain. He turned back. He had no choice.

The song filled him with an exquisite delight but also a subtle pain. He was right: the flower was not a thinking being, not in the way that he was capable of thought, but it did have an odd form of intelligence. It had a connection with him, and it would use him to serve its needs the way other flowers used color and scent. If he refused, the pain would become stronger. If he obeyed, the song itself was at least part of his reward. He realized that he was strong enough to hear this thing, but he was not strong enough to resist it. The plant had indeed expended much energy in finding him. It was weak now, and it needed him to bring it food, but even in its weakened state he could not resist it.

"You hear her." His guide put a hand on his arm.

"Yes," whispered Erba.

"And you do what she wants."

He thought of refusing again, and as soon as the thought crossed his mind, pain shot through him. He gasped, almost doubling over.

"Yes," he whispered, "I will do what she wants."

The pain stopped. He could feel the promise of it still, but also the promise of joy, that it would be as it was when he first set foot on this island, bright and beautiful. He did not think it would ever be bright and beautiful that way again, but certainly anything was better than the pain.

He knew what kind of food the plant wanted, and he knew how these people had kept it alive. He knew what the smell was, and he could see some of the remains of digested dinners around the bottom of the plant. He glanced behind him at the small people. They had been giving it members of their own band, one at a time; he would continue to do the same, until he could find a way to escape.

"You cannot feed her with us," said his guide. "Not anymore. We prune her dead leaves, we mound up her soil. She keeps all others from this place, except those you call here for her. She will help you call others to us. It is not often she needs the Great Food, but she needs it now. Now you will feed her the other, the man who came with you."

He wouldn't give Filfa to this thing, but why did they even need to ask him to do it? He realized that he knew the answer. The plant would get more nourishment from its food if he prepared it. He realized he was expected to link with Filfa's mind, and that now, under the plant's influence, he could do it. The plant would feed from its food's emotions. What could he do but stall?

He looked around him at the damp stone, the rotting vegetation. He hated this swamp and everything in it.

SHE HAD FOUND the oars, and by the time the sun rose she had learned to use them with at least some skill. The problem was that her arms ached; she was not accustomed to this sort of labor. Whenever she could, she let the current carry the boat. She found one waterskin beneath a thwart, but all the food was gone, and everything else with it—all the blankets, the fire strikers, everything. She came to the conclusion that Riessa and Kelern had put in to an island while she slept, taken everything, and then set the boat adrift. She didn't know how she could have slept through those events, and she didn't know why Sunrise had permitted Riessa and Kelern to abandon her, but then she didn't know much about the wolf. Although it made her nervous to be on her own, she was also relieved. With any luck she would never see Kelern again, and Riessa had proved the nature of her "friendship."

Forentel frowned. No matter what she did, it could never be right, never, and all because of what she was, neither Virsat not Tirdar, someone with no place of her own. She had tried to be a good daughter, but her father had never loved her, and worse, had wanted to use her. The only person who had loved her was her mother, and now she might not ever see Mareg again. She sniffled slightly. She had saved Riessa's life, and Kelern's, and they had left her. And she had saved Erba's life. Thinking about Erba made her feel even worse. Why had he left her in Hila? Why hadn't he even tried to speak to her? She could understand why Filfa would leave her behind, but not Erba. Something wet slid down her cheek, and she brushed it away angrily. Erba had left her. She never wanted to see him again.

The sun rising over the marsh was beautiful, she had to admit it. Little birds were wheeling and dipping over the water, feeding on the small insects that swarmed there. A large bird as white as pure sand was standing near a tangle of vegetation, dipping its head down every so often and coming up with a small fish. Forentel watched as they floated by, feeling hungrier and wishing Riessa had left at least some food.

"I don't suppose you can fish," she said to the wolf. Sunrise looked at her and panted, then stood up, leaned over the side of the boat and slurped up water. Forentel laughed and was rewarded with an injured look.

She made no attempt to pull in to any of the islands they passed on the leisurely current. The river was her best and only way of traveling, at least for now. When the sun had burned off the haze, it became hot. Forentel thought she was accustomed to heat, but this was different from Tireeran heat. This heat was moist and heavy, and it smothered her and made her head ache. As the day faded finally toward evening, she realized that she would have to land at an island. She needed food, and she needed to get out of the boat, to feel dry land, or what passed for it around here, beneath her feet. It would be better not to travel down the river at night. She was looking for a suitable island when she felt it.

She sat up straight and stared across the water. She

knew she was not hearing the call with her ears but with her mind. The wolf sat up beside her and then growled, a low, ominous sound.

"You're right," she said. "We won't go there; whatever that is, we should stay away from it."

Despite her words, she could feel the attraction. Whatever it was, it was on the island looming on the left in the dusk. It was trying to draw her in, to bring her to shore, but now nothing would have induced her to land there. She pulled harder on the oars, keeping to the slow current.

They drifted along the side of the island as the stars began to prick through the evening sky and the mist began to rise again off the marsh. As they drew level with the island, she realized what it was about the silent call that was so disturbing. It was not evil, no more than thorn poison was evil. This call was dangerous, far more so than thorn poison, and it was a trap. What was disturbing was the sense of something both familiar and tortured in the call. It reminded her of something. It reminded her of someone. It reminded her of Erba. She shifted against the oars and began to pull toward the island.

The wolf growled low in her throat again, and as Forentel continued to row, came over and stood above her. The next growl was louder and more dangerous. Forentel did not stop rowing.

"I have to get him," she said. "I can't leave him with—whatever that is. It's not just killing him. It's worse." He had left her behind without a word and without a thought, but she couldn't leave him, not in the danger she knew was there. The fear she felt was not for herself. It was for him. *I should leave him,* she thought, but she knew she wouldn't.

The wolf looked back at her, and Forentel felt a sudden heat. Sunrise would help her. She was not sure why, but she did know that she had an ally, for this time at least. She rowed to the island and beached the boat in a tangle of tree roots and branches that swept down to the water. The mess of vegetation would hide the boat, she hoped.

She could find Erba simply by following the call, which she felt as a huge, silent pressure in her head. It did not seem the wise thing to do. It would be better if she could ignore the silent call and follow other more physical signs.

Forentel set out along a path not far from the shore. She wanted to find the prince before full night, but already the dusk and the deeper darkness beneath the trees made it difficult to see. The path wound through razor-sharp, long grasses and spongy-looking trees. There was a smell of something rotting, which grew stronger the farther down the path they went. Ahead was a glimmer of light. As it grew brighter, she grew more cautious, and then at last she could see a group of huts ahead. Several fires burned outside. Forentel stopped, slipping back into the shadows. She looked back for Sunrise, but the wolf was nowhere to be seen.

There was a feast in the village. Tiny people came and went, carrying baskets and platters of food. At first she thought they were children, but when the firelight fell across one of them, she saw they were fully grown. There was one person of her size, sitting by one of the fires. She crept closer: it was Erba.

He was surrounded by the small people, and it was apparent that he was both an honored guest and a reluctant one. They brought him food, but he barely ate. Forentel looked for Filfa, but he was nowhere to be seen, and she wondered if an accident had befallen the older man.

Throughout all of this she was aware of the strange, silent calling. Although she could not see Sunrise, she was aware of the wolf helping her to resist the call and masking her from it.

She was aware of something else. She could sense Erba's mind, the tenor of his thoughts. He was miserable

and afraid and in despair. She thought she was able to read
him because of the singer and because of the wolf, but that
was not all. She felt him recognize her.

HE COULDN'T RESIST these people. They were going
to take Filfa down into the cave and feed him to that thing,
and he would have to help. Afterwards he would be here
for all of his life, his mind and his newfound ability coupled with the plant's to draw in new victims, to make the
minds of the victims acceptable as food.

   Outside of the circles of fire and torchlight, flying insects danced. The air was heavy with heat and water, and
he longed for the dry, crisp cool of a desert night. The little
people kept offering him food, insisting he eat. Occasionally he nibbled at something just so they would leave him
alone, but then he realized that the sooner the feast was
over, the sooner they would proceed to the cave with Filfa,
so he continued to accept their offerings. He tried to probe
his link with the plant, to see what he could learn, what
might be to his advantage, but he learned nothing. He sat
there in misery until something caught his attention.

   He didn't recognize it at first. It nibbled at the edges of
his thoughts, easing around the link he had with the plant.
It was featherlight, a touch that barely existed, but then he
realized what it was. It was Forentel.

   He wanted to warn her. He wanted her to stay away, but
he also wanted her with him, not that he thought she could
help, but simply to have the company of someone else of
his own kind. He wanted to share the misery. He didn't
know how it was possible for a Virsat, for two Virsat, to do
things he had always believed to be the province of Tirdar
alone, but here they were, and he was desperate for her
support. *Stay away,* he thought. *It will kill you.*

   Forentel blinked. She had heard the prince's voice as

clearly as if he had spoken in her ear. She did not wonder
for long how this was possible; those speculations could
wait. She already knew the thing would kill her if it could,
as would the small people. Could she just rush in there?
Even with Sunrise? She tried to send a thought back to
Erba, but she couldn't make him feel her thoughts the way
she had felt his.

While she hid, wondering what to do, several men took
Erba by the arms. He stood up, surrounded by a crowd of
singing, celebrating villagers. They were bringing someone else out of a hut, too, and even before she saw him she
knew it was Filfa.

In the torchlight, he looked terrible. It was hard to imagine that this shaky man with the bruised face, this man who
could barely stand without help, was an arrogant Virsat noble. His arms were bound behind him, but that hardly
seemed necessary. He swayed on his feet, and it took several of the small villagers to guide him past the fires and
down a trail. All of the village joined the procession, Erba
and his guides in the front, Filfa and guards following, and
all the others trailing behind them. Forentel waited until
the last of them had gone and then followed down the path
in the darkness, keeping back from the light of the last
torches. She felt something brush against her leg and
jumped, barely suppressing a cry. It was Sunrise; she could
see the wolf's eyes gleam in the darkness.

She would have tripped on the path but for the wolf's
guidance. Somehow the animal kept her on her feet, warning her without words of the roots and stones in the path.
The villagers led them down to the shore, a different part
of the shoreline from where she had hidden the boat. Then
they vanished. It took her a moment to realize that they had
gone into a cave.

She didn't want to go in. Despite her brief experience in
the tunnel beneath Illiana's cliff, being beneath the ground

was frightening to her. Not only that, but the thing was in there, the source of the call that she felt in her mind. It was strong here, so strong that it was difficult to resist it, even with the help of the wolf, who pressed against her legs, warm fur sticky against her. But she could hear the villagers inside, and she could feel Erba's horror and his desire. The combination made her skin crawl, but she hesitated for only another moment, to wonder why she would put herself at risk. She could sense Erba's fear. He couldn't reach out to her, but he needed her.

The little people crowded in the dark cave, and she tried to see over their heads and around them. They hadn't realized her presence, and she knew it was not only because Sunrise cloaked her thoughts but because everyone was so entranced with whatever it was that was going on in the front. Since she couldn't see, she opened her mind more.

There it was: Erba, in his terror and his joy, but also Filfa, in absolute horror and despair, and beyond them both whatever it was that was the author of all these emotions. She realized that she could also feel the people around them, at least in part. They were happy, and they were relieved. They had found what they had been searching for, and it was Erba. No longer would they be at risk. They were also avid for what was about to happen, for they would share in it.

A drum began to beat, a hollow sound. Her need to see overwhelmed her, and Forentel pushed forward. Now she could see over the heads of the crowd. She gaped, pushing forward still more to see the plant better. It reared up over the heads of everyone, even Erba. She had the sense that it was very old. She also recognized it as the source of the call. Beside the plant was the drummer, one of the small people, dressed in a cape of brilliant-colored feathers. Erba, too, had been draped in feathers. Filfa had not. He had been bound still more, with ropes around his ankles as well as his wrists, and he had been placed on the ground before the plant. As she watched, one of the long tendrils snaked down from the plant and twined itself around Filfa's shoulders, and he began to shudder.

Forentel could see more than the obvious. She saw the invisible tendrils pulsing, not only between the plant and Filfa, but between the plant and Erba. She could feel the hunger, and she could feel Erba's horror and his pleasure. She took another step forward. The people near her turned and looked at her.

They were all armed, men and women both. In one corner of her mind she thought wryly that this was a fine time to notice. But it didn't matter, because she felt something happen: the plant's attention shifted from Erba to her. It did not release Filfa, who had begun to sob, and it did not release Erba, but more of the invisible tendrils began to pulse toward her. Several of the men near her hesitated and then moved toward her.

"Stop!" She looked at the men nearest her and held up a hand. She spoke Virsat, but it didn't matter; they understood.

They stood back from her as she walked forward, until she stood before the plant. She saw Erba staring at her openmouthed, like one of Riessa's caught fish, she thought. She looked down at Filfa. She felt the tendrils between the plant and Erba break with a snap that was audible, somehow, to her mind. She was a far better partner for it than Erba, and the invisible tendrils coiled around her. Somewhere behind her was Sunrise, but she ignored the wolf's animal strength.

She looked down at Filfa and knew how to drain his life from him, how to torment his mind to give a wonderful emotional feast to the plant, before it began to digest his physical body. She was strong enough to link all of the villagers in this feast, so they could commune with the plant, their goddess.

She felt Filfa's terror as she began to direct the invisible
tendrils into him. He had never liked her; he had not even
seen her as human. He had suggested to Erba that they
keep her for a slave on their journey. This was her revenge,
made more delightful by the pleasure the plant fed back to
her. She could hear the little people calling out and singing,
clapping their hands, and the man with the drum was beat-
ing it again, its hollow boom echoing in the cavern. She
was vaguely aware of Erba crying, "No!" He attempted to
reach out to pull her away, but hands dragged him back. It
didn't matter, nothing mattered but this. It was what she
was meant to do. Then Filfa began to scream.

She drew in a sharp breath. Filfa lay on the ground,
glowing with unnatural light, sobbing and screaming in little pulsing jerks. She looked across the cavern. Everyone
in the cavern was entranced, caught up in the overflow of
emotion from the plant. She could feel their joy and even
some of their individual thoughts. Their old priest had not
been this strong, this capable, had not provided so much
pleasure. *She* would be very well served now. Sacrifices
could be lured in from far away, and would give more
nourishment; there would no longer be a need to sacrifice
one of their own. Forentel could feel it. She focused for a
moment on their trance, building it while she continued to
enable the plant to feed.

Then she turned her attention back to Filfa and focused
on him, sending the plant's tendrils deeper within him. His
screams became frenzied. Even Erba was caught. He was
horrified and disgusted at what was being done to his tutor,
but he was also thrilled. When she felt all around her to-
tally enmeshed, she stepped forward, grabbed the plant,
and pulled as hard as she could, ripping away one of the
smaller leaves. The stalk of the thing was smooth and rub-
bery under her fingers, and it was huge in circumference.
She could not get her hands around it. Frustrated, she dug

at it, gouging out pieces of vegetable matter. Vile-smelling fluid ran down her hands. She dragged down one of its huge leaves and began to rip it off. She felt the invisible tendrils fly free of Filfa and plunge into her.

Filfa stopped screaming. She was aware of a high-pitched sound within her own brain, behind her eyes, and she was tempted to stop her attack and claw at her eyes. She resisted, continuing to pull at the plant instead. Finally she jumped at it, trying to kick it and grind it into the ground. Pain streaked through her mind, and now she reached back for Sunrise, drawing on that tenuous bond to help her.

Other people were screaming now. One of the little men had grabbed her around the waist, and she kicked him, only vaguely aware when he fell away from her. She tore at the plant until agony made her stop, and she fell to the ground, curling into a ball.

The shouts and screams around her grew in volume, but she didn't look. She couldn't. The pain was so intense that she could barely keep breathing.

Someone picked her up and slung her over his shoulder. She opened her eyes, fighting nausea, and saw that it was Erba. He had her over one shoulder, and in his right hand was a spear he had wrenched from one of the villagers. In front of him, snarling at the crowd, stood Sunrise. Forentel blinked. Filfa was free of his bonds and was pushing toward the cavern entrance, stabbing left and right with a small sword, not much longer than a knife.

"Leave her!" shouted Filfa. Despite his success with the sword, he was not very steady on his feet. "Leave her! Erba, run!"

"Put me down," said Forentel.

"I'm not leaving you," Erba replied shortly.

"I said, put me down!"

The force of her tone was such that Erba did, surprised

at himself. With the wolf at her side, Forentel ran to one of
the torches and ripped it from its mounting. She swung it
from side to side, clearing a path for herself back toward
the plant. When she was close enough, she thrust the flaming torch into the plant and then turned and ran back toward the entrance. As soon as the flames touched the plant,
the agony in her mind abated.

There was pandemonium in the cavern. People were
shouting and screaming, most of them running toward the
plant to put out the flames. In the confusion they managed
to push out of the cavern.

"Our boat!" said Filfa. "Where is it?"

Forentel realized that she didn't know where her boat
was, either, in relation to this cavern. Someone did, however. The wolf pushed her large head against Forentel's
hand and then gave a short bark.

TWELVE

THERE WAS A PROPHET ON THE CORNER,
preaching to the small crowd of Tirdar gathered around. It
was the sort of scene that had been common in Tireera a
generation or so ago, Nedriff thought, but the old king had
cracked down on Tirdar superstition. Just what it was that
made these people such a good breeding ground for every
wild-eyed prophet or magician or trickster he would never
understand. Since Mirta's accession they had come back
with a vengeance from wherever it was they had festered.
Something would have to be done. He considered riding
his horse through them, but it wasn't necessary. With one
glance at him and at his mounted escort, they vanished like
water into sand.

Mirta was in his informal breakfast chamber when
Nedriff was shown in a while later. The remains of the

morning meal lay on the table, and Nedriff could not help
but notice that wine had been part of the new king's breakfast. Mirta was engaged now in reading some reports, a
task he loathed. His secretary was seated near him, ready
for whatever the king needed. Light streamed in through
the open windows and reflected back from the white
columns and the white marble floor, and Nedriff felt the
beginnings of a headache.

"Well?" said Mirta.

"There was another 'prophet' today, my lord; I almost
rode him down." Nedriff struggled to remain courteous. It
had seemed such a good idea to support Mirta in taking
the throne the way he had. He was beginning to regret it.
He had never intended that Mirta keep throne for too long,
but he had counted on a little more stability and a little
more time.

"Why should I care? They are Tirdar. They are foolish.
They have always been."

Nedriff repressed a sigh. He had truly thought Mirta the
better choice of the two brothers for his plans.

"Because," he said carefully, "they make the city unstable. They are only Tirdar, true, but Tireera depends upon
their labor." *You know this,* he wanted to add, *or you would
if you had not been drinking.* "You cannot, your pardon, I
mean, I do not believe it wise to permit this sort of thing to
continue. It is a kind of rebellion, my lord, and it *will*
grow."

"Rebellion. As in, armed rebellion?" Mirta pushed
aside the reports and focused on his general. "It is your
duty to see that does not happen. If you cannot, I will find
someone who can."

"I need your authorization, my lord, to take action
within the city."

Mirta stared at him for a moment. Nedriff could almost
see some of the thoughts trickling through his mind. In the

short time since he had come to power Mirta had become jealous of his authority and afraid of his own advisors. Nedriff, in command of the army of Tireera, was the unavoidable subject of some of this concern. Nedriff had done his utmost to reassure the king, all the more because his concerns were justified.

"Do what you need to," said Mirta at last. He turned to his secretary. "Draw up a paper of authority," he said. "Immediately."

Nedriff bowed. He knew the king wanted him out of the palace, and he was happy to oblige.

MAREG HELD UP a hand toward the priests, signaling *wait,* she was almost ready. This case had at first looked to be simple, and she wasn't sure why it was being brought before her. A small group of Tirdar was accused, she thought, of stealing from a Virsat estate, and of banding together for evil purpose. Such matters were usually dealt with by lesser judges and minor priests. It turned out, however, that these Tirdar were accused of treason. Mareg adjusted her long scarlet robe. It was lightweight silk, but during the heat of the day even this was too much. She nodded down at the two lesser judges who sat in carved seats below her dais; she wanted to be sure they were ready. When they nodded in return, she motioned to the priests.

The prisoners were brought in between two lines of guards, led by one of the senior priests in his white linen. The priest bowed before the statue of the Lady of Justice and lit another incense cone. Incense was one of the temple features Mareg could just as soon have done without.

"In accordance with the words of the Mighty Lady," intoned the priest in a bored voice, "we bring before her sworn servants, the High Judge Lady Mareg, and the

judges Lady Beha and Lord Jek, these prisoners, that they
may be judged. In accordance with the words of the Lady
of Justice, oh accused, we bring you before those who are
sworn to her but not of the temple, that you may may know
that you are fairly judged."

Right, thought Mareg. Ever since her conversation with
Illiana she had been considering Virsat justice more carefully, and she was less convinced than ever of its fairness.

There were five prisoners, and at first she barely
glanced at them. When they were brought to stand in the
circle of the accused, however, she did look more closely,
and she felt the blood drain from her face. Bilop the gardener was among them.

It was difficult for her to clear her mind and listen to
the charges and the evidence, but she did so. The accused,
it seemed had stolen various small items from Virsat estates. Bilop had stolen food and the king's horses' silver
bridles. These items were to be sold to provide funds for
an armed rebellion of Tirdar. The charges were read and
the evidence, which included some of the recovered
stolen items, laid out. One of the accused, a young Tirdar
boy barely into his teens, tried to defend himself, but a
guard silenced him by smashing his spear butt across the
boy's mouth. Prisoners were not permitted to speak unless the judges wished it. Then the final charge was
brought: assassination of King Rellaff by means of Tirdar
magic. Mareg and the assistant judges retired to consider
the evidence.

They lit incense before the statue of the Lady in the
meditation room and settled into their comfortable chairs.
A Tirdar servant brought bowls of fruit and left.

"I think we can dispose of this quickly," said Beha.
"There is no doubt of their guilt."

"Indeed," agreed Jek, "they confessed."

"Of course they confessed," agreed Mareg, in her turn.

"Did you look at them? They were all beaten, at the least, and some more than that."

"Naturally," said Jek. "Why would they confess, otherwise? It takes force to bring out the evil truth." He looked truly surprised.

It was the way things had always been done. Mareg herself would not have questioned it, had her mind not been set on this course by other events. She decided to take a different approach.

"You know Bilop, both of you. Do you believe these charges against him are credible?" She held up a hand. "Do not answer me immediately, but think of what you know of him."

She could almost see the thoughts going through Jek's mind. Many of the Virsat knew Bilop, had known him for years. She knew both Jek and Beha were considering the old gardener now in this light.

"No." Beha spoke first. "He is Tirdar, but still, he has never shown the least interest in most Tirdar foolishness, and certainly never in anything approaching rebellion. Or magic. He is quite sensible, for a Tirdar."

"That is true," Jek agreed. "It is possible that he was caught up in this all unknowing. And perhaps the others testified falsely against him. You are right to point this out, Lady Mareg, and I thank you." He bowed slightly to her without rising from his chair.

Mareg did not point out the inconsistencies in his argument: that force was necessary to bring out the truth from the prisoners, but the use of force had resulted in false testimony concerning Bilop. Probably Jek did not know Bilop's ancestry; few did. Almost certainly he would have considered a link to past Tirdar nobility culpable by itself. As for the charge of murder by magic, she knew quite well that her cojudges did not believe such a crime was even possible.

"We should have Bilop released," said Beha. "That old man has done nothing."

"Agreed," said Mareg.

"As for the others, I think we can agree they are guilty as charged." Jek spoke with authority. He was a younger man, advancing through the ranks of judge because of his family connections, which was usually the way. He was bored with the proceedings, annoyed by his red silk robe, and he wanted to get home to his new mistress.

"We have not questioned the others ourselves," said Beha.

It was a perfunctory statement. According to the law, they had option of doing this, if they thought it necessary. In this instance, both Beha and Jek obviously did not think it necessary. Mareg realized that there was nothing to be gained by having the other prisoners brought before them now. They would not deny their former confessions.

"We have no need," she said. "Since we are all agreed, we can call the temple scribe and have our decision recorded. Bilop is to be set free. The others will be imprisoned and then executed."

"Publicly as a deterrent?" asked Beha.

"Of course," said Mareg.

The official scribe was called in. The High Judge and the lesser judges left the temple.

It was late into the evening when Mareg returned to the temple. She went, not to her rooms in the temple, but directly down to the temple prison. She went without escort, carrying her own torch, and spiders and scorpions scuttled away from the light. The guards on duty were not unduly surprised to see the High Judge. She had made these kinds of visits before, on occasion, pursuing the interests of the Goddess of Justice.

"The prisoners who were condemned today," she said, "let me talk to them. One at a time, separately."

There was a room set aside for this. Only after they

brought in the first prisoner did Mareg think how little con-
ducive this room was to receiving true answers, and how
odd that she had never considered this before. There was a
large, deeply stained table taking up part of the room. The
straps and restraints at the corners left no doubt as to what
the table was used for. In other portions of the room were
various pieces of equipment, made more ominous by the
flickering torchlight. The prisoner began, understandably,
to tremble when she was brought in, and Mareg repressed a
sigh. She sent the guard out, even though it was against
custom.

"I will be quite safe," she told him. "I am protected by
the Lady of Justice, who will allow no harm to come to me.
Besides, you may wait at the end of the hall. If I need you,
I will cry out, and you will hear." These contradictory assertions satisfied the guard. When he had left, she made
herself as comfortable as possible in the room's only
wooden chair and turned to her trembling visitor.

The young woman was dirty, bloodstained, bruised, and
thin almost to emaciation. Her blonde hair was filthy and
matted, and there were purple circles beneath her eyes. If
she had stolen food, Mareg thought, it was understandable,
although it didn't look as though she had eaten any. She
looked completely incapable of magic.

"What is your name and for whom did you work?"

The young woman did not answer but fell to her knees.
Now Mareg did sigh.

"Get up," she said. "I won't hurt you." The young
woman began to sob.

Nothing was being accomplished, and Mareg felt frustrated. She rose from the chair and went to the sobbing
young woman. As her shadow fell across the prisoner, the
Tirdar woman sobbed and shook so hard that she began to
choke. Mareg dropped to her knees and, after a confused
moment, put her arms around the other woman.

The prisoner sobbed harder still, and Mareg didn't know what to do. Then the Tirdar threw her arms around her and clung there. *She's not much older than Forentel,* Mareg thought. She began to gently rub the other woman's back, going in small circles as she had when Forentel had been ill, but slowly and softly, afraid of the fragility she felt beneath her hands. Eventually the prisoner's sobs abated. Mareg drew off her cloak and wrapped it around the other woman, who was shivering convulsively.

"How old are you?" she asked.

"Sixteen summers," she whispered. "I think."

She wasn't a woman, Mareg thought, she was still a child, younger than Forentel, younger than Dreena, despite how she looked.

"What's your name, child?"

"Dayta. Dayta of Vitlernin. I work, I worked for Brezat Vitlernin."

"Tell me what happened." She made herself as comfortable as possible on the floor and wrapped the cloak more securely around Dayta.

It was not much of a story. Dayta had been born into Brezat's household, had grown up there. Her mother had for some years been a favorite of Brezat's. There was a possibility, Mareg realized, that Dayta might be Brezat's daughter.

"Lord Brezat called me to him," she said, "two years ago." She was no longer sobbing, and when she spoke she looked into some haunted distance, seeing something Mareg could not. "I did not want to go. My mother," she paused and swallowed, "tried to keep me from him, but Lord Brezat killed her."

Mareg drew in a breath, audible in the momentary silence, but Dayta didn't seem to notice.

"He had me for two years, and then he grew tired of me. He sent me back to work in the laundry. I was glad. But when he found me with Rell, he locked me in a storage room. He would not let them feed me, but Rell brought me food sometimes." She swallowed. "And then the steward caught Rell. Lord Brezat charged us both with theft and treason. And then with, with," her voice dropped to a whisper, "murder. Of the king. And he sent us here to die." She looked up at Mareg, her blue eyes filled with memory and absolutely no hope. "Do you believe me, High Judge?"

"Who is Rell?"

"He—my—he is charged with me, High Judge. And he did nothing but help me. And love me." The last was a whisper. "Do you believe me?"

"Yes," said Mareg slowly, "yes, I do." She had been trained to hear the truth, and she heard it now. "Who are the other two accused? Did you know them?"

"Yes, Lady. Gret is Lord Brezat's, too. He became friends with Ness, who is the daughter's daughter of Bilop's sister."

Mareg was surprised. She had not realized that the Tirdar would keep track of family lines with the same dedication and interest that Virsat did. How could she not have known these things? These Tirdar were, all of them, scapegoats. King Rellaff had been murdered, she had no doubt, but not by Tirdar, and certainly not by these Tirdar, who had neither means nor motive.

"I understand," was all she said.

"I am glad of it, lady. That someone, that you—you of all of them, lady, should understand this before I—we—die." She raised her eyes to Mareg again, and Mareg felt a chill.

"Why," she said. "Why me, why are you glad that I, especially, understand?" *Of all of them,* she thought. *Them.*

"Because of who you are." Dayta shrank back again. "You are her mother." She looked down at the stained stone floor. "The Delass," she whispered.

"I am the High Judge." Mareg frowned. "Here, that's
what counts." She rose to her feet. "You will go free." She
realized as she said it the problems she would face. "I will
speak to the king," she said, ignoring the disbelief and the
simultaneous hope on the girl's face. "And I will question
the others. If they are as innocent as you, I will overturn
their sentences also, but only if they are innocent." She
stood. "Guard!" she called.

She retrieved her cloak before the guard arrived to take
Dayta back to her cell and seated herself again in the chair.
The rest of the night was spent questioning the other three
Tirdar. She knew if she pursued the course she had em-
barked upon she could not turn back, and all things would
be changed. She realized she might be endangering herself.
She was quite probably endangering Nedriff, and she felt a
certain regret, but she trusted him to take care of himself.

Even so short a time as a few weeks ago, what she was
about to do would never have occurred to her. Even now, she
surprised herself, but it was not a choice. If she could
choose, she would choose not to do this. She remembered
the old-young face of the Tirdar madwoman, and she remembered her promise, but her promise was not to the Tirdar prophet; her promise was not even to her missing
daughter, the child she had not borne. Her promise was to
the Lady of Justice, to the vow she had sworn when she first
took service at the temple. Mareg sighed, wrapped her cloak
around her, and called for the guard again. When she left the
temple, it was just before dawn. She walked out into the
chilly streets of Tireera. She had spent all of her life here,
but she felt as if she were seeing the place for the first time.
She turned, not toward home, but toward the king's palace.

MIRTA HAD NOT slept well. He had not slept well since
his father had been helped into death, which was the way

he thought of it. Rellaff had said once, before he became ill, that if he ever became badly infirm he would not wish to live, and would welcome help moving into the next life. When it came time for it, however, he seemed to have forgotten those words. Since he had refused to act, Mirta had been forced to act for him. What was worse was the way he persisted in haunting Mirta's dreams.

Mirta rose from his bed and went to the window to look out over his gardens. Dawn had not yet broken, and the flowers below seemed to shimmer and float in the pale gray light. A Tirdar gardener worked silently, bent over his work, like a ghost. Mirta shuddered. He would have to call the royal priest and have him perform a propitiation of his father's spirit. These dreams and forebodings were beginning to erode his own robust health. He was so wrapped in his thoughts that the soft tap on his door made him jump. The tap was followed a moment later by the entrance of the Chief Servant of the Bedchamber, a Virsat noble whom Mirta had appointed. He looked surprised to see the king not only awake but up.

"I am sorry to disturb you, my lord king, but there is a visitor for you, who says it is urgent. A Virsat noble, a—"

"What could possibly be urgent at this time of morning? Send him away and tell him I will see him later." Mirta intended to soothe his nerves in the way he liked best before he dealt with anything of importance.

"It's High Judge Lady Mareg Friltera of Pentrat. She says she has come immediately from the Temple of Justice, where she has been all night, and she has information that you must have as soon as possible."

Mirta was intrigued, and more. Mareg had had a special relationship with his father, and she had attempted to continue that relationship with him. He had allowed her to cultivate it, because he thought it might prove useful.

"Show her into my breakfast room," he said. "I will join

her shortly. And have fruit, cheese, bread, and wine ready
for me when I do."

By the time he entered the breakfast room, the sun was
rising. He had bathed and dressed, but it had not helped his
weariness. When he looked at Mareg, however, it was apparent that she, too had not slept, and he remembered the bedchamber noble saying she had been at the temple all night.
His curiosity was overshadowed by a sudden premonition.

"King Mirta." Mareg inclined her head. *He looks terrible,* she thought. And then, as the probable reason came to
mind, *So he should.*

"Will you sit and eat with me, Lady Mareg? Or will
your news not wait?" He inclined his head toward the Tirdar attendant, and without waiting for Mareg's reply, said,
"Serve the lady."

Mareg accepted the slice of bread and cheese, realizing
how hungry she was after the night's work, and watched
with concern as Mirta poured himself a cup of wine.

"Tell me," said Mirta.

"Some Tirdar servants were accused of theft and rebellion. I know," she waved a hand, "it seems minor, and at
first I could not understand why they were brought before
me. Why bring them before the High Judge, when a lesser
could certainly have handled so simple a case? But then
they were charged with murder by magic. Of your father,
King Rellaff, sir. A feat of which none of them proved to
be in the least capable. As we all know, your esteemed father died when the gods called him. Someone wanted to be
sure they were condemned, and someone wanted to be sure
that I knew. I believe a message was being given."

"A message to you?"

"Yes, my lord, but not just to me. One of the accused
was Bilop. Your head gardener."

"Oh yes, I know the man; he is old and seems harmless.
I cannot imagine he was involved in any rebellion. Wait,

you say he was brought before you? My own gardener was brought before you?"

"I see you did not know, Lord King."

"Indeed I did not," Mirta's face darkened, and Mareg could almost read his thoughts. He trusted fewer and fewer people each day.

"The message was given to me, also, sir, because I am your friend. I believe I was not meant to determine its importance, or to inform you until the Tirdar had been put to death."

"And my authority usurped."

Mareg did not reply; this was precisely what she wanted the king to believe. Quite likely, and frighteningly, it was true.

"What have you done?" Mirta had put aside the wine, and his gaze was direct. He seemed again to take command, and to be the sort of man in whom his nobles had trusted.

"I questioned all the Tirdar. Bilop we released yesterday. Neither I nor the lesser judges were persuaded of his guilt. The others I questioned last night. All were innocent of the charges. I had them released."

"Who was responsible? Who brought the charges?"

"Lord Brezat Vitlernin."

"Brezat!" Mirta had half risen from his chair, but now he abruptly sat again. Brezat had been one of his primary backers, along with Nedriff Pentrat.

"My husband was not involved, Lord King, I am sure of it." She wasn't—quite the contrary. "But whoever was involved, King Mirta," she sat up straight, "I am sworn to justice. It was not being done."

"Indeed," said Mirta abstractedly, "most commendable."

"Will you give safety to those Tirdar who were Lord Brezat's? There are two of them."

Mirta stared her for a moment in astonishment. Then

the benefits of doing as she asked occurred to him. He would be sending a message of his own, and quite subtly, back to Brezat. He did not yet wish to challenge Brezat openly; he needed the man's support and his wealth.

"I will, Lady Mareg, I will." He smiled at her. "You are a worthy ally and a true friend. Would I had more like you." He would not take her word as to Nedriff's lack of involvement, however.

Mareg left the palace with exhaustion settling over her like a cloak. She knew the king would investigate her husband. She knew she should warn Nedriff that his involvement with Brezat was becoming dangerous. She hadn't decided whether or not she would.

THIRTEEN

$\mathcal{R}$IESSA KNEW SHE HAD FOUND WHAT SHE wanted, everything she had hoped for. This was a Tireeran she traveled with now, a man of the city. Not only that, he was a man of some wealth, or he would be. She needed to bind him to her, which should not be difficult; she had already made a good start. Then she needed to to make him take her back to Tireera. The thought of living a rich life in the city, so far from the swamp, was a dream come true. She did not despise Tireera as other Hilans did. On the contrary, the few Virsat they had captured and kept had instilled in her a longing to see the greater world and to better her fortunes. Anything had to be better than Hila, but Tireera was best of all.

She glanced at Kelern, sleeping beside her. She was glad she had let Frelenya—Forentel—talk her out of leaving him behind to die. He was a beautiful man, big and strong, with dark brown eyes and long, curly brown hair, normally tied back but now falling around his face as he slept. It was a good time for her to go through his pack, something she had had no opportunity to do in the past. She eased away from him, gently sliding out of the blanket they had shared.

It was just before dawn. They had camped on the high point of land, overlooking the marsh, in a small clearing. Kelern had ringed their spot with small fires to keep out any animals and to help drive off insects. It had worked, although by now most of the fires had pretty well burned down. The marsh birds were beginning their raucous dawn chorus, and Riessa knew she would have to hurry. Although Kelern seemed able to sleep through most natural sounds, waking only for anything out of the ordinary, she didn't see how anyone could sleep long through such an avian clatter.

The pack was right behind his head. Carefully she eased it away, watching him. He showed no signs of returning consciousness, and his breathing did not alter. She dragged the pack a little distance away and opened it.

Extra clothing: a cloak, another blanket, a shirt. Another long knife, leather thongs and cords, arrow shafts, arrow-heads, another bowstring. A pile of golden coins. Interesting. She had not known he carried these. Surely he would not notice if she took one or two for her own. She glanced over at Kelern: he still slept. A bundle of bound papers, with squiggles on the paper. The binding was leather. And a sheet of paper with things marked on it. She opened the paper up and turned it first one way and then the other, puzzled. A hand clamped down over her wrist like a vise.

"It's a map," said Kelern. "Surely you are familiar with the concept."

The map fluttered down from her hand as she tried not to squeak from the pain. "Let go!" she gasped, finally, when he showed no signs of doing so. How had he managed to wake up, get up, move, and get behind her so quickly?

"You are hurting me!" She tried to pull away, but his hand tightened more. With his other hand he rescued the map and then dragged her to him by her long hair and pulled his arm across her throat.

"It's supposed to hurt," he said. He released her wrist and took his arm from across her throat. She rubbed her wrist, glaring at him, not in the least embarrassed.

"I was just looking," she said.

"If you wanted to know what was in my pack you could have asked."

He watched her for a moment, seeing the glare turn into a sultry pout. She was beautiful, exotic, and she knew things about the marshes. She had made his days and especially his nights interesting. He was quite willing to have her with him as long as she did not become a liability. He knew her desire to go back to Tireera with him, to live as his wife and rule over a large estate, even though she had only the vaguest idea what that meant. He was willing to take her back to Tireera, too, if that proved possible, although it would not be as his wife. She was no Virsat, and she was not even Tireeran. She was a barbarian, a step below Tirdar. But this barbarian had her charms.

"That thing is a map?" Despite her outrage and her attempt to mask it with seduction, she was curious.

"Yes." Kelern was refolding the item.

"What is that other thing, the bundle of papers?"

"It's a book. It's a traveler's descriptions of the lands south of Tireera." He looked at her. "We have books on many things in Tireera."

If he expected the announcement to intimidate her, it did not work.

"You can teach me how to understand the magic of books," she said. "I will need to know that."

"You won't need to know." He was amused, despite himself. When he saw her open her mouth to reply, he held up a hand. "I will take you to Tireera," he told her, and then, when he saw the flash of triumph on her face, "if you do not delay me or attempt to sidetrack me. I must find the prince and his tutor. I am sworn to my king, and I must accomplish this task. I will not return to the city a failure." Finding the lost city of Dreffir, if it were not just legend, would be good, too. Then he would in fact have a claim on an estate, and he didn't see how Mirta could refuse him.

"Let's eat and then go," he said. "You are quite certain that this is the mainland, and not simply another island?"

"I am sure," Riessa told him.

It had to be the shore. It had to be the mainland, if she remembered the travelers' stories correctly. It had been very important, worth their lives, so she had been told, to avoid the island of the singer. So she had insisted they put ashore. They had meant to abandon Forentel, but they had not meant to abandon her in the boat, or to lose the boat.

Riessa had wanted to kill her. It wasn't that she had any ill feelings toward the city woman, quite the contrary. Forentel had saved her life. She simply did not want to leave someone so magically dangerous behind. But Kelern had balked at killing one of his own kind. He had agreed with Riessa that Forentel would hinder their progress, and he had agreed with her that they did not need a third person using up their supplies. He had not believed she was magic, however, let alone dangerous, and she was, he said, Virsat. While they argued, Forentel had slept in the boat, with the wolf beside her. And then the current had carried the boat away, without either of them noticing. With any luck she would drift right to the island of the singer, and that problem would be solved. It was good riddance to the wolf, too. Riessa had never thought to meet one of the spirit guardians, and she was relieved to see the animal go.

Even if they were on the mainland, it was still marshy. It was difficult going. Although Riessa prided herself on being tough, she was becoming tired. Kelern did not stop. They drank from his canteens as they walked, and ate a little bread as they walked, but they did not rest. Toward evening the insects became thicker, swarming in clouds around them.

"How do you know we are following the prince?" Riessa would have given anything to be out of the swarms of insects and also to simply stop and rest.

"They were in a boat," said Kelern shortly. "The current is carrying them. And they were going toward Dreffir, which should be downstream. If it exists."

"What if—what if they went to the island of the singer?"

"Then we will have to go there, too." Kelern glanced at her. "Or I will. With luck, this singer you fear will have done my work for me, but I will need proof." He glanced at her again. "I will be careful," he said. "I hope we do not have to go to this island, since we no longer have a boat. But if there is no sign of them farther downstream, we may have to turn back." He could tell she didn't like the sound of that. The truth was that he didn't, either. But his map was no longer of much use. He would need to find some local savages for information, and soon.

They spent the night much as they had the previous night, but this time without the ring of little fires. It was difficult for Riessa to sleep, out there in the open without even a fire to make things seem safer, but she had made her

decision, and she wouldn't leave Kelern now. Kelern
thought he had seen signs in the brush, signs that someone
had been by this way. Sure enough, shortly before dawn
there were sounds, not far away, sounds of something moving through the vegetation, and low conversation. Riessa
had fallen into a doze, but she woke with Kelern's hand
across her mouth for silence.

IT HAD BEEN Erba's boat they found, not hers. Forentel
managed to stagger to it and collapse into it while Erba and
Filfa tried to push it from the shore.

"Get up, stupid woman, and help us push!" shouted
Filfa.

She wanted to, but she couldn't. Waves of nausea rolled
over her, and she had a headache that stabbed lights into
her brain. She was aware of Sunrise standing over her,
growling low in her throat, of hearing Erba tell Filfa to
leave her alone. Then the boat rocked; they were in the water, and she felt it wobble as both men climbed in. She
knew someone took the oars, and they were pulling out
into the current.

She lay in the bottom of the boat with the wolf beside
her, listening to the men argue as they rowed. Filfa wanted
to toss her overboard. Although the wolf seemed to understand this and growled a little, it was Erba who refused,
pointing out that she had saved their lives yet again. They
kept at it so long that Forentel wanted to scream. Then she
felt something cool and wet on her forehead. Erba had wet
a cloth with river water and was sponging her face, and the
wolf was permitting him to do this.

"We have some drinking water," he told her. "Can you
sip this?" He held one of the waterskins to her lips. She
thought she would vomit, but the little bit of water that

trickled into her mouth had the opposite effect and settled her slightly.

"Let her heal herself," said Filfa sulkily, but Erba paid him no attention, continuing to sit beside Forentel, giving her sips of water.

As her headache and nausea eased, Forentel relaxed. The dark water drifted away beneath the boat. Was it her imagination, or was the river carrying them faster now? Eventually, despite herself, she fell asleep.

When she woke, it was full day. The wolf had been shading her face with her shadow. Forentel sat up abruptly, remembering the last time she had awoken in a boat, but this time she was not alone. Filfa was rowing, his back to her, while Erba gazed out over the river.

The river was indeed flowing faster, and the landscape had changed. The river was broad and open now. There were many islands, and some of them had marshy shores, but many were rocky and some were wooded, and there were clear channels between them. It was obvious now that they were moving downstream, carried by the current. The sky was high and milky overhead, and the weather seemed slightly cooler.

"How are you feeling, Lady Forentel?" Erba perched on a thwart. "We have most of our supplies, so if you're hungry, there's a little food. We left everything in the boat when we landed on that island, so it's still with us."

Forentel sat up and was accepting the hard cheese and water Erba offered with thanks when she realized what he had said. He smiled at the look on her face and then rummaged in one of the packs. Eventually he found what he was looking for and held it up. Her golden bracelet of nobility dangled from his hand.

"What!" said Filfa. He stopped rowing but took it up again at a hard glance from Erba. "She's no Virsat!"

"I knew you looked familiar when I saw you in Hila," Erba said "When I found this in your pack, I knew for certain."

"Then we are even, Lord Prince," she said. She took a bite of the hard cheese but made no attempt to reach for the bracelet. Now that she saw him again, in the light of day and away from the recent danger, she felt angry and relieved and confused. He had left her behind in Hila, he had—

Filfa stopped rowing again, and the boat spun slightly in the current. He looked more than grim; he looked furious, Forentel thought.

"She cannot be Forentel Pentrat! Only a Tirdar could do the things she did. That monstrosity—that plant—she connected with that abomination!" He paused, remembering that Erba had been caught, too.

Forentel swallowed her bite of cheese. "You are Virsat," she said to Filfa acidly, "pure Virsat, and you felt it." She took another bite of cheese.

Filfa's face darkened, and his eyes bugged slightly. Forentel watched with considerable curiosity, but whatever he might have said, Erba forestalled him.

"We're drifting, Filfa. You row; let me handle this." He turned to Forentel, still holding her bracelet. "Do you want this back?"

"No." She had forgotten it, once she had tucked it into her pack. She was going to say that she no longer identified herself as Virsat, but obviously that was not entirely true. She stared at the prince, hating him, knowing she didn't truly hate him, and hating herself for that, completely miserable.

She doesn't know what she is, Erba thought. *What is she? For that matter, what am I? I thought I knew.*

Forentel blinked and then swallowed. He hadn't spoken, but she had heard him. She stared at him, met his own stunned gaze. He knew. He knew she heard him.

"Erba!" Filfa twisted his head to look at them, and then pointed. Ahead of them the river broke up into several branches that parted around a large island. On one of these branches, closest to them, was a very strange craft.

The first thing Forentel noticed was how large it was: at least three times as long as their small craft, and much taller. It had sails, and a tiller as well as oars. The sails were set now, multicolored and cheerful, billowing out in the freshening breeze. Suddenly the sails luffed out. They could hear a voice shouting, and then the odd boat came about. It was obviously coming straight for them. They had been seen.

Filfa began to pull hard for the shore of the large island, but it was apparent they wouldn't make it. Their pursuer had too much speed and was rapidly overhauling them. Erba drew his sword.

"Keep rowing," he told Filfa, "and maybe we can make this hard for them."

Sunrise came and sat by Forentel, looking alert. What good would all this do, Forentel wondered. There were obviously a good many people on the approaching craft, and it had the speed to overtake them. They could see it better now, and someone seemed to be hanging over the side. It was a man with dark, braided hair and a close-trimmed beard. He was shouting something incomprehensible. Then he saw them clearly, saw Filfa rowing and Erba with his sword.

"Virsat!" he shouted. "Are you the Virsat from Tireera? Put down the sword!" He waved energetically.

Erba belatedly drew his knife with his left hand, struggling to keep his balance in the boat as Filfa still pulled for the shore. Forentel caught a glimpse of others behind the shouting man: women, she thought, and at least one child.

"Stay down," Erba told her. "I will do my best to protect you."

Forentel looked at him and then at the rapidly gaining boat; it didn't seem likely. She stood up and waved her arms back. "Yes!" she shouted. "We're from the city! Tireera! Who are you!"

"Travelers! Put down that sword; we mean you no harm!"

Sunrise put her paws on the side of their boat and suddenly launched herself into the water. Forentel could see the top of her head as she paddled toward land.

"Sunrise!" she cried, but the wolf did not even look back. She leaned over the side, toward the swimming animal.

"Get down!" said Erba, pulling her back.

Now they were close enough that they could plainly see the odd boat. It had a house on its deck, Forentel realized, and there were bulky things under heavy cloths, things that were tied down. She had seen the occasional trading ship that managed to come up the river to Tireera from some of the farming communities. Those had carried grain and fruit, but there was an undeniable similarity.

"I think they are traders of some sort," she said to Erba.

"You had better hope so," said Filfa, "since you have called them down on us."

Forentel ignored him. The boat was close to them now and it seemed huge, looming over them.

"We'll throw you a rope; you tie on. Then we'll send someone down to secure your boat, and you can come aboard."

There was no point in arguing. Erba caught the rope, followed shortly by a rope ladder. A young man with tightly braided black hair shimmied down this ladder as if he had been born doing it. For all Forentel knew, he had. He glanced around their tiny boat with a practiced eye, and then smiled at Forentel.

"Up ladder," he said, in broken Virsat. "You," he gestured, "all up. Old man first." He pointed at Filfa.

The boat didn't seem quite as large when they were on it as it had from below, but it was still impressive. Their host reached out to grasp Forentel's hands as she came over the side. His hands were strong and hard.

"Welcome to all," he said. "I am Willip, the master of this boat, the captain. And the father of all here." He turned and said something to the young man who had come back up the ladder. It was not in Virsat, but it sounded familiar. After a moment Forentel realized that it was Tirdar of a sort. The vowels did not sound the same as they did in the city, but now that she knew what to listen for, she could understand them. She glanced at Erba, and it was apparent that he had realized the same thing.

We can't let them know we understand them, Erba was thinking. *How can I tell Foreniel, how can I warn her?*

She met his eyes. *I know,* she thought, and felt the shock as he heard her in his mind. She glanced at Filfa. He had not realized yet that the boat people were speaking Tirdar, she had no desire to tell him, and she didn't know if she could speak to his mind the way she just had to Erba's. She was inclined to doubt it, and even the thought was distasteful.

"I am Erba, and this is my uncle Filfa, and my sister Forentel." Erba had sheathed his sword, but it was still in his hand.

"Welcome to you, then. We will bring your goods aboard and you shall eat with us. Then we will hear your story, and why it is you travel so far from your desert kingdom."

One of the women came up to them, smiling, bobbing her head, looking away and then back again. She reached and gingerly touched Forentel's hand, pointing to a hatch, and Forentel allowed herself to be led away. When Erba tried to follow her, Willip put out his hand to stop him.

"Your sister is safe," he said. "My women will give her

fresh clothing and bathe her. You will have the same. Then we meet for feasting."

The women took her down below the deck. It was strange, enclosed, and filled with odd smells, spicy and rancid together. There were entire little rooms down here, Forentel realized. It was a world of its own.

The women were laughing and tittering to one another. There were five of them who stayed with her, although several others seemed to come in and out. *How many are on this boat?* Forentel wondered. None of them spoke to her, and it seemed none spoke Virsat. They spoke to one another, though, and Forentel shamelessly listened in. They seemed to have no suspicion that she understood them.

There was a ceramic basin into which the women poured a little water. Then they pantomimed that she should strip off all her clothes. When she was reluctant, they reached to help her and then began to wipe her down with cloths they wet in the basin.

"She is good, if tall," said the oldest of the women. "Sometimes they like them tall."

"She is too skinny," said a younger woman. She giggled and pinched Forentel just below the ribs. When Forentel yelped and pulled back, they all laughed, and one of them patted her on the arm reassuringly.

"Radka, you know better! She must trust us."

"Perhaps," said the young woman sulkily, "but what difference does it make?"

"It makes it easier if they trust. Besides, he has said this is how it is to be done."

Forentel gathered that "he" was Willip, from the respect the older woman gave the word. Radka did not seem much impressed, however.

"I can't imagine he will get much for her," she said disdainfully. "Now that man, the younger one, he is something else again! I wish Father would consider keeping him!"

A chorus of giggles and agreement from the younger women greeted this remark, until the elder woman put a stop to it. All during the interchange the women continued washing Forentel. When they had finished, they began to perfume her, smiling all the while. The basin with its dirty water was taken to a little round window. One of the women opened this, and two of them helped tip the basin, emptying its contents out into the river. The heavy scent of the perfume made Forentel gag, and she tried to pull away, waving her hands, complaining in Virsat. It did no good. The women outnumbered her, and they were strong. Two of them gripped her arms, smiling while the others doused her with scent, rubbing it into her skin.

"There, there, it's good," said the elder woman. She stroked Forentel's hair. "We will get a better price for you down on the Big Island if you are clean and smell good. And see, we will give you nice clothes!"

All of this was said in Tirdar, but in soothing and encouraging tones. Forentel feigned both incomprehension and acquiescence, and also delight when she was shown the clothes. In reality she thought they looked barbaric: pants that fit her hips snugly but ballooned out below her knees, sewn with tiny bells. It would be impossible to walk anywhere quietly. Maybe that was the point. The shirt had long balloon sleeves that fit tightly around the wrists. Forentel felt like an inflated bladder.

They conducted her up the ladder again, pantomiming that they would soon be eating.

"Stupid city woman," said one of the women. "City people are all stupid."

"Not that you've seen many of them," answered another, "which is why they are worth so much."

If she had not waved at them, if she had not responded to their hail, Forentel wondered, would it have made any difference? She decided not. They would have been over-taken in any event, and Erba would have fought. They could have been killed, or at least wounded, as it was obvi-ous these people meant to keep them alive if possible, for their value. They had come to the house built on the deck. Forentel followed the gestures of the women and jingled her way inside.

The room, *cabin,* she learned later, had been strewn with cushions. There were low planks on which was ar-rayed a large number of dishes. Some of the men were al-ready seated there, including Erba and Filfa. She saw that they, too, had been the objects of the ministrations of the boat people. They were dressed in clothes similar to hers, but without the bells, and she tried not to wrinkle her nose at their perfume.

"We are traveling simply for interest, and for knowl-edge," Filfa was saying.

"In part," said Erba. "Our family is also interested in trade, and in information we can bring back and partner-ships we can establish." He smiled at Forentel, acknowl-edging her presence, and she smiled back.

"Your sister is beautiful," said Willip approvingly. "Many men will find her lovely. Ah," he said, when he saw Erba's reaction, "I meant no offense, if this is against your customs. I only comment."

He did mean offense, though, Forentel thought. And he had been testing them, testing the men, especially, in some way. She took her place on the cushions. She noted that their hosts did not permit them to sit together, but it didn't matter right now. She discovered she was famished.

She allowed herself to be served from various platters. Filfa was telling Willip about Tireera, obviously meaning to impress him with the richness and power of the city. Perhaps he also meant to suggest that Tireera could reach this far, and ensure their safety, but she could tell Willip was not impressed. She felt an edge of humorous contempt from him.

The feeling itself did not surprise her, but the fact that she was able to pick it up, when it seemed that neither Erba nor Filfa had noticed, did surprise her. She remembered Illiana saying that the ability to understand minds was something a few Tirdar could occasionally do. The boat people spoke a kind of Tirdar. Could she hear their thoughts? Could they hear hers? Unlikely, from what Illiana had said. She glanced at Willip from under lowered lashes. She needed to warn Erba and Filfa about the plans he had for them, but she would do what she could to gain more information first.

"Do you know of Dreffir?" Her question fell into a lull in the conversation, and all the men turned to look at her. It looked as though they might ignore her question.

"We might wish to establish trade with them, if the place exists." Erba came to her support.

"It exists." Willip chuckled. "But if you get there—*if* you get there—they will kill you. The city is rich, yes. They are all rich there, far richer than anything you could imagine from your Tireera. But they want nothing to do with anyone from outside, not from us, and they will not want you. If you go there," he repeated, "they will kill you." He seemed pleased by the prospect.

"How far is it?" Forentel asked.

"Not too far, but far enough. The river gets rough, very rough, and you cannot travel it for a time. Many," he hesitated, and made wavelike motions with his hands.

"Waterfalls," muttered Filfa.

"Ah, yes, perhaps. I did not have this word. Waterfalls. And there is jungle." He grinned when he saw their perplexity. "Like the swamp, but more plants, more trees, more," he waved his hands again, "everything. Animals. Insects." He smiled. "Do not go there. Stay with us now. We will take you to the Big Island and teach you something about trade. A very valuable lesson."

Forentel was not the only one who heard the mockery. Filfa frowned, and Erba looked edgy. Forentel realized, be-latedly, that he did not have his sword. All of them were unarmed. Willip seemed to realize he had made a mistake by alarming them.

"Ah," he said, "look! Our finest sweets! Eat and enjoy!"

The women were bringing in what looked like glazed fruits and pastries, and they placed large platters down in front of the three guests. Filfa reached for one and took a bite.

"Good!" he said.

Forentel watched the boat people watching them. There was an avidity trickling from the edges of their thoughts. She could not put a name to it, but she sensed danger. She jerked suddenly, filled with an astonished recognition, all the bells on her trousers jingling. She couldn't speak, and she didn't dare to, but she reached instead for the link she had before with Erba, the link to his mind alone. She tried to reach for Filfa as well, but there was no connection. It was too late anyway. Filfa's smile broadened and became silly.

"Very good!" he said again, reaching for more.

Doesn't eat those! Forentel sent the thought as hard as she could to Erba, screaming it silently. *They are drugged! These people mean to sell us on the Big Island!*

She saw Erba jerk in surprise as he received her message. His eyes widened, and he reacted immediately, reaching for the knife amidst the fruit. He was not the only one to react. Willip's head snapped around, and he stared at her.

"Stop them!" he shouted.

Filfa collapsed face-first into the food. Someone

grabbed Forentel from behind. She smashed her head back as hard as she could and heard a grunt: the back of her head had connected with someone's stomach. It did her no good. Her arms were twisted behind her, and she was hauled to her feet by one of the younger men. Looking over, she saw that Erba, too, had been subdued. Filfa was still asleep in the desserts.

FOURTEEN

$\mathcal{I}$T WAS DARK, DAMP, AND EVIL-SMELLING IN
the room. It was belowdecks, and it was small, and it had
bars.

"It's a prison," she said, when they were thrown in and
the door locked.

"They call it a brig on a ship," Erba told her.

"Let me put some water on your eye," Forentel said.
"They left us some." He had a gash along his left arm, and
his right eye was surrounded by the most amazing colors,
but otherwise he was unhurt.

"No." He drew away from her and went to look at Filfa,
who still slept. After a moment he looked up again. "Are
you hurt?"

"No." If he wanted to be curt, so could she. She was in
this mess because she was traveling with them, and she

was traveling with them again because she had rescued them from the island.

Erba sat back on his heels and looked up at her. "You truly are Tirdar," he said. "Aren't you? You have their powers." There was confusion in his voice.

She turned away from him. It was so very dim here; there was only one oil lamp, and it was outside their cell. Almost everything was in shadow, and she did not want to think about what might be in those shadows. She thought she heard things scuttling. To her surprise, she felt tears thick in her throat, and she fought them down. She didn't know what she was. She didn't know who she was. And it was more than obvious that she didn't know what she was doing.

"Everyone knows that Tirdar have no powers," she said. "They are an ignorant, superstitious people."

Erba flinched back from the bitterness in her voice. Looking down at his tutor, he felt truly alone, and he was tormented by a terrible suspicion.

"No," he said slowly, "those—abilities—are not just superstition. How could I, how could anyone, say that after what we have been through? But they aren't just Tirdar, are they? Could they be something that—that—" He stopped. "Are they something that perhaps are not linked to the Tirdar alone? Are you truly Lord Nedriff's daughter?"

"Yes." She chose to answer his second question. "The general is my father."

Erba came forward into what light there was, struggling to see her face. He felt a pang when he saw her expression. He had never liked hurting anyone, and he had avoided it as best he could. But he needed to know something, something he couldn't quite put a name to.

"Is Lady Judge Mareg your mother?" he persisted.

"In all the ways that count but one." Forentel raised her head. "A Tirdar woman gave birth to me. I am indeed part Tirdar, Lord Prince. Someone not truly human."

"No," he said, "no—" But she had turned away again. He couldn't say that Virsat didn't believe so. He couldn't say that *he* had never thought so, or at least that he had thought them a lesser kind of human. He could only say what he thought now.

"I do not think that about you, Forentel. Lady Forentel. I am sorry for—" He stopped, unused to apology. "I am sorry for treating you as a servant, when you are as noble as I." That was wrong, and it wasn't quite what he meant. In some ways, important ways, she was more noble than he was. The thought surprised him, and suddenly he laughed. "These people, here on this boat, they believe Virsat are lesser beings."

"So did they in Hila." Despite herself, Forentel felt slightly better. She sensed that something more was troubling the prince, something he would not disclose, maybe even to himself, but his edgy if ambivalent attitude toward her seemed, for the moment, to have eased.

"These people, or some of them, overheard what you said. When you spoke in my mind." It was one thing to discuss Tirdar abilities in the abstract, as he had with Filfa. It was another to admit they had affected him. "Perhaps it was Willip who heard you."

"Perhaps." What was he trying to say? "These people are Tirdar descended; you can tell from their language. That might explain how Willip heard."

"Yes." He wanted desperately to talk with her about scholarly matters, to pretend there was nothing wrong, nothing more important. He thought with brief longing of the days when it had seemed as if there were nothing more pressing in the world. "Can you distract these people, can you give them false thoughts, can you—"

Could she hurt them? He was trying to ask if she could hurt them. If she would.

"I will not harm them!" Surprised by her own vehemence, she paused. "I don't know if I even can."

"You were able to attack the plant."

"Yes. But not with my thoughts. I don't know if I can do that. And how would it harm them and not harm you? I'm sorry, Prince. I don't know much. The prophet at the shrine would have told me more, but there wasn't time."

"Thank the gods for that. If she had, there is no telling what further harm you might have caused."

The voice came from the floor in the shadows, where Filfa had been lying, forgotten. Forentel and Erba both started.

"You cannot trust a Tirdar."

"I am pleased to see that you have recovered, Lord Filfa," she muttered.

"He's not recovered." Erba was kneeling by the older man. "He can't sit up. He can't control his muscles."

"Except for his tongue," Forentel said acidly. "The drug will wear off eventually, I suppose," she added, "but I will see if I can hasten it, if you wish. If I can heal it." She had no desire to touch Filfa, to urge whatever drug this was to leave his body. She would, nonetheless. She drew a breath, gathering herself.

"Stay away from me."

"I will not harm you, Lord Filfa, whatever you may think."

"Save your strength," Erba agreed more diplomatically. "I have seen how your—healing—takes strength from you. I would think we have some time before we reach the place where they wish to sell us."

"The Big Island," Forentel put in.

"Probably they wanted to drug us all to make it easier for them to handle us," Erba continued. "We need a plan for when they come for us. We need to know more about the Big Island." He looked hopefully at Forentel. Unfortunately, she knew nothing more.

The rest of the evening and the night passed without anyone coming to check on them. They could tell that the

boat was no longer moving, except to rock gently. They
could hear noise above them, on deck, and they assumed
that they were docked at the Big Island. They shared the
water from the lidded bucket that had been left for them. It
tasted musty, and Forentel hoped it was free of any disease
demons, but it didn't matter. Filfa began to slowly recover
the use of his limbs. Despite Erba's objections, Forentel
put her hand on the gash on his left arm, urging the wound
to close, to reject any poison.

"It will take less from me now," she told him, "than if it
becomes infected later. All I will do is drive the infective
demons away."

Eventually, some of the boat people came for them.
They made no resistance, having decided that it would be
best if they waited until they were off the boat and had a
better chance of making an escape. It was dawn when they
were brought on deck, their hands bound behind them.
Forentel was given an extra guard, a nervous young man
who kept eyeing her and putting his hand to his long knife.
She was tempted to make a face at him, just to see if he
would startle, but she restrained herself.

Finally, they were escorted off the boat, down a long,
broad wooden plank onto a sandy shore. The sky was over-
cast, and the air so humid it was difficult to breathe, and
Forentel longed again for the desert. Tall, skinny trees
creaked in the breeze, their leaves whispering together.
Small knots of people, the villagers of the Big Island, eyed
them curiously as they were escorted to a large log building surrounded by open space.

Inside the building was a large room partitioned into
what seemed to Forentel like stock pens or cages. Some
people were already in one of these cages, sitting on the
wooden floor or leaning against the bars. She was shoved
into one of the empty pens with Erba and Filfa, and their
bonds cut as they were pushed in.

"We have made a mistake." Filfa looked around him at their pen, at the guards stationed at the doors to the big room. "We should have fought when we were on the boat. Our odds were better."

Forentel said nothing. She was tired of Filfa's complaints, tired of his air of superiority. She glanced at Erba, and it seemed that he shared her opinion, for he smiled slightly at her.

"Hey," Erba called to one of the men in the nearby pen. "Where are you from?" He spoke in Tirdar. There seemed no reason now to keep their knowledge of the language secret, and they needed information. But it was in vain.

"No talking!" said one of their guards, in the same language.

Forentel sat down on the wooden floor. It was formed of slats of wood, she noticed, so that it could be easily cleaned, the debris washed through to the ground below. She huddled down, feeling sick and cold despite the heat. She could feel the terror, despair, and even some of the drifting thoughts of people in the other pens. She tried to shut them out; her own thoughts were hard enough to deal with.

Erba looked around the huge room, taking everything in. The guards with their weapons seemed relaxed. It was obvious they expected no serious trouble from their charges. They often put their weapons aside, and in fact, there were other weapons stacked near the benches on which some of the guards lounged, talking. He glanced quickly away, lest anyone notice the direction of his attention.

Erba had never taken part in any military action. He had been trained in sword fighting, but he had never shown the interest or aptitude of his older brother Mirta, who was fascinated by all things military. He had preferred books and hunting. The closest he had come to an actual fight had been the unfortunate skirmish when the villagers from Hila had captured them, and his flight from his brother's men, and that scarcely qualified. Erba had never wanted to fight, let alone lead a fight, but now, looking around the room, he felt something harden within himself. He wanted to win his own freedom, true, and Forentel's and Filfa's, but he found himself speculating about the prisoners in the other pens. What had they done to deserve their fate, descendants of Tirdar or not? He noticed that people who looked as if they might have the capability to resist, men or women who looked strong, or who might be fighters or had any warrior training, were split apart into separate pens.

"The guards don't seem to keep us from talking to those with us in the same pen," he said softly to his companions. "They only keep us from conversing between pens. I could organize resistance if we could speak to the others. Look," he said in a lower tone, "how careless the guards are with their weapons."

"That's because there is nothing to concern them," said Filfa, "as long as they keep us apart. There is no way you can speak to the others."

Forentel looked up. "There is a way to communicate," she said.

IT WASN'T THE mainland. That became clear when they met their first villagers. It was difficult to understand them at first, but Kelern spoke Tirdar, and he soon realized that although this speech was different, it was comprehensible once you knew what to listen for. Riessa had far less trouble than he; her speech was closer to theirs.

They had woken to the sounds of approaching fishermen. Kelern had surprised them, appearing suddenly out of the bushes, taking one hostage before the unfortunate man realized anyone was near. Once he had determined their relative harmlessness, Kelern had released him. They had been both impressed and frightened, and Kelern had done his best to reassure them that they would be safe as long as they complied with his desires.

Riessa helped him make it clear that they were searching for two people, two criminals, and that there would be a reward for anyone who could give them good information. They had been taken to the nearest village where Kelern had had to kill one man who thought he could get the reward without giving any information, good or otherwise, and thought he had the strength and skill to take it. Kelern had made this unfortunate's death slow and painful enough to prove a sufficient warning to anyone else.

Now Kelern stretched, enjoying the bed that had been the village headman's, enjoying the sight of Riessa lying beside him in the morning light, still asleep. He had quickly determined that this island, called the Big Island with a lack of imagination that was suitable for such savages, was a local hub for trade and information. He planned to stay here a while to see if he could gather any more information that might be helpful to him.

There was a large trading town at the far end of the island—large by the standards of these people. He had been keeping clear of it, letting information come back to him, but it would soon be time to pay it a visit. He could live here like some barbarous king, but the only real life was back in Tireera. The sooner he completed his mission, the sooner he could go home.

Someone was knocking on the outside of the hut. The villagers had needed to be cured of their custom of knocking and then entering immediately. The cure had been easily achieved.

"Yes?" he called. "Come in." He smiled when Riessa

woke and hastily tried to cover herself with the sheet. He
didn't mind that the savages knew he owned an attractive
woman.

"I have news, Great One."

The visitor was the former headman. He stood in the hut
that had formerly been his and turned his eyes aside from
the new ruler of the village and his woman. Kelern tried
not to show his impatience. He had the villagers suitably
deferential now, and he did not want to spoil it.

"Yes?" he said mildly. "What is it? Don't be afraid."

"The men you are seeking, it may be that they have
been found." The headman had good reason to be afraid,
and he knew it, especially if his information proved false.
This Tireeran was almost supernatural in his fighting and
killing ability.

Kelern was out of bed, on his feet, and with his sword in
his hand in no more time than it had taken the headman to
blink.

"Where are they?"

"We are not sure, we do not know if it is really the men
that you seek—"

"Where are they!"

The headman fell to his knees. "In Trade Town! Willip's
pirates brought in two men that fit your descriptions. And a
woman with them. They are being held for sale tonight."

"I want your horse." Kelern was already dressed and
putting his pack together. "I will be in Trade Town before
evening."

"My horse! My horse—but—I need him—" It was the
only horse in the entire village.

"I need him more. If these are the men I seek, you will
have your house back, and your village. And here. You can
buy another horse, if you can find one." Kelern rummaged
in his pack and then tossed something in the direction of

the still kneeling headman. The man scrambled for the two small gold pieces on the filthy floor of the hut.

"Get me the horse now!"

The headman was on his feet, bowing as he hastened to leave.

"If you are coming with me, Riessa, get dressed. Don't stand there. I'm leaving now."

She knew better than to ask for more time. She was out of bed, dressing as fast as she could, gathering her possessions and stuffing them into her old pack. She hoped Kelern had found his quarry at last, for then it would be over, and they could go back to Tireera, where she could live the life she was born for. One thing bothered her: there was a woman with the two men in Trade Town. She had a solid suspicion that the woman was Forentel, and she had hoped to never see Forentel again. It didn't matter, she told herself. Even if it was Forentel, there was nothing the healer could do. She was a captured prisoner, just another slave for sale.

When she left the hut Kelern was already on horseback. He held out a hand to her and pulled her up behind him, while the villagers stood around gaping at them. There was no saddle, only an old blanket, and Riessa knew she would be sore and stiff by the time they arrived in town.

It was evening by the time they reached Trade Town, and Riessa's joints ached. Her skin itched from the grime of travel and insect bites. She was thirsty, and she looked longingly in the direction of a tavern, which stood at the edge of an open space. There were open-air stalls, filled with what looked like all kinds of goods. A clothing stall and another for what seemed to be just jewelry caught her eye. And of course there were food stalls. Torches flared, shedding light over everything, and people were wandering around, laughing, talking, purchasing items. Some men

with weapons kept a careful eye on the crowd. This was
city life, as she had always imagined it. When Kelern told
her that this was a backwater village compared to Tireera,
she had gasped in disbelief.

"This is just their market day. Here." Kelern helped her
dismount. "Let's get some food. We can eat it over there,
by the auction stand." He grinned when he saw how she
staggered from stiffness when she tried to walk.

There was an open space near the raised auction stand,
and people were already milling around there, under the
light of torches. Kelern left the horse in the care of a boy
who looked somewhat less than intelligent, but who believed in the promise both of more pay if the horse were
cared for and of serious harm if it were not. He purchased
two rolls with some sort of cheese in them from a vendor,
which they ate while making their way toward the auction
block. Kelern knew he didn't have enough gold to purchase
both Erba and Filfa if they were auctioned off, and he had
no intention of wasting his funds. He hoped to have con-
cluded his business before the sale even began.

"Wait here," he told Riessa. They had come to the edge
of the open space where would-be buyers crowded. "I will
be back for you."

She knew better than to ask to go with him. She
watched as he made his way through the crowd, headed toward the rear of the building where, presumably, the slaves
were kept. He seemed to slip between people without disturbing them, without them even noticing. When he was a
good distance ahead, she followed him.

He was almost too late. Kelern realized it as soon as
he got to the back of the building. He had wanted to pose
as a rich buyer, to bribe the guards to bring out just Erba
and Filfa, assuming that was who they were. It wouldn't
take him long to conclude his business and be gone, before the local guards could have time to react. If he were

too late, they would already have brought the prisoners out to the holding pen or even the auction block, where it would be much harder to do what he needed to. He spent only a brief moment berating himself for giving in to Riessa's desire for food and novelty. Then because he was honest with himself, he admitted it: he had given in to his desire to please and impress her. Because of that, he was just in time to see the guards beginning to lead the prisoners out.

They were being taken into a big holding pen in groups of three. Kelern pushed his way toward the guards. His hand was already on his sword, but he was smiling pleasantly.

"Excuse me," he said, genially, "I was hoping to take a private look at some of your merchandise."

"You can see them with everyone else," said the guard. "No private looks."

Kelern was beginning to edge past him. He didn't take the man lightly; the guard was young, strong, and with some obvious training, but Kelern knew he could take him if he had to. He thought he saw Erba; he and Filfa and Forentel were the last three to be brought out. Forentel looked pale, shaken, and ill, and Erba was half supporting her.

It was then that the pen seemed to erupt. Forentel suddenly straightened. Erba shouted and rushed the guard nearest him.

Simultaneously, all around the holding pen, men and women were charging the guards, leaping for the fence that surrounded the pen. Several of the prisoners slammed against the gate, wedging it open. Several others were right behind them, in what was obviously a coordinated attack. They rushed through the gate and back into the building.

It had taken the guards a few moments to realize what was happening, a few moments they could ill afford. But once they knew, they recovered with alacrity. There were only eight of them, and they shouted for help. Two ran to get the gate; the others were trying to fend off the prisoners and simultaneously round them up, but they were badly outnumbered. Under cover of this confusion, Kelern drew his sword and moved toward Erba.

Erba had wrested a knife from one of the guards, and he was wielding it with efficiency, having already stabbed the knife's original owner. Filfa had grabbed the sword from the same guard. There were a number of prisoners between Kelern and his quarry, and he realized that he might be mistaken for a guard himself.

"Help me!" One of the guards was attempting to fight off two prisoners, and he looked around desperately.

The struggling group was between Kelern and Erba, and there was no quick way around them. Kelern killed both prisoners in rapid succession. A quick swipe across the throat of one melded seamlessly into a stomach thrust to the other. When the man rolled away, moaning, Kelern cut down the guard as well with a casual backhanded slash. All around there were screams and shouts and the smell of blood.

Kelern noticed an odd thing: a little knot of armed prisoners surrounded Forentel, protecting her. She stood upright now, no longer leaning on anyone, but she had an abstracted expression, and her face gleamed with sweat, although she was not exerting herself at all.

Now there was more shouting. The group of prisoners who had rushed back into the building had returned with more arms. Knives, swords, clubs, and spears were being handed out and tossed to prisoners. Kelern hissed in frustration. There were too many people now in his way, and to make matters worse, some of the town's citizens had joined the fracas.

"We are free! We are free!" A woman was screaming at the top of her considerable lungs.

Against all odds, the prisoners had dispatched most of

the guards and were holding off the townsmen who were joining the fight. The town's armed guards seemed to be holding back. The scene was rapidly becoming a disaster. Then Erba leaped up on the auction block.

Erba felt invigorated, simultaneously more alive and more frightened than he had ever been, even when his brother's troops had almost killed him outside of Tireera. Here, he was not just reacting to events, he was acting. He was fighting, and fighting well, but this battle was no longer under his control, if it had ever been. Forentel had enabled them to organize and had enabled him to set up the plan. The effort had drained her strength, and now she could no longer link them all, not in the confusion of the fight. The battle plan was coming apart. The prisoners were not a trained army, and they were no longer acting in concert. Some of them were breaking for freedom now, others were looking for revenge against guards. They had achieved initial success through surprise, but that would not last. Even now, the town guards were at last reinforcing the slave guards. The prisoners would be cut to pieces, and nothing would have been gained. So Erba jumped up on the auction block.

"Stand together!" he shouted. He had a loud voice, a carrying voice. "Friends, stand together! Don't run! Remember the hostages!" If they presented a united bloc, and if they took some hostages, they could demand their freedom, and perhaps negotiate.

His reminder was just in time. Most of the remaining slaves rallied, drawing together near the auction block. A few of them grabbed a guard and subdued him with a knife at his throat. Two prisoners pulled someone out of the crowd that had gathered, a rich man, by the look of him, and terrified. What caught Erba's attention most of all, however, was the man fighting near the auction block, the man struggling now to hold off six of the freed prisoners. He had already killed at least four, and their bodies lay around him, forming a hazard. He was almost preternaturally good, and for a moment it looked as though he would prevail against the remaining six. There was something familiar about him; Erba knew him from somewhere.

"No! Don't hurt him! Kelern!"

It was a woman's voice. A woman came out of the crowd, trying to push her way toward the little skirmish rather than away from it. It was, Erba realized, the woman from the village, the woman whose life Forentel had saved through her healing. She ran forward, her dark hair streaming behind her, trying to push her way to Kelern's side, somehow managing to avoid being injured. Kelern Drilini, Erba thought. King's Guard. His brother's guard. He knew, with a sudden, absolute certainty what such a man was doing here.

Kelern looked up at the woman's shout. His distraction was momentary, however, and it appeared to cost him nothing. He killed two of his opponents with what seemed like barely a flick of his wrist. Erba, watching, felt a prickle of fear, but however good Kelern was, he was not skilled enough to fight free of the remaining four. One managed to get beneath Kelern's reach with his knife. Before he could finish off the Tireeran, the woman flung herself forward between attackers and attacked, and threw her arms around Kelern.

"No!" she sobbed.

The freed slave, nonplussed, pulled back, and Kelern thought for a moment that he had a chance, but it was too late, and he was taken.

If Kelern had reserved any tricks for a situation such as this, he was unable to use them now. He glanced with annoyance at Riessa. The slaves, panting and wounded, brought them both to the auction block, and to Erba. The other hostages were brought. Filfa and Forentel came to stand beside Erba, and Kelern looked up directly into Forentel's eyes.

"Let them go or you will regret it!" The voice had considerable authority, and its owner knew it.

The town had brought forth its prince, the local authority. The great man stood there, surrounded by his own guards, red with fury even in the torchlight. His guards had drawn weapons. There were archers with him, too, but due to the nature of the crowd, they could not fire without injuring their own citizens, or worse.

"Let them go, or we will kill you all! We will not have the name of great Trade Town destroyed!"

The citizens of Trade Town shouted out their agreement, much braver now that the leader was there with his troops. Erba repressed a smile. This was something he had counted on. He glanced at his hostages, then motioned for the local citizen to be brought into clear view. The prince obviously recognized him.

"We want our freedom," he called, his voice carrying over the shouts and angry mutters, quieting them. "We will release your merchant here," Erba made a guess at the man's profession, "and the guard." He glanced down at his hostages and saw that Riessa was trembling. "And this woman." He deliberately omitted Kelern from this list. "And you will let us go. Once we have gone, you can restore the great image of your town as a place of trade and not of piracy." He knew bitterness and sarcasm tinged his voice, and he drew a breath. It would serve no purpose to antagonize these people further. "But we will have safe conduct from here, and you will keep your word. If you do not, our hostages die. Your name is ruined. And no ship will ever dock here again for trade."

For a moment there was silence. No one in the huge crowd made a sound, save for the shuffling of feet, the

creak of the leather armor on the prince's men, and
Riessa's soft sobs. Then the prince shook his head.

"No," he said. "I do not accept. We make no bargains
with slaves. Trade Town will not surrender to slaves. You
all die."

He motioned to his men. The archers stepped forward,
bows drawn. People in the crowd began to scream, knowing they were in the line of fire, trying to pull back, but
wedged in by the people behind them. Erba felt oddly
calm. He had lost, but it did not seem to matter. He knew
he was about to die, and it didn't frighten him. He glanced
sideways at Filfa and Forentel, wanting to reassure them.
Filfa looked terrified, and Erba felt sorry for his old friend.
Forentel was another matter.

Forentel heard the prince's words, and heard what was
behind them. She knew he dreaded the loss of face, knew
he could not hold his position if he lost in such a public
fashion. She felt, too, the echoes from beneath this fear. It
wasn't just that he feared losing his own power, although
that was foremost. He was concerned about Trade Town.
He had been struggling to bring order out of chaos, struggling to find a balance between the merchants with their
own armies of bodyguards and the pirates who brought
their loot to the town. He was beginning to succeed, but it
could all be lost tonight with one false step. The slave market had been a source of disruption for a very long time.

"Wait! Stop!"

Forentel stepped forward to the edge of the auction
block. The torches around her lit her face, lit up the bronze
halo of her hair. She held up one hand in command or in
plea. She could feel the resonance of her words flow out,
not just the sound, but the intensity of her emotions. She
could sense an answer from the prince of the town, from
most of his guards. The archers held their fire.

"Listen to me!" She knew she didn't have much time.

"The good name of Trade Town depends on its fairness to all and on its reputation as a safe place. If you are a fair and compassionate ruler, your fame will spread. One of us is a prince of Tireera. Let us go, and your fame will reach that city. That is more valuable than any profits."

She didn't expect him to believe her. Claiming nobility was just the sort of thing someone would do in a desperate bid for freedom. It sounded feeble. It sounded laughable. No one laughed. The Trade Town warriors were staring, eyes huge, and pointing. Even the Trade Town prince took a step backwards.

"A spirit guide!" said the prince. He looked down at something just below the auction block and then back up to Forentel. "We are honored to have among us one of the chosen, and her guide. Of course you shall go free."

Forentel looked down to see what he could possibly be referring to. At the foot of the auction block stood Sunrise, fur raised.

FIFTEEN

$\mathcal{T}$RADE TOWN COULDN'T SEEM TO GET RID OF them fast enough. They were given clothing and provisions on a surprising scale, the promise of a boat, and escorted to the edge of town as soon as possible. They were not even offered a night's lodging, although the prince of the town spoke briefly and privately with Erba.

"Not that we would have accepted lodging," said Erba softly to Forentel, "not in this place." They were being escorted by some of the town guards, a few of them guards from the slave auction, who treated their erstwhile prisoners with considerable nervousness. "They may respect a healer and a spirit guide, whatever that may be," he glanced sideways at the wolf, who was trotting beside Forentel like a big dog and who gave him a big, wolfish grin, "and thank the gods they do, but they have no desire to spend much time with one. Which suits me."

It suited Forentel, too. Filfa had said nothing for a long time. He had eaten, and he walked with them, and he carried one of their now-bulging packs, but he spoke very little to Erba, and he said nothing at all to Forentel. He kept casting glances at Kelern but did not speak to him, either. Kelern and Riessa walked close together, slightly apart from the other three. Forentel knew she would have to talk to them. Surely Kelern would not persist in his mission now, after what they had endured.

A fair distance outside the town they stopped. They were in a cleared space, near a grove of trees for which Forentel did not know the name. The vegetation was so unlike anything she knew that it reminded her constantly of how far she was from home. She looked down at Sunrise, remembering how the wolf had come to her in the desert. Sunrise was a creature of the desert just as she was, but people in these strange places seemed to somehow recognize them both, to have expectations of them both, expectations that she did not understand.

"You may rest here," the leader of their escort told them. You may camp for as long as you wish, although," he glanced nervously at Forentel and at Sunrise, who yawned, showing off her canines, "perhaps you will not want to wait before setting out for Dreffir. When the rainy season comes, the river rises. We will have your promised boat prepared by tomorrow's noon."

Forentel was exhausted. Their escort was actually setting up shelters for them, two small tents. She frowned. Only two? She had no intention of sharing a tent with anyone, even Riessa. Perhaps especially Riessa, since she could feel a shifty menace from the woman.

She opened her mouth to question, and saw that Erba

had drawn aside with the Trade Town guards. Two of the guards had taken Kelern by the arms, and another was holding Riessa back. The guards were forcing Kelern to his knees before Erba. It had happened so quickly that Kelern had been taken by surprise, and Riessa had no chance to protest. It was obvious what was about to happen, and that Erba had made this arrangement before they left Trade Town.

"Stop! Stop, Erba, Prince, stop! What are you doing?" Forentel strode forward, pushing aside the swords of the startled town guards.

"What does it look like I'm doing?" Erba nodded to another town guard, who grasped Kelern by the hair and pulled his head back. Erba drew the knife he had been given. Kelern swallowed but said nothing and made no attempt to struggle.

"Stop it!"

Forentel took advantage of the uneasy awe of the townsmen. It helped, too, that the wolf rose to her full impressive height and came forward beside her. Even so, the guards did not release Kelern. Forentel stepped between Kelern and Erba, physically preventing the execution.

"You can't kill him, Erba."

"Lady Forentel, you forget yourself. I can kill him, and I will. This man has tracked me all the way from Tireera with one purpose in mind: my death. I intend to end his mission now."

Forentel looked down into Kelern's eyes. He stared back at her, afraid yet defiant. She looked deeper, trying to read there what it was that had made her so certain he must be saved, that he must not die, at least not now. She hated these new, strange abilities that rose within her; she hated them passionately and did not want to trust them. She didn't know if she could, yet all she knew was the sense of impending disaster if this man died. She became aware of Riessa, sobbing behind her.

"Stand aside, Forentel." Erba spoke more gently now. "I know one gently bred does not wish to see death—"

"Oh Erba!" Despite herself, she laughed. "After what we've seen together! Let him go. We will need him." Her matter-of-fact command achieved what desperation had not. The town guards released Kelern.

Filfa had remained silent through all of this, but now he shifted anxiously. Forentel glanced at him; something about him made her nervous, but perhaps it was only her dislike of the man. The past days had been hard on him, and he was old.

Kelern stepped back from them all. Riessa pulled away from her guard and ran to him. Erba frowned but let them go. Forentel looked away from the prince, but she could feel his turmoil. *I don't know,* she thought, *I don't know! I don't know why, but I feel we must let him go.* With her growing ability, she knew he heard her.

"Go." Erba waved his hand at Kelern. "Go, but don't let me see your face again. This lady," he nodded at Forentel, "has saved your life. Do not count on her doing it again. If I see you again, I will kill you."

Kelern stared for a moment and then laughed. "You will not," he said. Forentel didn't know if he meant they would not see him again, or that Erba could not kill him. Kelern walked to Forentel, with Riessa trailing reluctantly behind him.

"You are no true Virsat." In the depths of his eyes gratitude warred with a deep confusion and something akin to admiration. "But I owe you my life. I will not forget."

He turned and was gone into the dark trees before anyone realized it. Riessa gave a strangled cry and ran after him. They could hear her crunching through the woods, but there was no sound from Kelern. Riessa must have found him, however, or he her, for her cries stopped.

"Let them go," said Erba. "I hope you know what you are doing," he said to Forentel.

Again, Filfa said nothing at all. Forentel watched them putting their goods into one of the tents. The other, it would seem, was hers. She was exhausted, so deeply tired that her bones ached, but she couldn't go into the tent. She walked from the guards, who gave way for her with uneasy glances. She walked to the dark edge of the trees, where she found a large rock by virtue of tripping over it. She sat on this and stared into the dark forest.

She was not afraid of Kelern returning. Surely he would not be so foolish, and surely she had nothing to fear from him in any case. She put her head in her hands. After a few moments something pushed against her in the darkness. She smothered a cry when she saw the eyes gleaming back at her. It was Sunrise, who had found her in the dark. Tentatively, she reached out to stroke the wolf's head.

"Why did you choose me, and for what?" she asked. "What do they all want with us?" She hated that the wolf had found her, she hated the connection between them, yet at the same time was grateful for it, especially now.

Sunrise panted slightly. Forentel sighed. The wolf did not seem like a wild animal; she seemed more like one of the big hunting dogs from home, in attitude if not in appearance. *A tame dog,* she thought.

Sunrise sat up and growled. The sound was menacing and deep. Forentel felt a terror so stark that she stopped breathing. Sunrise stopped growling and relaxed. She looked at Forentel and gave a small yip. Forentel drew a shaky breath. It looked almost as though the wolf were smirking.

"Point taken," she said. "But why are you here? What is a spirit animal?"

She did not expect an answer. She was looking into the wolf's yellow eyes, and then she was falling into them. Her perspective shifted. There were concepts but no words: wilderness, wildness, and a sense of destiny. The wolf was no more or less spirit than she, but she had been searching for the one who would link with her, link to her and link her to the desert rulers, the ones in the city, and beyond, to the wider world of men. There was something that needed to be done, that needed this link; the desert demanded it. She was a bridge, but who was she, wolf or woman?

Forentel gasped for breath, pulling back. She felt the rock, solid beneath her, felt the humid night air. The wolf was still sitting beside her. Forentel reached out with a shaky hand and felt the fur beneath her fingers. The animal seemed unhurt.

"It's unsafe to be out here alone."

Forentel gasped and looked up, but the dark bulk leaning over her was Erba.

"You didn't even hear me come up. If you are going to be out alone and unprotected, you must be alert." He sat down beside her on the rock. "He could come back."

"I'm not alone," said Forentel, but as she said it she realized that Sunrise had gone. She could feel the wolf at the edge of her senses, curling into a ball not far from them on the forest floor, resting.

"I need to ask you," Erba shifted a little on the rock, not as comfortable as she was. "I want to ask you—"

Forentel tried not to sigh. She was so very tired. Why did they have to do this now? But obviously, they did.

"I want to ask you how it is you make me hear you. In my thoughts. What is it you do to me?"

"I do nothing to you." She slapped irritably at an insect. So many insects here, far more than in Tireera. "All I do is sometimes think thoughts at you, and you hear them." She heard the sharpness in her own tone, but she did not try to moderate it. "And you—you can sometimes send them at me. When you are upset."

"Can you hear my thoughts always?"

He tried very hard to hide the edge of fear, but she heard it. She almost answered *no,* but then she realized that she didn't really know. She tried to find what he was thinking, but there was nothing. She could sense his anxiety, and something else mixed with it, but nothing more.

"No," she said, "I can't. I certainly couldn't tell that you were going to abandon me in Hila. In that stupid village!" The words were out before she could stop them, and then there was no reason to hold back anymore. "I saved your life, yours and Filfa's, and you left me there!" She didn't know whether to cry or scream. Suddenly it was all too much.

Erba drew in a sharp breath. "Abandon you! No! I never would have have, I never—they told me, they told us—"

"They told you what?" She was standing up now, her hands balled into fists on her hips. She was thinking how she had saved them again on the island of the plant.

"Oh gods, Forentel. They told me you wanted to stay with them, to be their healer. That you were called by the gods, that you have a gift for healing."

"And you believed them!"

"You do have a gift for healing." It sounded weak, and Erba knew it. She wouldn't believe him; of course she wouldn't. He barely believed himself. "I am sorry. I am truly sorry, Forentel. I shouldn't have believed them, I should have insisted on talking to you." He was a fool. He was unused to thinking of himself this way, but it was so. He was a fool.

Forentel sighed. It was true. She could feel it in him, he had believed it. Despite herself, some of her anger drained away. She sat down again, abruptly.

"You did believe them." She looked down at the ground and barely refrained from putting her head in her hands. Why wouldn't he believe that a half-Tirdar girl would want to stay in some marsh village?

Erba peered at her in the darkness. She had read his mind. "You can tell what I think. You said you couldn't, but you can."

"No." Forentel sighed. She wished again for more time with Illiana. She needed to know more, so much more. "Although sometimes I know if you're uneasy, or afraid, but I imagine you do the same with others."

"True." Erba frowned in the darkness. He had always thought people could do this, that anyone could do this. Obviously that wasn't so. "Forentel," he said abruptly, "what will you do if—when—we reach Dreffir?"

"I don't know. I will try to learn what I can about," she hesitated, "what I am."

"Will you stay there?"

"No. I have to go back. My mother—Lady Mareg—" What was happening now, back in Tireera? "Besides, I am Tireeran. What about you? What will you do in Dreffir?" She remembered hearing her father say, more than once, that to defend you must sometimes attack. It seemed good advice just now.

"I have always wanted to find Dreffir." Erba's voice warmed slightly. "For years I've dreamed of it. A wealthy city, hidden far away, filled with mysteries. Maybe I will stay there." He had always dreamed of bringing back wealth and fame, but what was there for him now in Tireera? His brother sent assassins across great distances to kill him. And his father was dead. It was odd, but that fact had never seemed real before. He drew in a sharp breath. There had never been much love between father and younger son, but Erba had never imagined a world without his father in it, at the head of it. Even when Rellaff had become ill, Erba had always somehow imagined he would recover. Now he began to understand how profoundly everything was changed. His father was dead, murdered, and his brother wanted to murder him. He felt his throat thicken with grief, not only for his father but for himself, and for what he had lost.

"You have to go back."

Forentel's words pulled him back from the darkness of his thoughts. Erba turned to her, struggling to see her face in the darkness.

"There is nothing for me there." Even as he spoke he felt the grief increase. *Never go back to Tireera?*

"Tell me, Erba, what kind of king will your brother Mirta make?"

She could feel him fighting the sorrow, fighting the doubt, fighting the fear. He was so lonely and so afraid. Before she realized it, she put her arms around him. Then either he bent his head to her or she pulled his head down, she was never sure.

The kiss was long and deep, and his lips were soft. She had never kissed a man before, and this feeling was overwhelming. She tightened her arms. He wanted her, but he was afraid, afraid of her and of himself. Abruptly, he pulled back.

She couldn't take any more, and her head ached. She rose from the rock, saying nothing, and made her way back to the tents. He did not call her back. Behind her, she could feel Erba's grief and his rising fear. It was fear for himself and fear both of her and for her, but it was also fear for the city he had left behind, and fear for what he might have to do. He had spent most of his life avoiding responsibilities. Of course, she reflected, so had she. But as she lay down across the sleeping skin the Trade Town people had given her, she found herself thinking not of Erba but of Kelern. She remembered the intensity with which he had looked into her eyes tonight. Somehow, she knew she would see him again, that he had not abandoned his mission.

It was a gray and windy morning when Erba left his tent. They all slept late. He was still exhausted, having staggered in to bed only shortly before dawn. Filfa had been sleeping restlessly and had been muttering things in his sleep, something about a "bad bargain." Erba was grat-ified although slightly surprised to find that two of their Trade Town guards had remained, to take them to their boat. It was only as they were packing up their supplies that he caught a glimpse of Forentel. He stopped what he was doing and stared.

"It bothered me," said Forentel. "So I cut it off last night." She ran a hand through her now short, copper bronze hair. She turned back to what she was doing, fold-ing her sleeping skin into the large pack.

Erba continued to stare for a moment. It was obvious she didn't particularly care what he thought, and he real-ized that bothered him. But he also realized something else: she no longer had to try to keep it combed, or braided, and keeping it clean would be so much easier.

"A good idea," he said, and reached for his own knife. He grinned at Filfa, who watched him, shocked, as he hacked off his own hair.

That was the only levity they seemed likely to share for the rest of the day, and it wasn't much. The guards led them down a winding path back to the river, and there was a large, flat-bottomed boat with oars, a tiller, and a small sail with a removable mast just as promised. Erba felt grim at the sight of it. Would this journey never end? They had a map, however, which assured them it would: it showed Dreffir on it. The territory on the way to and surrounding

Dreffir was suitably vague. The map had various strange conceits: a notation for river monsters, for one. Erba felt they had seen the worst of any monsters when they had escaped first the plant and then from the Trade Town slave market. Since the Trade Town guards were anxious for them to be on their way, they piled everything into the boat and pushed out onto the river.

As the silvery water began to slide by beneath the boat again, and they settled into the journey, Erba felt depression seep into him. He wasn't even particularly interested in Filfa's demonstration of the use of the sail, although he watched carefully. He felt constantly aware of Forentel's presence now, even though she ignored him. And he kept hearing her question from the previous night. What kind of king would his brother make?

HE KNEW HE was losing the trust of the king. It worried Nedriff, but what really concerned him was that all the nobles were losing the trust of the king. Mirta seemed suspicious of everyone around him. Nedriff had it on good authority that king frequently did not sleep, and he knew from personal observation that Mirta drank too much wine. It had seemed initially that there was no choice. Rellaff would never recover, but he refused to hand over all power to Mirta. Something had needed to be done, and in a choice between Mirta and Erba, Mirta had seemed the best for his purposes.

He reached under his cloak and drew out another handful of grain for his horse. While the animal nuzzled its soft lips over his palm, he scanned the scrub desert behind him. The sun would be up soon, and he wanted this meeting to be over before then, if possible, so that he could go back to the city alone, claiming only an early morning ride to clear his head, as was his frequent custom. At last he saw the thin plume of dust, and then the horses and riders. The lead rider drew up near his escort, spoke for a minute, and then walked his horse forward, leaving his escort behind. A chance meeting in the desert, if anyone saw and remarked on it.

"You're late." Nedriff did not bother to keep the irritation out of his voice.

"What does it matter? It's overly cautious to meet out here; we could have been comfortable in your house. Or mine." Brezat shifted in his saddle and glanced behind him. He was a large man, thick around the waist from too many rich meals, but he was also a powerful man. His black hair was beginning to recede, accentuating a broad forehead, deep-set brown eyes with bushy brows, and a square face.

"It matters," said Nedriff, "because Mirta has his own guards, because he trusts no one, and because there are spies everywhere. I know my escort is safe and trustworthy." Nedriff had brought only two men with him. "I hope you know the same about yours."

"They are." Brezat waved his hand in dismissal, but his face darkened. He did not appreciate anyone doubting him, especially not his ally. "Nedriff, this cannot go on. I will not meet with you like this. We should not have to hide as if we are fugitive Tirdar. I say again, this cannot go on."

"My point entirely," said Nedriff dryly. "Mirta is becoming unstable. An unstable king, and such a young one. It was a mistake, I'm afraid, but not irreparable. If we are going to do something about this situation, my friend, we must be cautious."

"You have the army," said Brezat bluntly. "I can't see that much caution is needed, or at least not for long. I have the funds. A little planning: I give your troops the funds, and you, of course, administer them, and you remove Mirta and replace him with me. With you supporting me, and the troops behind you, we cannot fail."

"We won't fail. But there is more than a little planning involved here, Brezat." Nedriff dropped the reins and walked a short distance from his horse, forcing the other man to follow him. He stood looking off across the desert, while the other man shifted irritably. Brezat, he reflected, was not an easy man to deal with, but he needed him. It would have been easier if he could have cemented this alliance with the marriage of his elder daughter to Brezat.

"We will have the support of most of the nobles," said Brezat. "Those we can cannot win to our side, we must dispose of. It's simple."

"At exactly the same time as Mirta has his accident," said Nedriff. "Any sooner will warn Mirta, and he is edgy enough these days. Any later will give them time to react, and we cannot take the chance." He saw the way Brezat sniffed dismissively and frowned. "Believe me on this, my friend, it's not only dangerous, but it could be fatal. There are some of my troops loyal to the king, and there is his guard."

"I trust you to take care of it."

"Fine. But I need half the gold now."

Brezat stared at him. The dawn wind ruffled his cloak. He drew his brows together. "I can have it by nightfall," he said. "I will have it brought to the Temple of Justice, as we agreed, to the storeroom of your wife's chambers. Make sure she is away. Are you sure she never goes there?"

"She will be away. There is nothing in the storeroom she wants, merely old chests and furniture."

"You will not get the other half until we are successful."

"We have already agreed on that. And Brezat," Nedriff raised his voice slightly as the other man turned away. "Say nothing of this to anyone. Take care you are not followed."

Nedriff watched as the other man rode away. He waited before taking his horse and returning to his own escort. He did not trust Brezat not to betray them both through a careless word or worse, something overlooked, an action Brezat considered unimportant. Brezat needed him to achieve his goal of sovereignty over Tireera, but he believed success was all but achieved. Mareg had warned him about Brezat, warned him that Mirta had very good reason to distrust the noble. If only he could act without Brezat, Nedriff thought. But he could not. He needed Brezat's funds for his troops, to ensure the loyalty of those he had with him and to buy the loyalty of those who might feel a mistaken allegiance to their king. Brezat expected that once he was securely installed as king, he could then dispose of his ally.

He is so transparent, Nedriff thought. *How fortunate he does not realize it.*

MAREG LEFT THE house well before dusk, carried in her chair, with her out-walkers before her, waving their plumed fans. The occasional cry of "Make way for the High Judge" echoed across the Tireeran streets, where people were venturing forth again after the heat of the day. Soon the torches would be lit, and Virsat of all classes and free Tirdar would meet for their evening meal and then go out to shop or drink wine and visit friends under the torches in the pleasant cool of the night.

Tonight was the Festival of the Stars, the Virsat celebration of the beginning of time, when the gods lit up the sky with stars so they could see to create the world. The Lady of Justice had then placed the moon and the sun in the heavens so that mankind could see the difference between the ways of the gods and the ways of evil. The city would be celebrating, but in the Temple of Justice it would be a solemn event.

Tonight was the night of the Great Rite of Seeing. The priests, and the High Priest in particular, would be gath-

ered at the temple, with many of the high Virsat nobles in
attendance. The king would of course be there. Mareg suspected that Mirta put a great deal of stock in the prophecies
of the High Priest, something she herself did not, although
she would listen respectfully. It was an impressive ritual,
whatever else it was, and when it was over they would be
free to join the celebrations in the city, if they so chose.
Most Virsat nobles had parties planned.

Mareg did not. She would put in an appearance at the
palace, since the king had invited her, but she would not
stay long, and she had no plans to go anywhere else.
Nedriff was not coming with her to the temple. This was
not unusual; he had missed the Seeing on previous years,
but now the new king might take his absence amiss. This
year she had already determined to go home as soon as she
could, as she wanted to speak with Nedriff again about his
continued association with Brezat. She had warned him,
after she had pardoned the Tirdar, but he had shrugged off
the incident.

The great hall of the temple was already filled with the
smoke of incense when Mareg entered. The king was in his
carved stone chair, and the altar and the stool for the High
Priest had been prepared. Mareg bowed before the king,
and Mirta nodded to her as she went to the seat for the
High Judge. As she walked, she could not help but notice
how many Virsat nobles were absent. It did not bode well
for the new king.

The priests came in with the tinkle of tiny bells and the
jangle of temple musicians playing the stringed rittan, the
sacred instrument. The acolyte placed the crystal bowl of
water on the altar. There was chanting and ringing of bells,
during which Mareg let her mind wander. Before she returned home, she decided, she would go to her chambers.
She had left her favorite cloak there. Not that it mattered,
particularly, but it had been a gift from Forentel, one her

daughter had selected for her years ago, and she would feel better when she had retrieved it. She missed Forentel, and there had been no news of her. This was something she could not discuss with her husband, as Nedriff refused to let her mention it.

She knew others thought of Forentel, however, others from a rather unexpected quarter. Tirdar who saw her on the streets would sometimes bow to her. It was not because she was High Judge; she knew better than that. Once, a Tirdar woman had come up to her with flowers, and from curiosity she had told her escort to let the woman through.

"Why do you bring me those?" she had asked.

"Because you are her chosen mother," had been the answer, "and because you will see true justice done."

Mareg had never mentioned this incident to anyone.

"I see the path of the year ahead," the High Priest moaned in his most theatrical voice.

Mareg suppressed a grimace of distaste. She doubted that anyone had ever truly seen anything in the bowl of water or had ever prophesied the future. No Virsat, at least. *Perhaps Tirdar could do this,* she thought, remembering the woman in the desert shrine.

"The way is long, the way is lit by the stars," intoned the priest. Mareg fought a yawn.

And then suddenly, the priest's voice changed. It was as if a different person spoke, it was not the theatrical intonation to which they had become accustomed but a harsh croak, as if something that was not human spoke from out of the priest.

"It's the end of what we know. It is coming from the south, from down the green river, from the lost lands. Tireera must change. The Virsat must change. To live, Tireera must change."

Every person in the room was frozen. The voice, harsh and emotionless, had rooted them all in place.

"Many will die if they refuse the bridge, if they are un-ready. King and nobles and commoners, Virsat and Tirdar, all will change." The priest stopped speaking and swayed where he stood. He began to collapse, and two of the junior priests rushed forward to catch him.

"There must be a true king," croaked the priest. Then he fainted.

There was a commotion around the High Priest, with the juniors trying to give him water, fanning him. Nobles had risen and were chattering, others were leaving already. The Seeing was either a disaster or an amazing success. Mareg glanced toward the king's chair and saw that Mirta had turned ashen. Even at a distance she could see his wide eyes and the sheen of sweat on his face. He looked, she thought, like a prisoner who had just lost his case before her, like one condemned.

"The High Priest has been taken ill," said one of the junior priests, raising his voice to carry over the pandemonium. "The stress of the prophecy has taken him, but he will recover."

In fact, Mareg noted, he seemed to be recovering already. He was sitting up and looking around him, confused. Would they attempt the Seeing again? She doubted it. When she looked back to see Mirta again, he had left.

There was no point in staying. She might as well go home now, even though it was early, and find Nedriff. She rose and headed for the long staircase that led to the lower, more public areas of the temple. She would call for her litter and her out-walkers. Then she remembered her cloak. She reversed her direction and headed back toward the stairs.

The stairs were now crowded with Virsat nobles who were leaving, loudly discussing the Seeing. A few seemed to think they had heard a true prophecy tonight, and were concerned, but most appeared to believe that the High Priest had put on a particularly good show.

"Clever," said a woman, "to think of fainting like that, and the unusual voice."

"It's not traditional," said her male companion.

"All the more effective."

It was Lord Wickern and his wife. If they saw her, Mareg realized, she would be drawn into this discussion. She reversed direction again, but this time she headed for the smaller stairway at the side of the great temple room. This was the stairway used by the temple servants, to keep them out of the way of those doing the true business of the Lady of Justice.

Mareg entered her rooms from the back, through the little servants' door. This door was unlocked. *It should be locked,* she thought. Not that it mattered much, for the whole temple was guarded, and there was nothing of especial value in her outer rooms. Her inner chamber, with her books and scrolls, was locked. Nonetheless, she must remember to tell someone. There was her cloak, in the corner. And she could see the door to the storeroom. It was open. How odd. She had never used that room; it was filled with old chests and crates and odd bits of furniture. She had never bothered to have the servants empty it, as she had never needed it. But now, someone was in there.

She felt a brief flare of fear, and she reached for the dagger at her belt. Then she flattened herself against the wall, in the shadows. After a few moments, a young man came out. He was dressed as a temple servant, but she recognized him as one of Lord Brezat's private guardsmen.

Mareg's fear intensified. She drew herself as tight to the wall as she could, while her mind raced. She scarcely breathed. If he found her, he might kill her. She would fight, and she could call for help, but she knew it would be too late. Someone of his training and strength could kill her easily before help arrived.

He didn't notice her. Hidden in the shadows, she held

her breath as he went by, but it was apparent he expected
no one to be there. Mareg stayed frozen against the wall
long after he had gone. When at last she moved, she found
that her hands were trembling, and her legs were weak.

She would not have noticed that anyone had been in the
storeroom had she glanced in casually. But the evidence
was there, behind an old pile of half-broken stools. There
was an old chest, and behind it, another. Most of the items
in the room were covered with dust. The first chest had
clean streaks in its dust; the one behind it was mostly clear
of dust. Mareg opened it.

It was full of gold. Pouches and pouches of gold coins.
Mareg closed the chest and sat back on her heels for a moment, thinking. Then she stood up abruptly and left without her cloak. She had no desire for her husband or his ally
to know she had been anywhere near her chambers this
night. Especially when they discovered, as they eventually
would, that the gold was missing.

SIXTEEN

*K*EEPING TO THE RIVER WAS SAFEST, THEY thought, and by unspoken consensus they decided to stay on the river without putting in to shore for as long as possible. The boat had a good anchor, a large, smooth stone with grooves around which heavy line had been wrapped. There was a lot of line, so they were able to anchor well offshore in the evenings. They had rigged a shelter in the back of the boat from an oiled cloth that was apparently for just this purpose.

Forentel spent a fair amount of time alone in this shelter, letting the two men talk. Erba sometimes tried to bring her into the conversations, but she avoided involvement whenever possible, and Filfa tried to discourage her. She couldn't forget the kiss, and the memory of the way Erba had pulled away from her burned in her mind.

She preferred to spend her time with Sunrise. At least the animal appeared to like her presence. She didn't know what to think about the wolf any more than she knew what to think about herself. She hoped there would be answers for her in Dreffir.

Despite the city's presence on the map they had been given, she was beginning to doubt either its existence or the possibility that she might ever reach it. She was also afraid of what she might find if she did reach it. What if they were all like her there? It would be, she thought, a city of monsters.

The river had broadened out again, and slowed. There were vast fields of water flowers, whose long stems reached way down to the riverbed, but whose heads poked above the surface in a profusion of pink, white, and yellow blossoms. From a distance they saw something vast in one of the reed beds, a huge animal with a round head and tiny eyes that stared at them and then submerged completely. They kept their distance from it, hoping no more were close by.

"What if we ran into one under our boat?" Forentel wondered, but neither man answered.

One morning Forentel woke well before dawn. She had elected to sleep on the deck that night, giving the men the shelter. Through half-closed eyes she saw Filfa making his way back to the shelter.

Sunrise had curled up beside her during the night, keeping her warm and fending off the disturbing dreams that had begun to plague her. The wolf did not stir as Forentel rose and made her way to the bow where she settled herself with her cloak around her. Although the others left her alone, she did not feel truly private unless they slept, when she knew she had her thoughts to herself, as she did now.

So she was supposed to be the Delass. *A bridge. A bridge to what?* She closed her eyes, feeling the gentle rocking of the boat in the river. At the edges of her mind she thought she could feel the approach of the sun; soon it would be dawn. They would have to go to shore sometime soon, as their supplies were beginning to run thin. Could she find out what was on the shore before they visited it? Could she be true to whatever Illiana thought she was, could she bridge that distance? If there were other people there, people of Tirdar descent, perhaps she could. But how? When she had made contact before, she had known who it was she was seeking, and why. Now she didn't even know if anyone was there.

She sat and let her mind drift, in a gray haze that was close to sleep. She was peripherally aware of the birds beginning the dawn chorus, of the little insects that flitted over the water. She could sense a vastness, the impression of many nonhuman lives, but she did not dare let herself be drawn in. There were other human minds out there.

There were many of them. She received only vague impressions, but they were there. She struggled harder. She could not read their individual thoughts, but the minds of some of them were fierce, filled with feelings of delight in battle, thinking of raids, the emotions hard and strong. She sent her mind after them. These people were intense in their love of winning, of proving their worth through besting their enemies. She reached farther. She felt it was younger men especially, and even boys, seeking to prove their manhood, but also older men, needing to maintain their reputations and their mastery. The women were fierce, too. The women took pride in their men, wanted them to take advantage of anyone they could, to prove their strength. It was becoming clearer now, the way these people thought; it was becoming so clear, and in another moment she would be able to feel their individual minds, their individual thoughts.

The snarl brought her out of her trance, and Forentel

opened her eyes. Sunrise was standing on the deck in the light of the rising sun, all the fur on her back raised. In the water near their boat were dozens of swimmers. Most had knives in their teeth, and they were almost at the boat.

Forentel screamed. Erba was there before she could draw breath to scream again. His sword was already in his hand.

"Get the bow and the quiver!" he shouted when Filfa emerged from the little shelter a moment later. Filfa dashed back inside.

"The anchor." Erba sounded completely calm. "Get the anchor up, Forentel, and row, if you can. Get us out of here."

Forentel ran for the anchor. It would not come up at first. It seemed to have caught on something, and she pulled at it desperately. She felt the boat rock, and Sunrise was snarling loudly. She glanced up and saw that some of the swimmers had reached the side of the boat and were attempting to climb aboard. Filfa was firing arrows as quickly as he could. Some of the swimmers cried out, and two of them sank without a sound beneath the surface.

Sunrise crouched down, and as one man came over the side, she grabbed his arm in her mouth. She snarled again, and the man began screaming in hoarse bursts of sound. Then Sunrise was backing away, and Forentel saw that she had a hunk of flesh in her mouth.

Forentel felt slightly dizzy. She turned back to the anchor and tugged again. Still nothing happened. She kept pulling, feeling muscles strain and pop, and behind her she heard Filfa shout, a shout that was broken off suddenly. Erba was shouting, too, and the boat was rocking, and other people were screaming. She put her back into pulling at the anchor and felt it begin to give. She hauled harder, and it began to rise. River weeds streamed from it: the reason it had become entangled. She stepped back and started to pull it toward her and into the boat.

One of the attackers swam around toward her. He was a small brown man with a knife in his teeth, which did not stop him from grinning. His thoughts radiated anticipation; Forentel did not want to probe any more deeply than that. The anchor was almost in her hands; it hung from a short length of line, dripping with water and weeds. The swimmer reached for the side of the boat, and Forentel swung the anchor. It caught the man on the side of the head. He flailed, and the knife fell from his teeth. He sank beneath the surface, and a red stain began to spread across the water. She had a fuzzy impression of pain, fear, and then suffocation.

She drew back, feeling sick. She had just killed a man. Bile rose in her throat, and she thought she might vomit, but she pulled the anchor all the way over the side and onto the deck.

There was a battle on the deck. A few of the swimmers had managed to climb over the side. Sunrise was uninjured and seemed to be holding her own, in large part because the attackers were afraid to go near her. Two of them were managing to hold her off, however, by crouching and feinting with their long knives.

Filfa had dropped his bow and was struggling hand to hand with one of the attackers. He was unarmed, but somehow he was managing to keep his enemy at bay, trying to get the knife he wielded. But even as Forentel watched, Filfa slipped on the deck. His attacker was joined by a second, and then Filfa was down.

Erba had both his sword and a knife taken from an attacker, and he was faring far better than his tutor. There was a small heap of bodies at his feet, and as Forentel watched, he ran another attacker through with the sword and almost simultaneously swiped the knife sideways with his other hand, cutting a long arc across someone's stomach. The second man fell back, screaming, into the water.

The move had looked almost accidental, but there was no way it could have been.

There were still more swimmers in the water. So far she had been lucky, having had to deal with only one attacker, but obviously that was going to change soon. Forentel left the anchor on the deck. She ran to the stern, avoiding the fight as best she could in such a tight space, and tore the oiled cloth down from the shelter supports in her haste to find the sail. Erba had told her to row, but she knew she could never outdistance the swimmers by rowing. Besides, a breeze had sprung up. Panting, she managed to raise the sail and trim it. She hauled hard on the tiller, and the boat swung away from the island.

One of the attackers had seen what she was doing and ran across the deck to her. She could feel his emotions without even trying: rage and fury, both at what had happened to his friends and because his prey might escape. This was a disaster, but he thought he might redeem himself. If he could bring home the heads of the men and a live female captive, he could keep his reputation despite the loss of his warriors. With a shock, Forentel saw herself in his eyes as both exotic and desirable, a prize.

The surprise was dangerous. The attacker saw her momentary confusion and took advantage of it to come in close. With one leap he was beside her. He grabbed her throat, choking her, pulling her against him and away from the tiller. The sheet slid from her hand and the sail lost its trim. The boat, which had been picking up speed, coasted to a stop, sail luffing.

Forentel pulled ineffectually at the hands around her throat. For a small man, her captor was incredibly strong. He pulled her so her face was mere inches from his, her body tight against him. He released her throat and grabbed her arms with one hand, twisting them behind her. He was grinning. She looked into his eyes and saw the grin reflected there, too. He rubbed his body against hers, leaving no doubt what he wanted with her, as if she couldn't see it in his thoughts. Then he lifted his fist and punched her in the side of the head. As she slid into darkness she heard growling and then a scream from right above her.

Erba saw Forentel raise the sail and saw the savage grab her. He thought of anyone not Tireeran as a savage, but these people seemed to fit the definition better than most. He could feel the fierce rage and joy rolling off of them; it seemed part of their nature.

When Forentel raised the sail and the boat responded, Erba had managed to shove several of the savages into the water. The boat was moving quickly, and he knew they would be left behind. He blessed Forentel as the boat picked up speed. Filfa was down and needed help, but he couldn't go to his friend until he had dealt with the three men attacking him. He was engaged with one of the savages when the wind spilled out of the sail and the boat stopped. He saw the savage grab Forentel, but there was nothing he could do. He risked a glance to the side and saw the wolf tearing out the throat of one of the men. Good; one less for him to deal with. Then Forentel's captor hit her hard on the side of the head, and she dropped into his arms like a sack of grain. He could almost read the man's mind; he thought he could help his friend kill Erba and then take their heads, and then take Forentel with him back to his village.

Erba felt a fury come over him. His opponent seemed to have had some training in sword skill, for he had been using his long knife almost like a sword, and he had been keeping out of Erba's reach. Erba had been treating him with caution, but no longer. He fought like one possessed. He fought for his own life, but it was more than that. He fought to go to the aid of Filfa, but he also fought because the thought of Forentel in anyone else's hands was more

than he could bear. His opponent was dead almost before
he knew what he had done. He yanked his sword free of the
body and turned, expecting to meet the remaining barbarian. He heard a scream and realized that he was too late.

The wolf stood over the bodies of Forentel and the barbarian, and Erba stared, frozen. Sunrise had ripped out the
man's throat and also part of his chest. Erba could see the
man's heart, still pulsing erratically. The deck was awash
in blood, and the wolf was snarling. Erba swallowed. He
wanted to go to Forentel, but he also wanted to back away.
He scarcely dared breathe with the wolf's yellow eyes on
him. Then the animal turned away and bent over Forentel.

Erba had crossed the deck in the time it took to breathe.
He was beside the wolf before he realized that Forentel was
in no danger from the animal. Sunrise was sniffing her face
and gently licking her, but she stopped and looked up at
Erba. Erba froze again, seeing something in those eyes, an
intelligence both alien and familiar. Then the wolf moved
aside.

IT WAS DARK when she awoke, and her head hurt so
much that it was hard to open her eyes, so for a while she
didn't. She simply lay there, breathing, hurting. Then she
became aware of voices, of one voice in particular. After
another age of time and pain, her head cleared a little
more, and she realized it was Erba's voice. She remembered the attack, she remembered the man who seized her,
and she opened her eyes.

She was on the deck of the boat, wrapped in a blanket.
Erba was sitting beside her, a darker shape against the
night. A crescent moon was over his right shoulder, and the
stars were beginning to prick through the velvet darkness.
The warm bulk against her side was the wolf. There was
another dark bundle; she could barely see it against the

deck. She realized, after a moment, that it was Filfa. Erba was still speaking, saying something in a low voice, a murmur. After another long moment the words made sense. He was praying.

"If ever you have heard my prayer before, Lord Falcon of Brightness, hear me now," he was whispering. "Do not take them from me; they are all I have. I promise you, I promise—" His voice broke, and he sobbed, gently caressing Forentel's hair.

Forentel tried to sit up. It was mistake, and she moaned. Erba's sobs ceased abruptly, and he leaned over her.

"Forentel! You're awake! Are you all right? Can you see me?"

"I'm going to be sick." She suited the action to the word, turning her head. There wasn't much to come up, but she felt a little better when it was over. She felt Sunrise shift against her side, a comforting warmth. The wolf whined.

"She saved your life," said Erba. He put an arm around her shoulders and helped her to sit up.

It was too taxing to sit up unaided, and she leaned against him.

"Are they gone?" she whispered.

"They are. Except for one. He will not be a problem." His voice was grim, and but she didn't have the energy to ask for an explanation.

She could hear the water rushing against the side of the boat, and after a moment she realized they were under sail; Erba had tied down the sheet. They were sailing in the dark, with no one at the helm. Adrenaline shot through her.

"Where are we?" She was struggling to pull away from him now. "Erba, we can't sail at night; we can't see where we're going!"

"I'll set the anchor soon. I wanted to be well away from those savages. Well away." He leaned forward and gently brushed the hair away from her eyes. "I'll set the anchor now," he said, and left her.

She sat on the deck, half covered in the blanket, still feeling the touch of his hand on her face. After a moment she could hear him on the deck, taking down the sail, and then the sound of the anchor hitting the water. She sighed with relief as she felt the boat cease its progress.

The night didn't seem quite as dark now, although perhaps it was only that her eyes were more accustomed to it. She could see the outline of the shore, comfortingly far enough. And she could see the bundle on the deck that had to be Filfa. She remembered seeing him go down in the fight. Erba had said nothing about him; surely he would have, if his old friend had died. She felt suddenly cold and drew the blanket around her. If Filfa had died, it was because of her. They would not have been attacked at all, if not for her. Erba returned and crouched by her on the deck.

"Filfa," she said, trying not to look at the dark mass on the deck. "Is he—?"

"He's alive, but he's badly hurt. Very badly." She heard the quiver in his voice despite his attempt to hide it. "I wanted to ask you to help him, if you are well enough."

That was, of course, the reason for his gentleness with her, his consideration. He needed her help to heal Filfa. Her head still hurt, and she felt shaky and weak, but if Filfa still lived, she had no choice; she must try to heal him. Sunrise gripped her wrist gently with her teeth as she tried to rise, and she had the distinct impression that the wolf wanted her to stay where she was, wanted her to rest.

"Let me go," she said to the animal. "I have to." The wolf released her, and Forentel, unable to walk, crawled to Filfa.

She wasn't sure what she had expected, but whatever it was, this was worse. He was indeed alive, and he was even conscious, as she discovered when she tried to move him.

He moaned, and even in the darkness she could the whites of his eyes. She could feel a thick wetness on his shirt and on his trousers. There was a horrible smell.

"Light," she said. "I need to see." She knew they shouldn't give their position away to anyone who might be on the shore, but there was nothing for it. She needed to see her patient. Erba lit not a torch but a candle and shielded it from the shore.

Forentel gasped. Filfa's shirt and trousers were soaked with blood. She drew his shirt away and saw the jagged wound that started just above his waist. She reached for his trousers to pull them down. Filfa tried to put his hands over hers.

"No," he said. His voice was barely more than a whisper.

"I have to," she said. "I'm sorry."

Gentle though she was, he cried out in pain, and then she saw the cause of the smell. His abdomen had been pierced, and worse. Even in he light of the candle she could see the loops of his intestines. She drew back, feeling sick.

"Heal him, Forentel, I know you can." Any remaining skepticism Erba had was banished by his need.

She could sense his eyes on her as she bent over Filfa. The first thing she felt was a flash of annoyance. Erba had done nothing to help Filfa, nothing but give him water and wrap him in a blanket, as he had her. Then her annoyance vanished. There wasn't anything else he could have done. She reached out gently and put her hand on Filfa, and tried to do as she had done the previous times. She tried to send her mind, her thoughts, into the ruined body before her, to help it heal.

She felt herself sinking down, following the flow of his blood. She tried to call on the strengths that Filfa had within him to heal him, but there were none left. Whatever had been there had been drained by his wounds and by time. Every organ in his body was affected. When she tried to follow his blood, it was thin and weak, most of it drained from his wound. She started to pull back. She would have to tell Erba that she could not help him. Filfa would die. She realized that Filfa knew this already; perhaps approaching death made it easier for her to feel what was in his heart. He still did not like her, but he desperately wanted her to save him, and yet he knew she could not.

"She has the magic, Erba, she has it." Filfa's voice was barely audible. "She has it, but she can't use it for me." The words came out in a moan.

"She will," said Erba earnestly. "We have seen what she can do; she'll save you. You will, Forentel, won't you? You must! Don't fear, Filfa, she will."

"Erba, I can't."

"Forentel, you must." Erba set the candle down and took her shoulders and looked into her eyes, willing her to see how important this was. "I know Filfa has not been kind or courteous to you, but he meant nothing ill, truly; it is just the way he is. He meant nothing ill toward you," he repeated.

"He did," said Forentel, "not that it makes the least difference. I would save him if I could, Erba, especially since I . . . since it is my fault he was wounded." She hadn't meant to say it, but it slipped out. "I felt people on the shore, I was trying to see if I could understand what they were like, so we would know, so we would have warning. I think I must have called them to us."

She didn't wait for his reaction. She turned from him and bowed her head over Filfa. She put her hands over him, not touching him but just slightly above his wounds, and she sent her consciousness down into his ruined body.

Filfa didn't have the strength to heal. She already knew it. She knew it was hopeless, yet she had to try, so she began to pour her own strength into him, hoping it would be enough. There were all those places where the blood was still leaking out; she must try to seal them. Somehow she must close Filfa's intestines back into him; how could that be possible? And she must strengthen his heart, and stop the leaking of all the other fluids for which she had no name.

She could feel Filfa's strength increase, but it was not enough. She poured more of her own resources into him. She had been shaky to begin with, and now she knew her own strength was failing, and not just her strength. She was dimly aware of the world outside her bond with Filfa, but she could not return to it; she could not break free of this link. She could keep Filfa alive a little longer, but that was all. She could not save him, and when he died, so would she, if she did not die before him. Part of her wanted to die with him, in penance for having cost him his life, for having brought down this attack on them. Part of her wanted desperately to live, but she could not break free of the bond she had formed with Filfa, not in her already weakened state.

Then there was a presence with her in this odd no place, something warm and comforting and strong. Someone wanted her out of there, wanted to save her, wanted her alive, cared about her. Something was whining, pulling at her. Forentel opened her eyes to find Sunrise licking her face. She was lying on her side, and her clothes were covered with blood; apparently she had collapsed across Filfa before Sunrise pulled her off. She put her arm shakily around the wolf and then looked up into Erba's white face. Her headache was back.

"I can't save him," she said and closed her eyes.

"That's what I tried to tell you, but you never did listen when you didn't want to, Erba," Filfa said weakly. "Never, since you were a small child. Even a witch as strong as this one hasn't got the power to stop death. But she did give me some strength for a little longer."

"Filfa, save your strength. You will recover—"

"Stop it, Erba. Listen to me. I will not recover, and I have not much time left, only what the Tirdar witch gave me. The attack was not her fault; at least it may not have been. I signaled the shore." Filfa began to cough.

"What—you don't know what you're saying." Erba was cradling the older man.

"I know exactly what I'm saying. I signaled the shore. I thought—" He coughed again. "I thought Kelern might be there." He fell silent, breathing slowly. Forentel could feel his life ebbing away.

"Why?" Erba sounded lost. "Why? He would kill us."

"Not us. You. But he promised me he would not. He promised he would take you back to Tireera. I never thought we would get this far. I promised your brother you would not reach Dreffir, that it would not happen. That you would be safe away from him, you would never challenge—" He coughed again, this time for longer. "I thought you would be safe with me, we would go away from the city, live a new life. It would be all right; Mirta would forget us. But Mirta sent Kelern; he knew you better than I. And now Dreffir is close, so very close. So I made a bargain with Kelern not to kill you but to take you back. You must not go to Dreffir, you must not." He fell silent. The only sounds were those of his slow breathing and Sunrise panting softly.

"Why?" said Erba again. "Why can't I go to Dreffir? Why must I not reach Dreffir? Uncle, why?"

When there was no answer, Erba reached out and touched the other man's face gently. Then he sat back on the deck and put his face in his hands, sobbing in great rasping shudders.

Forentel watched him without moving. She closed her eyes again, still lying on the deck. There was an empty space where Filfa had just been, but a sense of him lingered, moving away, as if on some unfathomable journey. He tugged at her, as if she should follow him, but she pushed the faint tendril of contact away, and then it was gone.

Erba's sobs continued. She could feel that he was wounded, too, in his soul. He grieved far more for Filfa than for his father. She understood. She understood, too, not just his sense of abandonment but of betrayal. His pain was intense, and it exhausted her further just to be near it. Still lying on the deck she reached out and found his hand, covering it with hers.

SEVENTEEN

QUEEN SIRIKANYA OF DREFFIR LEANED across the table to pour another glass of fruit juice for her visitor. She needed no servant to perform this task. Not only was the queen accustomed to performing these little tasks herself, but her visitor was more than a close friend. The visitor was her sister. The sisters had never adhered to formality in private. The sunlight streamed in across the carved wooden table, strewn with the remains of breakfast in the queen's private quarters.

"It has been so long since anyone has come so far; are you sure, Siri?" Sariya accepted the glass and tried not to gulp it. She had been out with her troops since before dawn, and she was thirsty. She liked to see the elephants herself, not just her own elephant Mae, but to check on the other handlers. She had known her own Mae for most of her life, since the animal was a calf. This was true for almost all the members of the elite Elephant Corps, but Sariya, as its commander, took nothing for granted.

"I am sure. It's not just what I have seen, but Larar has confirmed it."

"I can't dispute the Old Man of the Mountain. Our brother has never seen false yet. But why now, why after all these years? Our cousins to the north have sent no one, and even their Raffa has not reached us in decades. The link is tenuous, if not broken." Sariya had reasons more serious than idle curiosity behind her questions. If Dreffir faced a threat, it was up to her to meet it. "Their conquerors may be heading southward."

"Perhaps, but I don't think so. That's not what I felt. A few of them are coming to us for reasons of their own." Sirikanya held up her hand to forestall her sister. "One of them is the lost ones' Delass."

Sariya stared at her sister and then rose abruptly to her feet. "We had best be prepared," she said. "The times become more dangerous now."

"True," agreed the queen, "but there are many ways to prepare."

"I will see to the troops," said Sariya. "You see to all those other ways."

"I will." Sirikanya smiled fondly at her sister. "Don't worry. I will, indeed."

"I DON'T UNDERSTAND why he doesn't—he didn't—want me to go to Dreffir." Erba was calm now, not past grief, but in its lull.

He was sitting on the deck beside Forentel, with Sunrise lying nearby. He had brought water and some cheese for them, and Forentel had eaten. She felt a little better, although she was still covered in Filfa's blood, and she still had a headache. Erba had taken the body of his tutor to the stern of the boat and had covered it with a blanket. They would have to bury him, Forentel supposed, although she shied away from thinking about it. What she wanted most was to get clean.

"Finding Dreffir was a dream for so long. Filfa is the one who ignited my interest. He is the one who encouraged me all those years. Why now would he not want me to go?"

"There is something in that city that is dangerous to the Virsat." Forentel was feeling her way, thinking out loud. "It's why Illiana sent me there. Not just to learn about my family, although there is that, but because what I might learn there will change things. There is something there, and I think Filfa knew what it was." She looked at Erba. "It makes sense, as much as anything does about that place." She sighed with frustration. "I wonder if Dreffir is even real. I know we have the map, but maps can lie, since they are made by men." She sounded more bitter than she intended.

Erba was silent for a moment. Then he said, "It's real. And we are not that far from it." He raised his hand to fore-stall her comment. "Come with me. There is something you should see."

Forentel got to her feet and followed him. There were two bodies, as it turned out, at the stern of the boat. One was Filfa's, wrapped in its blanket and very much dead. The other was one of their recent attackers, bound and gagged, but still alive. He twitched and tried to draw back as Erba leaned over him, and his eyes rolled, showing their whites. There were cuts all along his arms and near his eyes. One of his eyes was swollen. Forentel gasped.

"What are you doing with him? Why is he still here?" She was horrified that someone, even a savage such as this, had been left alone and in pain.

"Information," said Erba shortly. "We need it; he has it. I questioned him before, but perhaps you can say if he's telling the truth." He didn't wait to see if she could or if she would agree but reached down and yanked the gag from the man's mouth. "Tell her," he said in Tirdar. "How far are we from Dreffir? Does the city exist?"

Their captive drew a deep and shuddering breath. When he didn't immediately respond, Erba drew his knife and squatted beside him. The man began to tremble.

"No! Erba, don't!" Forentel had no reason to feel kindly toward this enemy who had attacked them, who had wanted to kill and enslave them. Nonetheless, she had no desire to see what Erba might do to him. She had the strong impression that most of the cuts on this man's arms and face had not resulted from the recent fight. Forentel addressed herself to him.

"Answer him," she said. "Answer him truthfully, and he will not harm you." She could only hope the prince would honor her promise.

"The city exists." He focused on her face, carefully avoiding any glance at Erba. "Dreffir exists. They sometimes send—" There was an unintelligible word, but Forentel got an impression.

"An expedition?" she said. "Trade? Soldiers?"

"Yes," he said, leaving her to wonder which. "But they will not deal with us. They will only kill us."

"No wonder there," Erba interjected sourly. Their captive glanced at him, flinched, and looked away again. "How far? How far is it?" Erba reached down, grabbed the man's face, and forced him to look at him.

"Some days only," he whispered. "Maybe a half moon's time." Then he seemed to rally slightly and smirked. "But you will never get there. Fishtlar will swallow you, will smash you. And my friends will be waiting, and we will laugh! I will be there, and I will laugh! Fishtlar will do to you what I did to your friend." He glanced toward Filfa's wrapped body. "I will enjoy watching you die."

"I should make you die the same way, but I will not. Your death will be quick. If you have gods, you can thank them for that." Erba leaned forward and grabbed his captive's hair. Before Forentel could react, he had cut the man's throat.

Forentel swallowed against the sudden nausea and backed away. She had felt a tenuous link with the victim, and she hastily broke it. She had no desire to feel yet another man's life draining away. She staggered away from the flow of blood and sat down hard on the deck. Sunrise came to her and put her huge head on Forentel's lap. She tried not to watch as Erba kicked his victim's body into the water.

"I told him he was safe!" Suddenly she was furious. "Safe if he answered your questions!"

"Well, he wasn't. He would have killed us anyway, at the next opportunity. I did what I must."

"Next time you do what you must, be sure first that I am not linked to your victim, trying to understand him." She was surprised by the fury she felt. "He was our enemy, but he was not garbage; he was a man! I do not want to feel any more men die!"

The sun was rising now. Erba was standing in the growing light, staring at her with astonishment and concern. Forentel turned away from him and walked to the side of the boat with Sunrise following her. She could see now that they were anchored not far from the main current. The current had caught Erba's victim, and the river was carrying the body away. Forentel felt as if she were covered in filth that was more than physical. If only she could swim, she thought, she would dive into the river now and let it cleanse her. Since she could not, she did the next best thing.

There was a bucket on the deck. She grabbed this, leaned over the side, and filled it with river water. Then she stripped off her clothes and poured the water over her. She did this again and again, standing in the light of the rising sun, washing herself.

Erba couldn't take his eyes off her. She looked like a goddess, with the light of dawn behind her. When the prince continued to stare at Forentel, Sunrise growled at him, and he turned away.

Forentel ignored the prince. It was difficult because she could feel his attention on her like heat from a fire. It was also difficult because without even trying she could feel some of his emotions. Even when he turned away, his thoughts circled her, like a moth around a flame.

His feelings were knotted together; one thing she was beginning to understand was that, no matter what they claimed, there wasn't much that was simple about what people felt. Erba was grieving the man who had meant more to him than his father, and he was grieving Filfa's treachery as much as his loss. He was also disgusted with himself for the way he had treated his captive. Tangled up with these emotions were Erba's thoughts about her, and these feelings captured her attention.

Erba thought she was beautiful. Even covered with blood and filth, even bruised and exhausted, she still seemed beautiful to him. He wanted her, but it was more than that. He cared about her, and he did not want to see her hurt. He was astonished by these feelings. He wanted to protect her, but he also feared her as well as feared for her. He feared what she might see within him. He had no way to realize that the last thing she wanted was to see any more of what was within him.

Forentel left the bucket on the deck and stalked past Erba to the remains of their shelter. She rummaged in the pile until she found fresh clothing, and then she dressed without looking up.

Erba was scrubbing the deck, doing his best to clean

away the remnants of battle and death. He was more
shaken than he would ever admit to anyone. The fight,
Filfa's death, those things were terrible. What was almost
as bad was that he didn't want to continue. If he were truthful, he would admit to himself that as much as he wanted to
find Dreffir, he was afraid of finding it. Forentel's words
had awakened a suspicion within him that he couldn't quite
put a name to.

And then there was Forentel herself. He had spent time,
more than enough time he had once thought, trying to determine just what she was. He realized now that he might
have set himself an impossible task, and that both fascinated and infuriated him.

"How far are we from where those—people—attacked
us?"

Erba jumped, dropping his mop with a clatter; wrapped
in his thoughts, he hadn't heard her come up behind him.

"Far enough." He rubbed at his back. Her nearness upset him, and he was afraid she knew.

"I hope so, because we're going to have visitors."

Erba looked where she pointed. She was right. Several
sleek little boats were moving swiftly toward them. They
were not being rowed, they were being paddled in a strange
manner, by one person in the bow and another in the stern.
They were eating up the distance at an incredible rate.

"Are they friendly?" Erba shaded his eyes from the sun,
peering toward them.

"I don't know!" She glared at him. "And by the time I
find out, *if* I can, they will be here! You row; I'll get the sail
up." She ran for the mast, not waiting to see if he would
obey her.

Her fear was that the sail had been torn in the recent
conflict. It had not. She felt the boat begin to move as she
struggled with the sail, and she could feel the power Erba
put into his rowing. It was like a nightmare repetition of the

previous day. She could hear the shouts of those in the sleek little boats as they closed with her boat, but she could not make out the words. And it was true: she could not discern the intentions of their pursuers, and she didn't know if she could if she tried.

She managed to raise the sail. Erba's rowing had brought them out into the clear from the protection of the shore, and the wind caught the sail, just as the current caught them. They pulled away from the people in the little boats. Erba shipped the oars and came to take the tiller. He said nothing. Neither of them spoke, they just concentrated on the river and their rapid progress.

DESPITE HER POSITION as High Judge, or perhaps because of it, Mareg was not a religious woman. She had a healthy skepticism, if not of the gods themselves, then of human ritual and human manipulation of the divine. She had attended the rituals she must, and she had done so with all propriety, but her heart had not been in it. Now, she did not want to ask a priest for help, and she wasn't convinced she could trust one if she did, yet she didn't know what else to do. It only made matters worse to realize that the cause of her distress was political.

If only she could read the signs herself, she would need no help, but of course she could not. The High Priest could read the signs, supposedly, but she didn't trust him. The Priest of the Falcon could read the signs as well, but the Falcon Priest was the king's. The last thing she wanted was for Mirta to learn anything before or unless she wanted him to. Yet Mareg felt a need for divine guidance, and, more mundanely, she felt a need for counsel, and from someone who would not talk. Individuals capable of both reading the signs of the gods and of keeping quiet about it were in short supply among the Virsat of Tireera. After

much consideration she came to the reluctant conclusion
that she would need to see the Tirdar prophet again.

As soon as she made the decision, acting on it became
more difficult. Her husband had discovered that his gold
was missing. Although he had no reason to suspect Mareg,
he trusted no one, and she knew he was having her
watched. Escaping the city and going to the Dawn Shrine
began to seem impossible.

She was also afraid that Nedriff would uncover the hiding place of his purloined funds. She had hidden the gold
in their own house, at the back of the root cellar, hastily
buried. It had taken her many trips to bring the bags of
coins there safely, but she was not convinced they would
remain safe. She needed a better place for them. Now she
couldn't move them without her husband discovering what
she had done, and worse, Brezat might find out.

At least she was able to walk in the king's garden, and
she did so often. She did not dare approach Bilop's area, as
she was guarded by her own servants and also watched by
her husband's spies, but she had no wish to. She walked in
the garden in the evenings, hoping the quiet would help her
to think, and to sort out her thoughts. Her watchers, both
official and clandestine, became accustomed to this habit.

One evening she sat on the stone bench in a little thicket
of flowering spike bushes. The bushes were watered by
hardened ceramic pipes that had been set into the soil so
cleverly that most visitors didn't realize they were there.
Mareg knew only because Bilop had once pointed them out
to her and had showed her how the pipes opened up at the
roots of the bushes. This kept the precious water from
evaporating into the dry air. It was a private spot, and
Mareg sat there breathing in the perfumed scents from the
spike flowers.

She had come to the conclusion that there was no
choice that was best for Tireera. The old king had no

longer been capable of ruling, but when her husband and
Brezat had helped Mirta to murder his father, no good had
been done. Mirta was too unstable to govern well; perhaps
the Falcon god had taken revenge in this way for the murder of one of his own, although Mareg doubted this. After
all, Mirta was the Falcon's, too, and royal murder was
scarcely an innovation. Erba might have proved a better
ruler, but he was young in too many ways, and now he was
gone. Murdered like his father, some whispered, while others said he had fled with Filfa. In either case he was gone,
just as Forentel was gone. Mareg tried to ignore the sharp
pain in her heart that came whenever she thought of her
elder daughter.

"And now it appears that the next king will be Brezat or
Nedriff your husband, unless you can prevent it. But you
cannot think how."

The words, and something brushing against her knees
caused Mareg to start, and she jumped up, stifling a cry.
She looked down into the amber eyes of a desert cat, a
large, tawny creature that blinked up at her, tail twitching.
She gasped and tried to edge back from it. She could see
her own guards nearby, outside the little thicket of spike
bushes. They were looking around the garden, and a couple
were in relaxed conversation. It seemed impossible that a
wild animal as large and dangerous as this could have not
not only entered the garden but passed her guards. She
drew breath to scream.

"If you scream," said the cat, "you will call them down
on us. Then we will not be able to speak. You will not be
able to ask me those questions you so much want to ask."

Mareg knew her mouth was open, and she closed it with
a snap. This was not possible. She closed her eyes just for a
moment. When she opened them again, the cat was gone,
and Illiana, the woman from the shrine, stood there. She
was young this time, with dark, curling hair, and she was

dressed in ordinary Tirdar clothing. She seated herself on the bench where Mareg had so recently rested, and patted the stone beside her. Warily, Mareg sat.

"How?" Mareg croaked. She swallowed and tried again. "How did you get in here?"

"Oh, I am not really here," said Illiana cheerfully. "If you had screamed or called your guards, they would not have found me."

Mareg stared at her for a moment more, and then, without warning, leaned over and grabbed Illiana's arm. It felt solid enough. She said so.

"You feel quite present to me," she said. She dropped the other woman's arm, resisting the urge to wipe her hand.

"Keep your voice low. They out there cannot hear me, but they can hear you well enough." Illiana settled back comfortably. "Do you want me to attempt to explain how it is I am both here and not here, or shall we discuss what is on your mind?"

"I, I—"

"Good. We shall discuss the reason you wished to see me. I am not certain you would understand the other, in any event." She smiled again. "I am not certain that I can explain it. So, the problem remains; you believe the next king will be Brezat if you cannot prevent it."

Mareg drew in a deep breath. Questions about Tirdar magic would have to wait. She had been incapable of going to Illiana, but the prophet had somehow come to her.

"Brezat will be a terrible king," she said. She drew another breath. "I think my husband wants the throne himself. Unfortunately, he will not be much better."

"Would he be better than Mirta?"

"Yes," said Mareg slowly. "For a little time, perhaps. But I do not think he can govern well for long. I wish there were someone, someone who could govern the city and all the outlying villages, someone who could govern justly."

She was sick of all the family interest that lay like a swamp beneath this matter of governing.

"Do you mean govern both Virsat and Tirdar?"

"Of course." Only after she spoke did Mareg take the time to think about the question. She realized that this was, in fact, what she had meant, but it was not the way most Virsat nobles would have heard the question, let alone answered it. The evening breeze ruffled through the blossoms and blew some of them to their feet. The sun had set abruptly, and it was turning cool. Mareg shivered.

"Will General Nedriff govern both peoples fairly?"

"He will not." Mareg shivered again.

"You wanted to ask me to read the signs, High Judge, to read the signs for the future of Tireera, of this ancient city. You did not ask me to read the signs for you, or for your family, as so many would have, but for the sake of the people. Yet the two are intertwined."

"Are you saying the signs show that Nedriff will be king?"

"I am not. The signs show he wishes it, but it must not be."

"Brezat would be worse." Mareg felt only a faint wonder to find herself talking of these things without explanation. Illiana obviously needed no explanations. In an obscure way, Mareg was grateful. "Brezat has only self-interest to answer to."

"There is one person only who can govern fairly and with dispassion."

Mareg looked her question.

"You," said Illiana, smiling.

Mareg stared at her and then laughed.

"Lady Mareg!" called one of the guards. "Are you well?"

"Yes, yes, I merely laughed remembering something." After a moment's wait, it became apparent that the guard would not come into the thicket. Mareg sighed, and turned back to Illiana, half expecting to find her vanished. "I cannot govern," she said flatly. "I am not royal." Although, she thought, that would not slow either Brezat or her husband. "And I am a woman and therefore not suited."

"You are more suited than anyone." Illiana was no longer smiling. "You care about the city and all in her. You would govern fairly. You *will* govern fairly."

Mareg heard the stress on the word *will* and swallowed hard. She had wanted Illiana to read the signs for her, but she had not wanted this.

"Do not be so concerned. You will not govern forever, only until they return. Surely there have been women who governed as regents among the Virsat. And we Tirdar have always had queens."

It was true, there had been women as regents. Mareg had no desire to be one of them, and besides, for whom? "Until who returns?" When Illiana did not answer, she raised her voice. "Until who returns? You are not making sense!"

"Lady! Lady Mareg!" There was the sound of guards running toward the thicket.

"There must be a bridge between our peoples," said Illiana, "if we are to live together as we must." She smiled and patted Mareg gently on the arm. It felt very real to Mareg. "You will need those funds to keep the government running. Don't fear, you will do well, when you must. You are regarded with respect, lady, by Virsat and Tirdar alike, and also with admiration."

A guard was pushing into the thicket, but Illiana seemed unconcerned.

"Forentel is still well," she said. "She will reach out to you when she is able."

Mareg gasped. Two guards were beside her now, but there was no sign of Illiana. Suddenly, another guard shouted.

"Look there! A desert cat!"

Mareg and the guards ran from the thicket. Sure enough, a large, tawny animal was leaping over a hedge in the dusk. When the guards turned to run after it, swords drawn, Mareg called them back.

"It did not harm me," she said. "It only frightened me, but I believe I frightened it more. Besides, you will never catch it."

EIGHTEEN

*W*E ARE PULLING OUT OF THE RIVER HERE.
Or as soon as we see a good spot to land. And then we'll
scout, or I will." Erba barely glanced at her when he spoke,
but his tone was adamant. He had withdrawn into himself
over the past several days, speaking to her when he must,
but guarding his thoughts and his emotions. His grief still
leaked through, she could feel it, especially at night, when
he slept on the deck under the stars and left the shelter to
her and to the wolf, but there was a shell of brittle hardness
around him.

They had not buried Filfa. They had not dared to put in
to shore to bury him. According to tradition, he should have
been returned home, his body given to the Falcon Priests
for their rites, and then, after two moon cycles, buried in
the family tomb. Obviously, this was impossible. In the

end, Erba had whispered some words to Filfa, something that Forentel had not been able to overhear. Then he had wrapped his tutor's body in a cloak, weighted it with weapons their attackers had left behind, and cast it over the side. Forentel had gone to stand beside Erba, watching while the body sank. She could feel Erba's grief and torment like a wound, like a disease. She had reached out and gently put her hand on his shoulder, but he had turned away.

"We need to get off the river now."

"Why?" She knew they needed to land soon, but why the rush to pull over immediately? "The current is good here. It's the fastest it's been, and we are making good progress. If Dreffir exists, we will get there faster this way." Forentel was tired of the tension between them, and she wondered again why it had to be so difficult. He wanted her, and more than just physically, but he pushed her away. He needed comfort, but he was afraid of her. All she wanted, for now, was a friend and a helpful traveling companion; it was that simple. It didn't appear she would have one in him.

"The current is too fast. It will bring us right up on Fishtlar. We don't want to do that. We will want to go around."

She had forgotten the savage's warning. After her experience on the island of the plant, she should have known better than to disregard this information, sketchy though it was.

"What kind of monster will this Fishtlar be?" she wondered. She was not in the least eager to face whatever it was; going around it, if possible, seemed an excellent idea. To her surprise, Erba grinned.

"I think I know exactly what kind of monster it is," He sounded smug, pleased with himself, and not inclined to let her in on the secret. Forentel was disgusted.

"It won't get us, though, not if I can help it." Erba seemed unaware of her reaction. "Strike the sail. Look over there; I think we can put in there."

"There" was a small sandy beach in the midst of a green so intense that it almost hurt the eyes. A profusion of trees and long grasses spilled out into the river. As Erba rowed in closer, a huge square head topped with little ears broke the surface of the water. The enormous gray animal regarded them with tiny eyes before it grunted and submerged again. They had seen these before, from a distance, but never one so close. Sunrise barked at it. Forentel tried to hush the wolf, fervently hoping they had done nothing to disturb the strange beast.

They beached the boat. Land felt strange to Forentel; it had been days since they had come off the river. Their food was running low, but they hadn't wanted to risk it, not even after they were fairly certain they had left the land of their attackers behind. Erba began immediately making up a pack for traveling.

"I won't be gone more than a few days at most," he told her. "I suggest that you camp back into the jungle a little. It's tempting to stay with the boat, but that might make you a better target. If Sunrise will stay with you," he looked slightly askance at the wolf, who was rolling in the sand, "you will have some protection."

"You're right, I won't stay with the boat." Forentel began to grab items and stuff them into her own pack. "We aren't splitting up. I'm coming with you."

"You will stay here, where you will be safe. I command it."

Forentel stared at him for a brief moment. Erba stared back, knowing he was provoking her, not even convinced any longer that staying here was best for her, or safest. Had he decided that she would be safer here simply because he so much wanted to have her with him?

Then she laughed.

It was suddenly too much. He had lost everything, his family, his homeland, and his purpose. He tried against all odds to remember that he was a Virsat prince, a prince of Tireera, and that was impossible in the face of laughter from the one person left to him.

"Laugh, then." He glared at her. She wasn't even a pure Virsat. "Go anywhere you want, I will not stop you. But you will not follow me! You have no need for me, since you have your mysterious Tirdar powers." He spat the word *Tirdar* at her as if it were bad-tasting. Then he turned on his heel and marched into the jungle.

Forentel stared after him, frozen with shock. She could feel Erba's upset and turmoil, but it did not stop her own hurt. She stood completely still, listening to him crash away through the vegetation. After a moment she could no longer hear the sounds of his progress over the cries of the birds and the other animal noises.

Something chattered right over her head. When she looked up, a rain of sticks and leaves came pelting down, followed by screeches. There were several furry things in the branches, small creatures with vaguely human faces. They swung by one long arm from the trees, or even more amazingly, by the tail, as they screeched to one another and threw things at her. Forentel took several steps back, away from this tribe of tiny hostile tree dwellers, but before she could more than wonder how to defend herself, Sunrise appeared beside her. The wolf barked twice, sharply, and the furry forest people retreated into the trees, flinging themselves from branch to branch as they fled, still screeching.

"Well, Sunrise," she said, when they had gone, "I guess it's just you and me. I hope. And I'm not even sure where we're going." It occurred to her to take the boat and go back out on the river, but she was reluctant to do so. Erba's warning made the land seem a little safer than the river right now, by a small fraction. As she carefully packed up everything that might possibly be of use that she could carry from the boat, she realized that she might never see

the boat again. It also did not escape her attention that Erba
had taken the map.

HE REALIZED HE was being foolish. The jungle was
dense, green, filled with strange plants and noises, and it
was hot. It gave heat a whole new meaning. He had to take
his knife and hack his way through the thick foliage, and in
no time he was drenched in sweat. The hard work helped to
drain his anger and make him uncomfortably aware that he
had acted like a petulant child. Losing his family was no
excuse; after all, Forentel had lost hers, too. Stomping off
in a huff in the midst of a strange jungle was not at all the
same thing as stomping off in the palace in Tireera. He realized that he might have left Forentel in danger. He
needed to go back to her. He even, he thought, suppressing
the wince he couldn't avoid, needed to apologize to her. He
would never have his old life back again; that was lost forever, but he could build, somehow, a new life. He had best
start now.

It was easy to follow his trail backwards. He had left a
huge swath through the vegetation. As he trudged back, a
swarm of something ran through the trees overhead,
shrieking and chattering. Eventually, he came to the little
clearing at the edge of the shore. The boat was pulled up
there, beached as he had left it. The sail was still rolled up
on the deck, but the covering for the little shelter was gone.
It was obvious that Forentel had taken what she could.
There was no sign of her or of the wolf. Erba spent a little
while calling her name, and even calling for the wolf before he thought to do the obvious and attempt to track her.

It was hard going through the jungle. For whatever reason, Forentel and the wolf had not left such a wide trail, or
such a clear one. Attempting to slip between trees and
vines the way she apparently had, Erba was soon out of

breath, drenched in sweat, gasping, and stuck in something thorny. He gave up trying to imitate her methods then and fell back on hacking with his knife. This was slow going but at least he could proceed without getting stuck again. Then her trail vanished.

He couldn't understand it. The ground was harder here, less amenable to holding footprints, but she hadn't passed by that long ago. There should be at least some bent or broken plants, but there was nothing. He wished he had a sense of smell like the wolf's. He spent more time calling for her, but there was no response. All that happened was that a flock of brilliantly colored birds took to the air, wheeling and calling overhead, making him realize that he could be alerting things far more dangerous than birds to his presence.

Finally he stopped. He sat down beneath one especially large tree with several trunks and wiped his face. He pulled out his waterskin and drank, trying to think rationally. He took out the map, feeling another twinge of concern. Forentel had no map, and she would be lost without one. After he had pored over the map for a while, he realized that he was lost in the jungle *with* a map. He thought he remembered in which direction the river lay, and in which direction it ran. He set off at an angle, hoping to intersect with the river, but farther downstream, where he had a pretty good idea what he would find.

Hours later, he knew he was right. He could hear the river up ahead and to the right. Furthermore, the terrain was becoming slightly more open. Black rock outcrops showed through the soil in some places. He had seen no sign of Forentel, but he hoped she would have gone back to follow the river, too. Now, however, dusk was approaching, and he was still in the jungle. He could hear things back in the trees, and he realized he needed to get somewhere safe for the night.

* * *

SHE HAD RETURNED to follow the river again, but from the shore, not the water. It seemed somehow easiest. Besides, Dreffir was supposed to be a river city, as Tireera was, so following the river had to be a good idea. Nonetheless, it was hard work. The shoreline was not open but was choked with brush and swamp, and more clouds of insects. As the sun began to wester, Sunrise kept closer to her and seemed nervous. A strong image of stopping for the night came into her mind. The wolf was concerned about her and wanted her safe. So she stopped in a relatively open spot and set up her camp. She ate a little of the remaining food and offered to share it with Sunrise, but the wolf turned up her nose at the hard cheese. Forentel fully expected the animal to leave to hunt some dinner for herself, but instead, the wolf lay down in front of her shelter. She lay awake for a long time, unable to sleep, hearing the noises from outside. Eventually, she drifted off.

Something roared, a terrifying sound that made her sit bolt upright, heart pounding. It was pitch-dark in the shelter, but the roar had been distant, so after a while she lay back down. Then, much closer, something screamed. She reached for her knife when she heard Sunrise growl, but when nothing more happened, she lay there tensely. She was certain now that she would never sleep, so it was with a sense of disoriented astonishment that she heard the wolf growling again, and opened her eyes to find light seeping through the gaps in the shelter. Something was crashing in the bushes, and the sound was coming closer. Forentel grabbed her knife and pushed her way out of the shelter and into the light of dawn, ready for an animal attack, or savages or monsters, or whatever the jungle could serve up to her. What she did not expect was what did come out of the jungle.

At first she did not recognize them. Sunrise did not attack them but only growled and then backed up. It was a man, seriously wounded, with blood soaking his clothing, and he carried something. She had a flash of horror that it was Erba, but it was not. It was Kelern, and the thing in his arms was Riessa, or what was left of her. Forentel gasped.

"Can you help us?" Kelern's voice was a raw whisper. "The Falcon must have brought me to you." He sank down, at the end of his strength, and placed Riessa on the ground.

Forentel felt the familiar compulsion to help, but looking at Kelern, she wondered if it would be possible. At first glance it seemed that part of his head had been torn away, but on closer examination she could see it was a big flap of his scalp. His curly brown hair hung from it as if it were a wig. There were wounds in the side of his head, too, as if something enormous had tried to chew him. His left shoulder was a pulpy mass of flesh. How he had managed to carry Riessa was a mystery.

Riessa was even worse. Part of her side had been ripped away, and with a sense of familiar horror Forentel realized she could see part of the other woman's intestines. She swallowed against the nausea, and then put her hand against Riessa's cheek. Her skin was cool to the touch, and for a moment Forentel thought she was dead, but then she saw Riessa's chest rise and fall slowly. But it was her face that was the worst. One eye had been ripped from its socket.

"I don't know if I can help her." Forentel's voice came out strangely. "What happened to you?"

"Animals," rasped Kelern. "Like the desert cats but bigger. There were several of them, one bigger than the others, with long hair around its head and face." He paused, gasping for breath. "They worked together, like dogs in a pack, but they did not expect me to fight them. I did, I fought them, and then I dragged Riessa into a tree, and when it be-

gan to get light they left. And I followed the sound of the
river. And found you. The Falcon brought me to you.
Please, Lady Forentel—"

"Hush." She sat down beside him and put her hand
against his torn head. Perhaps he was open to her because
of the pain, perhaps it was something else entirely, but she
had no trouble feeling her way into his wounds. She could
see immediately that she might be able to save his life. She
went back into her shelter and pulled out her cloak and
wrapped him in it, as he had begun to shiver. Then she
went to Riessa.

She really couldn't understand how it was that Riessa
was alive. Here, too, it was easy for her to reach down inside her patient. She had done this before with Riessa, and
whatever the channels were, apparently they were still
open. There was barely a flicker of life inside all the pain.

"I can't save her." Forentel spoke more to herself than
to Kelern.

"Try." It was a whisper.

Forentel stared at him, surprised. What she saw in his
eyes surprised her even more. Kelern felt a responsibility
for Riessa. It wasn't love, and it wasn't even affection, but
it was there. Without a word, she turned back to Riessa.
She closed her eyes and was almost immediately inside
Riessa, seeing with her other sight.

She had to work fast. She could feel that strange door
opening, the one through which Filfa had gone, and the
long passage behind it. If Riessa was to stay on this side of
the door, she couldn't hold back. She poured all of her energy into repairing what she could, drawing out the little
that remained of Riessa's own strength and adding everything she could from her own. Finally, when she stopped,
she opened her eyes.

She was weak, shaky, and covered with sweat, barely
able to focus on her patient. But when she did, her eyes

confirmed what her healing sense had told her: Riessa would live. Somehow she managed to close up the terrible rip in Riessa's side. Her empty eye socket was no longer dripping pus and blood but was smooth and healed. She breathed evenly now, asleep.

Then Forentel turned back to Kelern. She knew as soon as she looked at him that she would have no time to recover before attending to him, not if she were going to save him. He had been losing too much blood. Without hesitation she crawled over to him and put her hand against him.

It was like plunging into a river of sharp spikes. Where Riessa's pain had been deep and all-encompassing, Kelern's pain was sharp, immediate, and inescapable. But Forentel could swim in this kind of river. She couldn't link with Kelern quite the way she had with Riessa, but it didn't matter. He wanted her there, so he lent her his strength and did not make her search for it.

His strength was considerable, but it wasn't enough. She stopped the bleeding, and she actually began to knit the skin and scalp back into place, but she could not continue, not with both of their strengths so depleted. She felt herself begin to sink and drift, graying, attenuating, thinning out toward the doorway that waited there. She could almost feel what was there on the other side of that doorway, another land, another place much more interesting than this hot jungle, a place where there were people waiting for her.

A force slammed into her like a shock of lightning. That the force was immaterial did not diminish its power in the least. It was warm, golden, and vital, and it pulled Forentel back from the shadowy doorway through which she had begun to drift. It was Sunrise. The wolf wasn't going to let her leave. Forentel had a sense of a warm tongue lapping at her face, of fur against her mind rather than her skin, a sense of comfort, and more than comfort, strength.

The wolf was giving her the strength to continue the healing. She fused their strength together and continued until she knew that Kelern would be able to finish the healing on his own.

When she withdrew from her trance she found herself lying on the ground, so weak she couldn't move. Sunrise was lying half over her, and sprawled near them was Kelern. From the corner of her eye, she could see Riessa, still stretched out, apparently asleep. An ant walked across Forentel's face, but she had neither the energy nor the will to brush it off. She blinked, trying to encourage the insect to leave. Then a hand came down and brushed it away.

"I can see what you did here," said Erba. "You have healed them, healed my enemies."

"Erba," she whispered. "How did you—?" she wanted to ask how he had found her, but she couldn't seem to put the words together. Beside her, she felt Sunrise stir, recovering a little more quickly.

"I am sorry that your work must be wasted," said Erba, "but I cannot allow them to live." He was out of her field of vision again, but she heard it as he drew his sword. Not his knife, but his sword. It seemed he would execute Kelern as a Virsat noble. Forentel doubted that Kelern would appreciate this fact.

"Stop it!" she cried. She forced herself to roll onto her side and began to try to lever herself up off the ground. As she did, she saw Kelern rise to his feet. She gasped in astonishment; had she poured that much healing into him?

"Don't fear, Lady Forentel," he said, "I intend to frustrate our prince and take his head back to his brother."

Forentel saw that Kelern had drawn his sword. The two men faced each other, and then Erba lunged forward. There was the scrape and clash as the two weapons met. She could hear one of the men panting.

She tried to sit up, and after a moment, she managed it.

She wanted to to go to the men, to crawl forward, if necessary, but Sunrise sank her teeth into the cloth of Forentel's trousers. This both held her back and steadied her. Erba and Kelern were moving warily around each other.

"Stop it! I said, stop it!"

She couldn't get to her feet, but she could put considerable force into her voice, and she did so. To her surprise, she actually caught their attention for a moment.

"I will not let you kill each other. Erba, stop!"

"This man intends to kill me." Erba's voice was cold. "You heard him. I will not permit that."

It was true. Kelern had said he would take home Erba's head.

"Kelern." She managed, by sheer will alone, to stagger to her feet, where she stood, swaying.

Kelern looked at her with concern. "I will help you, lady, as soon as I have finished with him. Have no concern for me, and please, have no concern for your own safety. I owe you my life, and I will let no harm come to you."

She wanted to say something, anything, to stop the fight, but before she could think what words could possibly accomplish this, they were at it again. Kelern had leaped forward, taking Erba just slightly by surprise, but that was all he needed. Kelern came right in under Erba's guard, and was going for his throat. Forentel screamed.

"Kelern, stop! You must stop! Please! I command you! Stop!"

To her absolute astonishment, he did.

"I obey you, Lady Forentel, even though it costs me my life."

"Erba," said Forentel, sharply, "stop it, now! Drop that sword!" The command in her voice surprised her. Apparently, it surprised Erba, too, but he obeyed her without hesitation. He did not drop the sword, but he pulled back.

"I will have your word of honor, both of you." Forentel

drew a breath. It was difficult to stand upright without swaying. "There will be, if not true peace, at least a truce between you." When neither of them responded, she lost patience. "I mean it! There is enough of this. You both owe me your lives, if that is the justification you need."

She was tempted to say that she didn't care what they did, and she would go to Dreffir alone, but to her surprise, they both lowered their swords. They nodded warily to each other. Then Kelern came to Forentel and dropped to one knee before her.

"I owe you my life, and I pledge to you that I will always protect you. I am bound to your service now, Lady Forentel. I will hold you up, in any way that you require."

She looked down into his eyes, seeing something strange there. It was gratitude, but it was also awe, and something more. There was a warmth and and a fire in his eyes that she had never seen before anywhere, born of the intimacy of healing.

"Good," she said "because I think I'm going to faint."

The last thing she heard, before the world grayed, was Sunrise barking. The last thing she saw was Kelern's eyes, and the last thing she felt was his arm around her.

When she regained consciousness, she was lying with her head pillowed on a cloak. Sunrise was stretched out beside her. Someone had put a cool cloth on her head. She found that what she really wanted was food. Almost as soon as she thought this, Kelern was there, with cheese and a waterskin. He helped her sit up.

"You need to rebuild some strength," he told her.

He stayed by her while she ate, companionable in his silence. Erba was seated beside Riessa, who was now awake, and he was talking to her in a low voice. Riessa had one hand over her missing eye. When she felt Forentel's gaze, she turned toward her.

"I thought I was dead. Why did you save me?" Riessa pushed herself up and glared at Forentel from her one eye.

"You were dying, yes, and you were almost dead." The last thing she had expected from the Hilan woman was hostility. "Kelern asked me to do what I could."

"So you saved me, but you left me one eye. And scars." She ran her hand over the twisted flesh of her side and abdomen. "I am hideous!"

Forentel stared at her, taken aback. She couldn't think what to say. "I did what I could, and you are alive," she finally said. It sounded weak. "Perhaps if I had known more, I could have helped you more. I'm sorry." But why should she feel guilty? She had truly done her best.

Kelern had a different reaction. He rose from his place beside Forentel and stood over the village woman.

"Watch what you say!" he snapped. "The lady Forentel healed you and saved you, almost at the cost of her own life. You owe her thanks!"

Forentel swallowed. Kelern had felt responsible for Riessa, and had asked that she save her. She had thought he might love Riessa, but what she heard now in his voice didn't indicate it.

"Healed her and saved her," said Erba, thoughtfully, to Kelern. "You told me the large cats ripped her open, so her bowels showed." He turned to Forentel. "You saved her, but you did not save Filfa, whose injury was not as great." There was accusation in his voice.

Forentel stared at him, shocked. She felt much better now that she had eaten, and anger gave her more strength still. "I did what I could for both of them," she said. "I do not hold back what I can do."

She got to her feet and turned from them all. She was furious and near tears. She had almost died today from trying to save lives. No, she *had* saved lives. She had said that

she had done what she could, but she didn't really understand just what it was that she could do. It was then that she
noticed Sunrise was missing. Kelern would have gone to
search for the wolf, if she had requested it, but she would
not. She stood aside from all of them, letting them pack up
the supplies. When they had finished, Sunrise had returned, blood on her muzzle. Forentel got the distinct impression that she was pleased with herself. At least
somebody was, she thought.

NINETEEN

$\mathcal{T}$HEY FOLLOWED THE RIVER AS BEST THEY could. Although they often could not see it, they could hear it, as the current was moving faster now. The men carried all of their belongings, which was fine with Forentel. She was not entirely recovered from the toll the healing had taken on her. Riessa was much weaker still, and had trouble walking. Some of the muscles in her side were twisted now, so that she limped, and she could not seem to keep her balance or judge distance well with her missing eye. Forentel insisted that they stop for frequent rests, but she kept her distance from the Hilan, despite her impulse to try to help.

Sometime during the afternoon they came upon a trail that seemed to parallel the river's course. Kelern thought it was an animal trail, but they followed it all the same, grateful for anything that made their progress a little easier. As they walked they heard a roaring in the distance.

"That," said Erba, "should be Fishtlar."

It was a temptation to continue his aloof and irritated attitude, but Erba resisted it. He told himself repeatedly that Forentel had truly done all she could to save Filfa, but repetition didn't make him believe it. He knew she had been justified in her dislike of his tutor, and he could not shake the suspicion that this had held back her healing. Sometimes she seemed so fragile, but at other times her growing power frightened him. He wanted to protect her, yet he wasn't able to trust her. What made matters worse, and what irritated him even more, was the attention Kelern was now paying to her.

Now he glanced up to see how his remark about Fishtlar had been received. Kelern was walking slightly ahead of Forentel, protectively. Riessa was behind Forentel, struggling to keep up. None of them replied. Forentel held up her hand for a rest and then began to pick out some of the sticker bugs that were clinging around her ankles. Riessa sank down into the long grass. Sunrise sat on her haunches, watching them.

"It's a waterfall," said Erba. "Fishtlar is a waterfall. It must be a big one, from what we have heard."

"Then we had best go around," said Kelern flatly. He went back to studiously ignoring Erba, giving his attention to the immediate surroundings and making it clear that Erba was lucky to be ignored.

Erba glared at Forentel, feeling things slip farther from his control. Nothing was as it should be. Although he couldn't get Forentel from his thoughts, she didn't seem to hold him in much regard. And then there was the wolf. Forentel was not a true Virsat, and that animal was an abomination. He kicked viciously at a root and looked up to find Forentel watching him.

Forentel could feel Erba's thoughts. As clearly as if he had spoken, she felt his confusion and his fear. She also felt his attraction to her and his ambivalence. She felt it, and she understood it. She was not a true Virsat. Why couldn't she have been a normal Virsat, someone like her sister Dreena, perhaps? What would Dreena think if she could see Forentel now, out in the jungle with this strange assortment of companions, and with an animal? Forentel hated herself for what she was. That she couldn't help being what she was made it worse.

She looked down and found the golden eyes of the wolf looking back up at her. She had a link with an animal. No Virsat would ever have such a thing. She was a freak, and Sunrise made that status all the more clear. If only she did not have the wolf following her, perhaps she could pretend, at least, that she were normal. Just as she had felt Erba's thoughts, she knew now that Sunrise felt hers. A deep sadness and hurt flowed out into her, and then the wolf turned and was gone.

Forentel almost called her back, but she didn't. The wolf had always come and gone according to her own whims; she would return when she was ready.

They were back on the trail again, with the trees leaning over them, and they had to push their way through. The roaring had become part of the background, part of the air, something they no longer heard so much as felt. When it grew to a thunder, they couldn't speak to one another, but it was still a shock when they came suddenly out into the open and saw what was before them.

To call it a waterfall seemed the most unimaginative understatement. Forentel stopped completely and stared. When she could think again, she thought it was fortunate they had not followed the river directly, and that they were approaching this incredible marvel obliquely. At first all she could do was look and wonder.

They stood on a rock outcrop, with Fishtlar spread before them. The river they had followed for so long had branched out, and they hadn't even known it. Now all the branches came together again, falling in thunderous streams over dark rock cliffs. Stream after stream spread across the cliff face, across a horseshoe of cliffs, tumbling down and down, for what appeared to to be miles, into misty distances below. Colored birds in some of the trees wheeled and flew near the glittering rainbows of some of the nearer streams. Fog and mist boiled far below. It was some time before she realized that she was wet: the spray from the monster had soaked them all.

Forentel turned to her companions, all doubts and concerns for the moment dispelled by wonder. Riessa was staring at the falls, an odd expression on her face. Sunrise was still nowhere to be seen, and both men were no longer watching the torrent of water but had their eyes on something behind them.

"They won't believe this back in Tireera!" She found she had to shout to make herself heard over the incredible thunder of the water. The men still did not turn. Riessa was now looking behind them, too, and with a sinking feeling, Forentel turned.

Arrayed across the path and into the jungle, cutting them off from any escape, was a squad of warriors. They were all dressed alike in a uniform of short cotton kilts and belted shirts. All were equipped with short swords, and some with bows and quivers of arrows. One man, in the front, apparently their captain, had a short leather vest. He motioned at them in unmistakable sign language: *come.*

They were desperately outnumbered, so they went. Erba and Kelern were both relieved of their swords. One of the men made as if to search Forentel, but she could feel his indecision, and when she glared at him, he drew back, so she kept her knife. None of them touched Riessa.

The soldiers took them back into the jungle but down a different path. Finally, when the roar of Fishtlar had been somewhat diminished with distance, they stopped. Kelern tried to place himself near Forentel. The captain walked over and looked at them all in turn. No one spoke. At last the captain turned to Kelern.

"Who are you, and what do you do here?"

It was Tirdar speech. There were even more differences from the speech of the Tirdar of Tireera than the speech of the Hilan villagers or the pirates, but it was Tirdar, nonetheless, and comprehensible.

"I protect this lady." Kelern now moved to stand directly beside Forentel.

The captain considered this and seemed to accept it, for he turned to Forentel.

"Your purpose!"

Forentel stared back at him. It might be wisest not to be honest about what had brought them.

"This woman needs help," she began, looking toward Riessa. "We were hoping—"

"We are looking for Dreffir." Erba interrupted her, stepping forward.

Forentel had the distinct impression that Erba wanted several things: to draw attention from Forentel, to claim the leadership of their small group, and also, to prove something to himself. Whatever it was he had meant to do, the captain now turned all his attention to Erba.

"Yes," he said. "It is as I thought. You wish to find the holy city. You shall find it. We will take you there. And there you shall remain, if our great queen lets you live."

None of the soldiers answered any of their questions. They were taken down a new trail, surrounded all the time. The captain had informed them that they would not be bound as long as they made no attempt to escape. If they attempted to escape, they would be shot. Looking at his

men, with their lethal-looking short bows, Forentel had no
reason to doubt him. Apparently, none of the others
doubted him, either, for they made no attempts.

They walked without stopping, at a rapid, steady pace
that soon had Forentel exhausted. When Riessa stumbled
and would have fallen, one of the soldiers caught her and
hoisted her like another pack across his shoulders. Riessa
made no complaint. They walked under an endless
canopy of trees. Some of the long-tailed little people
Forentel had seen before swung through the branches, but
she realized now they were animals. She caught tantaliz-
ing hints of their thoughts. More colored birds flew
through the trees. It was a strange and enchanting place,
and Forentel wished she were there under better and different circumstances.

At last they came out again into the open, just as the sun
was setting. They were on the bank of the river again but
nowhere near the falls. They were on a ledge looking down
across a valley. Below them was a city, shining in the light
of the setting sun.

Around the city were fields and a broad road leading toward it. Tiny black dots moved toward the city; people,
Forentel thought. Domed buildings reflected the light,
gleaming.

"That's gold," whispered Kelern. "Some of the buildings are covered with gold."

"Dreffir," said Erba. He was looking down at the city of
his dreams, the legend. It did exist, and he had proved it. If
only Filfa could have seen it. "It's Dreffir," he repeated.

"The holy city," there was pride in the captain's voice.
"Now that you have seen her, you will never leave."

They camped for the night overlooking the valley, and
the next day they started the long trek down. It took them
days. They came across squads of soldiers several times,
and Erba realized they were patrols. The countryside was

crisscrossed by moving patrols from Dreffir, so there was
no chance that any strangers, let alone any invaders, could
approach the city without it being known in advance. He
wanted to know everything about the city before they
reached it, but all of his questions were ignored or turned
aside by the soldiers and their captain. Kelern had no better
luck than he. The women were treated with cool courtesy,
although Erba could see many sideways glances directed at
Riessa; she made the men uneasy with her disfigurement.

The jungle opened out as they came down into the valley, and farmlands were spread out around them. The land
was so lush that Erba kept blinking, not believing all the
shades of green. They were guarded more closely now that
they were in more populated lands. As they approached
what turned out to be a village on the road to Dreffir, the
captain insisted on tying their hands.

"I am a prince of Tireera," Erba protested. "I will harm
no one; I give you my word."

It made no difference. They bound Kelern, and they
even bound poor Riessa, he saw. But when they came to
Forentel, everything changed.

Forentel saw them tying Kelern's hands. He did not
complain the way Erba had, which she thought showed at
least a little sense, as she already understood that protest
would do no good. These soldiers had their orders, and she,
as a general's daughter, knew what that meant. They also
had avoided any attempt to get to know them or understand
them. They had not engaged in conversation with their captives, and they did not respond to questions. They kept to
themselves. So when one of the men came to her with rope
in his hands, she sighed and held out her crossed wrists.
And looked into his eyes.

His name was Pontu, and his mother was ill. He wanted
very much to finish with this patrol and be able to see her,
as he was afraid it might be too late. He didn't even want to

think such thoughts, but he couldn't help it. He was worried, too, about his sweetheart, Wilasa. She was soon to have his child, and then, if her family approved, he could perhaps wed her. She wanted to marry him, but her family wanted better for her than a poor soldier. He needed some way to convince them, but he was unlikely to find it out here on border patrol.

Forentel drew back and gasped. The soldier—Pontu—dropped the rope and stepped away from her, his eyes wide. His dark skin had paled.

"Lady," he whispered. He touched one trembling hand to his forehead. "Royal one, I did not know. Forgive me."

Forentel stared back at him. She had not meant for it to happen; it simply had. In the past it had taken effort on her part to touch another's thoughts, but this had been effortless. Either her abilities were growing, or there was something special about this man, Pontu. All she knew was that she felt embarrassed and more than a little frightened.

"You have nothing to apologize for," she said.

"What is the matter here?" The captain himself came over, frowning.

"This Lady," said Pontu, "she is of the Family."

"Nonsense," said the captain. He picked up the rope, and then he, too, looked into Forentel's eyes.

The captain's name was Corop, and he was a career soldier in his middle years, with a wife and one cohusband. His wife Meetar had five children, and she swore the two oldest were his. Corop wanted to leave the army and retire, which he would be able to do in three more years, with his pension. The only problem was that he could not abide his cohusband. That, and he was afraid civilian life might bore him.

"You don't have to farm," said Forentel before she thought, "just because your wife and cohusband do." In a certain way Corop reminded her of her father, and she could never imagine Nedriff farming.

Corop gasped and dropped the rope in his turn. "How can this be?" he said. He recovered more quickly than his trooper, however. "However it is," he said, "the queen will know. And that is where we are going. I am sorry for the discourtesy, Lady Forentel, to you and your companions." He turned to his men. "Set them free," he said.

They walked into the village, escorted more than guarded now. Whichever it was, it seemed no friendlier to Forentel. Instead of being treated with cool and condescending distance, they, and especially she, were now treated with nervous and uneasy respect. She couldn't keep her thoughts from what she had done, and not only what she had done, but how she had done it. She was terrified now of speaking with anyone or of looking at anyone directly.

The village was well laid out, with straight streets that ran between neat little houses with thatched roofs. People stood aside as they marched past. They were beautiful people, Erba thought, tall, most with light brown skin and some with paler skin, all dressed in bright colors, some with flowers in their hair. They did not seem afraid or intimidated by the soldiers. If they were Tirdar of some sort, they did not act like the Tirdar of Tireera did when Virsat troops passed through the streets. They smiled and waved in a friendly manner.

They were taken to a slightly larger building and shown inside. Seated on woven mats, they were offered fruit and strange, spicy bread, and given cool drinks. Forentel was served first, and no one met her eyes. Not even the members of her own party, not even Kelern would meet her glance. She felt isolated and alone, but she hid her misery and forced herself to eat. If only Sunrise were with her, she would have at least some company, but she still hadn't seen the wolf, and now she was afraid she never would.

"If you will come, please, Lady, and companions."

Corop stood before them, averting his eyes from Forentel. "We have suitable transportation for you to the city. It is not right for the Lady to walk through the gates."

Every time he said the word *lady,* Forentel heard the respect and the title, and she assumed the others did, too. She avoided looking at them, feeling even more alone.

The transportation proved to be not horses but a cart drawn by mules. One of them brayed at her. To make matters worse, it transpired that she was expected to ride in the cart, driven by one of the soldiers, while the others were to walk beside the cart. Despite her apparent status, no one paid the slightest attention when she protested, so she found herself seated in the cart while both Kelern and Erba, a prince and a soldier of Tireera, walked in the dust. Even Riessa was forced to walk. All other traffic drew aside for them, even though the road was now broad and well-kept. After a little time on the road, the city walls began to grow larger, and then to loom over them. They came to the gates of Dreffir at sunset.

The open gates were massive, made of wood carved in intricate designs; Forentel had never seen so much wood. The stone into which they were set was equally intricately carved. Two enormous and impossible stone animals, obviously mythological, stood alert at either side of the open gate. They were unlike anything the Tireerans had seen before, with tiny tails behind them, but massive tails on the fronts of their faces, which they held curved upwards. Two gorgeously uniformed guards stood with crossed spears, barring their way.

"Let us pass," said Corop. "I am escorting this Lady of the Family, and her companions."

He held out his hand to help Forentel from the wagon. As she descended, she could feel the eyes of the guards on her.

"These are barbarians," said one of them. He did not bother to lower his voice, and it was plain he did not expect any of them to understand. Either that, or he did not care if they did. "And this one is the Lady?" He grinned. "You have been out in the jungle too long, Corop. You have brought us more pirates and slaves and misfits." He chuckled. "And you wanted me to bring these to the queen herself?"

These were the people Illiana had sent her to find, Forentel thought, the people she had been sent to learn from, the people who could help her. They were no kinder than the Virsat, no more understanding than the Hilan villagers, or the pirates. She glanced at Kelern, who had flushed darkly, and at Erba. It had been Erba's dream to find Dreffir, the lost city. And she looked at Riessa, who stood, glowering at the ground, all but ignored, despite her obvious pain. Something hot rose up into her throat.

"We are no more barbarian than you," she said, stepping forward. "You should have some faith in your fellow soldier." She glanced at Corop. "He may not outrank you, but he is a good man, and he knows his duty. Dreffir is known as far away as Tireera for its knowledge and the aid it can offer." That wasn't entirely true, but Forentel had a point to make. "This woman," she nodded at Riessa, "needs care. She has been made to walk here, but surely now you can help her."

The gate guard stared at her as if a dog had suddenly spoken. He looked once at her, and then, quickly, at Riessa. Forentel could almost see his thoughts: Riessa was a swamp woman, and malformed, ugly. But he had the reputation of his city to uphold.

"She will be given aid," he said. "You all will. Since you are of the Family, Lady," he barely contained his snicker of disbelief, "you will be taken to the queen. The others will be cared for here."

"I do not leave the lady's side." Kelern stepped forward. He had no weapons, but it did not seem to matter. There was something in his voice that made the guard look at him sharply.

"They all stay with me," said Forentel.

But in the end, they did not. Kelern stayed with her, and so did Erba, but Riessa was led away by a young guardsman, with assurances from Corop that she would be cared for. They were taken through the city on foot, which amused Forentel after her ride in the cart. Corop accompanied them, with his small squad.

The streets were broad and paved, perfect for horses and carts, and running along the edge of the streets were walkways just for people. They seemed to be in a public area, for when Forentel stared in amazement at the gilded buildings and wondered aloud about who might live there, Corop smiled.

"They are temples," he said. "The gods live there."

The drifts of incense that wafted out gave support to his words. Torches were being lit along the streets. Ahead of them, at the end of the broad avenue, was an enormous building, surmounted by spires and domes that gleamed in the light of myriad torches.

"The palace," Forentel whispered.

Beside her, Erba frowned. He told himself he was not intimidated. He was a prince of Tireera, son of the greatest civilization in the world. It was hard to remain convinced of this, however, in the face of the grandeur they were approaching.

"You will be taken directly to the queen," Corop told them.

Erba's frown grew deeper. He had hoped at the least to be able to bathe first, to do what he could to appear more presentable. He drew in a breath and stood straighter. It didn't matter. He was still his father's son.

"Queen Sirikanya is the daughter of the gods," Corop told them. "You will treat her with the greatest respect.

When you meet her, you will kneel. All of you." He looked pointedly at the men. "And you will not meet her eyes."

They walked up the broad steps that led to the palace, with guards and soldiers lining their path, through the huge doors and into a hallway lit with the light of myriad torches and oil lamps. Gold glittered everywhere. The stone walls were carved with scenes of men and women and animals in graceful poses. Some of the eyes of the carvings flashed in the light, and Forentel realized they were set with precious gems. Here and there a pot of incense smoked. There were many people in the hall, all of them beautifully if simply dressed. All of them stood back to let their small party pass. At the far end of the hall was a carved stone chair, with someone seated on it, surrounded by armed guards. As they approached, Forentel saw that some of the guards were women.

Corop halted them just below the high, carved chair. He saluted, bringing his closed fist smartly across his chest to his shoulder, and his men did the same. The guards around the queen stared back impassively, spears grounded.

"Queen Sirikanya," said Corop, unnecessarily, "the Daughter of the Gods, the Royal One of Dreffir."

They were being pushed down to their knees by their escort. Forentel did not resist, although she felt Erba stiffen beside her. There was a rustle from above them, and then footsteps. The queen was coming down to them.

Forentel had the sense of someone standing over them. Corop had said not to look the queen in the eyes, but he hadn't said not to look up at all, and she couldn't help herself.

Queen Sirikanya was not what she expected. She was slender and beautiful, a tall woman of middle years, with long black hair wound up around the top of her head, and she was dressed in soft, shimmering silk. But what struck Forentel was the warmth that seemed to emanate from her.

Without meaning to, she looked up and directly into the queen's eyes.

Time stood still, and the room and everything in it vanished. She was aware of the warmth she had felt before, but also of sorrow, and a certain sense of strength and steel. But most of all, there was wonder.

"It's true; they didn't lie, and they didn't mistake it. You have come at last."

It was a moment before Forentel realized that the words had not been spoken, except in her mind. She was aware of the room around her again, of the men kneeling at her side. And then the queen leaned over, took her hands, and pulled her to her feet.

"This Lady is a daughter of my line, and she will be treated as such. Welcome, child."

Forentel found herself enfolded in the queen's embrace.

TWENTY

W HEN THE QUEEN HAD RECOGNIZED Forentel and lifted her to her feet, Erba had not been surprised. Everything seemed to fit together now: the long journey from Tireera, even his flight from his city. He had the uneasy, frustrated feeling of being caught up in something greater than himself. He put the thought from his mind and rose to his feet.

"Lady," he said to the queen, "I am Erba, Prince of Tireera." He bowed slightly from the waist, the courtesy of one of high rank to another. Queen Sirikanya was a beautiful woman, he thought, despite her age. He smiled charmingly and looked into her eyes.

She knew him. She was another, like Forentel, who could reach into his thoughts if she would. By sheer force of will he tore his gaze, and his thoughts, free of hers. Now he knew why he had been warned not to look into the eyes of the queen.

"Welcome, Prince," she said, "to the city you have sought for so long."

Later, when Erba and Kelern were alone in the apartment they had been given, Erba couldn't help himself.

"The queen is a witch," he said.

Kelern, in the process of examining the carved chest that stood in the corner of the common parlor, looked up at him.

"You will speak well of our hostess," he said. "As long as she treats Forentel well, I have no quarrel with her." He stood and walked over to Erba, looking at the prince critically. "If you believe this queen to be a witch, what is it you think of Lady Forentel? Forentel is of the line of the queen."

"Don't tell me you really believe that." Erba was disconcerted, and despite the truce between them, he did not like having Kelern so close to him. He could not forget that Kelern was his brother's man, sent to kill him.

"Then why would she say it?" Kelern knew he made the other man nervous, and he enjoyed doing so.

"I'm sure she has good reason. We don't know how the currents of power run in this place. I suggest you take care, Kelern."

"I intend to take very good care. I suggest you do the same." Kelern smiled faintly when he saw Erba shift slightly away from him. "You have nothing to fear from me, Prince, as long as you do no harm to Forentel."

"You appear to hold Forentel in very high regard. Higher than you do me, certainly, and higher, I suspect, than you hold my brother. Your king." Erba was curious. He knew it was more than stupid to bait a trained assassin, but he couldn't help it. Kelern's fanatical loyalty to Forentel disturbed him.

"The Lady Forentel saved my life. I know she saved

yours, and I do not know what happened when she did so, but when she saved mine, I felt, there was—" Kelern paused. He was not accustomed to saying what it was he felt, and in this case it was so far outside of anything he knew or was accustomed to that he was even more at a loss for words than usual.

"She saved me," he said, finally. "I do not mean only that she saved my life. When she healed me, our minds, I felt—she showed me what is real in life, what is good." Kelern's eyes looked away into the distance, and they held an odd fire. Erba barely breathed.

"They say Queen Sirikanya is the daughter of the gods," Kelern continued. "Perhaps she is. One thing is certain, however. Forentel is the child of the gods. She saved me. She may save Dreffir, if it is in need of saving, and she will be Tireera's savior. She is sent by the gods, and I will serve her and protect her to my last breath."

Erba stepped back. Kelern was frightening in his intensity.

"The Lady Forentel has all of my loyalty and service. I hope that is clear to you, Prince Erba."

"Perfectly clear," said Erba. He fought aside the urge to rush out to find Forentel, to keep her away from this man. It would be useless, and Forentel had shown she could take care of herself. He wished he could stop thinking about her.

"YOU NEVER DELIVERED it. Breaking your promise has brought us to this!" Nedriff kept his voice low, although he was angry enough that he almost did not mind if the guards heard. He glared across the tiny cell at his co-conspirator.

"You are the one who stole the funds," whispered Brezat. "I should have known better than to trust your greed. You took the funds and betrayed me to the king."

"Idiot." Nedriff felt some of his anger drain away. He should have known better than to trust Brezat. This was no one's fault but his own. "If I had betrayed you to the king, why would I be here with you in this cell? I involved myself with a fool."

Any further conversation was cut off by the arrival of more guards. Nedriff did not fight having his hands bound the way Brezat did. It galled him, but he knew it was futile, and he would not give Mirta's guards the opportunity to treat him as they did Brezat. He was not entirely out of options, as it happened. Once he had discovered that the promised funds were not in the storeroom, he had begun another plan. It was not as well thought out as what he had worked out with Brezat, but it would have to do, especially now.

They were taken to Mirta's private audience room, the smaller one off his bedchambers, not the larger, formal one. They had expected to be taken to the Temple of Justice, or at least to the main audience chamber. Mirta, Nedriff thought, would have wanted this done in public, but the king had become increasingly afraid to be in crowds.

Mirta was seated on the dais seat, surrounded by guards, and guards were posted all around the audience chamber. He was taking no chances with his own safety. None of this was surprising. What caused Nedriff to stumble and catch his breath was the figure seated just below the king.

Mareg had been staring out of the window at the darkening sky. A mound of papers lay before her on a low table, but she was not looking at them. An autumn storm was blowing up, as it was the season for the sharp, brief, vicious rainstorms that occasionally lashed the desert, also filling Tireera's cisterns. She had not been able to refuse the summons of the king, not as a private citizen, but certainly not as High Judge, when the king demanded her services to rule over a case of treason. She had been expecting it. The king's guards had brought her straight from the temple to the palace, through the streets where a brisk wind had been blowing, predecessor of the storm. Now she sat below the king on the dais, and slightly above Beha and Jek, who had been called with her.

His wife looked pale and tiny, sitting below the king, Nedriff thought. She was refusing to meet his eyes, and he had a sudden queasy feeling. He knew Brezat's eyes were on him, and he knew Brezat was even more convinced of his treachery now. They were taken to stand in the corner, surrounded by armed guards. Nedriff kept his gaze on his wife, not the king, but it was hard to ignore Mirta, and finally he stopped trying.

The king looked terrible. There were huge circles under his eyes, and his face was puffy. His hands trembled, even at rest. Nedriff would have placed a significant bet that he smelled of wine, too.

There were rows of benches drawn up in the audience, filling a large portion of it. The reason for this soon became clear: Virsat nobles were filing in, having been hastily called by their king. Outside on the terrace, and out in the hall, troops of the regular army were assembling. The only reason for meeting in this smaller audience hall was that Mirta had become less and less willing to leave his private apartments. He was afraid of being in public, so he had called the public here. He was afraid of crowds, so he had crowds of guards, but he had also called crowds of regular troops to protect him from the crowds of guards. Nedriff repressed a smile.

"Noble lords and ladies." The speaker was Mirta's official herald, a sallow young man with an excellent voice, appointed to the position after his predecessor, the herald of the old king, had met with an unfortunate accident. The new herald's name was Yessip, and he looked less than happy to be fulfilling his duties today.

"Noble lords and ladies," he said again. The room, which had been filled with whispers and speculation, quieted.

"You are brought here today to hear charges of treason against two Virsat, and to hear their sentences."

So much for a trial, thought Nedriff. This was only to be expected, however.

There were shocked murmurs. Virsat nobles turned in their seats to stare at Nedriff and Brezat, and others turned to stare at Mareg. The High Judge must preside over any sentencing of Virsat for high crimes, but the family connection added a juicy layer of scandal and drama. They waited for one of the lesser judges to read the charges. Yessip was in the act of handing the papers to Lady Beha, when Mirta jumped from his chair, stepped down, and took the papers from his hands. There were more murmurings among the spectators until Mirta began to read.

"The charges against the Lords Brezat and Nedriff," Mirta began, "are of treason and embezzlement." He strode down the remaining steps and onto the floor of the audience chamber, crossing to the corner where Nedriff and Brezat stood.

"Don't tell me you didn't do it!" he said. "My spies have assured me that you did! You conspired against me! And you stole the monies for the army! I know you did it. You are going to take those monies and bring back my disloyal brother from wherever you are hiding him!"

Now that the king was close, Nedriff knew he was right: Mirta had been drinking. It was also apparent that he hadn't been sleeping, or bathing for that matter. Nedriff refrained from wrinkling his nose.

"Don't deny it! Do you deny it?" Mirta seemed unaware that he sounded ludicrous.

"Of course I deny it!" Brezat was indignant. "It's ridiculous!"

No, it isn't, thought Nedriff. *It's just unfortunate that we don't have the monies because of you, Brezat.*

"How dare you speak to me like that! I know what you

have done. I have proof." Mirta was slightly unsteady on his feet, but he waved his hand at one of his guards, who came forward with more papers. Mirta took them. "Conversations," he said, more calmly, "reports of conversations between you, Lord Brezat, and General Nedriff." He waved them in the air.

"Reported by someone completely trustworthy, of course," said Nedriff dryly. He found the whole scene both repulsive and amusing in a strangely twisted way. He smiled. The smile infuriated Mirta.

"More trustworthy than you!" said the king. "You have taken those funds and paid the troops to follow you against me." Mirta seemed oblivious to the fact that he was contradicting his prior assertions. His voice was lower now, venomous. The assembled Virsat had no trouble hearing him, however. The room was utterly silent.

"I know because of what you did before. You were the one to plan, you were the one who helped me kill my fath—" Belatedly, Mirta realized what he was saying, but it was too late, and he could not call the words back.

Nedriff felt the blood drain from his face. He had known Mirta was becoming more and more unstable, but he had never believed the king would incriminate himself. That mattered, but of more immediate importance to Nedriff was the fact that Mirta had just condemned him. Since Brezat was accused along with him, Brezat was, by implication, guilty.

Brezat realized this. He took advantage of the moment of shock and astonishment that had paralyzed the room. He leaned forward and grabbed the spear from the guard nearest him. Before anyone could react, he ran Mirta through the heart with the spear.

"Nedriff should have finished the job," he said.

Pandemonium broke loose. Nobles were screaming, some running for the doors. Guards were charging for-

ward, too late to save Mirta, not sure what to do next. One
of them grabbed Brezat, and another wasted no time cutting his throat with a sword. Brezat's blood spurted out,
mixing with Mirta's. From the terraces outside, Nedriff's
regular troops were trying to get in, but running afoul of
Mirta's palace guards and of the nobles stampeding out.
Yessip the herald was screaming, his voice carrying over
the shouts and screams of others, until someone hit him
from behind, knocking him unconscious. Heightening the
confusion, the storm broke with a crash of thunder almost
directly overhead, and the blazing brilliance of lightning.
Torrential rains poured down, soaking those nobles who
managed to get as far as the terraces, and soaking the
troops trying to get in.

"Stop!" Nedriff's voice was at full strength, the voice he
used to command his troops in the field. "Everyone stop
now! There will be order here!"

It worked. People turned to him, desperate for some authority in the disaster. Only the storm did not pay attention,
but the thunder crashes were no longer directly overhead.

"Let the troops in, and keep the nobles in," he commanded the palace guards. "You," he said to the captain of
the guards, "take the king's body to his bedchamber. And
take that," he pointed to Brezat's body, "out." He was
happy that Brezat had been killed; the man had become too
dangerous. Brezat had advanced Nedriff's plan a little, and
he had also managed to remove himself, which was handy.

The troops entered the room from the terrace, crowding
the small chamber, and nobles edged back from them.
Nedriff strode to the dais and stood below it.

"There is nothing to fear." His voice carried over the
room. If it did not exactly calm the nobles, at least it quieted them further. "Tireera is safe, you will all be safe until
a new king is elevated. There will be peace and order. The

traitor Brezat is dead, the leader of the conspiracy. We will take steps to make sure the others are caught immediately."

He motioned the troopers to surround him, and a squad came forward, swords drawn. For the first time since Mirta's assassination he looked up at those still on the dais. The three judges looked back down at him. None of them had been harmed in the confusion.

Lady Judge Beha's lips were white, and her eyes were huge. She looked ready to faint. Lord Judge Jek was not much better off. Even from below him, at a distance, Nedriff could see the sweat on the man's brow, see him shaking. Mareg was different.

His wife was pale but composed. Her eyes were wide with shock, but she wasn't trembling the way Jek was, and she wasn't in danger of losing control as Beha was. She met his glance. In that moment Nedriff knew with absolute certainty what had happened to Brezat's funds. He knew with absolute certainty how Mirta had come by his information, and he knew also that this trial had been arranged, if not in its particulars at least in its generalities, and not by Mirta. Nedriff turned to his own captain.

"Arrest the Lady Mareg," he said. When his troopers stared at him, he repeated the order. "Arrest her," he said. "She is a traitor."

To Nedriff's utter and complete astonishment, his troops made no move to obey. Instead they looked up at the dais, at Mareg. Nedriff looked, too, and then felt his stomach plummet.

"No," said Mareg. "Arrest the general. He has plotted to kill the king, two kings, and to take Tireera for himself. Arrest him."

"Yes, High Judge," said the captain.

Nedriff did not intend to make it easy. As two of his own troopers turned to him, he punched one right below the rib cage, doubling the man over. As the the soldier fell, Nedriff pulled his spear from him. He did not have the space to use the spear as it was intended, so he used it instead as a staff, catching the second trooper in the face with the shaft. The man screamed and fell to the ground, writhing. For a moment, he was alone, ringed by his own reluctant troops, but then five of them rushed him, and it was over. The spear was pulled from him, his arms were wrenched painfully behind his back, and his hands were tied. He stared up at his wife, breathing hard.

"Tireera is under the protection of the gods and the Lady of Justice," Mareg said. "The Council of Judges will hold the government until there is a new king, and I will head the council. I am regent."

She nodded at her two colleagues, and Nedriff noticed that they did not seem entirely surprised by the turn of events. He had no time to notice anything more, because he was being taken away, out into the wet streets. There was no point in resisting. At least, he thought, the rain had stopped.

MAREG WAS IN the king's study. She did not intend to stay here, or to attempt to govern from the palace, even though that was what the priests had initially suggested, and the council of judges, too. Governing from the Temple of Justice could antagonize the other gods, and Tireera had always been governed from the palace. That, Mareg had insisted, was because it had always been governed by a king. She was not a king and she would never be, nor was she the queen the Tirdar looked for. She was simply regent, chosen by the Lady, until a new king was found. At last they had agreed that the business of government could take place in the common rooms of the Temple of Justice.

But she had had to return to the palace. The king's seal

had been lacking, and no one wanted to retrieve it. Touching it was unlucky, unless the holder and user of the seal was the ruler of Tireera. This meant that Mareg herself must go and retrieve it.

The seal was right on Mirta's carved wooden desk, the same desk that had been Rellaff's. The desk was solid wood, heavy and old, worth a fortune in and of itself. Mareg trailed her hand over it, admiring it, and then picked up the seal. She glanced at the doorway where her escort waited: three of the King's Guard and two from the temple, and prepared to leave. Then she hesitated.

It had been three days since the assassination and her assumption of power. In all of that time she had not seen her husband. She had had reports of him, of course. He was in the prison but held in comfort as befitted a Virsat noble, accused or not. There was always the concern that some of his troops might try to free him, but that concern did not seem urgent. The army seemed to accept the pronouncements of the priests of all the temples, including, significantly, the Falcon Priests. But Mareg knew that he would need to be tried and sentenced. She had been avoiding that thought, but now she decided that she might as well question him, and question him here. Using the king's study for such a purpose would unsettle him. She looked up.

"Bring me General Nedriff," she said. "I will question him now."

When they brought him in, however, he did not seem unsettled. He was surrounded by temple guards, her own guards, and she had more of them outside the door. She was seated behind the heavy desk, with its bulk between her and her husband, and she had a scribe from the temple, an official scribe, with her. Nedriff did not seem intimidated by any of this. He did not look like a man who was in all probability going to be condemned.

"I was wondering when I would see you again, Wife," he said.

Now that she saw him, Mareg was almost overcome by a wash of feeling for him, but most of it was not gentle. This was the man who had killed the old king, who had installed and then plotted against the new. This was the man who had caused her favorite child to flee the city, the man who had imprisoned her in her own house. Nonetheless, he was her husband. She tried to push her emotions aside.

"You are seeing me now," she said. "You are here to answer questions concerning your actions and Brezat's, to determine whether you have acted against Tireera and her king."

"Are you going to condemn me now, Mareg? Is this my trial?"

"No, Nedriff, no on both counts. But I must have, the council must have, some answers."

"You have already decided my fate. You have called me traitor."

Mareg sighed. Why had she thought the place of questioning would make the least difference to Nedriff?

"It certainly looks that way," she said tartly. "Are you a traitor, Nedriff?"

"Must we do this with all of them here?" Nedriff nodded at all the guards; his hands were bound, and he couldn't gesture.

Mareg hesitated. She should be safe enough. His hands were bound, and the guards would be right outside the small room.

"The scribe stays," she said. "He is our witness. The rest of you," she nodded at all the guards, "wait outside."

When they had all left, all but the scribe, Mareg looked at her husband. She did not feel safe enough to cut his bonds. He had to be uncomfortable with his wrists tied behind him, but he still managed to look relaxed.

"You are the one who told Mirta." Nedriff found that he was still surprised when he thought of this. He was not surprised that she had had the strength to make such a move; he had long known that his wife had considerable strength of character. What surprised him was that she had involved herself in political machinations. She always seemed somehow above such matters, interested only in justice and temple affairs.

"Justice will not be served, Nedriff, unless such political dealings are first put to rest."

It was as if she had read his mind. Nedriff flushed, something he did not do often. It galled him. Mareg was as noble as he, and had her own high position, but nonetheless he had thought that he knew her, and even to an extent that he controlled her. To find she was capable of such a thing made him question his own abilities.

"You were the one." He said it again.

"Yes, Nedriff, I was. You were planning to kill Mirta."

Nedriff was silent for a moment. Then he shrugged. "Yes," he said. "We planned to kill Mirta, Brezat and I. And yes, I did kill Rellaff, at Mirta's request. You could have been queen, Mareg."

Mareg looked back at him, saying nothing. The only sound was the scratching made by the pen of the scribe, as he wrote furiously across the papyrus. Mareg wondered what her husband really thought. Surely he must guess that Mirta had meant nothing to her. He should have, since he was king, but he had become king through murder, through patricide. That the Falcon and the Lady had punished him was not surprising.

As for her feelings for Nedriff, Mareg wasn't sure. They had shared a life for so long. She knew that her husband was surprised at her actions, shocked that he had misjudged her, even mortified that he had. To him, this was of more importance, or of equal importance, as the danger he now faced.

She had always known that he was selfish and control-
ling as well as brilliant. It had never particularly mattered
to her before, but that had all begun to change when he had
forced Forentel, the child of her soul, to run from the city,
to run for her life, for surely a marriage to Brezat would
have killed her. The Tirdar prophet had assured her that
Forentel still lived. She hoped this was true, but she could
not be sure. She blamed her husband for her the loss of her
elder daughter, the child of her heart.

The silence grew longer. The scribe had stopped writ-
ing, and still Mareg said nothing. Nedriff shifted uneasily.
At last he could stand the silence no longer.

"Will you condemn me, Wife?"

Mareg had been staring off into the distance, looking
out the small study window at the bright blue sky. She was
regent now, and she would be a good one, a fair one. She
turned her gaze back on her husband. There was no gentleness in it.

"No," she said. "That will be up to the Council of
Judges. But you should know, General, that you have condemned yourself."

TWENTY-ONE

$\mathcal{E}$VERYONE TREATED HER WITH THE UTMOST courtesy. Forentel had an apartment that was stunningly beautiful, with walls and furniture in shades of yellow and silver. It had its own bathing chamber with a small pool and sweet-scented oils. She was given clothing made of the wonderful, multihued silk that the people here loved. She had a personal maid, who answered ordinary questions and was careful not to look her in the eye. She had not seen the queen again since that first night, except at a distance. Instead, two days later, she was taken to see one of the local priests. It was not a thing she would have chosen.

"It's an honor," her maid told her. "Larar is the Old Man of the Mountain, the teacher of silence."

Forentel tried to look impressed and knew that she failed. The truth was that she felt more alone than ever, now that she was finally in Dreffir. Dreffir was a city with strange ways, where the people rose early and lit incense to their gods and then went about their business. For the first day she had been bathed, fed, and no more, and now they were taking her to a temple. She would rather see Queen Sirikanya. But most of all, she found herself missing Sunrise and wondering what the wolf was doing. The animal had been a bigger comfort than she had realized. Also, and despite herself, she missed Erba. The prince had proven to be deeper than she had suspected, and they had shared so much together.

"The Old Man is advisor to our blessed queen," the maid told her.

Forentel perked up. This was a little better. A royal advisor would be someone worth talking to, and she knew quite well from her own experience how powerful such advisors could be. Her father was one, and her mother, Mareg, could have been, if she had wished to involve herself in political life. She tried not to think about her parents; such thoughts would have to wait.

She was taken to one of the temples, a spired dome that shimmered gold in the dawn light. The streets were already filled with people, many of them quietly entering or leaving temples.

"The raffa will see you soon, lady, please wait here." The temple servant, a cheerful boy, smiled at her, and for a moment Forentel's heart leaped. The raffa? How could Illiana be in this place? When she was shown at last into the presence of the priest, she realized how foolish her hope had been. Of course it wasn't Illiana. *Raffa,* she remembered, meant "prophet."

The prophet, the Old Man of the Mountain, was in fact old, but not as ancient as she might have thought. He was bald, whether by nature or by design she couldn't tell. He was tall and slender but muscular, draped in a golden robe that hung to his ankles and left his right shoulder bare. His blue eyes twinkled in his dark face.

"Welcome, welcome!" He smiled at her, and she saw that a few of his teeth were missing, but his smile was charming for all that, and he looked her directly in the eye. "You are the new Lady of the Family, the one Queen Sirikanya has been waiting for, for so long. I don't suppose you have had any breakfast, have you, not so early in the morning? Please, please, sit down, and let me get some tea for you. I am the raffa, but they must have told you."

Forentel felt overcome, but pleasantly so. She let herself be shown to a wooden chair padded with comfortable cushions. While the priest poured a steaming cup of something fragrant, she looked around her.

The room was simple. It was situated high up in the temple, and it looked eastward, so it was filled with the light of the newly risen sun. There were only a few items furnishing the room: the chair on which she sat, another like it, and a small iron brazier, with which the priest was currently busy, and a bed, a simple pallet on the floor. Also on the floor, in a corner, were two large pottery bowls. One was empty, the other filled with water. Near them was a huge, flat cushion. Two hooks on the wall appeared to hold the priest's clothing. It was rather austere, she thought, for a royal advisor.

Then she looked at the walls. They were wood, and they were covered with carvings. Mostly they were carvings of animals and landscapes; mountains figured prominently. This made sense, Forentel realized. This priest was known as the Old Man of the Mountain. Some of the animals were the mythical beasts she had seen depicted before, the enormous animals with tails at at either end, but most of them were cats, large cats that looked very similar to the desert cats at home.

"I see you are admiring my carvings. I did them myself." He smiled modestly. "The cats are appropriate, of course, for the Shrine of the Dawn, but I must admit that I have a fondness for them, myself. That is understandable, since Bellist chose me."

He smiled and glanced at the bowls and the cushion on the floor. Forentel felt a sudden flash of horror, and almost jumped from her chair. One of the cats actually lived here, in this Shrine of the Dawn, so unlike its Tirdar counterpart in Tireera. At least the animal was not present. The priest did not remark on her reaction, although he could scarcely have missed it.

"Of course your own Family, Lady," he continued, "has more commonly been chosen by wolves."

Forentel drew in a breath and swallowed hard. She found, to her surprise, that she was blinking back tears.

"As you were chosen." The priest made it a statement. He smiled at her gently. "But you did not know it was a trait of your kind, and you rejected your wolf partner."

"What is my kind?" The words came out suddenly. It seemed like rudeness, but she couldn't call them back, and she realized that she didn't want to. The pain had become too intense. The long journey to find this place, trusting the whole time that it even existed, and losing so much in the process, and then not to have answers; it was all too much, and she was angry. Anger was better than tears.

"You are a human being, child, as are we all." He held up a hand when she frowned. "You are a daughter of the great line, the queen's line. Only those of the queen's line, and some of the priests, can see into thoughts. That is the great line. I see you do not understand what that means. When I say 'the great line,' what I mean is that you have great responsibilities as well as great gifts. You never learned what that meant when you were growing up, so you have much to learn now. That is why you are here. Fortunately," he grinned at her, seeming more like the young boy who had ushered her in than an old man, "I believe you will be a quick study. Here, please drink this; it is only tea. And then I will do my best to explain to you."

Forentel accepted the tea. It was delicious, and it did help with the hunger pangs she felt. It did more than that. It soothed her, as she knew it was meant to. Since the raffa seemed unafraid to look into her eyes, she looked into his. Then, to her surprise, she found herself telling him about growing up, about her dreams, about the sense of being an alien in her own family. She told him about her father and about Mareg, and then she told him about meeting Illiana, and the visions in the water. She felt the familiar horror as she did so, but it was somehow muffled, not as sharp.

When he said nothing, only looked at her with compassion, she found herself telling him about Sunrise, and about her journey. Lastly she told him about knowing the things that people thought, and how she did not wish to know these things, and how she was afraid of what she could do. Finally she was done, and she sat silent, exhausted. She was surprised at herself. She had not realized how unhappy she had been, not until she told him. She wondered if she should apologize, and she was trying to find the words, when he spoke.

"That is a lot for one person, any one person to endure. But you did, and you are here. You are strong." He touched her gently on the shoulder in sympathy. "You know now that the Tlrdar of your country are all that remain from a city of our people. Long ago, our civilization spread far to the north, but over the years we lost contact with many of our settlements. You are the heir of our people, Forentel, and the heir of the Virsat conquerors. You are the Delass. The bridge." He looked at her.

"I am beginning to understand what that means," Forentel said. "I don't want to be a bridge. I just want, I just want—" She wanted to be herself, to be accepted, to have an ordinary life. She didn't know how to say all that. "I don't want to be a bridge between two peoples. I don't know how to go about it, and I don't want it."

"Quite understandable. But you are, and can be, a bridge to more than that. You can bridge the kingdoms of humans and those of the animals, and even of the plants."

Forentel remembered the island, and shuddered. "I don't want to," she said again. "Can you teach me how to get rid of this—ability?"

"You cannot get rid of it. You can control it, but that you can do only if you accept it. You must embrace it, Forentel. I am sorry, child, but you will find that you have no choice." His blue eyes were sympathetic. "I have some of these abilities, too. I am the raffa, like your friend Illiana, and the gods have laid this upon me. Do you want to control it, Forentel? Sit quietly, and let your mind open to everything there is. Let your thoughts open out. You will see the connections, with a little practice, and you will be able to manage them. Do you want to try it? I can help you."

Did she want to try it? Forentel pondered this for a moment. She knew he was right; she could never get rid of this ability, this curse. The only chance she had of having any sort of life of her own would be if she could learn to control it. She was wavering on agreeing to try, when something came through the hanging beaded curtain and into the room.

It was a cat very like one of the desert cats of home, only larger. It was a brilliant orange in color, with dark black stripes and slightly rounded ears. It came waist high to the priest, and it gave him a gentle push with its large head before turning wild green eyes on Forentel.

"Bellist!" said the priest, reaching to scratch behind the animal's ears. "This is Forentel, a lady of our Family."

Forentel found herself staring into the animal's eyes. She could feel a sense of connection, of communion, the same sort of thing she had felt before, with so many, but especially with Sunrise. But this wasn't Sunrise. What made it worse was a sense of inquisitiveness, as if the cat were pushing to the edges of her mind. It was not unfriendly, but it was unnerving.

"I, I think—later—I will come back—thank you, Raffa!"

Before she could stop herself, Forentel turned and fled. She ran down the stairs and through the hallways of the temple, ignoring the startled looks she got. She remembered the way to the door and emerged, breathless, on the main steps, where her escort waited. They took her back to the palace without questions, for which she was grateful.

For a time she wandered her apartment. She glanced through the scrolled books the servants brought her, when she asked for histories of Dreffir, but she couldn't read them. Although she spoke Tirdar, the Dreffir language, she could not read it, and the thought of the knowledge there just beyond her reach was frustrating. She was told the queen was busy with affairs of government and would see her later. So with nothing else to do, Forentel sat in the small window seat and gazed out over the gardens of the palace and the rooftops of the city beyond.

Dreffir was a pleasant place. The city was beautiful, and what she had seen of it was clean and well-kept. The people were cheerful. But no one spoke to her, and when she spoke to people, they did not look her in the eye. She found she was more homesick than ever before, perhaps because she had the time to be. She missed Erba, but when she asked after him she was told he had been taken to see the sights without her. So she looked out the window and let her thoughts drift across the journey she had taken and everything that happened. She found herself thinking of Sunrise and wondering where she was.

She was drifting now in a strange, suspended state. It

seemed to her that she floated out of her window, out over
the palace gardens. She knew she didn't really, and in fact,
if she looked back, she could see herself seated in the window. This did not seem strange but somehow reassuring,
normal. She floated over the city, seeing the people below
her buying things in the market quarter, children laughing.
She floated above the gates of the city and out over the
fields. In one field she saw an animal, huge and gray, with
a tiny tail behind it, moving whole trees with its long forward tail. *Its nose,* she thought, *that's its nose.* And then,
They aren't mythical.

She missed her home, she missed Tireera. Most of all
she missed her mother. If only she could see Mareg, somehow talk to her, tell her that she was well. Tell her that she
had found Dreffir. She strained to see northward. And then
she felt Mareg. She knew immediately that it was her
mother.

Mareg was in her chambers in the Temple of Justice.
Forentel could see her. Her head was in her hands, and she
was not looking at the papers spread before her. She was
thinking of Forentel, wondering if her child still lived.

I am here! Forentel cried into the silence. *I am here, in
Dreffir, and I am well! I found Dreffir, Mother! I found it!
And they are good to me here!*

"Forentel?" Mareg raised her head and looked around
her. "Forentel?"

Forentel tried to throw herself into her mother's arms.
She wanted to bury her head against Mareg as she had had
done when she was little. It was impossible, she knew. She
was so far away. Nonetheless, her thoughts clung to her
mother. And then, to her utter surprise, she felt Mareg's
arms around her.

"My child! It's really you!"

Forentel sobbed. She could see her mother clearly, as if
she stood in the room with her. And her mother could see

her. Forentel saw, in a tumbled sequence, all that had happened. Her mother was free, her mother ruled in Tireera. She was safe, and the city was safe.

"And you are safe, child of my heart!"

Forentel felt the tears come, and then she was being pulled away.

"Come back!" cried Mareg.

I will! she cried. She was being blown away by strange winds, the essence of herself pulled back into the hot rich lands, away from her desert.

The jungle seemed to call to her, the great, hot, tangled forest. She was aware of the murmuring thoughts of the people in the city of Dreffir and on the roads and in the villages, like a buzz. The forest seemed richer somehow, more compelling. She had to go into the forest.

She felt something within the forest: the sense of interlocking lives, a community. It was everywhere, she knew, but it was clearer there somehow. She wanted to understand it. She let her mind thin out and expand, seeping into the other minds. She became part of the chattering troop of tailed animals in the treetops, and she became part of the little family of large striped cats that rested in the shade, waiting for night, while the mother played with her cubs. She could feel the thin, silvery cord that bound her back to her own body, in the window in the palace in Dreffir, but that cord was stretching ever thinner.

She was a bridge, yes, but not just between two cultures and peoples. She was a bridge between humanity and the tailed animals in the trees, and the great cats of the jungle and the pale dolphins that swam there in that great river, distant, but not too distant, really not distant at all because nothing was distant or removed from her. She flowed out, becoming linked even with the trees and the flowers that twined and grew in their highest branches. She had come here looking for something, for someone, but it didn't mat-

ter, because she had found all this. And who was she, what
was this odd, thin strand that linked her to something back
there in the hum and buzz of the city? She would break it,
be truly free.

She didn't know who she was any longer. She reached out
to snap the odd strand, but something stopped her. Something strong pulled her back. It was a presence deep and
strong, a presence that she knew, that was linked to her as she
was linked to all things. But this was more intense, immediate, and individual. It did not want her to break the strand.

It was Sunrise. She recognized the wolf, and then, as
she did, she recognized herself. She was Forentel, and she
was in a room in the palace in Dreffir.

For a moment she resented it. She resented being
shown, and remembering, that she was an individual, confined by that body back in one specific place. But then she
remembered that Sunrise was an individual, and bound in
time and space, and no less valuable for that. No, she was
more valuable because of it. And yet the wolf was here,
too, wherever that was.

Forentel was glad, and the joy she felt, and the relief,
flowed over her. Sunrise was glad, too. Out in this no place
that was every place, it was as if the wolf breathed on her,
rubbed fur against her. Forentel could almost feel the fur.
She *could* feel the fur.

She was lying on the floor in the room in the palace.
People were talking in worried tones, and someone was
trying to touch her, to help her, but couldn't, because there
was a wolf in the way. Sunrise sat over her, licking her
face, keeping everyone away from her. Forentel tried to sit
up. She managed to get her arms around the wolf, but she
slid back to the floor. Someone tried to catch her, but Sunrise growled and snapped.

"The queen," someone said.

Everyone moved aside. It was indeed Sirikanya, who

said something, softly, to the wolf. Sunrise let her get down on the floor, and she put her hand on Forentel's head.

"You are cold as mountain snow," Sirikanya said, "and no wonder. What were you thinking, bridging out so far like that? You spread yourself too thin; you might never have come back."

"I wouldn't have." Forentel was surprised at how thin and weak her voice was, as if she had left most of it somewhere else. "I wouldn't have, but for Sunrise." She managed to get her arms around the wolf again. It felt very natural. She knew she should be surprised that the animal was here, but she couldn't get her thoughts around the question. Then something else drifted into her mind.

"He said I should do this, I should try, the priest, the raffa, said—" What exactly had he said? She couldn't quite remember.

"Bring me that blanket. And that carafe of water, and the fruit from the bowl there." Sirikanya's tone was matter-of-fact. "And then leave us."

There was a little flurry of activity. A blanket of soft spun wool appeared, and the queen wrapped Forentel in it, with Sunrise watching every move but not interfering. Footsteps and voices receded, and there was the sound of the door closing.

"Drink this."

Sirikanya propped her up and held a porcelain cup to her lips. It was cool water, and Forentel sipped it gratefully. She found that she was thirsty, and the act of drinking helped to bring her back to herself.

"Now eat this."

"This" proved to be small squares of the blue fruit, the melon she had loved in Hila, which the queen held out to her on the point of a tiny knife. It was sweet and delicious. Forentel found that she wanted more. She sat up and took the knife and the bowl from the queen and finished the fruit.

"That's better," said the queen with satisfaction.

Forentel put the now empty bowl down and looked at the wolf, who was stretched out on the carpet. Sunrise looked back at her and yawned.

"How did she get in here?" Forentel found that she could think more clearly now, and could frame questions.

"She came when you called," said the queen, settling herself more comfortably on the floor, her back against some cushions. "She was never far from you. Noswi alerted me. My own wolf," she added, smiling when she saw Forentel's eyes widen, "but I felt it when your Sunrise entered the palace. I doubt anyone could have stopped her. Fortunately, my people know better than to try."

Forentel reached over to stroke the wolf's fur. Sunrise had saved her life, and she would never again deny the bond between them. But she was still confused.

"I should have made time for you sooner," said Sirikanya. "Perhaps I've forgotten what it's like to be so young." She smiled. "When you can't wait for things. I had only just heard that you left my brother so precipitously. It never occurred to me that you would attempt to bridge on your own, let alone so widely."

"Your brother?" Forentel felt muzzy and stupid.

"Larar. The raffa. He is my brother." She sighed. "You are a member of my Family, too, Forentel; that is obvious from your abilities. I share some of them, and so does Larar, although you have more than either of us."

"Can you hear thoughts?" Forentel had to know. "Can you do it without even meaning to?"

"I could, but I do not. I will not permit myself to do so. You can control this, also. It is an ability given to our line by the gods, but they gave us also the means to control it. It is easier, of course, when you look people in the eye. That is why, in the beginning, our people would not meet our glance. Now it is only tradition and courtesy. Forentel."

She leaned over, deliberately looking into Forentel's eyes. "Don't be afraid of what you can do. You will learn how to control this with practice."

Forentel sighed. A great sense of love and peacefulness flowed from the queen and surrounded her, but there was nothing more, no feeling of the queen trying to enter her thoughts.

"I don't want to be a bridge," she said. "I didn't ask for this." To her surprise, Sirikanya laughed.

"Of course you didn't; no one would ask for this. But you aren't alone, Forentel. And one thing I know for certain: bridges don't stand by themselves. They need anchors, and shores to which they connect. One of those shores, one of those anchors, is here. In Dreffir, with us. With me."

Forentel felt tears welling up and tried to fight them back. She was tired of running, of traveling, of not understanding. It was true: they would teach her here in Dreffir. She looked at Sirikanya. And they understood, and cared.

"You are Family, child. You may stay here as long as you want." Sirikanya gently gathered Forentel into her arms. Forentel stopped fighting the tears. Tireera was home, but so was Dreffir.

TWENTY-TWO

SHE SUPPOSED SHE WOULD HAVE TO BECOME
accustomed to the revulsion she inspired. It was hard, as
Riessa had always prided herself on her looks and considered her beauty her main asset. She knew she was clever,
but that had never counted for much, not by itself. Her
beauty and her willingness to seize any opportunity, those
were what counted. Now, that was gone. She had nothing
left.

Kelern had left her, too, without a backward glance, although that was to be expected, considering what she
looked like now. It was infuriating to know that he had
transferred all the devotion she had hoped for to the
Tireeran woman, who didn't even service him in bed. She
knew she should be grateful to Forentel for saving her life,
but she couldn't be. If Forentel had never come to Hila,

Riessa would not be here in Dreffir, crippled. She knew this wasn't a fair assessment, but it didn't matter. She hated Forentel.

Riessa had spent too much time sitting on the straw pallet that was her bed in the healers' building. The healers in Dreffir had several of these buildings, with rooms of various sorts for the ill and the injured, and Riessa had been housed in one of the dormitory rooms for those who were healed or mostly healed.

"You are healed already. The healer who treated you did an excellent job when she saved your life. What you need more than healing is to learn how to manage with the eye and the abilities that remain to you. You are more capable than you think now," the Dreffirian healer had said. He was not unsympathetic, but he obviously did not expect to spend much more time with her. "What you need most is a way to earn your livelihood."

He had introduced her to the dormitory cooks, and she had learned to clean the kitchens and the cook pots. She still lived in the dormitory, but she spent as little time there as possible. When she could, she went to the big courtyard to watch the Queen's Guard practice.

At first she stayed as far back as she could, hoping not to be noticed while she watched the men and women practice. She had never seen women warriors before, nor known that they even existed. One of the guards had noticed her standing in the shadows every day.

"Do you want to learn how to throw a spear?"

The question had come from behind her, and at first Riessa wasn't even sure that she was the one being addressed. The woman behind her, grinning, was one of the Queen's Guard. The troop was in the process of leaving the courtyard, but this one trooper had remained behind. Her name was Gura, and she had not been in the least repelled by Riessa's appearance. She had shown Riessa how to cast a spear and had taken time to practice with her. Riessa found that when she learned to compensate for her missing eye, she could cast accurately. Amazingly accurately. Gura had taken her to meet the guard's commander, and Riessa had then found herself living in a room off the barracks, cooking for the guard and practicing arms in her off hours.

She wanted to join the guard, to become one of their troop, but she knew they only tolerated her and felt sorry for her, so she tried to be grateful for what she had. It was hard. It was very far from the life she had envisioned when she left Hila. When she learned about the Elephant Corps, she had wanted so much to see something so fabulous, but she didn't know how to ask. She did find out where to go, and so one morning well before dawn she managed to sneak out of the city to the field near the elephant barracks.

Some of the elephants were already out, and the sight of the enormous animals made Riessa draw in her breath. She crept as close as she dared, hiding behind a bush. One of the elephants was picking up dirt with its, no *her* trunk, and showering herself with dust. The sight made her want to laugh. Riessa was not sure just how she knew the animal was female, nor how she knew why the elephant enjoyed this dust bath so much, but she knew. When the animal turned and lumbered right toward her, she did not back away. She stood still, entranced, looking into the small, wise eyes so high above her.

"It seems you have a gift for elephants," said a voice. A woman slid down from the immense height of the animal's back.

"You are Riessa the barbarian," the woman said.

Riessa did not take offense. The Dreffirians called anyone not of their city "barbarian."

"I am," she said. "How did you know?" She inspected the woman in front of her.

The elephant warrior was an ordinary-looking woman

of early middle age. Her black hair was cut very short, and her blue eyes were set in a face crinkled and lined by exposure to sun and weather. She was covered with dirt from the elephant's recent "bath," and now she dusted her hands on her short leather kilt.

"It's my job to know these things," she said. "It's also my job to see who might be good with the elephants." A long gray trunk wound itself into her short hair, and she laughed. "I guess Mae thinks it's her job, and according to Mae, you have the touch. Would like to work with the elephants, Riessa the barbarian?"

"I don't think they'll let me." Riessa wanted nothing more, but she knew quite well what she was. She saw herself suddenly in another light, too: she had been self-centered to the point of cruelty, at least in the past. She deserved to be what she was and nothing more.

"I think I can arrange it. I'm Sariya, commander of the Elephant Corps. There is more to you than you think, Riessa the barbarian, and according to Mae you have good qualities. We can always use people the elephants like."

ERBA HAD WANTED nothing more than to find Dreffir. That seemed like an age ago, when he was someone else entirely. Now he wanted to leave it. The whole place made him edgy. It was not simply that he worried about Tireera and what his brother might be doing at home, nor was it entirely that he was homesick. It was not even that he needed the privacy to grieve fully, although there was that, too. He knew he was uneasy in part because of the presence of so many of Tirdar descent. He was ashamed of himself for that, especially knowing that Forentel was half Tirdar, but he couldn't help it.

He knew quite well now that the fabled Tirdar abilities were not myth or rumor. The idea of his thoughts being invaded, even inadvertently, did not bother him as much as one other disturbing discovery. It appeared that he could occasionally overhear the thoughts of others. He didn't know why these people didn't learn to put some sort of mental barrier up; with all the evidence of a sophisticated civilization around him, he thought they should certainly be capable of it. Perhaps they were not susceptible to over-hearing each other accidentally by virtue of their Tirdar blood, but they should learn not to leak their thoughts all the same. It made things quite unnerving for a visitor.

He wanted to talk to someone Tireeran, but the only true Tireeran in the entire city save himself was Kelern Drilini, and Erba had no wish to see Kelern more than was neces-sary. Kelern had given his word word not to attack him, but he was not about to offer Kelern any friendship or confi-dences. Kelern would not attack him because Kelern had given his word to Forentel, and Kelern had become fanati-cal on the matter of Forentel. The almost religious devo-tion with which he regarded her was something else that made Erba uneasy. Thinking of Forentel made Erba realize that she was the person he really wanted to talk to, the per-son he felt the closest to.

Erba walked through the streets thinking about Forentel. It was dusk, and there were lights being lit within the houses and torches being lit on street corners. Wonderful smells of cooking food drifted out of dwellings. It was the first time he had been allowed out on his own, completely on his own, in the weeks since they had arrived in Dreffir. Forentel had been taken into the queen's family, and she was learning whatever it was she had to learn to control her strange abilities. Erba had been offered the opportunity to study with one of the priests, but he had rejected it as po-litely as he could. He was not Tirdar, and he had no need of whatever it was the priests might wish to teach him. On the one hand, he couldn't understand why he would reject the knowledge he had come so far to find, but on the other hand, he felt the seductive pull of Dreffir, submerging him, submerging his identity as a Tireeran. It would be so easy to melt into this city, to forget everything else. He fully intended to go home someday, and he needed to remind himself of who he was.

He stopped in front of a tavern, watching the patrons go in and out. The place was much more elegant than the taverns in Tireera, and there were tables set for dining outdoors, in the evening's cool. He watched a woman with copper bronze hair sit at a table. She reminded him of Forentel.

Forentel was accepted here, and she seemed much more at ease now, especially since the wolf had returned. He was afraid she still saw him as the rather selfish and self-centered child she had taken him for at first. He had been self-centered, he had to admit it. He wondered whether or not he had truly changed, but the real question was why he cared what she thought. He couldn't decide what he felt about her. He hated that Kelern was obsessed with her, but he had to admit that he, too, thought about her almost constantly. It was not acceptable, he knew. If he ever managed to return to Tireera and take the throne from his brother, he could not bring back a wife who was part Tirdar.

He stopped, shocked by his thoughts. Was he truly considering marrying Forentel?

Wrapped in his thoughts, he had wandered into the little area of outdoor tables and benches that the tavern had set up. One of the serving girls caught his eye and motioned to ask him if he wanted dinner. He considered it for a moment, but then he saw something from the corner of his eye, and turned.

It was Forentel. She was here, at this very tavern; perhaps her presence was what drew him. She was seated at a little table near the door, and there was someone with her.

At first he could not see who this was, as she also had several attendants, obviously guards, who stood near her, two tall women with sharp faces and weapons at their belts. Then Forentel's male companion shifted in his chair and Erba saw him clearly. It was Kelern.

The Tireeran soldier leaned forward in his chair. Never taking his eyes from Forentel, he reached out and poured something from a carafe into a delicate porcelain cup and handed it to her. As he did so, his fingers brushed hers.

Erba could feel the intensity of Kelern's emotions. Kelern adored Forentel, he worshipped her. Forentel was touched by this. She liked him, and she—

Forentel looked up, looked across the space and caught Erba's glance. She had felt him thinking of her, he could tell. She had drawn him here, and now she was reaching toward him with her thoughts. He felt concern, and something else, something more.

Erba turned on his heel and strode away from the tavern, oblivious to the startled looks that followed him. He didn't want to know what Forentel thought of Kelern, he didn't want to know what she thought of him. He told himself that he didn't want to think any more about Forentel at all. And then the knowledge came, the knowledge that he had been avoiding for so long, that had been sitting in the back of his brain, waiting for the chance to ambush him. His link with Forentel made it clear. He was part Tirdar himself.

He was here in Dreffir, the center of a rich and powerful civilization, and now it was clear to him. He needed to secure Dreffir's help, the help of its queen, in going back to Tireera and taking the throne from his brother. But he was part Tirdar. Dreffir was his inheritance, too. And he loved Forentel. He could deny it no longer.

* * *

FORENTEL FELT THE pressure of Erba's attention, and she felt his distress when he turned away suddenly. She knew he would run harder if she tried to touch him with her thoughts, as she had been learning to do. It was strange: he had touched her with his thoughts, but he didn't realize it; that was what had alerted her. She turned back to Kelern.

"Wait here," she said. She stood abruptly and motioned her attendants to stay.

It wasn't hard to find Erba in the crowd. His thoughts leaked out behind him like a little trail of smoke. She saw him stop suddenly, and she felt the force of his self-revelation. Then he turned and saw her.

She didn't know what to say. She had planned on comforting him, on saying something soothing and banal, but pinned by his gaze she could say nothing. She felt his confusion and his love and his unhappiness, and she realized she didn't need to say anything. She had been as blind as he. She went to him and put her arms around him.

I love you, she heard in her thoughts. It was a moment before she realized that the thought came in both their voices. Then Erba's arms were around her. Around them people laughed and talked and more lamps were being lit in the warm evening. Someday they would go back to Tireera, but before then they had much to learn, about Dreffir and about each other. They would do it together. Dreffir felt like home.

Epic, romantic fantasy from the author of
The Sword of the Land.

THE BLOOD OF THE LAND

NOEL-ANNE BRENNAN

With her baby kidnapped, her lover missing, and
her deposed cousin making war against her,
Rilsin's only hope lies in a princess who may be
her salvation—or an enemy worse than any she
has ever encountered.

"A wonderfully strong female protagonist."
—*Booklist*

0-441-01154-3

Available wherever books are sold or at
penguin.com